How
The Multiverse
Got Its Revenge

How
The Multiverse
Got Its Revenge

BOOK TWO OF THE THORNE CHRONICLES

{ K. Eason }

DAW BOOKS, INC

DONALD A. WOLLHEIM, FOUNDER
1745 Broadway, New York, NY 10019
ELIZABETH R. WOLLHEIM
SHEILA E. GILBERT
PUBLISHERS
www.dawbooks.com

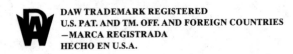

To the Maenads and the Adventurers

Acknowledgments

Sequels are hard, y'all. They're even harder during a pandemic. Thanks to the fantastic folks at DAW, especially Katie and Joshua, whose professionalism and expertise and just plain enthusiasm got this book cleaned up, dressed, and ready to go out in public.

Thanks to my amazing agent Lisa Rodgers, who always gets the jokes and finds the plot holes.

Thanks to Tan, who always reads the shitty first draft, and sometimes the second and third (slightly less shitty) drafts, too.

Thanks to Loren, my co-op partner in Borderlands 3 (and real life) who always has my back whether we're battling bandits or getting through this remote-teaching quarantine.

And most of all: thanks to all the people who wanted to know what happened next.

CHAPTER ONE ≡≡≡

var Valenko, former crown prince of the Free Worlds of Tadesh, now in permanent exile-asylum on Lanscot, was herding sheep for Grytt when the fairy appeared.

She looked like a small woman, short as a mirri, but of course without the distinctive, limbless spherical environmental suit mirri used when interacting with oxygen-based atmospheres, *and* without any daughter-buds, so really, there was nothing mirri-like about the fairy at all, except that human women did not, in Ivar's experience, come in that particular size. Here we must note that Ivar was unfamiliar with children of any age, his single experience having been limited to a visit with the Princess of Thorne, when she had shown him a pondful of fish and thus, quite inadvertently, saved him from an assassin's bomb.

But Ivar knew, somehow, and with firm conviction, that this was *not* a child. He was reasonably certain, as he drew a bit closer, that she was also not a woman, or at least not entirely human. He knew, in a sort of distant, textbook way, that there were no such things as *partial* humans, but he did not hold to those views with any conviction. He had almost as little experience with women as he did with children, having spent much of his post-adolescence in cryostasis, captive and laboratory experiment of Vernor Moss, former Regent of the Free Worlds of Tadesh. He had, because of Moss's machinations, skipped past much of the maturation process in which one learns, or is taught, what is and is not possible. This fluidity of perception made him especially receptive to new experiences, but also exceptionally ill-suited to most forms of social interaction. Grytt and Messer Rupert were the exceptions, in Messer Rupert's case because he had experience as a tutor and general molder-of-youthful-spirits (he had done rather well with Rory); and in Grytt's because she did not have especially high expectations of people in general.

Grytt did, however, expect Ivar to mind her sheep, which meant keeping them safe. Although Ivar knew (in that same, distant textbookish way) that it was really the dogs, Bobby and Edmund, who were responsible for sheep-safety, he also knew that sheep were not stupid. If there was something dangerous, they could usually tell; it was just what to do about it that sometimes confused them. Ivar shared some sympathy with that.

And so, when he saw the fairy, he looked at them, first: the sheep, and then the dogs. The sheep did not seem to notice the woman at all, which suggested that she was, in fact, real. (Sheep tended to ignore people unless there was food involved). Bobby and Edmund cocked their fluffy black-and-white ears at her, and Bobby even sniffed in her general direction, but no hackles came up, and no growling ensued, so Ivar decided it might be all right to approach.

So he did.

The fairy woman was sitting on a flat rock, the largest and flattest on a slopeful of rocks, almost at the pinnacle of the hill. It happened to be Ivar's favorite sitting-stone as well. He was not sure how to feel about finding someone else on it. (The wonder that there was anyone out here at all had already passed out of his awareness). She was dressed impractically for following sheep around the hills, and entirely in green, which set her at vibrant odds with the late summer grasses. She wore some kind of dress with a close-fitting bodice that dissolved into a skirt made of strips and panels of cloth overlapping like scales or feathers. Even from her position on the rock, sitting with her legs dangling, the skirt moved restlessly around her legs, as if it had a mind of its own. The hose she wore were also green and embroidered with tiny gold butterflies. Her feet were bare, and possessed of longish, shapely toes that seemed to have an extra joint.

The woman, he realized, was *entirely* green. Hair, which she wore long and intricately bound up in silver and gold threads. Eyes (except for the white part, and the pupil). And her skin, which was really the telling feature. The color could be paint—he had thought it must be, knowing as he did that human people did not come in green—but now he was certain that green was her natural shade.

She smiled, green lips breaking over teeth small and white as pearls, only sharper.

"Ivar Valenko," she said.

His patronymic was not exactly secret, but it also wasn't meant for, as Messer Rupert put it, general consumption. Ivar was *supposed* to be dead, and probably would have been, except for Rory; and if it became widely known that he wasn't, Dame Maggie might say he couldn't remain on the farm with Grytt and Rupert anymore. Ivar knew what exile meant (textbook knowing, again). He ranked it just above extended time in cryostasis for desirability.

So he was not at all pleased that this green woman sitting on his favorite rock knew his name.

Messer Rupert had said *hello* was the preferred manner in which to greet people one did not know. The green woman had already violated that protocol. Ivar borrowed his manners from

Grytt, who usually snorted when Messer Rupert pronounced on etiquette, skipped the greeting, and went straight to the thing he most wanted to know.

"What do you want?"

The green woman's green eyebrows climbed. Her smile remained, if a little stiffer now, sharp as her teeth. "Most people ask *what* I am, first."

Ivar shrugged. He had learned if he didn't say anything for long enough that two things happened: one, he could not get into trouble for saying the wrong thing; and two, people tended to lose patience and say whatever it was they'd intended in the first place.

"You certainly didn't get a Naming, did you?" the green woman muttered. Her smile had turned into a husk of itself. "Charm is the first thing we hand out at those. Well. Not the first thing *I* hand out. I usually get stuck with great strength or physical prowess or whatever best fits the father's expectations."

That confirmed it. This was a fairy. Ivar forgot to be suspicious, or rather, he set his suspicions aside. Rory had told him about the fairies that had attended her Naming, and the gifts they'd handed out. He had thought, at the time, she'd been teasing him, even though Messer Rupert and Grytt had, when pressed, confirmed the account. ("There were unknown xenos present," Messer Rupert had said; and Grytt had made one of her faces, which was as good as a verbal confirmation.)

Ivar had been vaguely jealous at the time. His father, and later Moss, had been relentlessly dismissive of anything which did not conform to his worldview, including fairies, imagination, and cats.

He eyed the fairy. "What did you give Rory for her Naming?"

"I gave her the ability to play the harp, which I understand she subverted to good cause." The fairy smiled, this time without teeth or humor. "If I'm called for a prince, I give things like incredible strength and physical resilience, but there's not much call for brawny princesses. Bet *someone's* regretting that now."

"She's not a princess anymore."

"She's still Rory Thorne," the green fairy said, enigmatically. "To answer your first question: I want you to deliver a message for me."

Cold sweat prickled on Ivar's skin. He hated talking to people with very few exceptions, and four of those exceptions had left Lanscot almost two years ago. "You should talk to Messer Rupert or Grytt."

The fairy snorted. She sounded a bit like a sheep when she did it. "That's who I want you to tell. Rupert's the one who most needs to hear this, but he's also the one most likely to get fixated on what I am and where I came from and how I got here. Not my first choice. And *Grytt*, well, no. There's too much metal on her now. If Two or Five had come—but of course not, no, *Send Three, she travels best*," the fairy muttered. "But you can tell her what I say, too. She's sensible."

The fairy paused.

Ivar supposed this was the place he was meant to ask *tell them what* and continue the conversation. He said nothing.

The green woman grimaced. Her teeth were *definitely* pointed. Ivar revised his opinion about them looking like pearls. They were yellower. More like bone.

That was not comforting.

Then the fairy began to speak, and that was even *less* comforting. Ivar listened without interrupting. And when the green woman was finished, he ran down the hill to find Rupert and Grytt.

———

"I can stay, if you want." Grytt stood by the door, balancing on her mecha foot while she tugged her boot over the other. The polysteel toes flexed like claws, scoring tiny gouges in the tile.

"No," Rupert said, and then, regretting the terseness of the syllable, "Thank you. I will be fine. I can handle Samur."

"Huh." Grytt shifted her weight, one side to the other. The mecha limb had its own special boot, more for tidiness than for necessity. The mecha joints were hexed against moisture and cold and heat, but not as much against mud. Grytt's boots were an appalling, deliberately bright yellow, in contrast to her practical, drab coveralls. Her mecha hand winked from the frayed grey cuffs.

She frowned at him. "I'll be right outside."

Rupert nodded. Then he turned back to the quantum-hex viewing ball. It looked like a plain, polished glass globe at the moment, sitting on a base of plain iron which was etched all over with hexes. He had already fed it the appropriate coordinates. He made eye contact with his distorted reflection, composed his features, leaned forward, and whispered his personal code.

Quantum-hexes are as close to instantaneous communication as the laws of the multiverse permit. Still, it felt like minutes before a tiny white light appeared in the viewing ball's center, which meant there was contact on the other end. He supposed the delay was a matter of routing. There had been a time his code would have gone immediately to Samur's office. Since those days were long over, he expected that he would have to spend some time arguing with minor functionaries, or perhaps her personal secretary, or *maybe* whoever it was had replaced him as Vizier of the Thorne Consortium.

It was even possible the Regent-Consort would refuse his call altogether, at which point he would have to try plan B, which involved formal requests and triplicate paperwork and very possibly a bribe, if the clerk's assistant in the communications office was still amenable to such persuasion.

The viewing ball's glow shifted from white to live-coal red. A three-dimensional projection began assembling itself inside the viewing ball, pixels drawing together like cosmic dust, swirling into the face and features of Samur, Regent-Consort of the Thorne Consortium. There were lines around Samur's mouth now that had nothing to do with smiling or laughter, and the Kreshti fern on her desk had dark-edged leaves, as if it had been scorched. The last time he had called her, that fern had been out of frame. He wished it was this time, as well, and resolved not to look at it.

"Ah," Rupert said. They had not parted on genial terms. He was no longer certain of his permissions with her name, and chose to err on the side of formality. "Regent-Consort. Thank you for taking my call."

Samur (for that is who she was in his head, and if he allowed himself to consider it, his heart) tilted her head to one side. "Rupert," she said, in the same tone she might have said, *I appear to have developed gout.* That was, he knew, not a signal that they were on first-name terms again. He had renounced his titles when he had chosen to stay on Lanscot. She had nothing else to call him. "What is it you want?"

The fern flared a nervous yellow, at odds with the frozen blue of her tone. She was worried about something, probably Rory, and too proudly furious with him to ask.

So of course, Rupert answered that question first. "Rory is fine, as far as I am aware. I'm not calling about her. Is this communication secure?" He knew as well—and probably better than—Samur how simple it was to weave a few surveillance hexes into a quantum-communication viewing ball. He had, at one time, made sure of Thorne's arithmantic security.

"It is on my end." She permitted an eyebrow to float up her forehead. "What is this about, then?"

"I wanted to ask . . ." Rupert trailed off. He had grown unaccustomed to the circumlocutions of diplomacy with only Grytt and Ivar for company. "Regent-Consort, have you heard of a xeno-people called the vakari? Or a political entity called the Protectorate?"

Rupert had cause then to be glad of the fern. Samur was *not* out of diplomatic practice. Her face might well have been a mask, for all the expression she showed. The fern darkened to a bloody orange with white striations. She glanced down at it and made a move to nudge it out of the projection. Then she paused, withdrew her hand, and grimaced.

"If I asked how you came to know those names, would you tell me?"

Ah, yes. Answer a question with a question. Rupert found his own face assuming that porcelain blank of the professional advisor, ambassador, and handler of prickly personalities.

"Of course, Regent-Consort. Ivar told me."

"Ivar?" Samur blinked. Her mask cracked. "*Prince* Ivar? I thought he was dead."

Rupert composed his face into a noncommittal smile. "He is not. And today, he encountered an unusual personage in the south pasture, and it was from this personage he learned these names."

"*Pasture*," Samur said under her breath. She leaned forward, crowding the fern most of the way out of the projection. It remained a twinkling, kaleidoscopic testament to ire and amusement in garishly equal measure. "What sort of unusual personage?"

"A fairy."

Samur stared at him. Her mouth opened, then closed, then reopened. Rupert could sympathize; his own had done something similar, when he'd first heard that word.

"The green one," he added. "Number three. You recall her? Small, perfectly proportioned, entirely green."

"With pointy little teeth, yes. I never understood why she gave out harp-playing." Samur shook her head carefully. Her earrings, elaborate confections of gold wire and holographic pearls, shimmered like rain. "Are you certain? That the fairy was real, I mean. Wasn't—isn't—Ivar . . . a bit damaged?"

Rupert reflected on the wisdom of saying, *Isn't everyone?* and discarded the idea. They had almost, *almost*, achieved something like their old rapport, and he did not want to jeopardize that with ill-timed sarcasm. He cast a glance toward the yard through the still-open door. Grytt was talking to Ivar, two upright islands in a small sea of woolly backs and muttered bleats. The two-and-a-bit years on Lanscot had been good to Ivar, as they had been good for Grytt and for Rupert himself.

That was not what Samur wanted, or needed, to hear. Rupert leaned close to the hex-dish and lowered his voice. "He is a bit feral, sometimes, but he does not suffer from delusions, visions, or dementia. The fairy's visit was real. He described her in detail too perfect to be invented."

Samur's eyebrows floated toward her hairline. "So what did she want? This fairy."

"She had a message for me and for Grytt, which she could not deliver, Ivar says, because we would ask too many questions and her time was limited." Rupert steepled his fingers. "*Do* you know about this Protectorate and these vakari?"

Samur's lips pursed. "I do, though I have not encountered them personally. The political entity calls itself the Protectorate. The *people* call themselves vakari. Apparently they are quite advanced arithmancers with some strange cultural practices. We had heard about them through some of our other xeno allies—the k'bal have nothing good to say—but I believe the first actual contact was between a Johnson-Thrymbe long-hauler and a vakari military scout, near one of the J-T mining outposts. There were no shots fired, although things were tense until the translation hexes got communications sorted out."

A *year* since the Protectorate had been common knowledge in the Consortium and the Merchants League! Civil wars did have a tendency to refocus national attention, but he would have expected *some* sort of reporting on the Confederation's networks, or at least chatter on the public forums, on which he kept a lurking, curious eye. Even with the Confederation of Liberated Worlds' careful curation of its media, something should have gotten through.

Unless, as he suspected, the doings of people—human and otherwise—on the other side of a civil war were just not as relevant to the Confederation's network executives as whether or not the Tadeshi royalists would disrupt a convoy or attempt to retake a station. Let people think too widely, they might forget the immediate threats.

"The fairy told Ivar that the Protectorate are, in fact, Expanding." He was careful to pronounce the capital letter, the same way Ivar had said it. "But that in so doing they are invading the k'bal territories and winning. And that . . ."

Samur waited with admirable patience for Rupert to finish. When he didn't, when it was obvious that he had either misplaced the words or decided to forego them (and truthfully, he had not yet decided which), she snapped, "Rupert. *And what?*"

"We *will* be next. Human space. The Merchants League, Thorne Consortium, the Confederation, all the unaffiliated worlds. There is already armed conflict between the Protectorate and the Tadeshi royalists. The fairy says we need to prepare. You don't seem surprised, Regent-Consort."

"I'm not. I'm surprised *you* are. A political entity which thrives on expansion and does not mind using violence to achieve those ends is not likely to simply stop because they've reached a new boundary. You know how invasions work. We fought the war with Free Worlds of Tadesh, didn't we, to stop them from doing the same thing to us?"

"We started that war." There were layers to the collective pronoun. *We*, the Consortium. *We*, the duo of Rupert and Samur.

"Pre-emptively. We needed the momentum. You know they would have invaded us, if we hadn't."

He did know. He had been instrumental in the decisions leading up to war's declaration. "Does that mean there are plans to pre-emptively attack the Protectorate? I ask, Regent-Consort, because the fairy predicted that we will lose a war with the Protectorate, should it come to that."

"We—the Thorne Consortium and the Merchants League— won't be alone in a conflict. There are already alliances in place. The other xeno interests I mentioned."

Rupert reflected just how much he despised agentless, objective prose. Alliances meant negotiations, and sides, and *effort*. They did not just happen intransitively. "Yes. The fairy mentioned them, too. Piecemeal agreements between the Merchants League families and," and here he drew breath, and recited the alien words exactly as Ivar had said them, "some of the tenju spacer clans and the alwar Harek Empire, which apparently consists of both planets *and* stations, though there are stray seedworlds of tenju and alwar and clans who are still operating independently." He felt like an actor speaking lines in a foreign language.

Samur blinked. "You *are* well-informed. Or shall I say, this fairy is."

Rupert strangled a laugh. He did not feel well-informed. Quite the opposite. He felt as if his head had been firmly buried in the garden, somewhere between the cabbage-sprouts and the compost heap. "The fairy says no alliance will save us. And by *us*, I mean all of us. The Confederation of Liberated Worlds, the Thorne Consortium, the Merchants League, and whatever organizational units these new xeno friends of yours have amongst themselves. She says, even if we unite, the Protectorate will rip the multiverse apart before they let themselves lose a war."

Samur shook her head, a sharp, brief gesture. "That's silly. First, multiverses don't rip like cheap cloth. Second, there is no *we*. And third, the Confederation of Liberated Worlds is in *the middle* of human space. I think you're quite safe there, on your little rainy sheep-planet of a capital, at least from the Protectorate. The *royalists* should be your concern, Rupert. They're far closer to your borders."

Like all terrestrial planets, Lanscot possessed a diversified climate based on latitude and seasonal orientation to the sun. That most of the planet's landmass was concentrated in the middle third of the higher latitudes was a matter of chance, as was Lanscot's location on the edge of Tadeshi space closest to Merchants League territory (which is to say: where the Tadeshi were very unlikely to attack from, having no bases there), or its primary agricultural contribution to trade. Samur's problem with Lanscot was entirely that Rupert had chosen to live there over returning to Thorne.

However factual, none of that was relevant. What *was*, however: "Yes. About that. The fairy says that the Tadeshi have made new friends among some of what I imagine are supposed to be your allies, although she only said *xenos*. The Tadeshi royalists have acquired a weapon which will prompt the Protectorate into that full-scale warfare which destroys the multiverse as we know it."

Samur frowned. The fern darkened to an ominous, boiling maroon. "Which allies? What kind of weapon?"

"The fairy was not specific." Actually, the fairy had recited poetry, which Rupert was loath to repeat. So instead he summarized, perhaps too succinctly, "Something which will offend the Protectorate on a moral level." No, that was not the right word. "A *spiritual* level. And, ah. Something about the eternal identity of roses, however they are named."

Samur stared at him. "If Dame Maggie wishes to institute formal alliance talks between the Confederation and the Consortium, she should send an *actual* ambassador. But if this is a *personal* appeal for an alliance between the Consortium and the Confederation, it's at least creative."

Rupert could see Grytt on his periphery, standing in the open door. He supposed she had heard most of this exchange. Even from the center of the yard, even surrounded by sheep, her mecha audio receptors were sensitive. He could well supply her expression—the crossed arms, the scowl—without turning to look. He made a *wait, don't interfere* gesture, out of his own viewing ball's projective field, and heard her disapproving *huh.*

Rupert discarded formality on a rush of irritation. "This is not some kind of political pretense, Samur, nor some excuse on my part to re-establish communications between us. I am relaying the message as Ivar relayed it to me—"

"From a *fairy.* Honestly, Rupert. Just say you got your information from Maggie's intelligence networks and have *done.*"

There was a time Rupert could have kept a blandly polite smile pasted to his face for hours, a useful skill he'd first developed under Thorne's old king, Rory's father, who had tended toward obstinacy and a surfeit of poor ideas, and which he'd later honed to a survival art on Urse with the Regent Vernor Moss, who had been ambitious and intelligent in equal, dangerous measure. Now Rupert crumpled that polite smile into a grimace and leaned close to the viewing ball.

"From one of the entities invited to your daughter's Naming, yes." It was hard to say if they had been one species; they had not matched, except in the apparent humanoid femaleness of their presentation. "You do recall their attendance, and the gifts they conferred." All but the twelfth, who had whispered her gift to the infant Rory.

"I recall they attended because *you* invited them, and they were seen once and never again. Why should one of them reappear now, to Ivar of all people, bringing some doomsday warning? It seems very inefficient, doesn't it? And rather fantastic."

The floor creaked. Grytt was abnormally heavy, being a good portion mecha and therefore metal. It was a little alarming how quietly she could move.

Samur must have thought so as well; she recoiled as Grytt thrust her face over Rupert's shoulder. The fern on Samur's desk prismed through startlement, with a flash of embarrassment, before flaring straight into outrage.

"Grytt! I thought we were alone, Rupert, what is this—"

"Oh, stuff it, Samur." Grytt had been Samur's body-maid once, and before that a Kreshti reconnaissance marine. She had since raised one renegade princess and lost half of her body to an assassin's bomb *and* survived the coup on Urse, and therefore suffered no anxiety about formality or diplomacy. "Weren't you listening? Expansion's a pretty word for invasion, and the fairy just *said* this weapon's going be their reason to come after all of us. War isn't good for anyone. You're better positioned to get that information to the right people than we are, so do that, can't you?"

Samur drilled Grytt with a look that, had it been directed at him, would have curdled Rupert's stomach, and been followed by an argument. Grytt proved immune to both. Samur's face, and fern, cycled through a flush of anger and embarrassment before settling into a sullen acquiescence. "Then what will *your* job be, pray tell?"

Grytt raised her remaining eyebrow. "Us? We're just the fairy messenger service. Our job's done."

"Grytt," Rupert said, in a warning tone that he anticipated would have no effect whatsoever on its object, but which would signal to Samur that she did not speak for both of them. He leaned forward, and arranged his features into what he hoped looked like earnest appeal. "We also need your help."

Samur's fern turned entirely orange, shot through with pink, at odds with her gentle head-tilt and her even more gentle, "More help?"

Rupert was not fooled. He watched her eyes, and they glittered, hard as obsidian and just as sharp.

"We, I—the Confederation—" Rupert paused. *Requires* was not the right word, despite its accuracy. Samur would not respond well to demands. "We would like to meet these xeno allies of yours." The possessive pronoun was also not the correct word— the allies were Samur's by association, because Samur had recently married into the Larish family (a second cousin, in no danger of inheriting the chief operating officer's title, but still on the governing board), thus cementing an alliance with the Merchants League for Thorne. "We would be grateful if you could, perhaps through your husband, arrange a meeting."

"I suppose *the fairy* told you about our treaties with the Harek Empire."

Our. Rupert controlled a wince. "She did not. I surmised that Larish would secure a trading partnership with new markets and partners, whoever they might be. You just told me which one. So. Could you arrange a meeting with the Harek Empire?"

"We. You claim to speak for the Confederation? As its ambassador?"

Rupert was so very thankful Kreshti ferns did not register emotions across quantum-hex viewing balls. He composed his features in his best blandly sincere expression.

"Yes."

Samur raised both eyebrows. Her smile grew teeth. "I have *met* the Confederation's ambassador, Rupert. You look nothing like her. You used to be better at this. Lying to people, I mean."

"I am out of practice." Most of his negotiations concerned whose turn it was to do laundry, and Ivar and Grytt did not require polite prevarication. "And you have only met the Confederation's ambassador to the Thorne Consortium. We don't have an ambassador to your xeno allies yet, but I am certain that Dame Maggie will make the necessary appointment official, when she is informed of the fairy's message, and the implications, *and* of a need for the post."

"And you're sure it will be you."

"I am certain no one else will volunteer for the job." He also intended to badger Dame Maggie relentlessly until she capitulated.

"The Vizier of the Confederation of Liberated Worlds." Samur's smile slipped again into a brief, genuine amusement. Then it scabbed over and fell off, leaving a crooked expression, drawn up tight at the corners. "And what is my daughter's involvement in this?"

"We don't know that she is involved," said Rupert. "The fairy said nothing about it."

"Of course she is." Samur folded her hands neatly on the desk.

The fern shifted into sunset hues. "As you have pointed out, Rupert: the fairies have been concerned with Rory since her birth. I cannot see some other reason they would send an emissary now, though why they came to you and not to me. . . ." Samur snipped off whatever else she meant to say. Suspicion sharpened her voice. "Has Rory returned to Lanscot?"

"No."

"Then tell me where she is."

Rupert side-eyed Grytt. "I can't."

Samur's fern turned a terrible color, dried blood veined with necrotic green. "You can. You just won't. She's alone out there, Rupert. You left her alone."

In fact, it was Rory (and Thorsdottir, Zhang, and Jaed) who had left him, Grytt, and Ivar to pursue a life of "freedom from all this" on the edge of the Verge. Samtlet was a self-sufficient mining colony, run by an elected stationmaster and council, which had a constant need for people with small ships to patrol its space for pirates and smugglers and, when encountering such persons, liberate the illegal cargo and return it to the proper authorities.

You are going to be a privateer, Rory.

More like salvagers who sometimes intercept smugglers.

I cannot tell your mother that.

No, Rory had said, entirely serious. *You cannot.*

"She isn't alone," said Rupert. "She has Thorsdottir, Zhang, and Jaed with her."

But the point was not Rory's solitude or company. The point was her preferences, which she had made very clear to Rupert and to Grytt (and, truthfully, to a lot of other people in several governments): She wanted to get away from politics. To live normally. To learn what *normal* even meant.

He added, "She is well removed from the conflict between the

Confederation and the royalists," he said, because he could tell Samur that much. "She wants to live quietly, out of the way, and just be a person, for once, and not a political symbol."

"Oh, Rupert." Samur's demeanor softened, suddenly, and the lines around her eyes crinkled into genuine affection. "My daughter renounced her title, but that does not mean she isn't a princess. Things happen to princesses, whether or not they want them to happen. Wherever that weapon is, Rory is, too. I know it. That's a mother's gift."

"Samur's probably right," said Grytt, when the call had ended, and the quantum communications viewing ball had reverted to its neutral, spherical opacity. "Rory's in the middle of whatever is happening out there."

"Rory has proved herself to be adept at handling difficult situations." Rupert rose from the chair and went to the middle of the living room. There, he stopped. He had to pack, possibly for a long time. He tried to recall if it had been his turn to do the laundry, or Grytt's, and whether or not he could make the evening shuttle to the capital. He settled his best *I am thinking, please do not disturb* expression over his features and began to compose mental lists of necessary items.

Grytt had no regard for his expressions, or for his signaled wish for solitude. She came and stood in front of him, where it was impossible to ignore her. It was that tesla eye of hers. Rupert was glad it was blue, and not red; but it made an unsettling combination, paired with her dark brown original eye, particularly when they were both glaring.

"I'm not worried about what *Rory* does. I'm worried about you, Rupert."

"Me?"

"You." She made a disgusted noise in her throat, turned on her heel, and stalked into the hallway. Rupert heard a door rattle in its track. She emerged shortly after, carrying a battered duffel over her shoulder. She dropped it on the floor at his feet. It was either an offering or a challenge, or perhaps some of both. "When you call Dame Maggie, tell her to expect both of us. You're not going alone. Politics are dangerous."

"But your sheep, Grytt."

"That's what Ivar and I were discussing out there." She jabbed her chin at the open door, through which drifted the sounds of sheep as the dogs, assisted by Ivar, herded the flock back toward the pasture. "He can manage 'em. The lambing's done, and we should be home by shearing-time."

"You hate void-travel."

"Yes, I do. And war, and sleet, and those little cabbages that taste like feet that you keep insisting on making me eat. But we all make our sacrifices."

Rupert found himself unable to meet her eyes. "Thank you."

"Huh. I'm just going along to make sure you come back here when it's over. There's no way I'm going to do your share of the chores."

CHAPTER TWO

The *G. Stein* drifted, dribbling threads of plasma and small plumes of what had been atmosphere from a rather large hole in its engine core. Its registry declared it a civilian delivery vessel, owned by the Flora and Flowers Terrestrial Distribution (or FFTD), which was a subsidiary of the Sons of John Corporation, which in turn was a founding member of the Merchants League.

"That's odd," said Thorsdottir, because it was.

First, there was exactly one human settlement in the Samtalet system, a mining station bored into the seventh moon of the heavily ringed methane giant Kaosol, which was unimaginatively and rather misleadingly called SAM-1 (there being no SAM-2). SAM-1 had one hostel, two public houses, one of which served food with its alcohol, a gym, and a general store. No florists. No *demand* for flowers. SAM-1's greenhouse was very practically dedicated to food production, the materials for which came along with the bi-yearly resupply ships.

And second, *G. Stein* appeared to've fallen victim to pirates, except who would want to steal flowers? And yet, there the ship was, leaking plasma.

Beside Thorsdottir, *Vagabond's* pilot-navigator, Zhang, made one of those throaty grunts that might mean *I agree, that is very odd* or *Oh, here we go again.* Knowing Zhang, it meant both.

"*G. Stein*, this is *Vagabond*," said Rory Thorne, who, being neither pilot nor gunner, sat in the little folding chair at the back of the very small cockpit, operating communications on a jury-rigged board. Communications were supposed to run through the pilot's station, but Zhang had declared herself unqualified. Thorsdottir thought that was wisest. Rory was good at speech-making, and Zhang was prone to distress if she had to interact with strangers.

"I don't think they're going to answer." Thorsdottir had to concentrate to keep the reflexive *highness* behind her teeth. Rory was adamant that she be called simply *Rory* these days, and for Thorsdottir, shedding the custom of her profession was proving difficult.

"Sst. I'm trying to hear." Rory waved an impatient, imperious hand. Her head was cocked, her eyes unfocused, as if that would help amplify whatever sounds might be coming through her earpiece.

Thorsdottir exchanged a look with Zhang in the main screen's reflection. Rory Thorne might have given up her title, might insist that she was just a normal person, but she had not quite shed the habits of a lifetime of command.

That was all right. Thorsdottir and Zhang had not shed their habit of obedience to Rory yet, either. Thorsdottir thought she might be getting a little closer; Rory's tone elicited the smallest twinge of annoyance this time.

Vagabond did not have much in the way of long-range scanners. It had been a small Tadeshi military transport in its past life, and its scanners were mostly limited to *can I shoot at that* and *will it shoot back* and *can I land there*, all of which ran through a small (which is to say, intellectually limited) arms-turing. At Thorsdot-tir's prompting, the arms-turing began looking to see whether or not any of the external aetherlocks were intact enough for *Vaga-bond* to dock.

Her screen erupted into a cascade of anxious orange numbers.

Thorsdottir swore under her breath. "We're not looking at a Merchants League ship at all. That's a Tadeshi warship running a false ID."

Zhang glanced over. "Then I think we know why the ship got shot. That's what happens to warships. What we don't know is what it's doing *here*. We are a long way from the front." She put *Vagabond* into an evasive roll that got the ship pointed—as much as voidships *point* anywhere—on a vector aimed back at SAM-1.

"What are you doing?" Rory's voice cracked, sharp with old habits of command. "Bring us back around. If that's a Tadeshi warship, we need to know what it's doing out here."

Zhang stabbed a look at Thorsdottir in the screen's reflection.

Thorsdottir sighed. "We don't know about any passive de-fenses *G. Stein* may have left. Warships always have redundancies. Its arms-turing could still be tracking us, even if its primary tur-ing's offline."

Rory shot a glance at the center console, where the ship's main turing lived, and smiled. "*Vagabond* would've noticed that."

Vagabond's primary turing (third-hand, independently manu-factured by Johnson-Thrymbe) was a little less intellectually lim-ited than the arms-turing, and responsible for synthesizing whatever information scans brought to it, and for navigational calculations. It tolerated Zhang and Thorsdottir, and seemed marginally more fond of Jaed, but it *liked* Rory. In return, Rory seemed to think of it as an ally, rather than a collection of code. Thorsdottir thought that was romantic and not especially helpful. A turing was limited by its hardware, much as people were. Whatever a turing *wanted* to do, there were limits to what it *could*. This turing wanted to please Rory, and Thorsdottir suspected it might fudge data in order to do so.

Zhang did not take her eyes off her controls. "Whoever did this to *G. Stein* could come back. Since they destroyed a warship already, I think it is safe to assume they could destroy us, too. We're not dealing with simple pirates, pri—Rory."

Rory made that noise in the back of her throat that meant she was trying to be patient with these objections, and that patience was starting to slip. "Begging the question why they left in the first place, and who they are; if they're shooting royalists, they might be friends of ours. Or perhaps *no one* did this. Perhaps it's a catastrophic equipment failure."

Thorsdottir side-eyed Zhang. "I see a hole in the engine core. That suggests a torpedo's involvement. But it could be a ruse. An ambush. A ship *meant* to look crippled, to lure people in. The attackers might be leaving it as bait."

"Bait for *who?* There are no Confederation outposts in Samtalet."

"There's us," said Thorsdottir.

"We're not technically rebels. We're independent contractors employed by the stationmaster. And besides, you don't really think that ship was meant for *us*."

Thorsdottir wished, not for the first time, that she knew how Rory *did* that: how she always knew when someone was hedging the truth, or saying something they didn't quite believe, or flat-out lying. "No. But I think it's indicative of bigger problems than someone dodging system tariffs."

"Exactly," said Rory. "I was prepared to think a floral delivery vessel out *here* must be smuggling something interesting. But a royalist warship, *masquerading* as a delivery vessel—I think we've interrupted an *operation* of some kind, and I think we need to know what it is. So. Let's prepare to board.—What?"

Thorsdottir and Zhang looked at each other. Zhang let her breath out. "There could be survivors, and they could be expecting a boarding party."

Rory took a bite of air, precursor, Thorsdottir thought, to another *But you don't think so*. And then she blinked, and let the air out, and stared, narrow-eyed, at the bulkhead, as if she could see through to the ship drifting outside. "All right. Then we'll be prepared for that, too. But first, Zhang, find us a useable aetherlock."

That took a moment, and it was not Zhang who found it, but rather Thorsdottir's trusty arms-turing, still looking for things to target and shoot. It beeped an alert, and then red-lined the aetherlock and inquired whether or not it could fire.

"No," Thorsdottir told it, unnecessarily (arms-turings did not have audio receptors) and a little bit testily. She fed *G. Stein's* aetherlock's coordinates over to Zhang, who brought *Vagabond* alongside. The primary turing would deal with the actual business of docking, the fine and minute adjustments for which Zhang had not yet developed the reflexes (she had been trained for atmospheric piloting; the void-piloting was a skill-in-progress). Zhang, meanwhile, engaged the external video feeds. At this distance and these speeds, the turing could actually render an image. *Seeing* where they were going always reassured Zhang, even if it was blurry variations on grey.

Thorsdottir ignored the image; it gave her a headache. She wished, not for the first time, that Grytt could be pried out of retirement ("I like my sheep") on Lanscot. A former Kreshti marine would be far more useful than a Royal Guard in a hostile boarding situation. Oh, privateers boarded ships all the time, and this would not be Thorsdottir's first boarding, either; it was just that most of *Vagabond's* vict—er, *targets*—were not interested in a straight-up fight. They preferred to sneak around, and when cornered, preferred surrender to violence.

There came a distant, metallic *clang*, and a grinding sound that would have been alarming if Thorsdottir hadn't heard it before.

"We're locked on." Zhang looked unhappy.

"Excellent. Then let's get ready to board. Thorsdottir?"

A Royal Guard would say *Yes, Highness*. A Royal-Guard-turned-privateer said instead, "On it," as she released her harness.

She squeezed past Rory and the comm-station and dogged the hatch between cockpit and *Vagabond's* very small, very cramped crew section, where the final crew member remained in his harness, both hands clamped to the arms of his chair.

"You can let go now," said Thorsdottir.

"Huh," said Jaed Moss. He did not move. "What just happened? There was *rolling*. And a bang. Did we dock?"

Thorsdottir squinted at Jaed. He was pale, but not especially green, and there were two fever-bright spots on his cheekbones. Excitement, fear, but not explosive nausea. She grunted, shrugged, and shot a look at the cockpit.

Then she closed the hatch again, which was both safety protocol and good sense, if one wished to discuss Rory's decisions *not* in Rory's hearing.

"The delivery ship wasn't a delivery ship. It wasn't even a smuggler. It's a Tadeshi warship running a false ID, and someone shot a hole in it, Zhang took evasives as a precaution but its turings aren't firing. I don't know exactly what kind of warship it was. Zhang doesn't either. Maybe you'll know."

The spots of color on his cheekbones intensified. "Because I'm Tadeshi?"

Yes, Thorsdottir wanted to say. *Your political origins automatically confer specialist knowledge on military vessels.* Jaed Moss had come from station-born privilege, and although the Free Worlds had compulsory military service, Thorsdottir knew for a fact that Jaed had never served. There were advantages to one's father being the usurping power behind the Tadeshi throne.

Thorsdottir knew that Jaed was a little bit (a lot) sensitive about his familial background, and also probably a little nauseous from Zhang's flying, so she tried to be, if not kind, at least neutral.

"No. Because you told us that you used to have a poster of all the Tadeshi warships above your bed, and I therefore assume some expertise on your part."

"Oh. Well. I can look."

"Good. Then get out of your harness and come do that."

Jaed's eyes followed her across the cabin. His fingers plucked at his harness as if at a harp's strings. "Um. So someone got here first, shot up *G. Stein*, and now we're doing . . . what, exactly?"

Thorsdottir braced both hands against the hardsuit rack.

"Now we're going to board and see what they were hiding, or smuggling, or whatever they were doing." She kept her voice as neutral as a k'bal in a conflict.

Jaed pinched his lips together and watched while Thorsdottir popped the seal and released her hardsuit from its place on the rack. He had acquired, thanks to Rory, more than a little arithmancy; Thorsdottir supposed sourly that he was probably looking at her aura and seeing just how unhappy she was with the prospect.

The cabin hatch clanged open. Rory ducked through, smiling so brightly and sharply that Thorsdottir's heart dropped. Rory had looked just like that before she challenged the Prince of Tadesh to a duel to first blood to establish his worthiness to marry her. See how all *that* had turned out.

"I'll just be a minute," said Rory in a tone that dared anyone to argue. She kept the smile bared as she squeezed through the narrow space between the bunks and helped herself into her own hardsuit.

Thorsdottir bit her lip and craned her neck to see through to the cockpit. Zhang had cranked around in her seat, straining her harness and staring *do something* at Thorsdottir. They had all discussed, at length and in detail, why Rory should remain in *Vagabond* when they did hostile boarding actions. Practically, Rory was the back-up pilot, if something happened to Zhang. She was not experienced, or particularly skilled, with weapons, most of her practice having been confined to simulations and a long history of playing *Duty Calls*; but she had a good relationship with *Vagabond's* primary turing, which seemed to regard Zhang as a professional hazard.

Since Rory had decided *not* to honor their prior agreements, it fell to someone to argue with her, and from Zhang's expression, she expected that someone to be Thorsdottir.

Jaed was studying the former princess. "Rory. What's going on?"

Thorsdottir expected a *nothing*, which is what she or Zhang might've gotten; but Rory looked at Jaed, and hesitated. Then she raised an insouciant eyebrow.

"I heard a transmission coming from *G. Stein*. It's not on the standard channels, and I thought it was just noise. But there's a pattern to it that I can't pin down. It's like . . . a whisper. Or I'm just hearing feedback. Or maybe it's some arithmancer's grocery receipt."

"Or maybe," muttered Thorsdottir, "it's a battle-hex that will fry us the moment we breach the hull."

Rory grinned at Thorsdottir. "You sound like Grytt."

"Thank you," said Thorsdottir. "Where would this communication be coming from, though? Or who? Hardsuit comms won't penetrate a ship's hull. The main turing is down."

"I don't know. That's why I'm going with you to look."

"So you intend to leave *Zhang* on board as our pilot?"

Rory looked up sharply, as if Thorsdottir had shouted *please do not be stupid about this* (which she had in fact been thinking) instead of making a respectful, quiet-voiced query.

"Is that a problem?"

Thorsdottir wished again for Grytt or the Vizier (who, like Rory, had rejected his title and who, like Rory, Thorsdottir couldn't quite imagine without it). They had come pre-loaded with Authority, capital A, to which even a princess might respond.

Though since, through no fault of their own, they had left Rory to extricate herself from Jaed's father's coup attempt and imprisonment, their influence over her might be somewhat diminished even if they *were* here. Still. They had never hesitated to tell Rory what they thought, and so Thorsdottir—mouth dry, heart crawling up into her throat—said, somewhat sharply, "Yes. You're the agreed-upon back-up pilot. If you truly believe there are people over there, then Zhang is better prepared for a firefight than you are."

Rory's eyes narrowed.

"And if there is an arithmancer or a battle-hex, how much help will Zhang be?"

Well, first, Zhang's 'slinger bolts went where she aimed them, every time, with appalling accuracy. Arithmancers—even military, battle-hex wielding arithmancers—were susceptible to 'slinger bolts. Secondly, and more importantly, to Thorsdottir's reckoning, Zhang had a Royal Guard's paranoid caution, not a princess's curiosity.

The words backed up in Thorsdottir's throat. Rory demanded honesty from her—they weren't *friends*, exactly, weren't *staff* anymore, so what? Crew? Close associates? But not equals, not Grytt-or-Vizier level authority, not anyone who could say what was necessary. She wished for Rory to use that uncanny insight and just, for once, read Thorsdottir's mind.

Rory stared at her, expectant.

"I'll go," said Jaed. "Instead of Zhang. I can shoot, and I'm an arithmancer. In case, you know. Battle-hexes."

It was not often Rory was struck silent. She regarded Jaed with round eyes and her mouth just a little agape. Then her lips came together, and her brows leveled out, and her expression went smooth as glass. She slapped the seals closed on her suit with more force than necessary.

"You're half the arithmancer I am."

The utterance was not kind, in either sentiment or delivery, and shocking for that reason. Rory demanded honesty, and gave it in return; but she was usually better at diplomacy.

Jaed recoiled, red-faced and surprised and, Thorsdottir suspected, hurt. It was no secret to anyone that he had, at one point, entertained *feelings* for Rory, which she had ignored gently and completely, and that he had, some six months into the nascent courtship, given up. There was no rancor between them, but he could be sensitive to Rory's moods, even now.

Thorsdottir had intended a career putting herself between people (royalty, *Rory*) and harm (people with 'slingers or pointy things). Rory's choices had necessitated a change in Thorsdottir's profession, but the underlying principles remained. Put herself between someone about to do damage and someone who needed protecting.

"I agree with Jaed," she said, more loudly than the narrow confines of the ship and the proximity of her targets would warrant. "If you're going to leave Zhang here, then he *should* come with us. He's got a greater familiarity with Tadeshi warships than we do. And," she drilled her stare at Rory, trying to be one-eyed, mecha-eyed Grytt, "he's at least as good with a 'slinger as you are."

He was, in fact, better, Rory's aim being somewhat unpredictable. Thorsdottir saw the sentiment reflected on Jaed's face, along with a surprised and uncomfortable gratitude.

"Fine." Rory's face might've been the visor of her hardsuit, or one of the marble statues in the Thorne palace gardens. Serene, unblinking, utterly without pity.

Jaed, accustomed to sitting at comms when Zhang and Thorsdottir boarded vessels, was not as quick, or as practiced, getting into a hardsuit. Thorsdottir refrained from reaching over and helping him with the seals as he fumbled first one leg, and then the other, into the greaves and mag-lock boots. The transition from *station-bred second son of a usurping traitor* to *spacer* was a large step, perhaps even larger than the one from *Royal Guard*, at least when it came to handling the equipment.

Thorsdottir readied the 'slingers and stuck her head and shoulders back into the cockpit.

Zhang had lowered *Vagabond's* forward blast-shields; this time, the view of *G. Stein* was real-time, live, on the other side of the transparent polysteel porthole. Now Thorsdottir could see for herself the scoring on the hull, blackened and still glowing with little white pockets of flame and unlike any damage she'd seen before.

High-velocity projectiles left *holes* in a hull, if they got past the shields. They didn't set it on fire. Fire wasn't even supposed to *happen* in void. There was no phlogiston. Fire didn't, couldn't, happen without phlogiston. Never mind that fire didn't burn through metal, either.

And yet, clearly, some kind of fire *did.*

"Is that—*what* could've done that? Plasma? Some kind of battle-hex?"

"I don't know," Zhang said softly. "Neither does Rory. But she wants to find out."

Thorsdottir pitched her voice low. "What's this about a transmission?"

"She said she heard something and she wanted to investigate. You know everything I do, right there." Zhang flicked a worried glance over her shoulder. "Rory's told me to stay here. Please tell me you're taking Jaed."

"I am. If I can't have you, I need someone else to hold a 'slinger."

Zhang took a breath and swallowed. "He will watch your back effectively. I can't predict his value if you meet resistance."

"I can. A third target for an angry Tadeshi marine," Thorsdottir muttered. She was sorry the moment she said it.

Zhang's voice dropped somewhere between whisper and breathless. "I told Rory that I don't think anyone should board that ship. Whoever did this, did *that*"—and she thrust her chin at the scorched ship outside the porthole—"may still be out there, and *Vagabond* is no match for a warship."

Thorsdottir squinted past *G. Stein*, at the velvet void beyond. There were a lot of places a ship could conceal itself, beyond the reach of *Vagabond's* instruments. It was wise, for some version of the word, for Zhang to remain on board. Thorsdottir still hated it.

"Be careful," said Zhang.

"We will," said Thorsdottir. "We'll go quick as we can."

That was certainly true. But Thorsdottir did not add, *we'll be back before you know it*, or *we'll be fine*. She and Zhang demanded honesty from each other, too.

CHAPTER THREE

Void-stations, Rupert reflected, were all very much alike. He supposed it was a convergence of necessity, in the beginning; there were only so many ways to construct void-proof, orbiting edifices in which one expected people to live and work. The older models had all relied on spin to produce gravity, and so had been versions of a spoked ring rotating around a central spindle. Even after gravity-hexes, the shapes of the stations had not changed overmuch, with *down* being feet toward the rim. Lanscot's station was no different.

The beanstalk through which people traveled to and from the station stretched down to the planetside capital city like the tether to an orbiting ring-shaped balloon. From this vantage, the city below was a blur of light, and the beanstalk looked impossibly fragile.

Rupert traced his fingers along the bulkhead. The paint was pristine, new, of a shade meant to sooth an observer, blandly pastel and warmly organic. It was a valiant effort if, to Rupert's eye, not especially successful. He had thought himself prepared for a return to void living, and in the first twenty-four hours of resuming it, he had been too occupied with meetings to pay much attention to his surroundings. But the past two days of relative inactivity had reminded him how very much he disliked bulk-heads and deckplate and confined horizons.

People got into patterns of thought, of engineering, of politics. Seeing beyond those patterns was difficult. *Breaking* those patterns was almost impossible. Dame Maggie of Lanscot, former farmer, then local parliamentarian, then leader of a colonial rebellion that cracked the Free Worlds of Tadesh, was a woman capable of both identifying patterns and of shattering them when necessary. She had not disbelieved him when he had reported what the green fairy had said (though he had mentioned neither fairy nor Ivar as his sources). She had visibly weighed the likelihood of his information. (With her face concealed by the head-to-toe woolen wrap, this was mostly a shifting of eyes.) She had then invited him—and Grytt, who, true to her word, had accompanied him—to stay a few days on the station while she made inquiries about xeno contacts. The end of those few days was almost nigh, with a meeting scheduled this afternoon. During the endless several hours remaining, Rupert had elected to traverse one end of the station to the other.

Lanscot's station, like Urse, had an arboretum. But unlike Urse, the arboretum here had a second tier and a dome of clear polysteel which rose out of the otherwise smooth profile of the station like a blister. A person possessed of sufficient desire and stamina could climb a rather daunting spiral of transparent steps from the arboretum's second tier along the interior skin of the dome, until they reached a small platform, on which one might sit and observe the void, the planet, and passing ships from a single vista.

He supposed it was meant to be a place of reflection and peace. When he reached the top of the steps, he instead found himself sweaty and out of breath and, when he looked down and back, filled with despair. He had to get down again, didn't he? There were a great many stairs.

Still, up here he was far from the bulkheads with their aggressively appealing paint, and if he could not imagine that the star-spangled dark out there was Lanscot's sky as seen from his back garden, he could at least discern familiar constellations, and enjoy the absence of the intervening clouds.

So taken was he with the view that he did not immediately notice the other visitor to the observation platform. She stood where the platform abutted the dome, hands clasped behind her back, chin level, watching the slow dance of a docking ship and its guide mecha ten levels down. Rupert noticed her and jerked, surprised. The platform was made of the same transparent substance as the dome and the steps, and he was certain that it had been unoccupied when he began his ascent. Even the most cursory, fleeting glance would have revealed her. Nor could she have passed him during the climb. She had simply appeared.

Then he took a closer, more complete look, and understood how she had evaded detection. Rupert had been the Vizier of Thorne when last he had seen her, and that had been twenty years and a lifetime ago on a distant planet, but one does not forget a fairy. He was as impressed by the fairy's demeanor as Ivar had been, though he recovered from his surprise more eloquently.

"I was under the impression you did not enjoy travel," said Rupert.

She cut him a sour look, sidelong and from beneath lowered eyelids. "I think we have that in common. And yet here *you* are, Vizier."

Rupert opened his mouth to object that the title was no longer applicable and to assert himself as a private citizen. Then he considered that the fairy might know something he did not (yet) know, about decisions made by Dame Maggie and whomever she had consulted about his report, and said nothing.

The fairy was watching him more openly now, one eyebrow quirked, the corners of her lips pulled tight. Daring him to argue with her, Rupert thought. Viziers did not argue. They advised. They cajoled. Sometimes they engaged in diplomatic chicanery, which involved knowing when to remain silent.

He moved up beside the green fairy as carefully as if he were approaching Grytt's large, orange, temperamental cat. He was prepared for a metaphorical toothy hiss, so was surprised by her actual toothy unsmile. Her teeth, he noted, were very white, in the otherwise unbroken verdancy of her, and as sharp as the cat's. All of them. Then she turned her attention back to the vista. The stars spangled distantly on the black. Much closer, Lanscot's curve glowed below in the reflected light of the little yellow sun. Clouds swirled over the landmass like the wisps of grey hair. Rupert resisted the urge to press his nose to the transparent alloy and stare down at the planet in a vain attempt to identify familiar landmarks beyond his home continent and the glittering carbuncle that was Eden's Burg, Lanscot's capital city and voidport.

"I imagine you know that I have passed your warning on to the appropriate parties," he said finally, when he had decided she was not going to begin the conversation.

"Mm." She put the unsmile away and continued to look out the porthole without blinking. She appeared to be considering something, and Rupert briefly entertained an idea of trying to read her aura.

Auras were only electromagnetic manifestations of a being's emotional state, whatever the biology at the root of it. Just as each chemical produced its own unique spectrum, so did each emotion. While doing so brought an advantage in negotiations, it was also a risk, if the target was at all versed in arithmancy. Whether fairies knew about arithmancy, he did not know, but it seemed best to assume that any creatures capable of crossing great distances without voidship or tesser-hex and climbing to the top of a spiral staircase unseen might be able to detect someone sniffing around their electromagnetic emotional emissions.

Or they might be able to read someone else's. Rupert quickly assembled a concealing hex for his own aura, which would return bland unconcern to a cursory glance, and which would be obviously a shield to any arithmancer of skill, who would then have to decide whether to allow the shield to remain or try a counter-hex to break it.

The fairy cut him an amused, sidelong glance. "Why do you think I'm here?"

"I don't know. Perhaps because we are not moving quickly enough for your preferences on the task to which we've been set. Perhaps because there has been a new development." He paused. "Has there been?"

"Are you worried about Rory Thorne?"

"Of course I am."

"So am I."

"Why? It been quite some time since she was your concern."

"And how would you know that?" The fairy turned, propping her shoulder against the polysteel.

Rupert flinched. He knew very well that the polysteel was the same stuff as the opaque parts of the hull, hexed for transparency, no more likely to disintegrate and cast everyone into aetherless void. But it still looked as if she were leaning on nothing at all, and that if she tipped too far, she might fall into the void and down toward the docking ships near the center of the station's ring.

He closed his eyes briefly to banish that image. It was only when he reopened them that he remembered she'd asked him a question, and one for which he had no rational answer except *you haven't seen her since she was an infant.*

"Why would she be important to you? One human girl."

"A princess is not just a girl."

"She's renounced the title."

"Rory Thorne can no more renounce what she is than you can renounce what *you* are."

"And I am a Vizier, you say."

The fairy quirked an eyebrow, one shade darker green than her skin.

Rupert chose to take that as an affirmative. "Is that why you came to Ivar first? Because he is a prince?"

"Ivar was never a prince. Ivar was, and is, a person who prefers to pass unnoticed. No, I came to Ivar because I knew you would ask too many questions. Which you are doing, as expected." The fairy's eyes flickered like sunlight through leaves. "To answer your first query: yes. Circumstances are proceeding rather more quickly than we anticipated. You need to leave now."

"Then it is Dame Maggie to whom you should speak. I have no influence over how quickly she makes decisions about political appointments and forging new alliances with people she's never heard of before, or arranges passage to distant, unaffiliated systems."

"Oh. She'll have heard of those people by now." The fairy pressed one hand against the dome, and then, after a moment, both her forehead and her nose. "Look down there."

Rupert told himself firmly that the polysteel would *not* betray him, and then took a moment to reassure himself that the hexwork was, in fact, intact: no missing variables, no wobbling, only the rigid interlace of equations. Then he moved up beside the fairy and laid his own palm on the dome. The alloy felt neither warm nor cold, which was unsettling, but it was at least reassuringly hard and solid when he leaned against it. The fairy herself radiated heat, or reflected it, a little bit like standing beside a mirror in sunlight; where his elbow and shoulder came closest, he felt small spots of warmth on the edge of discomfort.

He looked obediently where she indicated. Down, in this instance, meant the station's docks. A ship of unfamiliar design was just nosing its way into a berth. There were characters stenciled onto the hull, numbers—which Rupert recognized—and a set of symbols he did not. Clearly some sort of alphabet, however.

He felt the tiny thrill he experienced every time he encountered some new thing he might learn. An alphabet meant a language, a language meant a people, and that ship therefore must belong to one of the new xeno species.

"Before you ask," said the fairy, "That's an alwar vessel, from the Harek Empire. There's a tenju clanship on the other side of the docking ring. Either one of them will do for your transport, but I think you'll be happier riding with the alwar."

Did that mean Dame Maggie's investigations were finished, and she'd decided to take his advice? Or was this Samur's doing, this first contact? Rupert took a bite of air, and chewed it up, and swallowed it. His meeting with Maggie would almost certainly be delayed, with two xeno ships arriving, unless she had known they were coming.

The questions kept piling up. Rupert set them aside in favor of the most important. "You said circumstances were proceeding more quickly than you had anticipated. What circumstances?"

"There are *rules* about how forthcoming we can be and how

much we can interfere." The fairy's tongue flicked out between her sharp triangle teeth, as if tasting the dry station air. "I am already a few toes over that line."

"All right." Rupert eyed her feet surreptitiously. They possessed the customary number of toes and they were bare, though she gave no indication of discomfort. "I could attempt to read your aura while I asked questions. You would need to say nothing, and I—"

"Would go blind. You cannot even *see* some of the colors in my aura. But I will confirm that your guesses have not so far been wrong." The fairy spiked a long glance through the dome, as if consulting a set of notes only she could see. "Time is so *linear* on this plane. We warned you, *I* warned you, so that you could forestall events and create a new future, but those events are happening now. Or will be happening. Or have already." She squinted and shook her head. "Time is linear, but it is also in flux. Just *hurry*, Vizier. Find Grytt, and get to Rory, and to that weapon."

Rupert swallowed glass and sand. His chest hurt from the rapid beating of his heart.

"Thank you," he said, because courtesy was important.

Then he went to do the fairy's bidding.

Grytt, meanwhile, was having her own adventure. She would not have considered it that, having a rather high bar for what she considered hazardous and stimulating, and that bar tilted toward things involving violence. Dealing with bureaucrats qualified in that category, which was why Rupert had been handling negotiations with Dame Maggie. He seemed certain he could both convince Dame Maggie to name him some kind of ambassador or legal something in the Confederation and, once having done so, secure an assignment to Samtalet, where he could avert the fairy's disaster.

Grytt thought Maggie's several-days' delay for "conducting investigations" was a diplomatic stalling tactic that would result in disappointment for Rupert. Maggie had personnel more instrumental to the running of a government and an insurgent war and making first contact. Grytt would have raised that argument with Rupert, except she did not believe in magic, and it would take magic to change Rupert's mind when he set himself on something. Grytt preferred practicality, and so when Rupert had gone off before his meeting (to pace the corridors, Grytt knew, though he'd call it *taking a walk*), she had taken herself down to the transportation center. Maggie was going to say no, and then Rupert would be glad that she'd gotten tickets to Samtalet the conventional way, by waiting in a line and purchasing them.

Grytt had passed her time in the queue engaged in watching passersby and attempting to guess their political affiliations and, from there, their purpose on the station. She had seen a set of matched suits—business, not environmental—in the Sons of John colors, a mirri with her orbiting daughter-buds, and a pair of k'bal who between them had five heads, and whose cranial vents hissed continually as they navigated the swirl of humanity. She had not yet seen evidence of these so-called alwar or tenju, although the station's extranet had declared there was a delegation on board *right now*, and was that not exciting?

Grytt supposed it was, for all shades of that meaning. She also supposed that the xeno visit was the reason that the voidport's normal ticketing windows were closed, and all civilian traffic was coming through *here*, where there should be only cargo, which explained this ridiculous queue which had been unmoving and twenty persons deep for—she glanced at the chrono-display hanging over the administrator's station—eight minutes and forty-seven (eight, nine) seconds while a florid man in expensive clothing made his case for why time, space, and interstellar vessels should adjust to suit his particular need for a direct tesser-hex flight, instead of requiring two transfers along the way.

"I'm sorry, sir," said the clerk in a tone that suggested he was neither sorry nor saying it for the first time (fifty-one seconds, Grytt noted. Fifty-two). "But as I have said, there are no direct flights. I can book you on the *Miracle One*, which will take you to Hennesh, and from there you can—"

There came a collective sigh from the queue, as twenty separate people heaved out the contents of their lungs through clenched teeth and flared nostrils. Everyone had heard this part of the conversation before.

Grytt just hoped he would not purchase one of the last pair of tickets on the shuttle going to Hennesh, which was a shorter journey to Samtalet than either the three-stop itinerary through Thorne (where Grytt did not especially want to go, even if she remained on the void-station and did not descend the beanstalk to the planet) or the connection through the Larish Point, which was little more than a Merchants League waystation and not where Grytt wanted to be stuck with Rupert for a day's layover. Even if Dame Maggie granted Rupert his title and his mission, Grytt was not counting on official transportation. The Confederation was in its infancy, and the majority of its vessels were supporting the war effort. She reckoned they would be lucky to get reimbursed for the travel.

If that overdressed idiot at the front of the queue ever concluded his business.

She considered marching to the front and bodily removing the obstruction. Her notoriety with the Confederation might keep her out of the brig, or at least get her out of it quickly, and she would be performing a public service.

She set her jaw and took a step sideways, out of the queue. At the same time, she noticed a growing susurrus rippling through the usual buzz of commerce and conversation, like a rising wind rattles through leaves and, if it blows hard enough, drowns out the birdsong. Not that the ambient racket of a station was like birdsong. It was a terrible metaphor.

"Excuse me," said a voice in an unfamiliar accent among what had thus far been relentlessly standard GalSpek, from just behind and below her left shoulder. That was her mecha side, and not the one most people selected as a first approach. So she assumed, at first, that the person intended to initiate conversation with someone else, someone possessing two organic eyes and a skull not partly patched with brushed metal. But the novel accent made her turn anyway, slowly and casually, as if she were just looking around. Novelty, at this point in her queueing experience, was of paramount importance.

Then Grytt saw her first alw, and it took every scrap of remembering how much she hated to be stared at to refrain from staring in turn.

(Here we interject: while it is well known that mirri and k'bal are not remotely bipedal or physiologically similar to humanity, it is equally well known that alwar—and tenju, whom we shall encounter later in this chronicle—share similar primary and secondary sexual characteristics with human physiology. This in turn has led to much speculation about species origin and where in their genetic pasts alwar, tenju, and humans diverged. Sexual and gender identities, of course, are not wedded by default to biology, but where it is known to the historical record what the subject's gender identity is, we will employ the appropriate pronouns.)

And so.

The alw was the subject of everyone's attention, except the overdressed man at the front. Grytt, for all her mecha-enhanced bulk, was not a tall woman, but this person came scarcely higher than her collarbone, and seemed frail as a weed. She wore practical spacer clothing: neat, close-fitting trousers, tunic, no broad swaths of exposed skin. She had black skin, truly black, like pitch or void, several shades darker than the charcoal dark of her hair, which was shaved at the sides and drawn up on top of her skull in a tail. Her eyes were an unsettling shade of garnet, and very large in her finely boned face. There were metal rings in her ears, several in each, confined to the upswept cartilage, leaving the scant lobes bare and unpierced.

A second alw stood beside the first. This one, though sharing the same relative dimensions, was much more fair-skinned, with the pinkish undertones found in some humans (Jaed Moss came to mind, and Thorsdottir). His hair was an inoffensive, medium brown, drawn back in a single, sensible braid that hung down his back like a pointing finger. His eyes flicked down the queue, lingering where Grytt knew the k'bal were standing, multiple headstalks tilted in what might be curiosity or deepest disapproval. This alw, too, wore nondescript spacer clothes, but over them he sported a jacket which looked like fashionable affectation, and while it might have been (Grytt had no idea of alwar fashion), she did recognize the gleam of ballistic cloth in tesla-light, and how it was just a little bit stiffer than ordinary fabric.

Fashionable armor, then, which made this alw either soldier or security. He was *apparently* unarmed, because that was the law on Lanscot Station, but Grytt had little faith that diplomats (which these two must be) would be held to the same laws as everyone else.

Grytt cocked her remaining eyebrow at the alw woman. "How can I help you?" There were probably polite honorifics she should be using. But then, this alw had approached her, hadn't she?

"You are Domina Grytt," said the alw. "I am Adept Uo-Zanys Kesk." She bowed from the neck without ever breaking eyelock. "I represent the Harek Empire, and I am here to collect you for transport."

Bureaucrats, whatever their designation, rank, or political affiliation, shared a certainty of their own importance coupled with the conviction that if they deployed their credentials, circumstances would align in the manner they wished. That really only worked, in Grytt's experience, if the bureaucrat had sufficient rank to compel obedience, which meant the audience had to be familiar with that ranking system. Grytt had no idea what an adept was.

"Huh," she said, unmoving, and resisted an urge to fold her arms. The adept knew her name, which lent weight to her credibility, but Grytt was well past jumping whenever a minor functionary thought she should, particularly from a strange species, *particularly* when she was suggesting that Grytt would just go off and get on a ship with her.

The adept, this Uo-Zanys Kesk (Two names! What was she, royalty?), composed her face into a smile that looked a little too small and tight for comfort. "I understand that this greeting may seem abrupt, and I will be happy to answer any questions you may have, but it is urgent that you come with me."

"Huh," Grytt said again. This time she did fold her arms. She speared a look at the other alw, whose hands had drifted a little bit toward his hip, where—aha, yes, there was *indeed* some sort of sidearm, mostly concealed by the sweep of his jacket. But he was not looking at her, which was either insulting or—no. There was some *other* threat.

By now the entire queue, including the overdressed yammerer, had gotten quiet and very attentive. Grytt's remaining flesh prickled.

"What's standing behind me?" she asked the armed alw.

At that, several nearby persons waiting in the queue turned their heads, and one man's hand flew to his mouth as if drawn by a magnet.

That sealed it: Grytt had to look, and so got her first glimpse of tenju.

There were four of them, all roughly Grytt's height: not especially tall by human standards. But they were broader than she, which made them formidable indeed. Unlovely, too, by human metrics; Grytt was reminded of Lanscottar feral boars. These particular tenju wore sensibly, identically constructed close-fitting trousers and shirts, obviously a uniform of some kind. They were looking at the alwar and grinning with nothing like humor or friendliness, and with prominent tusks.

Grytt liked them immediately.

She turned back to the alwar. The armed alw bared his own far less impressive teeth, grin or grimace, or perhaps merely professional recognition.

"They are no one of consequence, Domina," he said softly. His accent was light, lilting, vowel-heavy.

The adept with two names was feigning indifference with the same deliberate dignity as a cat might deploy when safely out of reach of a barking dog. "Please, Domina Grytt, if you'll come with me—"

"She can ride with us," said one of the tenju. His accent was more guttural than the alw's, as if the words were trying to avoid the tusks as long as possible, and then rushing past. "Going the same place, aren't we?"

That begged the obvious question, which Grytt was preparing to ask, when her mecha eye caught movement at the edge of the crowd that had gathered (all while pretending to have business near the ticketing office).

For a man so tall and lanky, Rupert never gave the impression of striding briskly. Grytt blamed his robes, which had been required on Thorne (some archaic costume to which tradition attached far too much importance), and which he persisted in wearing because of some misplaced sentiment despite the inconvenience of farmyards and sheep. He arrived, a little breathless, forehead beaded with sweat at the hairline, skin visibly flushed, which was no minor feat with his complexion.

"Grytt," he announced, as if she did not already know her own name. Then, apparently noticing the tableau, he swung wide to approach from her right side (the next woman in the queue yielded ground without protest) and take her elbow as he leaned close and put his mouth next to her ear.

"We need to leave now. With"—and here he glanced, finally, at the alwar—"with *these* people." Grytt rocked back on her heels. Rupert, of all people, would not forget something as basic as people's names. That must mean he did not know them. He also did not run in public. Confronted by two impossibilities at once, she erred on the side of second-guessing him.

"Does that mean we've got authorization? You're . . . Vizier now, or whatever?"

His hand darted toward his pocket and hovered there, over what Grytt supposed was his handscroll with some official and officious message in barely comprehensible prose that he could take out and wave at the skeptical. A strange smile ghosted his lips. "Vizier, for the moment, until the Confederation parliament comes up with a better title."

"And Dame Maggie's sending us to Samtalet with—" She cast a glance at the adept. "Adept Uo-Zanys Kesk?"

Rupert inclined his head. His heavy robes whispered seditiously among themselves as he reached into their folds. "The Harek Empire has business in that sector, and has offered to courier us to the station. Do you want to see the orders?"

She nodded, slowly, and Rupert retrieved his handscroll, unrolled it, and made a great show of entering an elaborate access code. Then he snapped the scroll straight and flipped it to face her. The document, naming Rupert Vizier of the Confederation of Liberated Worlds, certainly looked authentic. Fancy script, impossible diction, Rupert's name and title prominently associated with the official seal. There was even an amendment, directing him to proceed at once to Samtalet, to establish an embassy there.

She eyelocked Rupert over the rim of the scroll, on the precipice of apology, and saw the corner of his eye twitch. Not a wink, which would have astonished her greatly, but a tiny muscle-spasm that astonished her nearly as much. Rupert was a consummate diplomat, and a formidable card player, because his features were disciplined. She had no doubt that he'd arithmanced his aura into serenity, but that tiny muscle—that she could see only because of her mecha eye, and because she knew him very well—was a betrayal. Rupert was lying. The document was not genuine. And more alarming, Rupert was afraid.

Grytt could think of only one reason that Rupert would be in possession of a forged authorization, or casting himself and her on the transportational mercies of a xeno whose name he did not even know, *and* afraid at the same time.

Something must have happened to Rory.

She drilled him with a *we'll talk later* look, rerolled the scroll, and handed it back to him.

"Right," she said. "I'll go get our bags, then."

Asking what had happened, and what he knew, and what he'd done (corollary, how much trouble they'd be in later) would have to wait. They had a whole trip to Samtalet ahead of them.

CHAPTER FOUR ≡≡≡

B y the time Thorsdottir re-emerged from the cockpit, Jaed had finally gotten himself into his hardsuit and Rory was elbow-deep in the arms-locker. She thrust a 'slinger at Thorsdottir. "Ready?"

Thorsdottir took the weapon, checked charge and load, and clipped it to her chestplate. She pretended not to watch as Rory, and then Jaed, performed the same operation. "The damage to *G. Stein's* hull. Do you know what did it?"

"What damage?" asked Jaed.

Rory sighed. She finished adjusting her helmet before answering. "As I told Zhang, I do not."

Jaed's voice rose and sharpened. "*What damage?*"

"Something that burns without phlogiston," Thorsdottir said. "Something that chewed through the hull of that warship like, like . . ." She made a frustrated noise. "Like it was a *cookie.*"

Jaed's eyes bounced between Thorsdottir and Rory. "What, like plasma?"

Rory had been smiling faintly at the comparison of warships to cookies. Now she sobered again. "We don't know. If it's a battle-hex—"

"If?" Jaed said. "What else would it be?"

—"then it's one I haven't seen before, though I don't pretend I'm an expert in battle-hexes. But it's pretty clearly *not* the Confederation's doing."

"Who *else* would be firing on Tadeshi royalist ships except the Confederation?"

"Well. That's the question, isn't it? We need to get aboard *G. Stein.* The turing might still have some salvageable memory. If there is someone shooting up royalist warships that *isn't* us, then maybe we have a new potential ally."

Thorsdottir sighed. She remembered what Grytt had said about the enemies of my enemies.

"Or a new enemy," said Jaed, who evidently also remembered that lesson.

"Then we need to know that, too." Rory sealed her helmet's visor, which effectively ended the conversation.

Thorsdottir looked at Jaed, who jammed his helmet on with less grace and more force than Rory had. His eyes, pale and blue, blazed through the faceplate like stars.

Thorsdottir settled her own helmet over her skull with more care, visor already down. The seals engaged automatically. The HUD came online with an understated flicker. The suit-to-suit comms hissed to life, accompanied by a trio of green teslas, one for each suit in the link, and the larger, solid green bar that meant the suit was connected to *Vagabond* and—

"Zhang," she said. "Copy?"

"Affirm," said Zhang.

"Proceeding to aetherlock," Thorsdottir said. She cycled the seals. *Vagabond* shivered underfoot. Then the red teslas over the hatch went grey and dim, and the green ones lit up. Everyone crowded into the aetherlock.

There came a hiss, and a puff of what looked like steam.

Thorsdottir's hardsuit reported breathable atmosphere in *G. Stein*, and for a mad moment she was tempted to remove her helmet. Wearing it made her feel like there was something important happening just outside the range of her perception, despite 360 degrees of periphery segmented and displayed in tiny frames along the HUD's border. One of those frames held Rory, shifting from one foot to the other in silent impatience.

Thorsdottir unclipped her 'slinger and put herself between Rory and *G. Stein's* hatch. She knew, without looking, that Rory's eyes would be rolling behind her faceplate. There were some habits of royal service that she couldn't change. Any 'slinger cleared for void-use wouldn't have sufficient force to breach the ship's superstructure, but a desperate defender might toss a grenade through the gap, or risk ricochet and simply open fire, which would result in many bolts pinging around very small space. Better any stray bolts hit *her*.

The hatch irised open. Beyond it, *G. Stein's* emergency lights studded the crease between deck and bulkhead like little beads of blood.

Or rubies, Thorsdottir told herself sternly. Everything red need not be likened to blood.

Her inner Grytt, the existence of whom would have appalled the actual Grytt, observed that liquids would freeze at sufficiently cold temperatures, and that blood was a liquid, and that ships with failing life support got very cold. Thorsdottir silenced that Grytt in terms she would not have dared use with the real one and stepped on *G. Stein's* deck.

No one shot at her. No one threw a grenade. Thorsdottir's HUD had not misinformed her. "*G. Stein* seems deserted. I don't see anyone. The ship's life support seems to be functioning, too,"

Thorsdottir added, in case Rory or Jaed (mostly Jaed) had not noticed.

She led her procession of three up a very long passage to the first intersection. The section seals to the left—no, to the *port*—were irised tight. The starboard corridor, and the one proceeding straight ahead, remained pressurized and accessible.

Thorsdottir stopped. "Where are we trying to go?"

"The bridge," said Rory. "That's where the turing's memory core will be."

Thorsdottir looked at the bulkheads. There were no helpful signs to say where she was. There were only opaque alphanumerics, a code meant for the residents and no one else.

"And how do we get there?"

"I've been on a ship like this, I think," Jaed said. "A tour when I was a kid, some official thing, everyone in fancy clothes. I got lost."

"That is *not* helpful."

Jaed's voice took on a razorish quality. "We go up, Thorsdottir. Of course. The bridge is at the top of the ship. That I *do* know."

Up. Thorsdottir panned her headlamp both ways. This ship—all ships, anymore, that traveled in void—had gravity-hexes. Up and down became a matter of design. *G. Stein*, from the outside, looked like a pair of slightly convex disks welded together on the edges. There *was* no up. There was only *around*.

"Jaed. Don't make me ask."

"The corridors coil clockwise to ascend," he said.

"That means port," said Rory. "Left. We're going left."

"Jaed and I will take point." Thorsdottir hoped she sounded as fiercely obdurate as Grytt. "You're behind us, Pr—Rory." She paused, in case of argument.

"Mm," said Rory, in the same way she might acknowledge the

observation that her tea had gotten cold. She was staring at something only she could see, eyes focused somewhere vaguely *up* and *over there.* "I'm tracking that rogue transmission. It's coming from this way."

"Of course it is," Thorsdottir muttered. "Come on, Jaed."

She peered up the port passage as far as her headlamp would illuminate, 'slinger raised. Then she held her breath and darted across the opening. No one shot at her, or at Jaed, who remained to cover that passage while Thorsdottir forged on ahead. There was another intersection upcoming in four meters or so. As Thorsdottir maneuvered to see if the seals were engaged, the emergency teslas dimmed suddenly, as if someone or something conspicuously absent from the HUD had cast a shadow across them.

Thorsdottir held up her un- 'slingered hand. Jaed stopped at once.

"Did you see that?"

"Yes." He sounded unhappy. "But I don't know what I saw."

"Rory, Jaed and I will investigate . . . whatever that was we just saw. You wait here." Thorsdottir paused, leaving silence where there might have been a *Princess* or a *Highness.*

"Mm." Rory's gaze hung in the unfocused nowhere that an arithmancer's attention went to when they were busy.

Right. Thorsdottir began edging forward into the cross-corridor. There were section seals here, poised to close in case of emergency. The bulkheads continued the alphanumeric tradition. This one said C-15b. She panned her headlamp up, over the bulkhead, onto the overhead. Nothing. She was on the verge of declaring the shadow nothing more than a power fluctuation in the teslas, subcategory, *overactive imagination*, when another flicker caught her attention further up the starboard cross-passage.

She took a step toward it, exactly far enough to ascertain that no, it was just another dark patch likely due to a tesla malfunction and nothing more nefarious. She started to turn back, toggling the comm with her chin, drawing breath to report it was nothing.

She saw Jaed coming into the cross-passage. They locked eyes through his faceplate.

Then, abruptly, the section seal irised shut.

"Wait! What was that? *Thorsdottir!*" Jaed slammed his fists against the unyielding metal. "Rory!"

Rory heard both her name and the dull boom of Jaed's assault from several layers deep in the aether. The multiverse was composed of numbers, described by mathematics; Messer Rupert had said, somewhat whimsically, that math was the language of the multiverse. He was not *wrong* about that; but practically, when one was trying to navigate an unfamiliar corridor in a hardsuit *and* carry on a conversation, the math tended to mumble. Or rather, *blur*, because Rory saw the equations, rather than heard them: the pressure of the atmosphere inside the corridor, the concentrations of aetheric gases, winking in and out of visibility at varying intervals, with varying brightness. The mysterious transmission was winkier and dimmer than the rest, and harder to track.

No. It was *impossible* to track, with Jaed's shouting. And her HUD was flashing at her, too, something about a dropped contact—

Oh. *Oh.*

She slammed back into the primary layer of aether with an eye-watering blink.

Jaed hit the section seal a second time. "Thorsdottir!"

"Thorsdottir. *Thorsdottir,* do you copy?" Zhang was not shouting, but the intensity of her distress made Rory's chest hurt. "Jaed, what's happening? She dropped off the link."

Rory caught her breath—she always forgot to breathe regularly, when she was trying to arithmance and walk at the same time—and studied her HUD. The comm-teslas for Jaed and *Vagabond* were still green. Thorsdottir's was grey.

That could be a sudden equipment failure. Or it could be—well. Something that didn't bear thinking about, and which she had to consider nevertheless.

"Rory," said Zhang. Her voice was brittle, steady, on the comms. "I cannot raise Thorsdottir on the comm."

"Neither can we. Stand by."

Jaed gave up attacking the indifferent metal and rounded on her. The hardsuit's headlamp bleached his features, smoothed them, so that he looked like a mask of himself. "The seal

was it arithmancy

just *closed*. Why?"

didn't you stop it

The thirteenth fairy's gift to Rory, at her naming, had been to know the truth, however anyone tried to conceal it. But because one of the other fairy gifts had been kindness, and because she had been a princess until very recently and therefore accustomed to diplomacy, Rory squelched the urge to snap, *You, too, know some arithmancy, so why aren't you also partly at fault?* at him.

She held up a hand instead, *stay* or *wait* or perhaps *be quiet*, and went to the seal. The Tadeshi emblem was painted on the metal, a small portion of it on each petal of the iris. On the bulkhead beside the seal, there was a panel, complete with a card reader and a keypad. The panel stared back at her, blankly unhelpful. The keypad had clearly been designed for fingertips, not fingertips inside of hardsuit gauntlets. That didn't matter. All she needed to do was dip into the aether, and access the turing responsible for the locks—

Rory sank her awareness into the layer of aether where turing codes lived, the reality of machine intelligence. On a station, there were hundreds of these: little turings, each individual and not quite conscious and yet linked to the larger system. On a ship there was usually one primary turing, self-aware; intelligence dependent on ship make, model, and purpose. A warship's turing would be smarter than most. But the layer of *G. Stein's* aether on which there should be swirling machine-code-sentience was blank and dark, like staring into a deep hole whose edges and depth she could not see.

"The main turing's dead," she whispered. "I don't mean offline. I mean *dead*. And that's not even right. It's more like its intelligence has been destroyed, and its body, this ship, is carrying on in its absence."

"You're not supposed to be *able* to kill a warship turing like that. They're shielded and—it's just not supposed to happen. There are redundancies. Failsafes."

"And yet, it has." Rory prodded the panel with her fingertip. The touchscreen was unresponsive. "Maybe we can get the panel off and . . . I don't know. Open the hatch that way?"

Jaed's headlamp splashed down over her glove and onto the panel and the iris and the very edges of the Tadeshi device. "I can't do that. I have no *idea* how to do that."

"Neither do I." Rory closed her eyes. Then, having little hope of success, she cracked them open again and dropped her perception into the second aetheric layer. She did not know how to open a mechanical lock with arithmancy, but if Messer Rupert was right (and he always was) then there must be a way to do it. Math was the language of the multiverse. Just change a word, change reality, maybe, and she'd get the seal open.

First, she saw the mysterious transmission she'd been following, still present and brighter than she'd seen it so far, its equation rippling like a flag. Then, as had been its habit when noticed, it retreated deeper into the aether and out of sight, like ducking behind a convenient tree in a forest. She ignored it. No time for distractions right now. Rory pushed her concentration into the mechanism of the section seal itself. The equations here were harder, less forgiving. Usually there was a flicker on the variables, some hint of what could be changed. Here, she saw nothing except an alphanumeric line, black and static and *lifeless*. It was as if the moving parts of the seal had been fused.

Thorsdottir was on the other side of that seal, however, and so she had to try something. She did. And then she tried another something, and a third, and a fourth, to the same effect as Jaed's punches.

Then she saw movement: a flash, like light striking a mirror, small and fleeting (and unpleasant) as a needle-prick. She bent her attention that way, and saw another flash on her periphery, and felt another prick. It was a tiny hex, the tiniest she'd ever seen. And there were *many* of them.

That layer of aether turned white and solid. And then it, *they*, threw her out of it.

Rory blinked. Her eyes were watering in sympathetic aftermath. There was no *actual* physical sensation to which her body could respond. But her psyche prickled. So did her pride.

"I can't get it open." And then, because she knew Jaed would ask (Zhang wouldn't; Zhang would just despair quietly): "This was arithmancy. Is arithmancy.—Don't," she said, as Jaed turned toward the panel. "Don't touch that. It's—active. Some kind of battle-hex on the seal."

That wasn't exactly true. She was fairly sure whatever had just hit her was not a battle-hex, but she did not know what *else* to call it. Effective, certainly: that seal was not going to open. The very mechanisms were fused, and the little sparkling needle-stabs were actively making sure that they stayed that way. Jaed took a physical step back from the panel. "So there *is* an arithmancer on board."

"Or there was, and this is their parting gift to us." Rory's head was beginning to ache. She wished she could pinch the bridge of her nose. She settled for leaning her forehead against the helmet's interior.

Jaed peered into her faceplate. "Are you all right?"

I have just been attacked by a million invisible, tiny battle-hexes. Fortunately, Rory's fairy gift did not require *her* honesty, and so she said only, "Yes."

Jaed's gaze flicked down. His lips pursed, then moved silently, but with exaggerated deliberation, so that she could not misunderstand, and so that Zhang could not hear: "Your nose is bleeding."

So it was. Rory sniffed hard and swallowed. "Fine," she mouthed back at him.

Jaed was just enough of an arithmancer to know that was both true and not. His jaw squared off. "What now?"

Rory wished, sometimes, that people would try to answer that question themselves instead of soliciting her opinion. But then, she thought guiltily, she had a habit of ignoring what other people suggested if it crossed her own desires. Jaed probably just thought he was being efficient by asking her first.

This time, however, she did not possess the pertinent knowledge.

"I'm not the one who grew up on void-stations. You tell me. How do we get around a section seal?"

Jaed was momentarily quiet. The backsplash from his headlamp carved new shadows into his features. For a moment, he looked alarmingly like his father, and Rory felt her skin creep. Then he whipped around and dropped to his knees on the decking. "On a ship this size, there will be maintenance tubes. There are access panels at every intersection—here."

Rory was impressed. She wouldn't have seen the panel door. Or rather, she would not have noticed the seams in the bulkhead and thought *someone can get behind that*. Jaed pried the panel off and set it aside. There were numbers and letters stenciled on the back, where they would have been visible from the tunnel's interior. Rory could see the faint bleed of emergency teslas from inside the tunnel.

Jaed poked head and shoulders into the shaft. "On a station, mecha do the maintenance. But *military* ships use human crew, so the tubes have to be big enough for a hardsuit in case of emergencies. *And*, human crew means the tubes are numbered. My father wanted the military to go to mecha, because they're cheaper. That was one of the arguments he lost with the Minister of Defense." Jaed looked up at her. He wore a faint smile, brittle on the edges, that Rory didn't think he was aware of. "Which is good for us. We can count our way through the decks. So where are we going?"

This time, Rory had a ready answer. "We were heading for the bridge. Thorsdottir knows that. She'll meet us there, if she can. So—up, Jaed. We're going up."

CHAPTER FIVE

Thorsdottir resisted the urge to pound on the unfeeling steel. She clenched her fists and silenced her distraught hardsuit. The teslas associated with everyone else—Jaed, Rory, Zhang—were grey and dim. That was . . . bad.

"Jaed?" Her voice seemed small and thin in the helmet's confines. "Do you copy?"

She waited. The interior of her helmet remained silent, except for the puff of her own exasperation. A section seal didn't close like that without provocation, usually in the form of explosive decompression or a fire or, worse thought, some arithmancer's prodding.

Thorsdottir closed her eyes and counted to five. Then she thrust her chin harder into the toggle. "Rory? Jaed? *Zhang*?"

Then, very abruptly, the emergency teslas went out, turning the passageway into a weighted, hungry black that nibbled at her suit's teslas, chewing away the meager glow of the HUD. Her helmet still had its headlamp, which punched a pool of brilliance into the dark, and which would alert anyone out there where she was, so they would know precisely where to aim a 'slinger bolt.

Thorsdottir chilled and prickled at once, from her skin to her most interior organ.

"Zhang, do you copy?" she said, with no real hope of response.

This time, she heard the channel hiss. And then, more than that: a murmuring, almost inaudible. A voice, or at least something *like* a voice. But not the sure rhythms of normal conversation or the hammering cadence of troops calling orders. It was a more liquid utterance, less disciplined, wandering a range of tones and pitches, like a song. The melody resolved itself, suddenly, into syllables which sounded very much like *help me* and *this way.*

The hardsuits were supposed to be hexed against interference and external meddling.

The channel hissed again. This time, it took no imagination at all to hear *this way* in the whispers.

Then the emergency teslas on the deck lit up again in sequence, starting from the one nearest Thorsdottir's boots and proceeding up the corridor, one by one. Then they all went dark again, for a heartbeat, before repeating the sequence.

And again. And—

"All right," Thorsdottir said. "I'm coming."

She made her way through the darkened ship, herded by the emergency teslas until the passage coiled down and around almost a full revolution. The teslas stopped at another sealed hatch, the bulkhead beside which bore the label Cargo 15b. This seal was not an iris, but a thick, flat wedge of metal that had dropped from the overhead and which dragged itself up as she approached, revealing an unlit interior space. The emergency teslas seemed reluctant to trespass, and flickered nervously at the threshold.

Thorsdottir did not find that especially comforting. Her hardsuit told her that there was breathable atmosphere in the hold, and that its outer hull doors remained sealed, and that there were not, to its knowledge, any outstanding heat sources that might be a talented arithmancer wearing a hardsuit.

Of course, her suit had been hacked. That made its reports suspect.

Thorsdottir weighed the possibilities that, having led her all this way, a supremely talented Tadeshi arithmancer meant to kill her anyway. Then she dipped her chin inside the helmet and stomped forward into the cargo bay, leaving her emergency tesla escorts behind.

A new bank of teslas greeted her, blue-white and studding a series of brushed steel cases mag-locked to both deck and overhead, one row on each side, like an honor guard (or a firing squad). They were, as she got a closer look at them, easily identifiable as cryostasis units, the sort used for transporting perishable organics, medicine, and occasionally individuals (although that practice was generally illegal, except for the transportation of prisoners, and even *then* the legality depended upon the jurisdiction).

Thorsdottir examined one of the units, pleased, and then puzzled, to find its contents neatly labeled. She frowned. She was no scholar, but she had done well enough in botany to recognize the word *rosoideae*. The fiction of labeling smuggled goods as something other than they were made perfect sense, when she had assumed that *G. Stein* was a civilian vessel. Civilian, owned-by-a-florist *G. Stein* could have carried roses among its cargo without comment. But since its masquerade as civilian vessel went only as far as its false ID transmission, there would be no need to carry on the ruse into its cargo hold. Besides, cryostasis units like these were expensive, both in currency and in power consumption; and no one would waste that kind of hardware on decorative plants.

And there was still the matter of the arithmancer. *Someone* had hacked her suit. And someone had wanted her to come here to this cargo bay of falsely labeled roses. It was all very vague, but

Thorsdottir had been a guard to royalty and was accustomed to having incomplete information and needing to act anyway.

She peered down the bay's dim length, where she could just make out the columnar silhouette of a turing console bolted to the bulkhead at the far end, near the massive exterior aetherlock. Double-wide doors, meant for ease of moving cargo to some location with breathable atmosphere. She walked to it slowly, half expecting an ambush from the shadows, or those doors to pop open and suck her into the void, but nothing happened.

The turing console's interface had not been designed for hard-suited fingers. She stared, frustrated, at the tiny keypad and the turing's blank standby screen.

Which, as if it sensed her attention, produced the words, *help me*, at the same instant she heard the same sentiment wisp through her comms.

Thorsdottir swallowed dust and her own hammering heart. There were a couple of ways one could address an unexpected encounter. The 'slinger, while comforting, did not seem appropriate, or useful, or warranted. If something wanted to talk first, then that path was worth pursuing.

She engaged the ex-comms on her helmet, even though she suspected what-or-whoever had hacked her could hear what she said anyway.

"Who are you? *Where* are you?" She felt more than a little bit foolish, talking to a terminal in an empty cargo bay.

The screen blanked again. Then the word *rose* typed itself out, just as the predictable whisper returned.

Thorsdottir wondered if this arithmancer, this *suit-hacker*, was playing some kind of game, the rules of which they knew and she did not.

"You're . . . hiding in the roses? In one of the stasis units?"

rose

Not exactly a denial. "Rose? That's, what, your name?"

rose, the screen confirmed.

The name was . . . unlikely. This entire *scenario* was unlikely. Play along. Thorsdottir felt her lips arrange themselves in a smile of the sort one deployed with small children on the verge of a tantrum.

"Fine. Rose, my name is Thorsdottir. Where are you?"

rose

The only possible source of this limited conversation was the turing console. Thorsdottir knew that sentient turings were impossible, though she did not know the exact arithmantic reasons. Rory would know, of course . . . but maybe, *maybe*, Rory did not know everything.

"Are you in the turing, Rose? *Are* you the turing?"

rose

Right. If Rose was a turing, they did not seem to be very clever. Unless Rose was, well, *a rose*, which seemed even more unlikely.

Although, Thorsdottir reminded herself, Rose—turing, plant, whatever they were—*had* gotten her down here alone. Her smile flaked away. "What do you want?"

The screen blanked, and paused, and Thorsdottir had the absurd impression that it was thinking. Then:

flesh

That seemed fairly horrible, but Thorsdottir was also a little relieved. She was good at dealing with threats, and disinclined to be anyone's supper, *and* she had a working sidearm.

Although . . . flesh was an odd word to use, if ingestion was the intent. Meat would've been better. *Flesh* was living meat. Maybe if Rose needed Thorsdottir's flesh, it was because Rose did not have any of Rose's own.

The back of Thorsdottir's neck prickled tight. "For what, exactly?"

The screen remained blank. Perhaps Rose was simply too polite to say *I want to kill you.*

Then, after a long interval, the screen coughed up: *rose.*

"Right, I got that. That's your name. I asked what you wanted with flesh. *My* flesh."

The screen filled with a column of *roseroserose.* At the same time, the cargo hold's blue-white overhead teslas rippled like leaves in strong wind, spangling the crates with electromagnetic raindrops. Then they went out, bank by bank, until only the cryostasis units were illuminated, bathed in pools of white light.

It was, Thorsdottir thought, the equivalent of a turing throwing a tantrum, complete with pointing fingers and punctuated by shouts. It was also clear what Rose wanted Thorsdottir to do with her convenient flesh.

"I am not opening those," Thorsdottir said firmly. "Not until you tell me what the contents are."

roseroserose

"No. That's what the label says. That's not what's really inside, or . . ." Her stomach dropped. "Or *who.*"

The channel remained silent for a chain of heartbeats. The screen remained blank. Perhaps the turing was martialing patience, or reconsidering Thorsdottir's edibility, or deciding whether or not to short out her suit's life support. Then the screen lit up, revealing an official-looking document bearing the seal of the Tadeshi royalists and the word classified in bold red, on which the word *rose* figured prominently numerous times. Then the screen abruptly resized its display, and the official-looking document resolved itself into words that, as Thorsdottir began to read, turned her guts to cold jelly all over again.

She knew that honorable warfare was a diplomatic term, and that battlefield realities were different. She knew that collateral damage was inevitable and undesirable, but occasionally strategically necessary. And she knew that things in classified documents were rarely comforting. But there were some strategies that, if executed, would change the whole shape of a conflict.

What she saw on the screen was just such a thing.

It was a set of orders for the transport and eventual deployment of an alchemical weapon. A weapon which would, if she understood correctly, destroy an entire biosphere by infesting it with nanomecha which would alchemically transmute life-supporting molecules into lifeless ones, rendering the planet both uninhabited and uninhabitable. Except nanomecha were entirely theoretical, beyond even the most advanced alchemy and robotics. *Size matters, that's the problem*, Rory had said once, after a viewing of a poorly rated fantasy-horror in which nanomecha-borne disease infected a void-station and turned everyone into monsters that the handsome and none-too-bright hero had then been forced to kill. *We haven't figured out how to program them collectively.*

Well. Someone appeared to have solved that problem, and then sold the result to the Tadeshi.

"The roses," Thorsdottir said. "They're the weapon."

She didn't realize she'd said it out loud until the screen blanked again. Then a single word appeared in the center.

yes

Another length of Jaed's body disappeared into the maintenance shaft.

"Maybe I should go first," said Rory. "I'm a better—"

"Arithmancer? Yes. But I'm a better shot." Jaed wiggled all the way into the shaft. His voice, strained through the comm speakers, sounded a little breathless. "Not that I'll have a hand free to fire a 'slinger. It's tight in here."

"Zhang," Rory murmured, "We're proceeding to the bridge."

"Acknowledged."

Then she got down on her knees on the deckplate and followed Jaed into the shaft.

It *was* tight.

She spent the next thirty minutes staring at Jaed's boots, mostly vertical, occasionally canted at an alarming lateral angle. The shafts were minimally lit, either because of the EM damage from the unknown attacker or because it was assumed anyone in the shaft would provide their own light. The suit's headlamps did that, although they responded to the ambient dark by dimming themselves so as not to blind their users. The effect was rather like crawling through a metal tube filled with twilight.

Jaed's boots stopped. The tiny blue teslas on his heels stared at her like eyes.

"Bridge," he said, closely followed by a muttered, "I think. I hope. It's the end of the shaft, anyway."

There came a dull thump as Jaed wrestled with the access panel, followed by a vibration that Rory felt through her hardsuit as the panel hit metal decking. Then the ominous red of emergency teslas slivered down the shaft.

Jaed let out a squawk, and then an expletive. He did not move.

"What is it?" Rory asked sharply.

Jaed did not appear to be in distress, which is to say, he was not kicking or trying to back up or making wet gasping noises. He was, however, breathing a little bit hard, which could be blamed on the last half hour's exertions, or, Rory suspected, whatever it was he was seeing.

At least he did *not* sound as if he'd met a patrol of marines, or someone demanding he exit the shaft or they'd shoot.

Rory smacked Jaed's ankle. His foot jerked. Then, without comment (and now she *was* worried; Jaed was not especially taciturn), he crawled out of the shaft. Rory scrambled after him, and lurched out into—

Oh.

Rory had seen footage of uncontrolled decompression before, although mostly in the special effects of e-vid renderings, enhanced for extra drama and gore. She knew that human skin would resist the dramatic burst, and that people's insides tended to remain, well, inside. Vomit was not as appealing, so the e-vids tended to leave that out. It was much in evidence here, on the deck and on consoles and staining the fronts of uniforms that were all Tadeshi royalist military; there had been no attempt at maintaining the civilian fiction on board. She identified a captain's insignia on the woman sprawled in the center of the deck, and what appeared to be several other officer insignias through the smears of digestive effluvia. The blood, fortunately, was minimal, a trickle of red here and there, from nostrils and mouths, and from at least one wide eye Rory glimpsed, the white of which had gone entirely red.

"Don't throw up," Rory said, because Jaed was making unfortunate choking gasps inside his helmet. "Breathe."

She wondered why she did not need her own advice, and, ironically, felt a little queasy that she didn't.

"*Rory?*"

"Fine, Zhang. We're fine. The bridge crew isn't, though. Stand by."

G. Stein's bridge was far larger than *Vagabond's* pair of chairs and a jumpseat. The pilot's and gunner's stations were opposite the maintenance shaft, partly concealed behind the central pillar display with its multiple screens and the primary turing console. Rory stepped over the captain's outflung limbs. There was a cabinet marked with the universal symbol for emergency, and the more descriptive, neatly stenciled *Environmental Suits*. The cabinet appeared unopened.

Jaed panned his headlamp across the bulkhead, the overhead, the deck. He sounded steadier, as if his insides would also remain where they were, and also *firmer*. "What *happened* here?"

"I think that's obvious."

"But it's not. This decompression happened too fast. Faster than a ship's emergency systems would have reacted to an emergency. The crew should've had time to get to the suits, even if there was a breach or a fire. *And* the seals would've shut." He waved a hand at the bridge doors, which were closed, but without the spiraled iris of a pressure seal. "This had to be some kind of battle-hex."

He was right. Rory examined that realization carefully, as if it might explode and take the rest of the known multiverse with it. She knew that she was being unfair: she was annoyed with Jaed for seeing what she should have before she had, and *more* annoyed— and, let us be honest, *afraid*—because she had no more idea how this had happened than he did.

She stalked to the main pillar console. There was a body slumped in the chair, over which (whom? when did a corpse cease to rate human pronouns?) Rory leaned carefully. She peered into the turing screen, and then *through* it, into the aetheric layers. She could see the mathematical descriptions of the physical elements— polymers, alloys, circuits. On the next layer, where the usual workings of turings happened, there was nothing. She plucked one of the corpse's hands aside, gently and without looking at it or its owner, and tapped a sequence of keys.

The turing did not respond. But the screen coughed up a display, consisting of cryptic alphanumerics that all meant, essentially, *this turing is dead*. There were pieces of code, as if something had detonated inside the turing's primary system and blown its code into shards.

Rory's stomach turned again. She had seen a bomb's aftermath, in her childhood on Thorne, when her father had died. She had never been permitted to see what remained of her father, but she imagined he must've looked a little bit like this.

"*We* don't have any battle-hexes that can do this." She stated the obvious, in the hope that something better would present itself.

Something better did not. Something worse did, in Zhang's cool, practical voice: "*Then who else are the Tadeshi at war with?*"

Jaed made a noise like water on hot metal. "I'd have said no one. One war is enough. And *where* this happened—I mean, we're on the edge of the Verge out here. There's really *nothing* except SAM-1 and a few planets no one wants to live on and a lot of unexplored void."

That was not entirely true. "The k'bal have a couple of colonies on this edge of the Verge, if I remember right," said Rory. "And they're all arithmancers."

"The k'bal didn't do *this*." Jaed panned his headlamp over the bulkheads as if he could see through them to the void on the other side. "I mean, they're pacifists."

"Well, maybe *they* offended someone. Or there's, I don't know, such a thing as angry k'bal."

"Who then turned around and killed a Tadeshi ship? I don't think so. What about that transmission you intercepted? What if all this is sabotage, and the responsible arithmancer's still on board?"

"You watch too many e-vids." Rory was certain that was not the case. Almost certain. "The transmission disappeared when the seal closed behind Thorsdottir." She did not add that she had not exactly looked for it since then, either. Her sinuses still watered when she remembered the hexes that had thrown her out of the aether.

"It's either a saboteur or some unknown xeno-invasion from the Verge," Jaed said tartly. "Which do you prefer?"

"I *don't* prefer. That transmission was more like a whisper. Crude. Whatever did this—well, it's amazing, complex work."

"*It might be an act of war,*" said Zhang flatly. "*I am looking at G. Stein's hull right now. We do not know of a weapon that can inflict that sort of damage, nor who might possess it, but it seems reasonable that those same people might have other weapons that we cannot imagine.*" She paused. Then, in a brittle voice, as if she spoke with a chestful of broken glass, "*You should return to Vagabond at once.*"

"Not without Thorsdottir," Jaed said, but he was looking at Rory.

Rory nodded at him. "Not without Thorsdottir. Stand by, Zhang."

She cut the comms to *Vagabond.* She left her forehead resting on the switch, so that Zhang could neither hear nor respond. "Except, Jaed, listen. I don't know how to get the seals open without the turing. I don't even know how to *start.*"

"I might have an idea." Jaed circled around the main pillar. After a few seconds of staring at what seemed to be blank metal from close range, he popped open a panel and stuffed a hand into the console, as far as the hardsuit's glove permitted. His face worked behind the visor, grimace to scowl to squint-eyed concentration.

Rory knew from experience that the tactile interface on the hardsuits wasn't especially sensitive. Whatever Jaed was feeling around for would have to be big or obvious—

A small shower of sparks erupted from the console, like incandescent snowflakes. Every emergency tesla on the bridge went out simultaneously, dropping them into a sea of darkness with two little headlamp islands.

"Jaed."

"Um."

The deck shivered. Then the entire bridge lit up, every panel, every tesla, except for a significant pattern on the central panel, which remained grey and dim.

Rory blinked. "What just happened?"

"Manual system override." Jaed sounded a little breathless. "We're lucky. This is an older ship. The new ones don't *have* manual switches."

Lucky had not been a word Rory would've associated with this situation. Still, it appeared that Jaed had done something useful. That grey panel on the main console, though, worried her. "The turing is still dead. Shouldn't it be rebooting?"

"It should." Jaed straightened. He frowned at the pillar, then, after a moment, struck it with a closed fist.

The lights remained dim.

"That never works," Rory murmured. "Hitting things as a means of repair. Especially turings."

"You'd be surprised." Jaed flashed her a grin that faded as fast as it had appeared. "There should be a secondary turing, though. This is a warship. There's never one of *any* important system."

"The attack must have targeted the turings specifically, then, and taken them both out." Rory was caught between admiration and dismay. A battle-hex that could take out a shielded warship turing (two!) could either be a great help to the Confederation or devastate it completely. This was also the last settled system before the Verge, the very edge of human-held void. Chances were good (or very, very bad) that *G. Stein's* attackers had been xeno, of some new and hostile kind.

In the interval while Rory had been pondering the possibility of a new and hostile power, Jaed had crossed the bridge. He stood now in front of the bridge doors, which, to Rory's surprise, slid apart as he got close to them.

He let out a little whoop. "The automated systems are back online. Barring an actual breach in the hull, we should be able to just walk down to Thorsdottir."

Rory did not mention that Thorsdottir's hardsuit still did not register, or that, if there *were* saboteurs trapped in some sealed-off section, Jaed had just let them loose.

She said only, "Then let's go get her."

CHAPTER SIX

Rory discovered three things, as she descended the decks on *G. Stein*. The first was that the attackers had gone no higher than deck three. The second was that any fears of meeting survivors were unfounded. The third was that, however unprepared she might feel, picking through the aftermath of what had been a terrible battle, Jaed Moss was even more so.

"Breathe," Rory said, a repetition somewhere between ten and infinity. "Don't throw up."

"I *won't*," Jaed snapped—or gasped, more accurately—also a repetition between ten and infinity. He had so far kept that promise, despite some audible gagging.

The carnage on the lower decks was both worse and not as bad as on the bridge. There, Rory had been able to distract herself by wondering *how* exactly the battle-hex had accomplished the bridge decompression, in the most shielded and defended portion of the ship. *Here*, the cause of death in the corridors was much more apparent: a number of scorch-marks and burns reminiscent of the damage on the ship's hull, which suggested that the same sort of weapon had been used, and that it had much the same effect on Tadeshi marine hardsuits as it did on Tadeshi warships.

"Rory," Jaed said, and startled Rory out of her grim examination of yet another corpse. She looked away from her subject—faceshield cracked, helmet twisted at an impossible angle—and looked at Jaed, who was standing near a bulkhead on which there was a large splash of blood, presumably from the crumpled, armored heap on the deck, around which there was an equally impressively large stain.

Rory wished—quietly, carefully, in the farthest corner of her mind—that the teslas would all go out again. "Don't throw up, Jaed, just *breathe*—"

"I *am* breathing." He sucked in an audible lungful, then let it go. "Just look at this." He hovered a finger above a tear in the armor. The edges poked up like broken teeth, jagged and darkly stained.

Rory took her own advice (breathe, don't throw up) and looked at what remained of the person on the other side of that armor. "We already know whoever did this has superior weaponry."

"Yeah. But this isn't burn damage. This is *tearing* damage."

"So they're stronger than we are, too." This was the sort of information that Leadership (capital-L, which meant Dame Maggie and the Confederation parliament on Lanscot) needed to know. It was not something she wanted to examine in greater detail in the pitiless glare of the overhead teslas.

Rory stood up, perhaps too quickly. For a moment her vision sparked before it steadied, on a long inhale.

"Breathe," Jaed muttered. Rory was unsure if he meant that advice for himself, or for her. She took it anyway. It seemed hotter in her suit than it had on the bridge.

Jaed was still talking, something about the concentration of bodies, making a stand. Chatter, clearly, to hide his own discomfort. She wished he would shut up. She opened her mouth to say so—her kindness fully exhausted, along with her patience—and barely got her mouth shut in time, as bile surged up the back of her throat.

She closed her eyes and leaned against the inside of her helmet. Breathe, get her stomach settled, she was—had been—a princess, she was Rory Thorne, she would *not* throw up in a hardsuit.

She gasped. Her lungs burned.

"Rory?" Jaed's voice sounded thin, tinny.

Like a voice might sound in minimal atmosphere. She couldn't breathe because there really *wasn't* enough oxygen.

Several thoughts chased themselves through her head in the interval between heartbeats. The first was that there must be a crack in her suit, somehow, leaking her air. The second was that her HUD had advised no such thing, which meant there *was* oxygen and the suit had malfunctioned. The third was that her suit was lying to her, which it would not do unless it had been hacked.

She was sure she would have noticed a hacking attempt, but she was even more sure that she could not breathe, and the need was becoming acute. Her HUD said that there was atmosphere in the ship, and whether or not it was safe, it was her only option.

She slapped at the seals on her helmet, then grabbed and twisted. The suit resisted, or seemed to. She clawed at her helmet.

Jaed's face appeared, square in her faceplate. His mouth was moving in what appeared to be repetitions of her name, and the perfectly logical *what's wrong*, and probably *you can't just break the suit seal like that, who knows what's in the air.*

But then he grabbed the sides of her head, pushing her flapping hands aside, and *twisted*. The seals broke with a hiss, and then canned ship atmosphere, cold and dry and smelling of burned metal, burned meat, and blood, rushed into her suit.

Rory gasped, and sucked it into her lungs, and thought it was the best breath she'd ever drawn.

Then she collapsed into coughing. She hardly noticed when Jaed pulled her helmet off with more speed than accuracy, snagging her ear and sending a bolt of pain through the side of her head. Ears could be replaced, or sewn back on, and were not, in any case, as important as breathing.

Jaed held both her shoulders and somehow refrained from asking her anything. When she blinked the cough-inspired tears out of her eyes, she saw that his mouth was moving, and though his eyes were firmly fixed on her, she suspected he was talking to Zhang on his comms.

"Thank you," she said, when she could speak at all.

"What happened?" His voice echoed through his ex-comm speaker.

"My—I couldn't breathe. My suit had no air."

Jaed's eyes, which had been wide and horrified, narrowed, and at the same time, unfocused. He was probably checking her aura, which was a gauge of honesty but also of physical condition: a dying body's aura was more faint, or sometimes discolored, depending on the cause.

"Am I," she began to ask, but then Jaed's expression shifted to another one with which she was familiar.

It was the look of an arithmancer who has seen something both unexpected and unwelcome, and, judging from the sudden scattering of sparks across the skin of Jaed's hardsuit, hostile.

Rory recalled her own recent battle with impossibly numerous, tiny hexes, and shifted her awareness accordingly. It wasn't a particularly good idea; a mind focused on arithmancy tended to assume that its body was handling basic functions, and her body was not entirely recovered from interruptions to essential services. Nevertheless, she needed to *see.*

The trouble seemed to be the same as before, the mirror-flash shards of miniscule hexes, separate and uncountable and still moving and hexing together like a school of malevolent fish. They had already scored a hit on Jaed; the equations along the seams of his faceplate were blackened and smeared, which Rory assumed to be an attack on the seal integrity. As she watched, Jaed worked a counter-hex. The smeared edges of the equation sharpened, then flared a bright plasma blue which cooled into steely perfection.

Good, thought Rory: a teacher's pride in her student. But that pride proved short-lived. The school of hex-shards was collecting for another attack. She marveled that she could *see* them at all, or their movements. It was as if they were some kind of arithmantic disruption, or on some level, animated arithmancy.

Jaed, meanwhile, was preparing his own retaliatory strike. His arithmancy was flashier, or, as the less charitable might say, unrefined. He was attempting to eject the attackers from this layer of aether. It was a bold effort, made bolder by Jaed's unfortunately vivid hexes. If they survived this, she would need to teach him about subtlety.

And if he failed, well—he had a very good idea, and one she might also attempt. Rendering a layer of aether impossible to an arithmancer required a fairly sophisticated hex, and it was something she had tried only in practice, rather than practical application, same as Jaed. But she was feeling inspired. These shards appeared to work in conjunction. Perhaps that was both their strength and their strategy. Rory meant to make it their weakness, as well.

The shards drew together, clustering in a glittering cloud. They hovered for a moment, twisting back and forth, as if making a decision about who was the greater danger. Then they speared toward Jaed and swarmed over his hardsuit. From this in-aether perspective, it appeared as if they became a single, molten entity. Their underlying equations—what made them *real*—were still imperceptible to Rory in this layer of aether. In order to make her hex work, she'd need to see them. She hoped Jaed could withstand them for a moment or two. Time moved at different rates in the different aetheric layers. *His* moments would be minutes to her. And still, she had to hurry.

She sank one layer deeper, and then a third. *Now* she could see the hex-shards' code. It was extremely tiny, and very intricate, knotted around itself in dizzying equations that seemed to shift as Rory observed them. There were also a great many of them and, from a cursory look, they appeared to be identical. They also looked like nothing Rory had ever seen, not a turing, nor even a sophisticated array of battle-hexes. There was a helical shape to their arranging that was reminiscent of something alive, and suggested some truly innovative arithmancy.

A pity she'd have to destroy them.

Rory finished assembling her hex and released it. For a moment the alphanumeric string hung there, floating, stiff as a stick in a river. Then it wobbled toward the shard-code, which was beginning to flex and do something ominous, and probably awful, to Jaed. If Rory had been hacking a turing on this layer of aether, she would have expected some reaction, some security hex to come storming out to challenge the incoming code. But the hex-shards seemed oblivious, as if they had no reason to suspect an attack on this aetheric level. Or perhaps they were entirely busy dismantling Jaed's hardsuit.

Rory waited long enough to see her hex infiltrate the outer layer of the hex-shards' code. Then she withdrew, as fast as was prudent (perhaps a *little* bit faster) to find Jaed leaning against a bulkhead, suit steaming at the seams, visor raised. He was coughing savagely.

Rory winced in sympathy. But at least he was still standing, not choking.

"Jaed?"

He slid a glance at her. His eyes were bloodshot and red-rimmed, which made his irises a startling, plasma blue. "They ran. For lack of a better word. Disengaged and went *that* way." He waved fingers down the corridor.

It was the same direction she and Jaed had been heading. Of course.

"*What happened?*" Zhang's voice seeped out of Jaed's comms. Her tone was so calm, so quiet, that Rory guessed she'd asked that same question, without response, several times already.

"Arithmantic resistance," said Rory. "We handled it. We're continuing to Thorsdottir's last location."

Zhang hesitated. There were a dozen questions in that silence. But because she was Zhang, all she said was, "*Copy. I have not been able to reach her.*"

"Right," said Jaed. "What the hell was that? Or . . . those? What just hit us?"

"Arithmantic resistance," Rory repeated, a little more firmly. "Clearly not the same caliber of hexwork we saw on the bridge, or our suits would've—I don't know. Combusted. But it was some kind of battle-hex."

"Except it looked like a million little tiny separate hexes all working together. It was coordinated. How does that happen?"

"I don't know, but I've seen them before. At the seal. When I tried to open the hatch, they attacked."

"And you didn't see fit to *tell* me?"

"Tell you what? That what looks like a bunch of tiny little hexes just ganged up and threw me out of the aether?"

"Yes! Exactly that! Not *oh, it's just a battle-hex, I handled it.*" Jaed's lips razored white.

"I—uh. Sorry." Rory frowned.

"Is it that you didn't think I needed to know? Or that you didn't want to admit you *didn't* know something? Oh, never mind." Jaed pushed off the bulkhead and staggered, weaving down the corridor.

Rory started after him, still frowning. "What did they do to you?"

"Jacked the environmentals in my suit. Temperature regulation. Nothing permanently damaged. *Damn* it." There came the unmistakable sound of a gloved fist hitting metal. "The seal's still down."

An unwelcome pressure built in Rory's chest, one she had not felt since her imprisonment on Urse. "I thought manual reset should've opened everything."

"It would have, unless this was some kind emergency seal. Fire. Hull breach." He wheeled to face her. Behind him, she could see the tightly irised hatch. Emergency teslas, the same abused red as Jaed's eyes, glared from the perimeter. "We know the xeno attackers didn't dock at the aetherlock and board the way we did. Maybe this is where they punched through. Or maybe the little arithmancers locked it to slow us down. We'll have to go around."

"But there *is* an around?"

"Yeah," he said, and pushed past her, moving more or less steadily. "We're going to have to walk back through some of the bodies, though."

Rory did not want to ask how far it might be, or how much

delay they might suffer. She also decided not to comment on *arithmancers*, in the plural, even as she heard Zhang's audible, unhappy inhale on Jaed's ex-comm.

Not nearly as unhappy as the arithmancer(s) would be, Rory thought, when she caught up to them. Especially if something had happened to Thorsdottir. She took a deep breath, tugged her helmet back over her head, and followed.

CHAPTER SEVEN ≡≡≡

Thorsdottir glanced from the document on the screen to the cryostasis tubes with their frosted portholes. If the royalists were willing to ruin a biosphere and kill everyone in it, they were not interested in reclaiming that territory, but in making an example. The Tadeshi royalists were getting desperate, which meant the Confederation was winning. That was good. But if the royalists turned this into a *tactic*, sacrificing whole worlds on the altar of intimidation, the Confederation would crumble. This bioweapon effectively escalated the war to a level that would be unsustainable, and probably contagious as well; both the Merchants League and the Consortium would want their own version, so that everyone could mutually assure the destruction of everyone else.

Thorsdottir looked at the turing, having no better place to direct her questions. "Why are you telling me this?"

The screen continued to display the document. No whispers were forthcoming in her helmet. It was, in fact, profoundly silent, of the embarrassed sort that accompanies unanticipated or unwelcome questions.

"Because you know I have to do something about it, right? These roses. This plan to, what, wipe out a whole biosphere?"

The silence took on another layer, more thoughtful. Then the screen split itself into two windows, banishing the document to the right side. A blank, black column appeared on the left, along with a flashing cursor.

Thorsdottir waited, counting the blinks, until the screen spelled out *help* in slow letters, as if the typist was especially reluctant.

Help, in Thorsdottir's experience, came in two categories. The first required an obvious response. Extinguishing fires, or opening doors for the overburdened, and the like. The second category had more ambiguous solutions, particularly when the requester was also an anonymous arithmancer who had nearly cut her in half, forcibly separated her from Rory and Jaed, and hacked her hardsuit.

"If you want me to help you," she said, "you need to tell me who you are. And *where* you are. I need some honesty, here."

The screen remained, if not silent, then at least unresponsive. The *help* remained where it was. The cursor blinked. Then, *rose* and *here* appeared in rapid succession, the letters tripping over themselves in their haste.

The answer made sense, but only in an improbable, e-vid drama sort of way. Thorsdottir assumed Rose was answering her questions in the order she'd asked them; that meant the lethal roses— alchemically altered, in cryostasis and infused with nanomecha— were somewhere on the sentience scale.

Perhaps she should believe in invisible xenos, too, or ghosts, or, or *magic*.

Or. Thorsdottir frowned. When one is surrounded by evidence of the impossible, one might need to redefine one's understanding of the term.

The cryostasis tubes appeared to be intact, under her head-lamp's beam. All the teslas were lit that should be, and in the appropriate color. She ran her gloved hands over the seams that she could not see, feeling for gaps, wishing she dared break her suit seal so she could get actual hands into the investigation. Her HUD *said* there was atmosphere in the cargo hold, but if one of those tubes had cracked, there could be also contamination from the roses. Maybe. Or something.

If the roses (the nanomecha in the roses? Was there a difference?) were talking to her already, clearly the stasis wasn't working. They had already hacked her hardsuit's comm system. They had also asked for her help.

She returned to the turing console.

"All right, Rose. I'm going to ask again: why *me*? There were three of us who boarded. Rory would've been a better choice, I think."

The turing screen blanked completely.

Thorsdottir stared at it for an offended moment. Then she balled up her left fist and thumped the screen's frame. When that produced no results, she said a very privateer-ish word under her breath. It was only then that she noticed the entire cargo hold had gone dark, and that her headlamp was the sole source of illumination. Even the emergency teslas were out.

The next word she meant to say—a variation on the last— dried up on her tongue.

A faint and wordless keening swirled through her helmet. Thorsdottir checked her HUD, but there was no indication of any network, no magical reconnection to *Vagabond* or Rory and Jaed. The sound must be coming from Rose, and they were panicking.

Fantastic, she thought. *I have been hijacked by a rosebush afraid of the dark.*

Thorsdottir frowned and shook her head and, after a moment's consideration, thumped the side of the helmet with her fist.

"Stop that."

The keening stopped.

The deck under her boots shivered. The cargo-bay teslas, and the turing, flared back to life.

The shipping manifest, with its damning declaration of murderous flora, had vanished. In the middle of the screen hung one word:

coming

repeated until the entire screen was a tapestry of those six letters.

Thorsdottir knew hysterics when she saw them.

"Calm down," she said, in her best voice of authority. "Who's coming?"

The screen flickered, resolving into a grainy, colorless image, of the sort produced by security 'bots. The view was set high, with a distorted bubble-eyed view of two corridors. A squad of Tadeshi royalist marines in their angular black hardsuits trotted down one of the corridors in neat, high-speed formation. Their visors were down, opaque and intimidating, their 'slingers in hand. As they moved through the intersection and out of frame, Thorsdottir noted that the timestamp was from twenty-three hours ago, rounding up, and the alphanumerics on the bulkhead they passed were C-151.

The seal that had nearly bisected her had been at the C-152b intersection. This recording had happened one corridor away, though she did not know exactly how far, or where. She found herself wishing either for a ship's diagram (she looked: there was *not* one conveniently painted on the bulkhead, with an X to mark *you are here*) or for Jaed Moss to explain the design to her.

Her stomach knotted. She did not examine the cause—that she wished for Jaed, that she had not first thought of Rory—because the turing screen divided its image again. The now-empty intersection of C-151 remained on one half. On the second, another high-angle image showed more Tadeshi marines—or perhaps the same unit—approaching. They took up defensive positions.

Thorsdottir wished she could see what the Tadeshi did; this angle, this camera, was entirely insufficient.

As if she'd spoken aloud her request, the screen rearranged itself again. The first two images shrank to even quarters; the bottom half filled with a new vantage. This image had clearly come from one of the Tadeshi hardsuits. There were readings overlaid in a faded grey that would have been green on an actual HUD, which showed other linked suits. Thorsdottir supposed it was a unit commander's cam she was seeing. The knots in her stomach drew tighter. She already knew how this story ended. *Vagabond's* scans had found no one alive on *G. Stein*. The helmet-cam's frame faced a curve in the corridor, just past the ridged line of a section seal. There was no cover. The helmet-bearer sank down, apparently kneeling. A target's crosshairs appeared on the HUD.

Thorsdottir leaned closer to the screen, as if that would help resolve the images, and watched.

They came around the not-quite-really-a-corner in a blur of speed and unfamiliar proportions. Five of them, taller than human, upright, roughly bipedal, though they seemed more stretched out and thinner in the limbs. They wore hardsuits or armor, slick-looking, with triangular protrusions—what were those, *fins*?—jutting out at the joints (too many joints). Their weapons were familiar enough, long-barreled and held in both hands, some kind of rifle. But what came out of its barrel looked like something from an imagined future were there were energy weapons instead of projectiles.

The same imagined future, Thorsdottir thought grimly, where monstrous xenos attacked human soldiers.

The helmet-cam jolted. Its point of view toppled back, pointed up and at an angle. The fighting raged on the edges, while the suit-indicators on the HUD went out, one by one.

A xeno paused over the fallen marine. Thorsdottir got a clear look at the shape of its visor, which was frustratingly opaque. The head inside that helmet wouldn't be much larger than a human's, but it would be longer in the jaw, flatter overall. The xeno paused, head cocked as if listening. Then they moved out of frame, liquid and alien and not at all like a human would move. Thorsdottir's stomach, having exhausted its knot-tying skills, began to sink.

The skirmish continued in the top two frames, moving from right to left as the xeno invaders pushed the defenders back. The Tadeshi did some damage—Thorsdottir saw at least one xeno fall— but they were overmatched. The xeno beam weapons cut through bulkhead and armor.

There was no sound on the recording. That was the worst part. There should have been sirens, and alarms, and human voices shouting on the comms. Instead the Tadeshi fell in silence, one by one, and the xenos pressed forward. The battle passed through the left-side camera frame, the remaining Tadeshi falling back from the xeno advance toward the C-152a intersection, the first image Rose had shown her.

Then, suddenly, those seals irised closed, leaving that camera staring at two hatches squeezed shut like eyes against greater horror.

Thorsdottir imagined what had happened on the other side of that seal. The Tadeshi soldiers pinned against the steel and safety-hex, dying there as the xenos came down that passage and found them trapped. Who or whatever had triggered the seals had con-demned those soldiers to death.

A ship's turing could've done it. The bridge crew, the captain, making a decision to protect a bioweapon from hostile seizure and theft.

Thorsdottir glanced between the screen and the cryo-tube. Perhaps the same entity that had hacked her suit—working hypothesis, Rose—had condemned those soldiers to die. She wanted to ask that question, along with what the xenos were, who, where they'd gone. Instead, she took a breath and asked the questions to which she suspected she had answers already.

"Are they, the xenos, the ones you're afraid of?"

yes

Sensible. "Well, they're gone. You're safe."

no coming

"What, *now*?"

yes

Wonderful. Thorsdottir's grasp of celestial motion was somewhat vague, but she knew *void* was a very big thing, even in something as mapped out as a planetary system, and that ships did not just cross the vast swaths of emptiness in an instant (except by tesser-hex, and *that* took special buoys and gates). There had been no sign of any ships in the vicinity of *G. Stein*. There were places that ships could conceal themselves in a system—convenient moons, asteroid belts, planetary rings—but the actual getting from *there* to *here*, the sort done with plasma core engines and physics, took time. There were physical *laws*.

Those were the same laws that said nanomecha could not fuse with flora to create a sentient, living weapon. Perhaps there were *new* laws. Or perhaps the multiverse had just decided to make things up as it went along. But it made sense the xenos would return. The roses were a bioweapon. Xenos could see the value in such a thing. That made them the nasty sort of xenos, but then, perfectly human Tadeshi had been responsible for creating the rose-bushes in the first place, or commissioning their creation, with intent to use them on fellow humans, so no one had a prime claim to nastiness. But the xenos had known about Rose, somehow. *That* was alarming, although why Thorsdottir thought xenos, motives unknown, in possession of lethal rosebushes were more frightening than Tadeshi, motives very clear, she was not sure. At least the xenos had not *found* Rose, probably because they were looking for a bomb or something weaponish, and not a bunch of flowers.

coming, Rose repeated. *coming coming*

"Show me."

The screen offered a new image. This time, the hardsuits were recognizably human-shaped. The humans inside those suits were also recognizable, because one of them was carrying her helmet under one arm. Jaed had his helmet on, but his visor was up. Even with such poor resolution, Thorsdottir could see that his face was not happy. Rory wore that expression Thorsdottir knew very well from their months of imprisonment on Urse: scared and angry and intending to enact reprisals for both conditions.

Thorsdottir was so happy to see both of them she almost forgot to breathe. Then she recalled that Rose was unhappy about their approach, and that an unhappy Rose could be extremely dangerous. "Those are not xenos. They're human. They're my friends. They're *not* a threat to you."

The screen blanked.

no

That response was both emphatic and ambiguous. Then *help* reappeared and hung there, looking lonely and plaintive, to be joined by a flashing *coming*.

What the big, oddly jointed xenos with their plasma rifles had in common with Rory and Jaed in Rose's mind (minds?),

Thorsdottir had no idea. It seemed logical that, if Rose could differentiate among hardsuited humans well enough to select Thorsdottir and exclude Rory and Jaed, that Rose could also tell that Rory and Jaed were not xenos.

Rose was also clearly *afraid* of them, and it had some kind of control over ship seals, which meant ship systems, and for some reason *both* Rory and Jaed had broken their hardsuits' integrity. She could imagine a great many things that could go very, very wrong. Vented corridors. Violent evacuation of oxygen.

"Let me talk to my friends." Thorsdottir struck the side of her helmet, open-palmed, to eliminate ambiguity. "Turn the comms back on."

The comms remained silent.

"Please. Let me talk to them."

Nothing. Thorsdottir waited until she was sure that Rose was ignoring her or, more worrying, up to some lethal mischief. The camera feed showed Rory and Jaed rounding a curve of corridor. Thorsdottir *thought* the sign on the bulkhead behind them said C-152, which would put them on this level and thus between seals. If Rose was going to react badly, it would have to be soon.

Thorsdottir whipped around and ran to the set of doors that opened into the corridor. She hit the controls and was pleasantly surprised when they worked. As the door labored apart, she wrenched the panel off those same controls, reached into the tangle of wires, hoped her hardsuit was shielded against electrical shocks, and pulled.

The doors squealed to a stop halfway. Wide enough, she judged, for Jaed and Rory to get through. Good enough. If Rose needed her help, then Rose needed her alive, which meant they couldn't turn off life support or depressurize that corridor now without killing her, too.

Thorsdottir took a deep breath, and held it, and then, over the flashing advisement of *danger* from her HUD, opened her visor.

Her comms let out a squeal that sounded like a despairing wail.

Thorsdottir pitched her voice louder. "Rose, stop it! Let me talk to them."

The machine wailing stopped. Another yelling entirely filled Thorsdottir's helmet, slipped out her open visor, and began echoing in the cargo bay.

"*Thorsdottir!*" Zhang was, in fact, yelling. "*Do you copy?*"

"Yes!" Thorsdottir matched Zhang for volume.

"*I have Thorsdottir,*" said Zhang, still shouting. "*Rory, Jaed, do you copy? I have her.*"

It took a few confusing moments of cross-talk—it is easy to interrupt on comms, if one is not following the etiquette of saying *copy* and *over*—before it was established that yes, Thorsdottir could hear everyone and yes, everyone could hear Thorsdottir and also that everyone was fine and oh yes! Rory and Jaed had almost arrived at cargo bay C-152a.

Thorsdottir poked her head under the door, trusting that Rose would not, in a fit of panic or pique, slam it shut, just in time to see Jaed rounding the curve of the corridor with Rory half a step behind him.

She saw immediately that their reports of *fine* had been an exaggeration.

The part of Thorsdottir that had been, and still was, professionally and personally invested in Rory's (in Jaed's, in everyone's) well-being flared into brief heat. There were smears of dried blood on Rory's face, and on Jaed's, that meant there had been arithmancy and hexes traded, and that Rory and Jaed had lost at least one exchange.

"Thorsdottir?" Jaed had never been particularly pigmented,

but he was whiter than usual. "What *happened*? Where have you been?"

"I got hacked," she said. "What happened to *you*?"

"Someone attacked us with arithmancy." Rory was looking around the cargo bay, narrow-eyed, as though she expected someone or something to come leaping out.

Thorsdottir shot an accusing glare at the turing screen. All communication, video evidence, and documentation had vanished. A complicated fractal drew and redrew itself in the center of the screen in perpetual, pixelated motion.

"*Not* the same someones who killed the bridge crew, though," said Jaed. "After we lost you, we climbed up to the bridge through the maintenance shafts. Everyone there was dead. Looked like sudden decompression, but no one had gotten to their suits. No sign of a breach, either, and the main turing was dead. Some kind of super sophisticated battle-hex. If someone'd hit us with *that*, well. We'd be dead."

"Ah," said Thorsdottir. Some things were beginning to make sense. Some things were not. "The bridge crew was decompressed? Not shot or, ah, torn apart?"

Jaed flinched, and somehow managed to turn even whiter. "Not on the bridge. But we found some of that in the lower decks. How did you know?"

"Because—oh, look here. Rory, you should see this, too." Thorsdottir went to the turing console. She stripped off her glove and laid it down beside the keyboard. "I'm going to show battle footage," she said, and stabbed a sequence into the keyboard. She had no idea how to recall the recording. Rose knew. And if Rose decided not to play along—

The screen divided itself again, and the recording began to play. Thorsdottir let her breath out.

"Look," she said, mostly for Zhang's benefit. "Some kind of unknown xeno species boarded *G. Stein*. They're bipedal, too many joints on the limbs. Some kind of fins on the armor, maybe? And plasma beam weapons."

"Well," said Rory, "now we know what can rip Tadeshi armor apart. And what can burn through a ship's hull, if they have those weapons on a larger scale. I'm more curious why they attacked in the first place. Was this first contact, or just the latest in a series of conflicts with the royalists?"

"I don't know about that last part, but as to why they attacked—well. I think they wanted this. Look. There's a manifest. It's, ah. Just look." Thorsdottir reached past Rory, and with a few keystrokes and Rose's invisible collusion, recalled the shipping manifest and the associated documentation.

Rory peered at the screen. Then she jerked her face back as if she expected the turing screen to throw sparks at her. Thorsdottir recognized the expression, and her stomach dropped into her boots. When Rory got a look like that, she toppled dictatorships and upended years of careful treaties. "I've never seen anything like this."

"That's the second time today you've said that," Jaed said, and added, when Thorsdottir looked at him, "When we saw what'd happened to the turing on the bridge. The battle-hexes that took this ship down, Rory said, were—what did you say?—amazing, I think."

"Mm. I did. Zhang said it was an act of war. And *this* is, too, both of those things. Clearly someone's solved the technical problems of nanomecha. And of course they've been weaponized."

Jaed, for once, was not watching Rory. He glared instead at Thorsdottir. "So if the xenos came for the weapons, why leave without them? They breached the hull, they boarded, they killed a lot of people, and then they just, what, *left*?"

"How should I know? I don't think *we* chased them away. If I had to guess, I'd say they didn't know to look for murder-flowers. Maybe they don't even know what's *in* here. But I think they'll be coming back, maybe soon."

"I'm more interested in who's still on board," said Rory. She was still reading the document, level-eyed, level-voiced, projecting a dispassion Thorsdottir in no way believed genuine. "Jaed and I were attacked in the corridor by a type of arithmancy I haven't seen before. I would've said it was a hex left behind as a trap, but it didn't *act* like a trap. And it didn't look at all like the sophisticated hexwork I saw on the bridge, so now I don't think it was a product of these xenos. You can tell. Arithmancy has markers. What attacked us felt like a novice with a few good hexes and not much strategy."

Thorsdottir looked from the dried blood on Rory's face to the dried blood on Jaed's and decided not to remark on the irony.

Jaed did not share Thorsdottir's restraint. "Really, Rory? We didn't win. We're both sitting here breathing ship atmosphere. If we'd been attacked in void, we'd be dead. We got lucky."

Rory took her eyes off the turing screen long enough to skewer him on a stare. "It was *not* luck."

Thorsdottir lacked any fairy gifts for detecting lies, but she knew wounded pride when she heard it. "I think I know who did it. Same person who hacked my rig."

Rory stared at her. Jaed stared at her. Thorsdottir supposed Rose might be staring at her, too.

"I think it's Rose." Thorsdottir waved a hand at the screen with the classified documentation. "Somehow. The seal closed me off from you, and the emergency teslas lit me a path here—"

"Did you just give the weapon a name?" Rory interrupted.

"That's what they call themself. I don't know if they're one plant or all of them. Or all the nanomecha collectively. Anyway. We had a, uh, conversation before you arrived. Kind of. That's how I found the footage of the xenos in the first place. Rose showed them to me, when they asked for help. Rose is afraid of them."

"Fear is for sentients," Rory said drily. "At best, I'm guessing the nanomecha in those roses is networking to increase their processing power, with some rudimentary arithmantic defensive hexes programmed in."

"Rose is a person. Look." Thorsdottir pointed at the screen. "Let's talk to them. Rose. Did you bring me here?"

yes

Rory's face blanked in an appropriate expression of shock just barely contained by years of diplomacy. Thorsdottir hoped her own expression of *told you so* was similarly contained.

"*Why* did you bring me here?"

help

Thorsdottir looked at Rory and raised both eyebrows. "See?"

Rory pursed her lips in an expression eerily reminiscent of the Vizier, which indicated an unwillingness to pursue the current line of conversation. "If your Rose is concerned about the xenos, they've got reason. The battle-hex that decompressed the bridge and killed the turing was highly sophisticated. The fighting in the corridors was devastating. I mean, they have handheld plasma weapons, which means they've solved the Sendarin-Wu constant problem. Arithmancers of that caliber would have nothing to fear from, well, anyone, except the k'bal, and *they* are pacifists. They would be able to destroy these roses easily."

Jaed scoffed. "They still left without Rose, so maybe they're not as amazing as you seem to think."

"I don't think they're *amazing*. I just. How can you *not* admire that level of arithmantic expertise?"

"Because they ripped people apart," Jaed said flatly. "Because they decompressed a whole bridge. Or doesn't it count if it's Tadeshi they killed?"

Thorsdottir cleared her throat. "We all agree that something made the xenos leave. So either they weren't after Rose at all, or they didn't know what to look for, or something here scared them off. Rose hacked *all* our hardsuits. Maybe they can do that to the xenos, too. And we don't even know if they, the xenos, breathe oxygen. A suit breach for them might be lethal."

"Maybe." Rory frowned down at her helmet, which she had set on the console beside the keyboard. "Maybe you're right, Jaed. Maybe we got lucky."

Jaed looked surprised. He side-eyed Thorsdottir, as if checking that she'd heard the same admission. "Oh. Well. So how do we bring these roses back with us? I don't think these tubes are going to fit on *Vagabond*."

"We don't." Rory's face was composed again. "The roses are genocide-flowers. Anyone who gets them will want to use them. Therefore, no one can have them, and that means we've got to destroy them."

Thorsdottir opened her mouth to protest, but Jaed was faster. "Come *on*, Rory. You don't just—you can't mean that!"

The turing screen faded. Then, in the middle, in a large, white type, appeared the words *help rose*.

Thorsdottir was the only one to notice, Jaed and Rory being too busy glaring at each other again. She gritted her teeth and interrupted. She wanted to say, *I told Rose that you weren't a threat, and damned if you'll make me a liar.* But out loud, she said, "The xenos are afraid of Rose. That's a good argument for keeping them alive."

Rory paused, mid-breath, and turned to Thorsdottir. She cocked her head, as if she could hear what Thorsdottir had *not* said, and her eyes narrowed.

"Rose tried to kill me and Jaed." Rory's voice was quiet, even, dangerous.

Thorsdottir's voice was quiet, even, reasonable. "I don't think they did."

"Really."

"I think they fought back, but there's a difference between self-defense and assassination. They thought you were dangerous. You're an arithmancer. *Both* of you are. So are the xenos, or at least some of them, from what you said you saw on the bridge. So maybe that's the connection. Rose is afraid of arithmancers *because* they, Rose, are not that skilled at arithmancy. They're *scared*, Rory. And you're giving them reason to be."

Jaed cleared his throat. Thorsdottir and Rory both turned toward him, the latter expectantly, the former resignedly, both of them anticipating he would lend his support to Rory.

And so both of them were surprised when Jaed said, "Thorsdottir's right. There's nothing like Rose anywhere. They're unique. And besides." He pointed at the screen. "They're sentient, and they just asked us for help. That makes them a refugee, right?"

Rory opened her mouth to argue. Then she, too, looked at the screen. Reason leaked back into her eyes, and compassion: an echo of the princess Thorsdottir had known on Urse, before Vernor Moss had imprisoned her, before she had abdicated crown and responsibility and decided the multiverse could fend for itself.

"Rose," she said.

help rose

Rory looked slightly queasy. "You tried to kill us."

The screen remained blank. Then, slowly: *sorry.*

"Was it because we were arithmancers?"

yes

"Not much of a talker, are they?" Jaed muttered. "Reminds me of you, Zhang."

"Funny."

"No, but listen." Jaed looked more serious. "The roses are still in cryostasis. How are we even *talking* to them? Are the nanomecha somehow *not* frozen? Are they immune?"

"Maybe it's only some of them," said Thorsdottir. "It doesn't matter. Point is, we need to bring Rose with us."

"We can't, though." This time, Rory's voice was gentle. "Jaed's right. We don't have room on *Vagabond* for the units."

Thorsdottir opened her mouth to—she wasn't sure what. Argue. Protest. Volunteer to stay on board *G. Stein* and wait for a larger ship to return, which she knew would lead to argument, and for which she was already marshaling counterpoints.

"I just got a transmission from G. Stein,*"* Zhang said suddenly. *"It appears to be some sort of shipping manifest for roses accompanied by what appears to be a classified Tadeshi military document with a lot of numbers. Some kind of . . . passcode?"*

They all looked at the console.

"Rose," Rory asked, "did you send that?"

yes

Thorsdottir could not help herself. "Still think they're not sentient?"

"No. I don't. But that makes them *more* dangerous." Rory turned and eyelocked Thorsdottir. "We don't dare just leave Rose here and hope we can come back later. For all we know, that's what the xenos did, and they're already on their way. Or the Tadeshi, if they're checking to see what happened to *G. Stein*. If someone gets them, and the data on *this*"—she gestured at the console—"then they'll know how to use them. And we can't let that happen."

Rory slid a look at the console, and from there up the bank of tubes. "I don't know how much you can hear, Rose," she murmured, "or how much you understand, but listen. You have to understand that you're meant to kill people. That's your purpose. Do you understand?"

The screen remained blank for a few seconds. Then, slowly, it produced a *yes*. And then, immediately after that, *rose not want, rose not kill.*

"See?" Thorsdottir said.

Rory's features might've been cast in polysteel. "That's admirable. Nevertheless, we can't leave them behind, and we can't take them with us. So that does not leave us with much of a choice."

Thorsdottir shook her head. She did not trust her voice to behave. One did not *shout* at Rory Thorne, princess or no.

Unless one was Jaed Moss. "You are *not* serious! We can't—We are *not* going to do that. Rory. It's *wrong*."

"I'm happy to hear alternatives—"

"We purge the data from this ship and take the only copy with us! Or we just purge the data altogether. Then Rose can't *do* anything—"

"Until someone figures out the passcodes! Or whoever made them in the first place supplies a replacement. It's a risk we can't take—"

"Who the hell are *you* to decide this?"

Their voices grew in volume, tangling and tearing at each other like thorns against flesh.

Thorsdottir turned her face away from them and lowered her

voice to conspiracy. "Rose. Rory's right, but she's also wrong. We can't take *all* of you. But we can't leave any part of you behind that's alive. Do you understand?"

yes

"I can take a clipping. Will that be enough? Can you . . . survive?"

A moment, two, three, while Jaed called Rory a genocidal dictator and she called him a romantic idealist with no sense of history. Then Rose typed out a firm, large-fonted *yes*.

There came a great hissing from the bank of cryostasis units. But there was no corresponding gout of cold air, as there would be in a defrosting. Instead there was a deeper rattle, like the machine was trying to cough. The hissing stopped. The teslas on the front of the units turned from blues and greens to yellows and reds. A few of them were blinking. Then they began to go dark, one by one.

In the sudden absence of the subliminal hum of working machinery, Jaed's horrified whisper seemed very loud. "Oh, no. Rory, what have you done?"

"I didn't do that!"

They both looked at Thorsdottir, who stood up and walked briskly across the cargo bay to face off with the first cryostasis unit. The porthole was dark, now, the internal illumination dead along with the rest of its systems. Her own face stared back at her.

She balled up her fist and slammed it into the control panel. She succeeded in denting the alloy and scuffing her glove.

"Thorsdottir," said Jaed. "What are you doing?"

At least it wasn't Rory asking. Then Thorsdottir might've taken the query as a request (or an order) to stop. From Jaed, however, she took it as an obvious question deserving of an obvious answer.

"Opening this unit."

"That won't work." He nudged her aside and, before she could retaliate, pried the control panel off. He grabbed a fistful of wires. "This will. Sometimes. Just tell me what we're doing?"

"Thought you liked botany. Pull the damned wires."

"I do, but." His eyes widened. "You can propagate roses from cuttings. I have no idea if that works on frozen roses, or nanomecha-hybrids."

"Rose thinks it will. I asked them. They agreed. Then they killed the cryostasis units."

"They could've opened them first. Saved me some work."

The unit unsealed itself with another hiss. The door rolled aside. The rosebush looked very small and helpless: roots in a sack bundle, stems cut back, the whole thing wrapped in twine. Thorsdottir had a hard time believing it wasn't *just* a plant. But then, that was the point. And technically, until someone sent the command to the nanomecha, it was just a bush with a dormant transformative bioweapon inside.

Just.

"Jaed. How do I do this?"

Jaed, who had in his past life aspired to be a botanist, grimaced slightly. "Ideally, we'd have a nice clean sharp knife and some rooting hormones. Let's assume a bioweapon can survive a little rough treatment. Just—take the longest stem you can, all right?"

"Right." Thorsdottir reached in and broke off a length of branch. It snapped with an audible crack, like bone, and she winced.

Hardsuits did not come with an excess of pocket-compartments. Thorsdottir considered, then popped the chamber that held extra bolt clips for the 'slinger. She emptied one of the clips and passed the extra bolts to Jaed. Then she put the Rose cutting inside the clip and sealed it, and stowed it back in her suit.

"If you can hear me," she said, "I promise to get you some water soon. And some dirt."

She looked hopefully at her HUD, but there was no unauthorized blinking, nor any ghost-hissing on her comms.

There was only Zhang's voice, cool and terrified. *"There's a ship inbound. You have to get back to* Vagabond.*"*

"What kind of ship?" Rory asked. "Tadeshi?"

"Xeno," guessed Thorsdottir, a moment before Zhang confirmed, *"Unknown configuration. I don't know where it came from. It just appeared out of nowhere, and it's coming very fast."*

CHAPTER EIGHT

Grytt held a dim opinion of void-flight on a good day. She found it cramped, uncomfortable, usually cold. The alwar vessel (their liaison, the adept, had translated its name into GalSpek as *Favored Daughter*) had done nothing to dispel that opinion. If anything, the internal dimensions were even more cramped, designed as they were for a people significantly smaller than the human average. When Grytt passed through a hatch, her shoulder came a hairsbreadth from brushing edges. The tenju who had come with them—one, which was a compromise from the original offer of four, which was still one more than Adept Uo-Zanys Kesk had wanted—had to turn slightly sideways, accompanied by a muttered monologue whose sentiment Grytt understood, even if the words themselves escaped her. At least she did not have to duck. Rupert did.

The bridge, to which they had been conducted upon embarking (while their baggage, having changed custody, travelled elsewhere on board), at least possessed something of a domed overhead, as well as an impressive array of various-colored teslas (some blinking, some not) and screens. There was a central, bowl-shaped console, large enough for the crew to sit around, with a three-dimensional, translucent globe display projected in the hollow.

A ring of seats lined one of the bulkheads, in what was clearly meant to be an observational capacity. The adept had deposited them there before taking herself to the other side of the bridge and the central console to confer with an official-looking person who Grytt supposed must be in command.

The entire bridge had a rather unmilitary (which is to say, impractical) decor. There were inlaid designs on the bulkheads, apparently unnecessary to function, but which looked expensive and well-crafted. On a Kreshti warship, such ornamentation would have been reserved for visiting dignitaries' quarters and the conference rooms well away from the working environment. Grytt debated whether or not *Favored Daughter* was even a military ship; it could be a luxury liner, or a diplomatic vessel, from its level of opulence. But the crew's uniforms *looked* military, and the personnel traded gestures that looked like salutes, and at least four alwar carried sidearms and stood positioned so that if they must use those weapons, they would not strike the bridge crew, but rather hit the visitors.

So Grytt surmised that she, Rupert, and the tenju were guests, but also under observation. That seemed fair. She was grateful at least that the seats were made of a substance that did its best to conform to her dimensions within the limits of their own, though she didn't have high hopes for fastening the five-point harness, due to its alwar dimensions, when it came time to tesser-hex. Damn sure it'd chafe in inconvenient places.

Tesser-hex travel itself was dull no matter how comfortable the chairs or how attractive the decorations; much of it was spent traveling to the appropriate gates, which were really just fragile confections of wire and metal, built by the k'bal and etched all over with arithmantic symbols, through which a ship with the appropriate hex-codes could travel to another gate elsewhere. Then there would be a burst of dangerous speeds, at which point everyone would strap into their harnesses and wait through the actual hex—("Minutes," Rupert would say, scoffing, while Grytt scowled and thought "hours")—after which the ship would appear in a similar gate across the void.

There was no possible way a ship could get lost in void-space, said Rupert, the arithmancer, clearly intending to reassure her with his authority. Gates were fixed points, anchors, unmoving and unmovable. Grytt's bone-deep conviction that they'd go into the void and stay there was entirely illogical.

Grytt sucked in a lungful of dry, very ship-flavored air and pushed herself as far back into the alwar-dimensioned chair as she could. A buzz of what was presumably the alwar language surrounded them, as the individuals at the various stations got to work. It was a bewildering number, to Grytt's eyes; there was a joke in there somewhere, about the correct number of alwar required to traverse the void. She considered saying as much to Rupert, even began to lean his direction, before reconsidering. His attention was bent entirely on the techs and pilots sitting around the central console, over which hovered a hologram model of Lanscot's system, complete with the tiny station and a bewildering crosshatching of glowy lines. Grytt kept expecting Lanscot station to notice their absence, to call and demand their return. Either they hadn't yet, or the alwar had ignored them.

She glanced at the lone tenju. He, like every other member of his species that she'd seen, tended toward a muscular, stocky, *solid* physique, all with that slightly undershot jaw and the jutting lower tusks. They were uniformly formidable. Grytt hoped they were also interesting travel companions.

This one was focused on that hologram. She followed his narrow-eyed scowl to a moving blip in the hologram, which was moving to match *Favored Daughter's* heading as the ship left the station's immediate void-space.

"That your ship?" she said. "That blip?"

The tenju's eyes cut toward her. They were a clear, jewel-blue, remarkably lovely in that particular collection of features. His cheeks, more leathery than alwar or human skin, sucked in thoughtfully. The curse of a tesla eye, that she could count pores in a person's skin from a meter away. The tenju *had* pores, but there was no trace of facial hair, also like the alwar. Either those species did not grow beards or their razor technology was markedly more effective. Rupert was scrupulous about shaving, but there was always a little bit of a shadow.

The tenju decided that she was worth answering. "Mm. Yes." Then he turned back to the hologram in a whisper of braids and hooks.

Not a talker. Grytt could respect that. She supposed the tenju vessel intended to accompany them to Samtalet, since it was clearly following *Favored Daughter*. Both ships were queuing up for the tesser-hex, perhaps squabbling over the order of transfer. She wasn't entirely sure what the reasoning was, why these two groups—who appeared to have a testy, though solid, working relationship—had decided to go to Samtalet at all, much less play transport. Maybe they had their own fairy visitors. Maybe they knew something she and Rupert did not, about what was happening out there. She wished she could ask the tenju for a better explanation of what was happening, but this wasn't the place or the time or, clearly, the tenju to interrogate. She hadn't even gotten his name.

She distracted herself with the alwar instead. They were predominantly female, and both sexes shared a common physiology—humanoid, clearly mammalian, possibly primate—with at least as much phenotypical variation as Grytt was accustomed to see in human beings. Hair, eye, skin color varied from the predominant, obsidian black of Adept Uo-Zanys Kesk to the pasty-pale of one of her escorts.

The tenju she'd seen so far—all four of them—seemed a little more uniformly presented. Harder to see secondary sexual characteristics. Darkish hair, in all shades from mud to darkest charcoal. Skin the color of river-rocks, in all those variations. The one sitting beside her was a medium grey-green, which made him look, under the alwar teslas, as if he were vaguely unwell.

Perhaps he was. Grytt had, before her encounter with Tadeshi explosives, been prone to nausea on void-flights and to turning a similar grey-green. Since having most of her insides replaced with mecha parts, as well as both her inner ears, that didn't happen anymore.

She caught the tenju side-eyeing her. He probably thought she wouldn't notice, and she wouldn't have, except the tesla optic gave her a wider field of vision on that side. She let him observe, unchallenged. If he wanted to say something, he—

"You meet any veeks yet?"

—would do so. Which he just had.

She cocked her head and drilled him with both eyes, aware that it was an unsettling expression, and awarded the tenju a point for not flinching.

"What's a veek?"

On her other side, Rupert stirred and coughed, very softly. "I believe he refers to the *vakari*." He said it slowly, as if trying it out for the first time. "Veek is the slang term."

The tenju's jewel-blue eyes flicked past Grytt like twin plasma shots. He snorted. "They won't much like you. The veeks, I mean. All that metal on you. Mecha, right? Implants?" He paused and pasted an expectant expression over his features.

Grytt strangled a sigh. "Why is that a problem for these va-kari?"

"They're religious fanatics. Really strict about organic purity." The tenju hitched a shoulder. "I reckon it's an excuse for their Expansion propaganda. They're cleaning up the multiverse by taking over the rest of us for our own good. Keeping us all pure or some rot."

Expansion sounded like a nice way of saying *war*.

Rupert cleared his throat delicately. "Do you or your people know if the Protectorate intend to colonize, or to, ah, exterminate?"

The tenju leaned forward so he could better see around Grytt. He raked his gaze over Rupert. "What kind of a question is that?"

"I'm Grytt," said Grytt, and stuck out her mecha hand. She didn't know what tenju thought about handshakes. She might be offending him, but better he take offense at *her* than pursue his annoyance with Rupert. "This is *my friend*, the Vizier of the Confederation of Liberated Worlds."

The tenju looked at Grytt's hand. Then he took it in his own. She could feel, in a distant, impersonal way, that he was squeezing very, very hard. She applied pressure in return, sufficient enough to make him scowl and extricate his hand with some haste.

He regarded her with new respect.

"Hworgesh," he said. "Special attaché to Captain Ilsa. She's in command of the *Bane* out there."

"Bane to anything in particular?" asked Grytt.

"Anything that crosses us." Hworgesh grinned. He shot Rupert a look, accompanied by a single raised brow. "What's a vizier do?"

"A vizier is meant to ask questions. The answers help me effect diplomatic policy."

"Diplomat. Right." Hworgesh's tone suggested a rather unfavorable opinion of the profession.

Grytt bristled on Rupert's behalf. "What's a *special attaché*? Sounds kind of like a diplomat."

"It's not. It's—more like a representative of the captain. A proxy." Hworgesh pressed his lips together. "What's *your* title, then?"

"I'm just Grytt."

Hworgesh's eyes narrowed. Clearly he thought that answer insufficient. Grytt gazed back, impassive.

Rupert stirred, a deliberate restlessness that bespoke an unvoiced query and great self-control. He might as well have poked her.

"These vakari," she said. "Are we likely to meet any?"

"Might." Hworgesh flung a worried look at the hologram display. "Hard to say. They've been breaking through all over, that side of the Verge. They're cutting right through the k'bal."

"Are they responding to some kind of pressure?" Rupert leaned even farther forward, until he was bent nearly double in an effort to see around Grytt. Probably reading the tenju's aura. She sat back, pretending nonchalance. "Or is this an Expansion of aggression?" He pronounced the capital *E*.

"Well now, that's the question everyone's asking." Hworgesh looked like he wanted to spit, then thought better of it. "Veeks've always been bad neighbors. Always fighting on the borders. But something's riled 'em up. Maybe something internal. Maybe some new trouble. *You* know anything?"

"I'm sure we don't," said Rupert. Grytt could *hear* the disarming smile.

"Huh. That's odd, because the order came down to come get you two from." He made a gyroscopic gesture at the overhead. "On high. Some political favors called in—go escort these people to Samtalet."

"Ah." Grytt could hear Rupert's smile slip. "Was it a favor, perhaps, from an entity in the Merchants League?"

"So you *do* know something." Hworgesh looked grimly pleased. "Or at least, someone."

Samur. Had to be. Grytt did not look at Rupert, who had no doubt come to the same realization. "We got our orders," she said, to keep Hworgesh's attention focused on her. "You know how that goes. You don't ask why, you just . . . do it."

"Mm." Hworgesh eyed her knowingly. "Well, there's nothing in Samtalet except a mining colony. Too close by half to the Verge and the veeks. If someone wants you out *there*, maybe you should ask the reasons."

Rupert found his voice, only a little frayed on the edges. "Thank you, Special Attaché Hworgesh, for being so forthcoming."

"Just Hworgesh. Titles are for alwar, mostly."

And judging from his expression, alwar ranked only a little bit above vakari in his estimation. Grytt wondered if that was a species-wide opinion, or strictly Hworgesh's. She felt the first tweakings of a headache. There were too many variables in this first-contact business. She should switch seats with Rupert and leave all the chatter to him, except Rupert had settled back in his chair again. Perhaps he'd fed his curiosity for the moment. Ha. Not likely. *More* probable, he was just making a list of new questions to fire off like a 'slinger on fast-fire. Or he was brooding about Samur again. Either way, she didn't want to—

"Ah," Rupert said. Only that, but the tone made Grytt whip around as if he'd shouted a profane expletive.

Ah, indeed. Lanscot station had disgorged a pair of blips, which, as Grytt watched, began trailing *Favored Daughter* and *Bane*. Her stomach coiled in on itself, the sensation entirely independent of how much organic stomach remained.

One of the alwar, sprouting comms from both ears, jerked upright. He turned and said something rapid and unintelligible to the alwar captain.

"Huh," said Hworgesh, so quietly even Grytt's mecha ear had to strain. "Something about *you*, sounds like. Station wants us to turn around and go back."

Grytt said a word that generally did not make it into the Kreshti-GalSpek dictionaries. "Will we?"

"Not likely. The Empire doesn't like taking orders from us lesser beings."

The captain leaned over the comm officer. Then she turned and beckoned at Adept Uo-Zanys Kesk, who, after a pause bordering on insolent, left her post and approached. There was a brief conference. Grytt side-eyed Hworgesh, who was unabashedly leaning his whole self that direction. The tenju swore under his breath. Some expressions and utterances are universal in delivery and intent, even if their specific syllables defy comprehension.

Before Grytt could inquire whether it was the content of the conversation, or its volume, that inspired such ire, the adept broke away from the captain. She came around the bridge crew in a tight, quick circle, her fingers claw-locked on each seat-back in sequence, using them for both balance and pace.

Grytt's knotted stomach tightened into a singularity of anticipation. Beside her, Rupert drew upright into the stillness of dread.

If the adept noticed their distress, she gave no sign of it. Her voice and face remained inflexibly calm and courteous.

"Please fasten your harnesses," she said. "We will be tesser-hexing sooner than anticipated."

Huh. The central display was pretty clear that *Favored Daughter* was still a long way from the Lanscot system's gate. Grytt dragged the harness into place anyway, because one does not take chances on voidships, even as she suspected that this was a ploy to immobilize her, should the alwar decide to take custody of their guests on Lanscot's demands.

She *was* substantially larger. Perhaps they thought she would offer resistance. They weren't wrong about that, though she intended to wait until her captors were human, and resistance less likely to cause an intergalactic incident.

"We are quite far from the gate," Rupert said politely.

Grytt fired a look at his impassive profile. All his Vizier-ness must have rusted away in his two years on the sheep-farm. She'd ruined him. He might *look* the diplomat, but she could smell the suspicion smoking off him.

Adept Uo-Zanys Kesk laughed. An actual laugh, humor, and not a jagged emotional expulsion.

"We don't need a *gate*," she said, gently condescending. Her smile, unlike her laugh, contained sharp edges: all pride, Grytt thought, and contempt for the species that did. "We only used the one here out of courtesy. The Confederation traffic control systems have not been upgraded for random entry."

"Without a gate," said Rupert, matching her tone, "how do you compensate for the Ekandeosol Paradox?" And then, because the adept's face had blanked at the name, he rattled off a string of letters and operations.

"Oh!" she said, momentarily misplacing her pride and condescension in favor of a genuine delight. "You're an arithmancer. I can show you the equations, if you'd like."

Oh, thought Grytt, less delighted. *There are two of them.*

Hworgesh grunted and muttered, barely audible. "Oh yes, please."

"I would appreciate that," said Rupert.

"After the tesser-hex." Grytt reached over to fasten Rupert's harness.

Adept Uo-Zanys Kesk chuckled. "Indeed, Vizier. After the tesser-hex."

She sat down on Rupert's other side, advising them that the countdown would soon be visible on the central holo, which indeed, yes, there it was. Presumably those were numeric symbols, anyway. Funny little curls and spikes changing at regular intervals.

Grytt eyed it with some dread. The run-up to a tesser-hex is dull. The *actual* travel between void-points is not: the conventional manner to which Grytt was accustomed involved a great deal of turbulence and sensory distortion, which some people found exhilarating and which Grytt had reserved for second-worst sensation in the multiverse (the first being "caught in an explosion").

The alwar version of tesser-hexing was, remarkably, even less pleasant. This time, Grytt felt as though she were stretching, as if her flesh had become a membrane and someone was pulling, pulling, until she was *sure* she was going to rip, or tear, or *come undone*. The mecha part of herself, hexed to integrate with human nerves and muscle, reported no sensation, but Grytt became certain that if she moved, even the slightest bit, she would part ways with herself.

The *theory* behind tesser-hex travel, which Rupert and Rory had discussed with mutual fascination until Grytt had no choice but to retain some understanding of it, was that all matter and energy fused, somehow, in that between-place. There was indeed a possibility of *coming undone*, but the ships were battle-hexed to maintain internal integrity. What one felt did not reflect the reality of the situation. Grytt, who found that feelings often conflicted with, or at least distorted, material events, had been content to ignore them.

Now, for the forever-moment of the tesser-hex, she was left to wonder just how much difference there was between alwar physiology and human, how wide the gap in arithmantic understanding, and whether human flesh *might* come unglued in the passage, where alwar (and tenju) flesh would not.

And then, with a snapping sensation, the tesser-hex ended. Grytt closed her flesh eye. The tesla eye, pitiless, reported the bridge intact, no one melted, and a new display on the hologram.

"That," said Rupert, a bit breathlessly, "was amazing."

CHAPTER NINE ═══════

V*ery fast*, in the vast scale of void, is a relative term. Voidships travel *very fast* on an absolute scale of velocity,
though the degree depends on engine size and power-
to-mass ratios and other technical specifications unnecessary to
anyone except engineers. A Tadeshi corsair like *G. Stein* is faster
than a Tadeshi military shuttle like *Vagabond*; both of those move
more swiftly than a mirri corracle; a Thorne Consortium warship
(built by Merchants League shipyards) is faster still, and a k'bal
kite-skiff outpaces them all. The xeno vessel Zhang had identified
was moving faster than *any* of the aforementioned ships.

People running from a cargo bay to a vessel docked at an aetherlock run significantly more slowly on that same absolute scale, and
yet, because of the relatively short distances involved, may board a
ship, and that ship may shrug itself into the void and achieve several kilometers' clearance, before *very fast* makes its arrival.

So it happened with Thorsdottir, Jaed, Rory, and Zhang.

There was no time to remove their hardsuits. Thorsdottir and
Rory threw themselves into their respective stations in *Vagabond's*
tiny cockpit. Jaed, who should have gone into the back cabin and
availed himself of a chair and harness there, chose to stay in the
cockpit as well, preferring to brace himself between the bulkhead

and Rory's chair and trust to maglocked boots and the hardsuit's reinforcement for his safety. This was unwise, because although *Vagabond's* standard hexwork could counter and compensate for inertial shifts, there was always the chance the ship would execute a maneuver beyond their capability. At that point, Jaed and his hardsuit would become a large, free-floating projectile in a very small space and endanger everyone.

Vagabond's turing knew it. *Vagabond's* turing advised Zhang (and Thorsdottir, by proximity, since she could see Zhang's screen as well as her own) of the danger, and recommended "locking down the loose cargo immediately." A part of Zhang wanted to do that: grab Jaed Moss bodily and escort him into the cabin and strap him down, over all protests, because he was violating everything she knew about shipboard safety during combat and, if he would not behave responsibly on his own, he should be made to do so. Another part of her sympathized. Waiting for everyone else to do, or fail to do, their jobs, and being dependent on the outcome, would not have suited *her* especially well, particularly if she had just gotten herself out of a dangerous situation, as Jaed had.

And the part of her that was too pragmatic to indulge temper or sympathy simply noted that if such a lockdown became necessary—if something happened to the inertials—then there would be bigger worries than Jaed bouncing around the cockpit, and those worries would look more like torpedoes or missiles or whatever dreadful battle-hex a xeno warship could muster.

"Where did that ship come from?" asked Rory. "Was it hiding behind one of the moonlets?" The second of Samtalet's two resident gas giants, Perkele, had a small constellation of moons and jagged bits of former moons in orbit. It was also the nearest planetary body to *G. Stein*.

Zhang flashed Thorsdottir an incredulous side-eye. Rory was not given to asking questions when she could ascertain the answer herself. Anyone looking at the navigational screen could *see* that the xeno ship was, in fact, coming from a direction other than Perkele or its satellites, or the station, or in fact anything except the system's edge.

"No," said Zhang, after a moment, when it was clear Rory was not actually looking at the nav-screen. "The trajectory's wrong. They came out of nowhere. One second, nothing on the scans. Then, there they were."

"Thank you," Rory said absently. "I'm getting signal fragments. Not like what I heard on *G. Stein*, not like Rose's whispers. It sounds like there are two separate origins, which suggests two ships. *That's* why I'm not looking at your screen and am asking obvious questions."

Thorsdottir pitched her voice low, for Zhang's ears. "Rory thinks the xenos can tesser-hex without a gate."

Zhang shot her another worried side-eye. "Does that mean there could be more of them coming? Or out there already?"

"I wonder if SAM-1 can see what's happening." Jaed sounded grim. "I wonder if it's even still *there*, or if these whoever-they-ares already blew them up."

"I sent them a warning," Rory said. "I haven't gotten a response."

Thorsdottir had a sinking feeling about the station's well-being. SAM-1, like all stations, had a quantum-hex communication system. They could have already called for help, and received instant confirmation, but that help would still take time to arrive. Ship-to-ship conflicts were harrowing enough. Stations could not run away. She imagined a xeno boarding party on SAM-1 like Rose had shown her on *G. Stein*, and felt sick.

Then *Vagabond's* arms-turing beeped and Thorsdottir felt even sicker: the xeno ship was in *Vagabond's* gun-range already, which meant that *Vagabond* was almost certainly in range of the xeno guns.

"Should we keep running?" Zhang asked. "Or turn around and—?"

"Die by superior battle-hex," Jaed muttered. "Or superior weapons."

"Keep running," said Rory. "I'm trying to hail them. If we can talk, maybe . . ."

Rory did not finish the sentence. Thorsdottir finished it for her, in the confines of her skull. *Maybe they won't attack. Maybe they'll tell us who they are.* She touched the compartment on her hardsuit in which she'd stored Rose's clipping, as if for luck, or just to reassure herself Rose was still there.

Though Rory had given no orders about targeting the xeno ship, Thorsdottir busied herself with the arms-turing. The targeting scope could *see* the xeno ship, but it was having difficulty settling on a lock. Considering the xeno ship's vector—coming straight at *Vagabond*—and its sheer size—far larger than *G. Stein*—that failure seemed hex-related. She started to report as much, in hopes that one (or both) of the arithmancers on board could *do something* to let *Vagabond* at least get a shot off in the conflict.

She was forestalled by a metallic squeal that ripped through the cockpit. For an instant she thought they'd been holed, breached, that the sound was *Vagabond's* hull ripping open. Then she recognized comm-screech.

"Sorry," Rory muttered, "sorry, sorry."

The screech came down to a whine, which then resolved into words.

"Tadeshi vessel. Disarm. Cease forward momentum. Prepare to be boarded."

For a fistful of moments, Zhang and Thorsdottir and Rory and Jaed sat there, listening to the first words they'd ever heard from a species they'd never met, in a perfectly comprehensible—if oddly accented—GalSpek.

This was not, obviously, first contact for the xenos.

"Well, hello to you, too," Jaed said, under his breath.

Thorsdottir turned her attention from her arms-turing to Rory, and by proximity to Jaed, who clung to the back of Rory's chair with both hands, white lipped.

Rory looked more composed, but Thorsdottir was not fooled; there was an edge in her voice Vernor Moss would have recognized.

"Xeno vessel, please identify yourself. This is the free-trader *Vagabond*. We are on a salvage operation. We are not Tadeshi. Repeat. We are *not* Tadeshi. Please acknowledge."

"You assume that'll matter to them," said Jaed.

"I'm hoping it will," Rory snapped.

"*Vagabond.*" The speaker—male, female, impossible to say; the voice had an odd doubling, as if the transmission had lagged, and an echo as if he, she, it, or they were speaking from inside of a bucket—stumbled over the syllables. "This is Protectorate vessel *Sissten*. We repeat. Disarm. Cease forward momentum. Prepare for boarding."

Thorsdottir glanced at Zhang. So now they had a name. Neither of them had ever heard of this Protectorate in any briefing, back when they had gotten such things; nor in their months of confinement on Urse, as Rory's body-maids, with nothing to do but read and watch broadcasts, had they heard anything about them. They must be a very new problem, or a well-concealed old problem. Thorsdottir suspected the former.

"Ten minutes to the tesser-hex buoy," Zhang said. She might as well have said forever.

Thorsdottir coaxed the arms-turing into granting her manual control. She primed one of the aft missiles and pointed it in the general direction of *back there*. She didn't expect to *hit* the xeno ship, but she might distract them. Or she might get them to return fire, which would be catastrophic. Then again, she had seen what the xenos did to *G. Stein's* crew. It might be kinder to detonate into the void than to be boarded. It was also a very final solution.

Thorsdottir snagged Rory's eye. "Should I fire?"

Rory shook her head. "No. Disarm."

Thorsdottir disarmed the missiles. Her hands were trembling a little, and slick with sweat and cold inside the hardsuit gloves. There had to be *something* that someone could do. Not her, fine, but perhaps Zhang could execute an evasive maneuver, a roll or a jag or *something*. Then she remembered that Jaed was standing, unsecured and vulnerable to rapid and violent shifts in momentum, behind Rory's station. She swore, loud enough that Zhang side-eyed her.

"What?"

"Nothing. *Nothing*." There was no point in explanation.

The *Sissten*-blip on the nav-screen sped up suddenly, halving, then halving again, the distance to the *Vagabond*. The arms-turing squawked indignantly, finding its target entirely relocated and all its careful calculations spoiled. The primary turing wailed about proximity.

That was impossible. Thorsdottir did not pretend to understand all the physics of void-flight, but she knew about objects in motion and mass and acceleration.

"How," she began to ask.

"Arithmancy," Jaed said shortly. "Or magic."

"Give me visual!" Rory said sharply.

The main screen lit up.

A massive shape—*Sissten*, presumably—shot past *Vagabond* at ridiculously high speed, laced with threads of multi-colored lights. Then it stopped and spun and suddenly they were looking at it. Or it was looking at them. At least Thorsdottir assumed she was looking at the bow of the vessel. It had that same spear-head quality as the xeno hardsuit helmets, narrow end first. The threads of light became individual teslas studding the skin of a vessel the likes of which Thorsdottir had never seen before. It looked a bit like a ring, hollowed in the center, with several triangular appendages jutting out of the rims. It was big enough to encircle *Vagabond* several times over, along with *G. Stein*.

How that massive ship bled off velocity that fast, how it came around *that fast*—more magic. Clearly.

"Princess," she said. It was as much of a prayer as a lapse into old habit.

Rory did not answer.

Sissten appeared to shimmer, as if distorted by high heat.

Vagabond shuddered. Thorsdottir was thrown into her harness. Jaed was thrown into something solid: there was a *thump*, metal on metal, and an unhealthy scraping noise, and an expletive of which Grytt would have been proud. Every tesla and screen went dark. There were only the hardsuit teslas, which everyone wore except Zhang, twinkling in the dark.

"Our primary turing is not responding," Zhang said faintly. "Neither are the engines. We appear to have lost all momentum."

Thorsdottir resisted the urge to punch the arms-turing, which had died with the rest of *Vagabond*. She took a deep breath instead.

Jaed's tone could have etched metal. "*Amazing*, isn't it? This level of arithmancy."

Rory did not answer. The silence inside *Vagabond* grew and took on a life of its own, pressing inward until Thorsdottir thought she could choke on it. That massive ship was right outside, *right* there. What it would do next was anyone's guess—

Except she did know. The xenos had said very clearly what they intended.

Thorsdottir unfastened her harness and stood up, head ducked against the low overhead. She stepped past Rory and the dead comm station, and unclipped her 'slinger, and paused in front of Jaed. His gaze bounced from her face to her weapon and back. Then he unclipped his own, and nodded.

Rory broke her silence, finally. She twisted to look up at them, elbow and shoulder grinding against a seat and station inadequate to accommodate the bulk of her hardsuit.

"Sit down, both of you."

Thorsdottir's heart beat hard and fast, and not because there were xenos inbound. "They're going to board."

"Yes. So they said. Sit down." Rory took a bite of air. "You saw what happened on *G. Stein*. We can't meet them with force."

Thorsdottir swallowed her argument. She clipped the 'slinger back to her hardsuit with unnecessary force. It felt like retreat—no, it *felt* like surrender—to return to her seat. But she did, because Rory had asked, and because although Thorsdottir harbored a vague conviction that she would rather die fighting than sitting, she had a firm conviction that she did not want to die at all. Rory was usually right with her hunches.

Jaed stared at Thorsdottir with a mixture of defiance and disbelief. Then he, too, stowed his 'slinger. It took him two tries to clip it in place. Thorsdottir felt a stab of sympathy. She wished she could tell him that the shaking hands improved, but she did not think he would appreciate the knowledge.

"I don't think they want to kill us," Rory offered.

Jaed jerked his gaze off Thorsdottir's face and scowled at Rory instead. "How can you even say that?"

"Because they would have already. Be a leaf," Rory said cryptically. Then she closed her eyes as if something hurt. "Seal your visors, though, in case of atmospheric incompatibility. Zhang—"

Zhang was not wearing a hardsuit. "It's all right."

Rory's composure slipped. "No, it's not. Get back into the cabin. Close the hatch manually and get suited, fast as you can. But unless I call for you, *stay there*."

Zhang did not ask why; Zhang was not given to asking. She jumped from her chair, and after a moment, Rory heard a hardsuit rattle off its rack.

Rory felt a certain relief for that. *One* of her crew was unmutinous. Thorsdottir radiated disapproval, silent and spiky and very reminiscent of Grytt, which almost made Rory smile, which led in the next breath to a sharp pain beneath her ribs, somewhere near her heart. Messer Rupert had asked her to stay on Lanscot where it was safe (as if anything could be, in the midst of a multiverse-splitting civil conflict). Grytt had said only that sheep-farming was a good occupation, if one did not want excitement, which was really the same thing as safe.

She had wanted—not adventure, exactly, nor excitement, though privateering was both—but to do something not dictated by protocol or birth. And because of who she was—because declaring herself unprincess did not make her anyone other than Rory Thorne, she had had to go very far from Lanscot, from the Free

Worlds of Tadesh, from anywhere she might be recognized by anyone who cared.

Of course Thorsdottir and Zhang had gone with her. She had told them it was not required, that they, too, had a choice. But she'd known what they would say, even as she said it. They hadn't joined the Royal Guard to settle on Lanscot and tend sheep.

Nor, she thought now, with a pang, had they joined to die in a small, stolen ship in the hinterlands of settled void. She could be very wrong about the xenos' intentions. They might peel *Vagabond* open as soon as come knocking at the hatch.

Vagabond's teslas came back, in a ripple of color. The life support coughed back to consciousness. The engines appeared to be dormant, still, and when Rory looked, so did the primary turing. The tesla bank beside the smaller of *Vagabond's* two aetherlocks lit up in a countdown to pressurization.

The xenos appeared to be coming the civilized way, by pre-existing aperture, rather than making a new one with their plasma-beam weapons. How nice.

"I'm suited," Zhang reported, in something close to a whisper, as if helmet-comms could be overheard by invading xenos. She was clearly hoping that Rory would relent and command her to emerge from the cabin.

Rory did not. "Good. Stay there. Assuming they don't notice you, you can reboot the ship's powercore once we're gone." Rory had no clear notion of *how* one did that; her only experience thus far had been Jaed ripping at wires on *G. Stein*. That principle of destructive restoration would work on *Vagabond* too. She trusted Zhang to figure out how.

She did not let herself think about whether or not *Vagabond's* turing was dead in the same way that *G. Stein's* was, and *if* it was, how Zhang would be able to do anything with the ship to run nav calculations for high speed maneuvers.

"Prin—Rory," Zhang breathed, as close to arguing as Zhang ever got. "I don't like this."

"I know." Rory was aware that her conversation with Zhang was as much for Thorsdottir and Jaed's benefit. "But I have to believe, if they intended to kill us outright, they would have. And if they intended some kind of violence, they wouldn't be coming in through the aetherlock."

"If they—did you *see* what they did on *G. Stein*? Weren't you there?" Jaed's voice, low and furious, filled her helmet.

"I suspect the Tadeshi shot first."

"I wonder *why*."

"I don't. The Tadeshi thought they could win, and they were wrong. We *know* we can't."

Jaed sputtered.

"Leaf, Jaed. Be a leaf." Rory did not exhort him to trust her. He did anyway, and besides, it was Rory's experience that *telling* someone they had to have faith defeated the purpose.

Thorsdottir had been sitting at her station. Now she stood up. Jaed, who had taken Zhang's seat in her absence, also stood, and Rory saw that they meant to maneuver her into the back, somehow, and put themselves between her and the aetherlock.

"No," she told them. "I'll go first."

Rory wanted to believe Thorsdottir did not argue because she saw the wisdom of Rory's decision.

"All right,"

You're being stupid

said Thorsdottir.

The thirteenth fairy's gift had never been a comfortable thing.

Rory had thought it would grow easier, the farther she distanced herself from princesshood. But it was the opposite. Friends, it turned out, had more divergent opinions than Royal Guards did, and except for Jaed, tended not to voice them aloud.

"It'll be fine," she said, though the fairies had not granted her predictive powers. She wished they had. Pretty and kind were all well and good, but not as useful as precognition.

The aetherlock chimed. The tesla panels shifted from red to green.

Hands slick inside the hardsuit gloves, heart trying to crawl out her throat, Rory positioned herself in front of the lock as the iris flexed. A puff of atmosphere came in first, accompanied by a hiss like a dead comm channel. Rory's hardsuit, ever diligent, identified the incoming atmosphere as breathable, if not exactly the human-standard mixture. It wasn't toxic, like the mirri's, who needed their suits and their own aether supply. More like the multicranial, long-limbed k'bal, who could share human atmosphere, even if they found human gravity standards uncomfortable.

Except these xenos were not at all like the k'bal, when the hatch opened. They were as tall—Rory had ascertained that much from the *G. Stein* footage—but they had the correct (by human standards) number and disposition of limbs, and only one head. They entered the narrow aetherlock in a spear-tip formation, one taking point, two flanking. The latter pair held the plasma-spitting, long-barreled weapons leveled. The one in the front carried no weapon. Their hands were empty, open, with four digits: three overly jointed fingers and a thumb, all of which seemed to end in talon-points. Those might be features of their battle armor, or features of the hands which the armor accommodated. On one level, it did not matter. Rory had seen footage of what those talons could do to Tadeshi battle armor. They would have no difficulty at all with a standard civilian hardsuit.

The xenos stopped just inside and appeared to regard her, the wedge-shaped helmets pointing like fingers. Their visors were entirely opaque. The light slid off their hardsuits, fracturing into oil-slick hues, or settling into resinous black. That was armor, almost certainly hexed for that effect.

Someone—Jaed, she thought—caught their breath.

Rory had thought about whether to meet the xenos palms open and up, to demonstrate their emptiness and forestall any precipitous fingers on triggers. She revised her intentions and reached up instead to open her visor. The faceshield was transparent, but she hoped a bare face would signal openness, and not (she thought, as the visor retracted) offer a hideous insult. Her gesture had the simultaneous effects of rendering her intersuit comms listen-only, and of exposing her to whatever contamination might be possible with an alien atmosphere. It was the latter, she supposed, that incited Thorsdottir to swear with impressive creativity. Jaed only said, "Rory, *no*," and groaned.

Rory, for her part, ignored them. The xeno atmosphere tasted a little more metallic than that to which she was accustomed, and seemed both warmer and drier. She took several deep breaths. There was a peppery odor, and an eye-prickling discomfort like raw onions that quickly vanished.

The xenos made no reciprocal gestures. The one in the front cocked their head slowly, as if they had spotted something interesting and wanted a closer look. Then they raised their empty left hand and the two in the rear lowered their weapons.

"You will come with us," the foremost xeno said in accented GalSpek. The syllables, compressed (Rory supposed) by the helmet's ex-comms, still sounded strangely doubled, as if there were a fractional lag between the beginning and end of a syllable.

Rory stabbed her gaze at the imagined eyes behind that visor. Then she peeled off a fraction of her attention, and dipped into the first layer of aether, and tried for her first look at a xeno aura. Tried, because she saw nothing at all. The aura of each xeno was as blank as mecha. What if they *were*? Her gut congealed around that possibility.

Then she saw the glimmer of an equation, flicker-fast, and realized she was looking at a deflecting hex meant to block exactly the sort of exploration Rory was attempting.

There was an arithmancer under one of those hardsuits, or maybe under all of them. Rory suspected, however, that it was only the one in front who was running the hex, if only because if *she* had been the leader of a hostile boarding party, that's what she would have done.

She also suspected her own aura had just flared into a rainbow of realization. She considered deploying her own concealing hex, but another arithmancer might notice that, at which point these xenos would have information about her, perhaps too much.

Be a mantis-lion. Look like a leaf. Speak like, if not a princess, then at least a diplomat. She had no protocols for first contact (which this clearly was *not*, if these people spoke GalSpek), but she thought courtesy might bridge the gaps in custom of which she was unaware.

"How kind of you to invite us onto your vessel. But among my people, it is customary to perform introductions, first. I am Rory Thorne, citizen of the Confederation of Liberated Worlds. These are my crewmates. Our species is human. Whom do I have the honor of addressing?"

The rifle-wielding xeno on the left jerked, as if surprised, and turned to their fellow. The leader tipped their head the other way. Then they hissed, two short bursts of sound, soon echoed by the others.

They were . . . laughing. That might be a good sign; humor, and the ability to experience and express it, was something over which species could bond. It was also unnerving, since laughter, at least among humans and the mirri (the k'bal did not laugh), could indicate a great many unpleasant things.

Rory's teeth clenched. She had never particularly enjoyed being laughter's object, whatever its flavor. Her aura flared in response.

The foremost xeno took a quick, sharp step closer. Rory was forced to look up, if she wished to stare at their visor and not their torso, which, rather than being humanly flat, pinched into a vertical ridge starting just below the suit's collar and extended almost to the waist. It seemed to be a physiological cousin to the other strange fins that ran just past the joints on each limb, and along the top of what should have been hips.

The xeno's visor retracted, and Rory got her first look at a face—two eyes, what one might uncharitably call a snout or, less pejoratively, a wedge-shaped nose-and-mouth arrangement, where the nostrils were expanding slits. The xeno's skin was charcoal-dark, roughly textured and apparently hairless. Several ridges of what looked like skin-covered bone ran along the sides of its skull, ending in a spiked fringe jabbing off the back. There were no ears in evidence; Rory supposed them somewhere in the creases between ridges, or perhaps in some more novel location. The most startling features were the mobile plates, hinged to the skull at the rear of the jaw, which flared out as the xeno leaned over Rory. Then the lips pulled back with surprising flexibility to reveal a great many triangular and pointed teeth which were etched with elaborate carvings in varying shades of blue, from cobalt to cerulean.

Rory managed not to flinch back as the xeno dipped low and close to her face. The etching on those teeth really was very fine and precise. Lovely, even. And those teeth were very, *very* sharp. A carnivorous species, then. Or primarily so.

"Hold *still*," Thorsdottir said with quiet force on the comms, and Rory supposed Jaed had made some unwise move. That suspicion was borne out in the next moment, when the armed xenos, in tandem, raised their weapons. A 'slinger was made to throw bolts, and so staring at the wrong end of it was like staring at the empty eye socket of the hollow barrel. The xeno plasma weapon had a tip like a spear or an arrowhead, if someone had made either of those implements out of wire and filament, and left the bulk of them hollow. The plasma would collect there, and focus, and then it would burn through whatever it touched. Jaed, presumably, if he did not heed Thorsdottir's warning.

The foremost xeno raised their left hand again, and repeated the *put the weapons down* gesture more sharply this time. They closed their mouth, concealing the beautiful, terrible teeth. A ripple of color passed over their cheeks—subdued violet, watery green—in a spangling pattern, before settling back to the dull charcoal.

"My name is Sub-Commander Koto-rek ia'vakat'ia Tarsik. You may address me as Sub-Commander." The odd echo persisted, as the xeno spoke, so Rory supposed it was a feature of physiology, and not an effect of the helmet. "You are now in Protectorate custody."

Thorsdottir spoke for the first time. "You say that like we should know what that is, Sub-Commander. Or, forgive me, even what species you are."

The sub-commander's head tilted, an odd, sharp movement

that made Rory want to flinch out of range, and which drew attention to the xeno's pair of large, darkly undifferentiated eyes, like pools of pitch with a faint spangling in their depths that might've been reflected tesla-light or scattered pigmentation. The jaw-plates flared out a centimeter or two, in what Rory interpreted as an indication of forbearance. "We are vakari. I am a vakar."

"Huh," said Thorsdottir.

"Thank you," Rory interjected, before that *huh* produced anymore insubordinate friends. She repeated *vakar, vakari,* in her head, impressing upon herself the sharpness of the consonants, not unlike the silhouettes of their hardsuits. A sharp people, the vakari. Very pointy.

"Sub-Commander, thank you for the explanations. But I must ask, why have you intercepted us?"

The sub-commander gestured broadly at the aetherlock, the cockpit, the seal cabin hatch. "This vessel is not designed for cargo or storage. It is a Tadeshi military transport. But you are not Tadeshi soldiers."

"We told you we were salvagers." Jaed's voice crackled from the back of the aetherlock. Rory thought he must have opened his helmet; his anger was unmitigated by ex-comms, and echoed off the metal. "Not that you left us much, assuming you were the ones who shot up *G. Stein*. What are you even doing here? Samtalet is an unaffiliated system."

Rory wished Jaed a little less volume, a little more prudence, less success at achieving the courage to stand up for himself. Perhaps a better definition of what it meant to be brave at all.

The sub-commander's jaw-plates flared with a faint hissing. Annoyance, Rory guessed, or amusement. "This system proved unwilling or unable to defend its borders from Tadeshi traffic. Now it has been annexed by the Protectorate."

Jaed sputtered, but thankfully said nothing else.

Rory asked, in her best polite tone. "But Sub-Commander, I must reiterate, we are not Tadeshi."

"If we become convinced of that, you may be permitted to depart. Now come with us, please, Rory Thorne. We have questions."

CHAPTER TEN ≡≡≡

The k'bal, perhaps more than any other species, are obsessed with knowledge. The ancient human adage, *knowledge is power*, is widely held to be the first thing the human ambassador said to impress the k'bal as civilized. The great k'bal philosopher P'Tet posits that a species' relationship to the acquisition and disposition of knowledge, and the value placed upon it, determines its place in the hierarchy of civilization. In that hierarchy, humanity (collectively, the scores of all subset cultures averaged together) falls somewhere in the lower third, because although knowledge is power, so too is ignorance considered to be bliss.

The discovery of *that* proverb, according to accounts by the historian Kwel Qing Zanat, caused the k'bal ambassador to vent all of their cranial vents simultaneously, and to subsequently flee the room in a combination of embarrassment and horror. The intervention of the mirri was enlisted to repair relations, which succeeded only after the human delegation made clear that ignorance was sometimes conflated with innocence, particularly in children, where knowledge was meant to include both academic subjects and experience, which in turn led to a series of misunderstandings about the legal status of the human delegation and several demands by the k'bal to speak to a human adult.

Rory had never found the latter maxim, that ignorance is bliss, to be true. Messer Rupert had always presented ignorance as a handicap, at least in academic areas; the other variant, her innocence, had been an early casualty of her father's assassination, and later of Grytt's relentless pragmatism. One of the worst effects of her confinement on Urse had been Regent Moss's control of information into her apartments. She had not known about the Lanscottar rebellion until she had unwittingly helped to start it, and was left with the consequences of having done so. Whether one regarded ignorance as bliss or as deeply frustrating, one was not exempt from the results of that ignorance. Knowledge was power, and power could be uncomfortable, but it was far better than being surprised.

And now, once again ignorant—and her own fault this time, for attempting to withdraw from political knowledge—she found herself quite helpless and not a bit happy about it. In the two years since she'd renounced her title and gone into, if not hiding, then at least obscurity, Rory had discovered that the news came late and thinly to her. She was not *surprised* that she had never heard of the Protectorate before today, but she was both annoyed and alarmed at that lack of knowledge. It was evident that the first contact between human and vakari had taken place some time ago; the sub-commander spoke GalSpek, or at least had sufficient hexes to perform translation, and the vakari were aware not only of the *name* Tadeshi, but also able to identify a warship as of that manufacture, which in turn suggested a familiarity that was not congenial. Someone, *somewhere*, must have information about them more in depth than what she had.

But lacking that information, Rory had her own observations

from which to make conclusions. So what did she know? The vakari were bipeds. Rory was not a biologist, but she supposed some
significance there, when the other two xeno species with which
humanity had made contact, k'bal and mirri, were distinctly not.
(Another exception was the fairies, she amended, but she had
never found them in xenobiological treatises, either). Their physiology was not especially mammalian, but they breathed normal-
ish aether, and she hypothesized endothermic metabolism, as the
ship's temperature was not especially warm. With those teeth,
they either were, or had evolved from, some kind of predator. She
could not determine a clear sex, as the vakari were lacking mammalian secondary sexual characteristics, and she had insufficient
experience of vakari features to notice patterns of differentiation
that might be sex-linked. She was also entirely at a loss as to how
to assign gender, or how to even inquire about the subject. K'bal
had four genders that changed according to ambient temperature,
age, and mood; the mirri, being parthenogenic clones, were all *she*.
Vakari might be two, or three, or offended by the very concept.
She settled in her head on a temporary *they*, with revisions to be
made as she acquired more information.

The vakari ship maintained something close to, but less than,
a standard G. A cursory scan of the first layer of aether showed
Rory extensive hexwork in the bulkheads and deck, more so than
was standard on human ships. She had read about, but never observed, similar features on k'bal vessels. K'bal were arithmantically gifted, and arithmantically dependent (more than was wise,
Messer Rupert had said; and Grytt had added something about
eggs and baskets and diversifying one's arsenal when possible).
That said, Grytt *would* approve of those plasma rifles, in that she
would want to acquire one, and that she would want all of them
currently not in her possession deactivated or melted to slag. Rory

favored the latter alternative, but seeing no way to accomplish it, resolved to remain un-shot, which would involve not antagonizing her captors. She tried to imagine them as *hosts*, but the presence of the aforementioned weapons made that difficult.

She was aware that Jaed and Thorsdottir had followed her onto *Sissten's* deck, and that the two vakari soldiers had followed *them*, which meant the xenos had left no one on *Vagabond* and that Zhang might remain undetected. She was also aware when, just past a crossroads of corridors, that escort tried to divert left with Jaed and Thorsdottir. Tried, because Jaed lodged an immediate and vocal protest.

"Where are you taking her? No."

Rory turned around. Jaed was too busy glaring at the vakari soldiers, who were in turn looking at the sub-commander, to notice her. So Rory held up a hand, hoping the gesture was universally understood and that no one shot anyone.

Jaed ignored, or did not see, her hand. Thorsdottir, however, did. Her eyebrows plunged down and gathered in a knot over her nose.

"It's all right," said Rory. "Go with them."

There was a time, Rory thought, hardly daring to breathe, that Thorsdottir would not have looked at her like that (Zhang still would not), and she wished fleetingly that Thorsdottir had proved less adaptive than her partner in attempting to interact with Rory as an equal. Now was not the time for argument.

But Thorsdottir was also ultimately sensible. She grabbed Jaed's arm and pulled, and when that did not immediately produce results, inserted herself between him and the vakari soldiers.

"Come on," she said, and added something else, low-voiced, that Rory could not quite hear. Jaed's very pale skin flushed red, then washed white again. He threw a look at Rory, who regretted, not for the first time, that the fairy gift confined itself to revealing spoken untruths, and was little use for nonverbal communication.

Then Jaed and Thorsdottir went where the Protectorate soldiers indicated they ought: down a corridor that rapidly bent them out of sight. Rory listened as their footfalls on the deckplate receded to echoes.

The sub-commander had paused, was waiting, seemed to be observing this drama with amusement.

Rory cleared her throat and waited until the vakar's ink-black attention came back to her (hard to say *where* those eyes looked, but the rest of the face came in line, so). "Where are you taking them, Sub-Commander?"

The sub-commander's head tilted, another one of those sharp, short gestures, like a bird noting the sudden movement of insects. "They won't be harmed."

Truth, though Rory sensed a lurking and unuttered *unless*. She considered asking the logical follow-up question, where are you taking *me*, and did not. She would find out soon enough. As for whether or not *she* might be harmed in the near future, well, she supposed that, too, hinged on an unspoken *unless*.

So she nodded, and in case that gesture did not translate, said, "All right."

The vakar gestured the direction they had been going, and turned and began walking.

Rory, after a moment, followed. She did not see as she had very much choice.

The vakari soldiers marched Thorsdottir and Jaed briskly down the corridor. With her visor retracted, Thorsdottir's HUD was limited to a small array of teslas on the inner edge of the helmet.

The hardsuit was monitoring atmosphere, pressure, the presence of everyone else on its network. Jaed and Rory were there. Zhang was *not*, which Thorsdottir hoped was because Zhang was cleverly keeping herself off the network, and not because the Protectorate had, after removing what they thought was the crew, destroyed *Vagabond*.

The soldiers paused at the end of the corridor, where there was a large door that retracted into the wall, rather than irising like a normal hatch. The chamber on the other side was large, open in the center, lined along the edges with smaller rooms, the doors to which were open, except one, and the interiors of which were unoccupied (except for, presumably, the one behind the closed door).

It was not *quite* a jail, but it was pretty clearly some sort of holding area into which one deposited individuals one did not want wandering loose. A third vakar soldier stood up as they came in. That vakar had been sitting in front of what looked like a screen on a console, at which Thorsdottir now got a look: it was divided into as many sections as there were small rooms, all but one of which was blank. The single image appeared to be of a person sitting in the center of one of the cells: legs folded, hands resting on knees, back to the camera. The figure turned their head briefly, as if hearing them in the main room.

Thorsdottir stopped dead. She had been unsure of gender at first. Now she was also unsure of species.

"Sss," said the taller of their two escorts, and Thorsdottir twitched. The vakar sounded like a cross between a large, angry cat and a large, angry snake. She twitched again when she looked and found their visor retracted. So far all the vakari she'd seen looked very much alike in the shape and proportion of features, which is to say a bit like pictures of dragons Thorsdottir had seen in a bestiary, only upright and without the wings or tail. It made her curious what physiological features lay concealed under those fins on their hardsuits. Probably, given the rest of them, something sharp, spikes or bone ridges. She hoped the vakari did not harbor a similar curiosity about what lay under *her* hardsuit. She flicked a glance at the console screen. The occupant of the other room (oh, call it what it *was*: the cell) appeared to be wearing some kind of bulky outer layer, as well, so it seemed unlikely she and Jaed would be forced to strip.

The vakar guard who had hissed did not *look* angry, though it was difficult to assign emotions to their features. Their dark eyes were wide, the jaw-plates neither clamped nor flared out. They pointed at the 'slinger on her chest.

Thorsdottir considered, for a reflexive moment, resisting, even though she had seen the devastation on *G. Stein*. She supposed it was a sympathetic reaction to Jaed, who was scowling renewed rebellion at their captors.

"Give it to them," said Thorsdottir, and yielded her weapon to that open-palmed expectation. The soldier's fingers—four of them, taloned, extra joint—closed over the weapon. Their jaw-plates flared, and a spangling of cyan bloomed on the planes of their face. (Not cheeks, Thorsdottir thought. Cheeks were fleshy. Cheeks wrinkled.) They turned the 'slinger in their hand, careful to keep the business end pointed at the deck. They said something to their partner, who had Jaed's weapon, which elicited a hiss and a similar ripple of facial pigmentation.

The resident guard seemed to defer to the other two: head turned a little out of line, failing eye contact, not participating in the conversation. They were not wearing a hardsuit, though the shape of their uniform was the same as the soldiers' suits, with similar patterns on chest and shoulder that must be insignia or rank. The soldiers, having thus disarmed Thorsdottir and Jaed, left the room, taking the 'slingers with them. They appeared to Thorsdottir to be swaggering.

The remaining vakar pointed at the empty cell adjacent to the occupied one and laid their other hand on what Thorsdottir supposed was a weapon, although it did not look like the plasma rifles: it was small, cylindrical, smooth. It probably shot lightning, or high-velocity spikes, or acid. Or maybe it was just what it looked like: a club.

Thorsdottir wondered how strong this particular vakar might be, and how hard they could hit.

Jaed, who was evidently wondering the same thing, said from the side of his mouth: "There's one of them and two of us."

There were a dozen reasons why that was a bad idea. Thorsdottir picked the one most likely to work on Jaed. "No. They've still got Rory."

He made a strangled noise. Then he swore and followed her into the cell. He did not turn to look when the vakar sealed them inside. He began an immediate examination of the seams of the room and the tesla fixtures. His eyes had that not-quite-there stare to them, as if he could see through the bulkhead—which, come to consider it, maybe he *could*, with the right hexes.

Thorsdottir had grown up in a large family with a dearth of bathrooms, and had gone from there to royal service. She was not accustomed to privacy, exactly, but—"You *can't* see through the polysteel, can you?"

"What? No." He scowled. "Not how you mean. I can see *into* it. The structure of it. But by the time I can see *through*, I can't see this plane. At the moment I can't even do that. There's some kind of hexwork in here. I don't recognize the equations, though. I mean, it's *math*, but it's different."

She shrugged. Of *course* there was xeno arithmancy. "Can you get past it?"

"No."

"Then stop pacing and listen to me."

Jaed shot her a glare from the corner of his eye. Then he leaned against the bulkhead and folded his arms as well as the hardsuit would permit. "All right. What?"

"The person in the cell beside us? I don't *think* they're human. I saw two arms, two legs, one head, all in the usual places—"

"So, not a mirri or k'bal."

"—No. But I thought I saw *tusks*."

Jaed said nothing for a moment, clearly digesting the word and its implications. "The sub-commander knew the name Tadeshi, and that *Vagabond's* a military model. That suggests familiarity. Did my father know about these people? Did I just—not notice?"

"If you're asking, is it your fault somehow that you didn't know about this, if your father was involved with this Protectorate, then no. But I don't think he was. I think if the Free Worlds of Tadesh had been in contact or conflict with a new xeno species, that secret would've gotten out. I think this is *new*."

"The contact, or the conflict?"

"Both. The sub-commander said they'd annexed Samtalet. That suggests *they're* the aggressors. Although why, or what they want—I have no idea."

"Why is for people like Rory to worry about," said Jaed. "She wants so badly *not* to be a princess, except, you know, she's always a princess. Doing all the talking."

It was Thorsdottir's turn to dredge up a laugh. "It's what we expect from her. We're sitting here now, and I, at least, am half-assuming she's going to figure all this out. They could be doing awful things to her, but I imagine them talking, and her figuring out what's going on, and somehow fixing all of it. And I think that's what she expects will happen, too."

They shared silence, for a moment. Jaed's gaze flickered sidelong; Thorsdottir felt it brush over her profile, in its restless patrol of their cell's perimeter. She felt it return, and the weight as it settled.

"Why do *you* think the vakari killed the people on *G. Stein*?"

Thorsdottir shrugged, realized the gesture was largely obscured in a hardsuit, and pursed her lips noncommittally instead. Then, because she *knew* Jaed, and knew he would not just stop asking, "We *assumed* Rose was meant for the Confederation, but what if the Tadeshi were going to use them on vakari colonies or something?"

Jaed sputtered a word he'd gotten from Grytt. "Then why abandon *G. Stein* before they found Rose? Why attack and board at all? Why not just blow the ship up? Why come *back*?"

"Maybe the Protectorate didn't know what they were looking for. Maybe the manifest fooled them. Or they think because we showed up, *we* would know where to find Rose, and maybe that we have them. Which. Ah." Thorsdottir turned her head, made eyelock, and flicked her gaze down at the compartment on her hardsuit where she was keeping Rose's clippings.

Jaed's astonishment splashed over his face. Then that astonishment cooled, dried, hardened into something cannier. He tapped the side of his helmet and raised both eyebrows. Then he sealed his faceplate. Thorsdottir reminded herself that he'd worked for Dame Maggie and the Lanscottar resistance for months on Urse, while evading his father's increasingly invasive searches. He only *looked* like a fresh-faced innocent.

An impatient innocent: Thorsdottir watched Jaed's expression perform the facial equivalent of exasperated pacing for a few moments on the far side of his visor, before, with a careful tap of her skull on the helmet's interior, she dropped her own.

Her HUD came online, mostly green (you are alive) but with a not insignificant portion of amber (the atmospheric composition displeased it, as did the gravity). There were wobbly lines wrinkling the display at odd intervals, as if there were some kind of EM interference.

Arithmancy, perhaps. Some indication the vakari had hacked the suits with their admirable, awful arithmancy. Thorsdottir slotted that possibility into the ever-growing category of things over which she had no control.

"That guard out there might think this is suspicious," she said. "Putting the visors down. Might as well shout that we're talking about something secret on suit-comms."

"Well, we are." Jaed leaned forward until her suit, and presumably his, beeped a warning. "Are you telling me you *brought Rose with us*?"

"I didn't exactly have time to store them somewhere else, did I?" The HUD was still flickering. Hope fluttered in the back of Thorsdottir's throat. "But you know how good they are with hacking things.—Rose? Can you hear me?" If Rose couldn't answer, or if there wasn't enough of Rose *left* to answer, well, that was just how things were, and she and Jaed were no worse off than they'd been.

Another splash of astonishment widened Jaed's eyes. Thorsdottir noticed for the first time that Jaed had a fine spray of freckles on his cheeks, faint as milk. From their brief, brief stay on Lanscot, she thought. From the only time in his life he spent outdoors, in sunlight.

"Are they there? Can they hear you?" he asked, at the same time that Thorsdottir's HUD assembled a shakily pixelated *yes*.

"Yes." Thorsdottir frowned *hush* at Jaed. "Are you okay, Rose?"

The *yes* blinked. It seemed to be getting a little brighter.

She nodded, mouthed *fine* at Jaed, and said aloud, "Do you think Rose could invade *their* hardsuits? Or their ship? Maybe hack us out of this cell?"

"That depends on their arithmancy, I guess, and on whether or not there's enough of them left to contaminate anything besides your suit. Hold still. I have an idea." Jaed stepped around her, and, after a moment in which she drew breath to demand *what* he was up to, began picking and prying at something on her backplate. "Presumably Rose had been able to migrate out of the stasis pods by . . . doing something. Something which perhaps required open power conduits, or unshielded, unhexed systems."

"Jaed."

"There's a power-cell access panel back here. And if I can get it off, I can link our suits together, and—"

"And that gives Rose somewhere else to migrate. Maybe someplace else to reproduce?"

"I think they need something biological for reproduction. The clipping's got to mean something. Maybe the mecha have a limited lifespan outside of biology? Maybe without a biological anchor the command codes won't fully activate? I don't know. I *do* know that two suits with Rose are better than one.—Yes. *Yes.*" The second monosyllable rang triumphant.

Thorsdottir's HUD announced, via several flashing teslas, that Jaed had succeeded in removing the panel. Next came a great deal of rattling.

She cast her eyes at the imagined location of the surveillance 'bot. If their fellow prisoner's image on the monitor was indication, then it must be placed high, maybe over the door. She could not see any of the expected indicators. No strange bumps, or

lenses, or marks of any kind. Presumably Jaed, with his arithmancy, was more perceptive. Presumably his hex had blinded it.
Presumably—and here, Thorsdottir drifted from presumption into
hope, bordering on prayer—the vakari guard wasn't watching them
right now and getting suspicious about their activities.

Her own attention was drawn to an ominous flash, bright and
white and much like sunlight on ice, or a tesla flashing alert, above
the door.

Well. That solved where the surveillance 'bot was, anyway.
And whether or not the vakar had noticed.

"Jaed." He wasn't looking at doors or for 'bots. He was tugging
on her suit, as if he were wrestling with it, and maintaining a muttered monologue.

"Don't have the right cables. Just need to expose a wire—and
there. Can Rose cross—Oh. Yes. I see they can. Hi there, Rose.
Come on over.—They're on my HUD. Typing at me."

"*Jaed*. Is that your doing?"

"What?"

"Look up. Above the door."

She assumed that he was looking; the thumping about on her
suit ceased, though that did not entirely reassure her. She did not
want to deal with whatever came next with *panel ajar* still blinking at her.

"Uh oh."

"So it's not you."

"No. My hex isn't working. It's . . . gone. Something made it
gone."

"Another arithmancer."

"Really good counter-measures. Could be automated." He
closed her back-panel with more force than she thought was entirely necessary. Then he came around and peered up at the flash.

He retracted his visor and squinted up at the 'bot, as if he could peer through it. "Hey. Don't worry, okay? She had a short in her suit. I was fixing it. That's all." He gestured at Thorsdottir. Thorsdottir noticed he'd removed the suit glove, and that his bare hand seemed very small and frail, poking out of the suit, clutching a small nest of wires, the ends of which still dribbled sparks.

Unless the vakari guard was both especially trusting and not particularly bright, Thorsdottir supposed they would notice and take alarm. *She* was alarmed—sparks were never a good sign. "Did you destroy your glove?"

"What? No. I'm just leaving my suit unsealed a little bit longer."

Thorsdottir drew breath to demand *why* he would do that—because it seemed unwise, damaging a hardsuit on an alien vessel, and because she was accustomed to Jaed doing things she thought were unwise. But she let her breath out, words unspoken.

"Rose," she said, by way of both query and explanation.

yes, said Rose.

Jaed, lips pressed thin as a blade, only smiled.

The tesla above the door stopped flashing.

Then the cell dimmed, then brightened, then went black for two very long blinks.

"That was fast," Jaed said, admiring. "Even for nanomecha."

But then the deck jerked underfoot, and he skidded along the bulkhead until he fetched up hard against Thorsdottir.

"That wasn't Rose," Thorsdottir said. "That was an impact. I think this ship is under attack."

CHAPTER ELEVEN ≡≡≡

"There is nothing new in the multiverse" is an adage that, like most of its genre, is not especially illuminating, but which finds its way onto beverage containers and cheap garments and into the mindset of people under the mistaken impression that indifference indicates sophistication. Nonetheless, there is some truth to the maxim. The multiverse tends to repetition, at least in its physical construction. There are only so many ways physics and alchemy can conspire to create a planetary system, for instance.

And so Samtalet was, on one level, nothing new: a standard yellow star, a scattering of planetary bodies, including the gas giants Kaosol and Perkele, around the first of which orbited an extensive ring system with rocks large enough to mine. The SAM-1 mining installation made its home in the seventh of Kaosol's moons, also called (somewhat unimaginatively) SAM-1.

When *Favored Daughter* tore a dainty hole out of voidspace and slid into the Samtalet system, she did so conservatively: coming in at the system's edge, beyond the outermost orbit, clear of known debris.

Grytt knew this because she was listening to Rupert and Adept Uo-Zanys Kesk, mostly the latter, who was at least as delighted as the former to pontificate on the finer points of arithmancy. Grytt was glad that the eye on that side of her head was a tesla. It couldn't glaze, or glare, or otherwise betray her impatience. It could, however, show her Rupert, and *he* appeared to be raptly attentive. He wasn't faking, either. Grytt could tell.

She occupied herself instead with the main display, which *Favored Daughter's* turing had assembled as a holographic representation above the central console.

Grytt knew the general arrangements of planetary systems, and she had familiarized herself with Samtalet when Rory relocated there. The novelty in *Favored Daughter's* rendition was a combination of orientation—they had not, obviously, come through the system gate—and composition, because in addition to planetary bodies, there were smaller, non-orbiting bodies marked in flashing rings.

She leaned forward to her harness's limits. "Are those ships?"

Even as she inquired, another flashing icon appeared on the hologram, this one uncomfortably (to Grytt's perception) close to *Favored Daughter*, parallel to their plane and vector and, evidently, matching speed.

Hworgesh pressed into his harness, as if he could attain clearer vantage from the extra centimeters such a move afforded him.

He side-eyed Grytt and stabbed out a finger. "That one, just came in? That's *Bane*, my ship. *That*—" he indicated a purple-ringed blip, "is a Protectorate vessel. Can't read the name from here, but it's got a purple ring, so it's veek. The alwar always make their enemies purple."

Purple? Grytt squinted, which was unhelpful for her meat eye and a signal to her mecha one to telescope its focus. It was a bit like looking down a 'slinger's targeting scope. The rest of the bridge withdrew to the blurry edges of perception. Ah, yes, purple. She made a mental note: tenju vision was superior in distance color-perception, at least. And alwar had a prejudice against purple. That was something Rupert would find interesting.

Now that she could perceive color, she also noted two red-ringed blips. She jabbed her mecha hand at the hologram. "And those?"

Hworgesh's gaze snapped from the hologram to Grytt's finger, which had caught and reflected the ambient illumination in such a way that it appeared to possess a light of its own.

"Tadeshi." His gaze moved from her finger to her face, and he grimaced. "I can't read the markers from here. Can you?"

"I can't read alwar," she began to say, before realizing that the tiny column of characters beside the blips was not ship-names, but designators of speed, direction, mass, and energy emissions. She picked the one closest to their relative position and adjusted her fingertip accordingly.

"The smaller one looks dead," she said. "Minimal energy output. Looks like a little warship, maybe a corsair? *That* one"—and she pointed to the larger red-ringed dot, which was holding position on the far side of the Protectorate ship—"is alive and really big, whatever . . ." She trailed off. "I think that's a Tadeshi dreadnought."

Hworgesh spat something unintelligible.

At the word *dreadnought*, Rupert and the adept stopped talking. At the same instant, several bright yellow streaks appeared on the display, streaking from the dreadnought toward the Protectorate ship.

"That's bad," said Grytt.

"Yes," said Rupert, for once devoid of extraneous verbiage or even sufficient volume to reach Grytt's original, organic ear.

She shot him a sharp side-eye. His face had collapsed on itself, the skin sagging off the precipice of his nose and cheekbones.

She felt much the same way Rupert looked. A dreadnought was a serious commitment of personnel and resources for the Tadeshi royalists, and if Dame Maggie's intelligence was to be trusted, they were getting a little short of both. If that ship was *here*, there was something of great importance that the Tadeshi were prepared to fight to get.

Grytt squashed the sick certainty that the something was a some*one* named Rory. The Tadeshi would *love* to get their collective hands on her, but not so much that they would send one of their capital ships. This was something else: the weapon the fairy had told Rupert about. Bet on that.

The bridge held its collective breath, except for a single alwar crew-woman who, after a staccato exclamation (Grytt bet, correctly, that she had called out "they're firing"), murmured a monologue that sounded like countdown to impact. But before the yellow streaks could reach the vakari ship, they simply . . . vanished.

The captain barked a query. A different crewperson responded, light-voiced and mostly obscured by the central console.

"Veek battle-hexes," Hworgesh said. "Best in the multiverse. It'll take more than a mass-driven rock to punch through them."

"The Tadeshi have more than mass-driven rocks in their arsenal," said Grytt. "They've got missiles. Warheads."

"Might as well be rocks."

The vakari vessel released its own set of streaks in an unremarkable white, almost lost on the hologram. It seemed to Grytt's admittedly novice perception of such things to be moving a little bit *faster* than the Tadeshi's yellow missiles had been.

"You ever seen veek whitefire before?" Hworgesh sound both grim and satisfied. "You're in for a treat."

A liberal interpretation of *treat*, Grytt thought; the white streaks made contact with the dreadnought, and a few of the readouts changed rather abruptly. The dreadnought began, if not a retreat, then at least a reconsideration, maneuvering to put itself behind the dead ship. As it did so, it fired again, another barrage of yellow, accompanied by a few fast-moving green specks.

"Plasma weapons," Hworgesh said, and repeated his earlier observation: "They'd be better off just throwing rocks. Veek battle-hexes are *nasty*."

"Wait," said Grytt. Something was changing on the vakari ship's readouts, a general shuffling of digits that seemed unusually random. Before Hworgesh could make further comment, the crew-woman who'd first called out did so again, in tones of surprise. At then the yellow streaks struck their target.

The purple dot that was the Protectorate ship registered an immediate, violent change in position. No further white streaks were forthcoming. The vakari ship's readings abandoned their randomized dance and began a steady decline, which, Grytt noted, Adept Uo-Zanys Kesk was watching with a growing incredulity.

Another set of yellow streaks followed the first, and again, made impact. The vakari ship failed to respond, and though a few of the readings steadied, a few others continued their dive toward zero.

"Excuse me," said the adept. She unhooked her harness and was halfway across the bridge before Rupert could finish the reflexively polite "of course."

There was some sort of conversation ongoing across the bridge between the adept and the captain. Grytt watched the body language evolve from heads together to facing each other to squared off, with mouths moving rapidly and often simultaneously. The crew kept about its business, pretending oblivion.

Hworgesh grunted. "I'd trade a tusk to hear what they're saying."

"I can hear it," Grytt said. "I just can't understand it. The mecha ear," she added, when Hworgesh squinted at her, one-eyed and dubiously. "It's got quite a range."

"People know you can do that?"

"People don't ask."

"Huh. Well." Hworgesh sat back. "I'm *guessing* there's a policy dispute of some kind. Adepts aren't military, but they carry government weight. This have to do with your *diplomacy?*"

He pronounced the word sound like a bad smell.

"Probably." Rupert gave himself a visible mental shake and slipped his diplomatic mask back into place. "We are supposed to proceed to SAM-1 to establish an embassy there for the Confederation of Liberated Worlds. I imagine that the fact that the Tadeshi are currently at war with the Confederation, and now appear to be engaged in hostilities with the vakari in this very sector, is likely the source of the captain's concern."

"Huh." Hworgesh did not sound convinced. "Well. Maybe she'll tell you herself. Here she comes."

Here, indeed: the captain had disengaged from her conversation with the adept, involving a pointing finger and sharp words whose meaning seemed to be *stay right there, I'll be back to deal with you in a moment*. Then she crossed the bridge with the jabbing steps of profound irritation and stopped in front of Rupert. Then she pointed at him. She was unarmed, Grytt noted, though the way her un-pointing hand twitched toward her hip suggested that was not always the case.

Whatever Hworgesh said, this *was* a warship, and the captain, a soldier.

An angry soldier.

"You," the captain said, in more heavily accented GalSpek than Adept Uo-Zanys Kesk's, "Vizier. A word. With me, please—not *you.*" That was aimed at Grytt, who was already releasing her safety harness. "I require the vizier only."

She said *vizier* the same way Hworgesh had said *diplomacy.*

"Uh oh." Hworgesh looked brightly from Rupert to the captain and then to Grytt. His eyes glinted with ill-concealed curiosity.

Grytt, meanwhile, had already discarded several retorts as inappropriate to an ambassador's head of security, or attaché, or whatever Rupert was calling her on his forged credentials. She contented herself with standing up and, since that motion brought her uncomfortably close to the captain, staring down at her.

"It's all right," Rupert said smoothly, entirely unruffled, his tone at odds with the round-eyed glare he jabbed at Grytt over the captain's head. "I am happy to come with you, Captain."

And so Grytt sat down again, while Rupert unclipped his harness and rose and followed the captain and the adept—who threw Grytt a furious, sympathetic scowl before she stalked away.

Hworgesh looked vaguely disappointed. "He'll be fine. Captain might yell a little, that's all. She won't lay hands on a *diplomat.*"

"What about the tenju? What if we were on *Bane*?"

"I'd say you should get up and follow him."

Rupert felt better now that he was in trouble. He knew what to do with angry people who *weren't* trying to shoot him, and, like Hworgesh, he was certain the captain meant him no actual harm. Unlike Grytt, he had not noticed the wistful drift of her hand toward an absent sidearm; if he had, he might have been less sanguine as he followed the captain back across the bridge, where he and Adept Uo-Zanys Kesk fell into her wake like the recalcitrant offspring of a furious mother duck. The captain led them to a room just a door down the corridor from the bridge, which was probably spacious by alwar standards, and seemed extravagant even to Rupert, who had to duck slightly to come through the door. It was an ovoid space, which was unusual enough on a ship, but it was also *big*. The overhead in here was easily a half-meter over *his* head, which seemed excessive. Elaborate, intricate murals covered most of the bulkheads, depicting (mostly) female figures in varying costume engaged in pursuits that likely held significance to the alwar, more than a few of whom wore robes like the adept's, with their hair in that same distinctive topknot. A holographic projector dominated the center of the room, rising from the center of a table like some kind of primitive effigy. Around the table, a ring of chairs was bolted to the deck, the surface of which had an actual *carpet* on it worked with geometric designs of unusual, uncomfortable dimensions in varying shades of red, black, and a vivid mid-range blue.

The captain did not suggest anyone sit down, and so Rupert did not. He stopped when the adept stopped—just inside the door—while the captain stalked to the projector and with angry jabs summoned a three-dimensional, slightly translucent detail of the bridge display, with the battling ships enlarged so that Rupert could make out the surface architecture. The silhouettes were familiar from the years of the war he had overseen when he had served Samur and the Consortium. The Protectorate, outlined in violent purple, was faintly avian in design, with angles that, if they translated to the ship's interior, would make it a rather jagged place.

"That is *Sissten*," said the captain with no preamble whatsoever. "It is a vakari ship, a—how do you say—" she glared at Adept Uo-Zanys Kesk and spat out a stream of syllables.

There were hexes that helped with translation (or hindered it).

Rupert had used them from time to time in his duties for Rory's father, when negotiating with other humans who maintained private languages other than GalSpek. He had never used one for a first contact situation, for obvious reasons, but the *theory* should work. He diverted his attention to the appropriate layer of aether and assembled and deployed a hex, hoping that the relative time-lags between layers and the captain's demands on the adept would conceal his activities.

He surfaced to find both alwar staring at him. The captain looked less than amused. Adept Uo-Zanys Kesk wore a small, unsurprised smile.

"Did it work?" she asked. "Your hex?"

"It did." Though Rupert perceived GalSpek, the liquid alwar syllables lingered like an echo.

"An arithmancer." The captain said the word like Hworgesh had said *diplomacy*.

"As I suspected," said Adept Uo-Zanys Kesk. "The discourtesy is ours, Captain. We should speak the language our guest understands. And we should make introductions. Vizier, this is Captain Kahess Trylor."

"Captain Kahess is fine, or just Captain," snapped Captain Kahess, in her accented GalSpek. "Vizier Rupert, I have questions."

It was at this point that Rupert decided two things: that an alw's first name was sufficient for formal address, and consequently that he would shorten Adept Uo-Zanys Kesk to *Kesk* in his head, if not aloud without invitation (and so too shall this account, reader), because after their arithmantic conversation, he felt a familiarity to and with her that bypassed the formality of family names and title.

He bowed instead, in the Thorne Consortium manner, slightly and from the waist. "How may I assist, Captain?"

"You may tell me the truth. Make sure he's telling the truth," she said to Kesk, who pursed her lips and said nothing. Her gaze slid sidelong at Rupert, thoughtful. The rings in her ear glinted in the light.

It was the look one arithmancer gave another, a measuring of potential. Rupert kept his own expression bland, and quietly shored up his own defenses. He did not *intend* to lie, but he was also not going to take the option off the table when he had no idea what the captain intended to ask, or why she was so upset.

"The captain was saying," said Kesk, "that *Sissten* is a Protectorate interceptor. They are designed for surgical strikes rather than line warfare. Its presence here suggests the Protectorate was intending to, well, intercept something, not to engage in battle."

"They destroyed the Tadeshi corsair." Kahess did not bother with GalSpek. "You can't see that *here*"—she jabbed at the hologram—"but our scans show damage on the hull consistent with a Protectorate attack."

Rupert elected to hoist one eyebrow, which might be surprise or acknowledgement, and then wondered if the alwar—who also possessed eyebrows—would understand the expression.

Adept Kesk's mouth lifted slightly in one corner. "That the Protectorate and the Tadeshi are at odds is well known; the Free Worlds borders on the Protectorate Expansion, and there have been skirmishes. But Samtalet is out of *both* of their territories by a significant margin. So—"

Captain Kahess interjected. "So why are they here, Vizier?"

"I don't know. I assure you, Captain, that their presence here is an unpleasant surprise to us both."

"And yet, they're at war with your Confederation."

Yes, thought Rupert. *It is my Confederation. Only mine, and for which I bear sole responsibility. Is there a question?* He noted simultaneously that his irritation was unusual—he really *was* out of practice with diplomacy—and that he retained enough facial and vocal discipline to conceal it. All that emerged from his lips was, "They are, Captain. Though as you have noted, Samtalet is very far from the front. Nor is Samtalet *part* of the Confederation."

"So there must be a reason they're out here."

"One assumes so."

"Then what is it? Because I am finding it hard to believe the Confederation *doesn't* keep close intelligence on its adversary."

Rupert wondered what sort of systemic competence the Harek Empire maintained, if the assumption that what one *should* do, diplomatically and politically, was in fact what one *was* doing. The alwar must be very organized people, or very good at bureaucracy, or at *least* maintain an effective network of spies. "If such information exists, I assure you, Captain, I am not privy to it."

"You were the Thorne Consortium's vizier during *their* war with the Free Worlds of Tadesh."

"I . . . was." Apparently the Imperial intelligence machine was *very* well-informed. How uncomfortable.

"So why would they send you, an *expert* in Tadeshi warfare, out to Samtalet unless they expected something like this?" Captain Kahess waved her hand at the holographic display.

"Honestly, Captain," Kesk interjected, her voice pitched between conciliatory and exasperated. "The battle out there is between Protectorate and Tadeshi. It's got nothing to do with the Vizier, or the Confederation. You may have answered your own question: the Vizier is here in Samtalet, with his expertise, to ascertain the reason for the Tadeshi interest in the region."

The adept, at least, used his title correctly, pronouncing its capital letter. She also earned a scowl from Captain Kahess for the interjection. And, to Rupert's considerable discomfiture, she still wore that tiny, secretive smile, as if she and he were sharing a great secret at the captain's expense.

Kesk had not yet attempted to breach his aural camouflage. Either she believed him, or she was allowing him the opportunity to lie for her own benefit, which suggested she knew the truth. Or suspected it.

Rupert found a small smile setting up residence on his own lips: he had *missed* this, living among sheep, Grytt, and Ivar.

Fortunately for the fledgling diplomatic relations between Harek and Confederation, Captain Kahess did not notice Rupert's smile. She had, however, noticed Kesk's, and took immediate offense.

"You're going to tell me it's *coincidence*? You saw what just happened. The Tadeshi missiles got through *Sissten's* shields."

"That happens. The vakari are not invincible."

"Did you not *see* the readings?" Kahess flailed in the general direction of the vakari ship on the hologram. "The shields just went down. Nothing even *hit* them. That's a battle-hex. The Tadeshi do not have anything that sophisticated."

"I did see." The balance of Kesk's voice tipped toward exasperation. "This is *precisely* the conversation we were having on the bridge. I also told you *then* that I thought the hex was a single deployment, rather than sustained and built into the dreadnought's defenses, for the very reason that its configuration does not match anything we've seen the Tadeshi produce."

"And you couldn't hazard a guess how many of those they might have, either, and I *still* want to know where the Tadeshi *got* that hex."

"You *can't* think that *he* had anything to do with that."

Rupert elected to overlook both Kesk's tone and her expression of amused incredulity. "I assure you, Captain, I am not a battle-arithmancer."

"Of course you aren't. But you *are* at war with the Tadeshi, and you're an expert, and you're a diplomat. So where, from whom, are they getting that kind of hexwork?"

"I don't know."

A prickling sensation crawled over Rupert's scalp. It had been many years since his examinations, but he recalled the circumstances of his last experience of it. Kesk had just pierced his hex.

"He is telling the truth, Captain."

Rupert had learned that, although prevarication and evasion could guide a conversation in the desired direction, if those options were not available, aggressively unvarnished truth could accomplish the same goal. It was the difference between a scalpel and a battering ram, but one used what one had available.

"I've never seen a battle-hex like that before, Captain. Nor have I seen reports of such being used on Confederation ships. Or, for that matter, League ships or Thorne Consortium ships or *any* human vessel. It may be a hex designed particularly for the Protectorate, by parties unknown to us."

"I did suggest as much, Kahess," Adept Kesk murmured.

Ordinarily Rupert would have offered a sympathetic glance (for who among us has not experienced the frustration entailed when our expertise is ignored?), but his scalp, and pride, still prickled. Instead he gazed at the captain with composed candor as she in turn transferred her scowl to Kesk, even as she aimed another question at Rupert.

"Why are the Tadeshi attacking the Protectorate out here, right now, *with a dreadnought*?"

"Again, Captain, I don't know." And then he added, somewhat

reluctantly, because playing dumb can occasionally have the un-fortunate side-effect of convincing people of one's incompetence, which can be detrimental in long-term negotiations: "Perhaps the Tadeshi were transporting someone, or something, of interest, that the Protectorate tried to intercept. Or perhaps did intercept, given the damage to the corsair. Perhaps the Tadeshi want that something back."

"But you don't know what." Kahess thrust her face up at him. If the disparities between their heights disturbed her, she gave no sign of it. "Because listen to me, Vizier, the Tadeshi are pirates on a good day, and if they have a weapon like *that*, then they're a threat to everyone, no matter the size of the vessel."

"I—have no idea what that ship was carrying."

"He is telling the truth," said Kesk, "which I have *also* sug-gested, before this embarrassing confrontation."

This time Rupert glanced at the adept; although *I told you so* often crosses the minds of political advisors, it rarely crosses their lips. Clearly, Rupert needed to recalculate the nature of the rela-tionship between a ship captain and an adept.

"The Vizier is not here to intercept some shipment of arms for the Confederation," the adept continued, in the tones of someone who is repeating herself. "We are not at cross-purposes. The Con-federation is not our enemy. *That*"—and she pointed, not at the wounded *Sissten*, which had been Rupert's expectation, but instead at the drifting, crippled Tadeshi vessel—"should be what concerns us. The Tadeshi and vakari are clearly fighting over something. We should know what."

"And as *I* have said," snapped Kahess, "I'm not taking this ship into a firefight to satisfy your curiosity."

"I assure you, it is not *my* curiosity—"

"It is until it's got an official Senate seal on a set of written orders."

At this point Rupert realized several things: that Kesk had reverted to her own language, and that although she might be reading his aura, she had either neglected to, or declined to, destroy his translation hex. He suspected the latter; Kesk did not seem the sort of woman to *neglect* things. She wanted him privy to the conversation, and she was trusting him to be clever enough to maintain the illusion of ignorance. Because it was clear that the captain thought herself safely unintelligible. He was not sure Kahess even recalled his presence in the room.

"You said he had ulterior motives for being here. You said—"

"He does. But it's got nothing to do with the Tadeshi and whoever their new allies are, and *that* is why *we*—you and me and this ship, this Empire ship—are out here. Not this alleged *favor* we're doing for the Merchants League."

Interesting. *Usefully* interesting.

Kahess snorted with a well-worn disgust. This argument had happened before, clearly, and several times. "This supposed secret weapon of yours again."

"Not *of mine,* and not *supposed.* We have intelligence indicating something was smuggled out of Protectorate space, by the Tadeshi, headed for Samtalet. What we did not know was for whom it was intended. I think that dead ship out there was carrying it. I think the vakari have it now. I think the Tadeshi have sent that dreadnought to recover it. And thus this interests the Confederation at least as much as it interests the Empire."

"How do you know that? Bah, don't." Kahess made a pushing away gesture. "Do *not* say it's classified."

Kesk raised both eyebrows and, deliberately, stayed silent.

"Well, fine, what do you expect us to do about it? *Favored Daughter* and *Bane* together can't defeat a dreadnought."

"I *suggest* hailing the vakari and offering our help."

"To the *vakari*. Help. You're *out* of your mind."

Rupert felt a bit like the murals on the bulkhead. Meanwhile, on the hologram, the Tadeshi ship continued its attack on the vakari vessel, which had coughed up another whitefire attack despite its fluctuating readouts. Rupert wished he knew more about ship engineering and what those numbers meant. He suspected the captain would know, but he could hardly come out and ask—

". . . and why he *is* out here." Kesk switched back to GalSpek. "Why are you, Vizier? Out here in Samtalet, I mean. It's not to establish an embassy."

Rupert's face flushed. He really *was* out of practice, if he had lost the thread of their conversation. He fell back again on truth for his strategy, albeit this time a bit less unvarnished. Quite varnished, in fact. Shiny with it.

"Retrieval of important Confederation personnel," he said, and added, with the half-beat pause intended to convey the word *intelligence* could take the place of the entire prepositional object, "I cannot give you more detail than that, Adept. Captain."

"I'm afraid you may have to," said Kesk. "Because retrieving your *personnel* now aligns with Harek Imperial goals. We became aware of a Tadeshi plan—"

"*Alleged* plan," Kahess muttered.

"—to acquire something from Protectorate space, the route for which would pass through Samtalet. We assumed a weapon. It was convenient to honor a request from our Merchants League allies to ferry you out here, and to play along with their clearly fictive embassy excuse, because it put us in the area. But now here *you* are, Vizier, telling me you intend to acquire Confederation personnel, who I infer may possess information useful to both our governments, or perhaps even *be* the thing the Tadeshi meant to acquire. I believe you understand that the more details we possess, the better our chances of success."

It was unfortunate, Rupert thought, that he was woefully short on detail. "I am seeking the Princess Rory Thorne," he said, because it was true. "She has been operating in this system as a, ah. Salvager. We received word that she was in danger, though the specifics of her situation were not relayed to us."

Adept Kesk raised an eyebrow, but did not challenge his choice of descriptors for Rory, nor remark that his prose was unusually objective. Perhaps that was expected of spies and intelligence operatives.

Grytt was going to—laugh, perhaps, that he had come to this. Or say, *better you than me*. Or, most likely, swear herself blue that she had let him leave her sight in the first place.

"And this princess." Captain Kahess tried out the title, working her mouth around the unfamiliar syllables. "They know about this weapon?"

"That would be something to ask her," said Rupert. "If we succeed in the extraction, I am certain the Confederation will agree to an information exchange."

Kahess's eyebrows shot up. "*Extraction*? Are you telling me she is on one of those ships?"

"She may be," Rupert said, with a serenity he did not feel, and which he was certain his aura did not reflect. "Though the hostilities of the Tadeshi suggest they do not yet have possession of her. And it is of paramount importance that the Tadeshi do not acquire her."

We should note that the Vizier was in no way *certain* of Rory's whereabouts, and that he still maintained some hope that Rory was on SAM-1 and nowhere near the murdered ship or the battle. But the fairy's pair of portentous warnings, coupled with Rory's predilection for finding the center of politically fraught situations, made him fear that she was somewhere on one of those ships. Rupert had also judged that the alwar concerns about sophisticated battle-hexes, potential super-weapons, and Tadeshi aggression concerned the Confederation, and saw an opportunity to acquire intelligence that might ameliorate any penalties Dame Maggie might otherwise bring down on his head when she caught up with him.

In other words, Rupert was operating on a hunch, or as Grytt would say, *from the gut.*

We leave the reader to consider what it is that guts typically process.

Before Kesk could reply, an interruption by the holographic display showed the dreadnought disgorging another barrage. These streaks, however, were marked orange, and flashing, and appeared to be very small ships.

"Breaching pods," Kahess said flatly. "The Tadeshi are going to board that Protectorate ship. If your princess is on it, Vizier, she's in trouble."

CHAPTER TWELVE

T he ship bucked a second time. Thorsdottir threw an arm out, planting a palm on the bulkhead, and grabbed for Jaed with the other hand. She had intended to brace him but instead, he caught her. His knees were flexed, his hips centered neatly under his shoulders.

Thorsdottir felt a gawping stare break over her face.

Jaed twisted up the corner of his mouth like a wet rag. "Drills." His voice tilted into a singsong recitation of someone official-sounding: "What to do in case of grav-hex failure and/or hostile action against Urse." He dropped back into his normal tone. "Did a lot of these when Thorne was trying to kill us. Not that your warships ever *got* to Urse."

"We did drills, too. Only it was *you* who were trying to kill *us*. And we were mostly drilling *on* Thorne against bombardment from space or a palace invasion, so gravity was not an issue—ah!" This time the deckplate rattled, as if it were contemplating unbolting itself from itself. If there were arithmancers involved, that might be a possibility.

Jaed rode out the upheaval with an unblinking grace, all his attention fixed on her face. "Bombardment from space is barbaric. That would destroy a biosphere. We would never—" Jaed's gaze dropped to her hardsuit pouch, in which Rose's clipping resided, and his face flamed and blanched. "Never mind. We would destroy a biosphere."

"Stop saying we. You're not Tadeshi anymore." Thorsdottir bent her own knees, sank her weight as if she were preparing for an opponent's rush and attack. That helped. She took her hand off the bulkhead and tested her balance. Definitely better.

Until, at least, she looked up and Jaed's scowl threatened to knock her over again. "Of course I am. What else would I be?"

"Whatever you like." Thorsdottir took a tentative step toward the cell door. "This ship's taking fire."

"Yes. And we're locked in a cell. There's not much we can do about it."

That annoyed Thorsdottir precisely because it was true. She had been confined before with Rory on Urse, and she had not much enjoyed the experience. "Be ready anyway. Someone's going to come through that door eventu—"

The teslas went out completely. The dark was absolute, solid, like a hard-edged blanket, slapping the breath from her lungs.

The hardsuit's headlamps activated at once, punching into the black. Something about the vakari bulkheads absorbed the glare, gave it back satiny and unblinding.

Jaed was already at the door. He had his hand (back in its glove) pressed where the access panel should have been, had there been one on the inside of the cell, and his head tilted inside his helmet in a listening attitude. His eyes were closed, his brows knotted in concentration.

Thorsdottir stayed quiet. Rory *looked* where she hexed, and was impervious to noise and other distractions. Jaed seemed to need to listen. Could one *hear* the equations—? Thorsdottir shook her head. *She* couldn't. What she could hear was alarms, which seemed to pick an intolerable pitch no matter what species they served, howling somewhere on the deck. Perhaps the power loss had not been ship-wide. Clearly it had not affected the alarms, only the teslas. Perhaps—

The door exhaled sharply and sagged in its track. It was not entirely open, but it was wide enough that Jaed—whose eyes opened with considerably more speed and snap than the door—could jam his fingers into the crack. "Hurry, help me."

Thorsdottir pushed Jaed aside and wedged her very much human limb, in its hardsuit case, through the gap. Then her shoulder, and her hip. Grytt, Thorsdottir thought, would've ripped the door open like paper. It was almost enough to make her wish for her own mecha enhancements, if not the manner of the acquisition.

She remembered the vakari guard armed with that cylindrical weapon. With luck, that guard was distracted. Without luck, well. Better the guard hit *her* than Jaed, though why Thorsdottir was so certain of that, she could not have articulated.

That certainty was soon tested. Thorsdottir's hardsuit flashed a warning—*motion detected*—and then something cylindrical cracked down against the arm and shoulder that she'd pushed through the gap in the door. For a moment she thought an incredulous *that's it?* as the cylinder skidded down her hardsuit. The vakari were idiots, arming a guard with only a truncheon.

But then two things happened to readjust Thorsdottir's perception. The first was her HUD's sudden panic, *BREACH* flashing in all squared-off capital letters. The second was the eruption of blue lightning where the vakar's weapon touched her, clearly something like electricity but also hotter, more *liquid*, that flowed up to her elbow and down to her glove. Then the lightning found the breach-site, which Thorsdottir herself could not quite *see* (the lightning was too bright, and the HUD was flashing, and the crack in her suit was very small), except by the flash where the weapon's discharge bled into it.

Then the pain hit, a phrase which was as inadequate to the experience as saying, "it's difficult to breathe underwater."

Thorsdottir's vision tunneled. Her breath puffed against the visor's interior, bringing fog with it. She found herself on her knees on the deck, outside of the cell. Her throat hurt. Her vision was wet on the edges, sweat or tears that cleared when she blinked. Sound came from a very great distance. Her arm—she could not feel her arm. That might be worse, although given her last memory of it, she would not complain.

Something (someone, that was a hardsuit) slammed into her shoulder and then toppled over her. She tried to get out of the way and, at the same time, *see* what was happening. The main teslas in the room were still out, which left little islands of headlamps and a roiling sea of dark. Blue lightning arced from some short distance away (the HUD could've told her, but her vision was in rebellion, and refused to focus), and Thorsdottir flinched. The guard was still out there with that weapon.

That begged asking why it was over *there*, and not zapping her *here*—

Jaed materialized in front of her, face bleached by his headlamp and still looking whiter than normal. His visor was up, she saw, which was *stupid*, there was a vakar with a lightning-stick out there. His lips flapped and writhed, but she heard nothing coming through them. She stared at him, uncomprehending.

His face creased with exasperation. Then he struck the side of her helmet, hard enough that her head bounced off the interior. She should have felt irritation, certainly, but also some discomfort.

She felt neither, and harbored a dim certainty that that, too, was a bad sign.

Jaed pushed his face up against her visor. His mouth moved.

OPEN THE VISOR

She did, when she remembered how. It labored open, taking the HUD and its warnings with it. Cool air rushed in and brought the sounds of the room with it. Scuffling, the ragged snarls of breath dragged hard and fast through teeth, the meaty thumps of bodies bouncing into each other and into harder surfaces. Thorsdottir smelled ozone and burning meat—oh. *Oh.* That smell was her, wasn't it? Her stomach clenched as someone, not a human voice, screamed.

Jaed's gaze flicked that way. He had both hands on the side of her helmet. "The other prisoner's fighting the guard. They got out of their cell on their own. Come on. Let's go. Get up."

Jaed had not asked if she was all right. That must mean either he knew the answer already, or the answer did not matter.

Rose, she thought. What had that arcing-sparking weapon done to them?

"Come *on.*" Jaed was pulling at her; she could see his gloved hands gripping her upper arms. She glanced down at the breach-site in her suit, just a flicker, and then looked away. Her hardsuit was blackened, smoking a little from the crack on her forearm.

Just as well she could not feel her hand right now, she decided firmly, and rocked off her knees, onto her heels, and lurched to her feet. Jaed participated far more in that process than pleased her; her balance was suspect, her hardsuit sluggish, and the sudden change in altitude resurrected the roaring in her ears and reduced her vision to Jaed's twin blue moon eyes and the flat, grimly scared line of his lips. Her stomach clenched again, this time around empty acid. Bile burned the back of her throat.

"Come on, come on," he said in jagged, airless bursts, as he propelled her across the deck. The battling xenos had fetched up near the central console. The vakar appeared to be losing. Their weapon trailed sparks and lightning and Thorsdottir found herself staring at it, waiting for it to strike the other prisoner, waiting for that flash of contact. But then from the dark came a *crack*, of the sort that sounded both organic and final.

The shuffling, snarling, heaving sounds of conflict stopped. The weapon-stick fell, end over end, and clanged against the deck, and then rolled a short way.

Heavy, ragged breath came from a stationary location in the dark.

The ship heaved suddenly and the emergency teslas came on. The vakari, too, must consider red to be the color of alarm; the room turned bloody, dim, adding to Thorsdottir's blurry-eyed nausea.

"Come *on*." Jaed tugged at her. He was not looking at the center console with the resolve of someone who has decided that not looking at a thing is the same as that thing not being there. Thorsdottir had found that to be universally untrue, and so she *did* look.

The vakari guard was definitely dead, crumpled against the main console, head bent and neck twisted. Now Thorsdottir knew what was under those triangular panels on its uniform. Spikes studded the backs of their arms, wrist to elbow, and presumably also between the double knee joints, and the hard convexities of their hips (though the latter two fin-like portions of their uniform remained intact). The jaw-plate was evidently detachable. Probably a natural vulnerability. The color of vakari blood was impossible to guess under the influence of throbbing red teslas, but there was a great deal of it in a spreading pool, and an accompanying metallic odor.

The door was in front of them. Whether it would open automatically, or at all, was another matter. Thorsdottir was not at all sure she could help, if it came to another attempt to force it.

But that might not matter.

The other xeno had gotten up and come around the far side of the central console, and now stood between them and the door. He (assuming humanoid secondary sexual physiology, which Thorsdottir did, unconsciously and in this case correctly) stood a little shorter than Jaed, and broader. His hardsuit, helmetless, was of an unfamiliar design that seemed more concerned with visible armored plating and with intricate painted designs, some of which had been damaged. There were scorch-marks on the torso and upper chest.

Someone's suit was proof against vakari lightning-sticks.

That xeno had taken possession of said lightning-stick, and now held it loosely in his right hand. Five digits, Thorsdottir noted, four fingers and a thumb, in the usual disposition and numeration of joints. She was not a biologist, conventional or xeno, but that similarity seemed significant. Illogically, it disposed her *better* toward their fellow captive, as did the fact that there were no spiky growths or extra joints, and—

Well. She had been right, thinking there were tusks. They were shortish, perhaps a fingertip upthrust from his lower lip, and predictably sharp. The rest of his features were human-ish, emphasis on the *ish*. A single protruding nose with two nostrils, a pair of eyes (narrowed, in what Thorsdottir assumed was hostility, suspicion, or pain), a single horizontal mouth with that formidable dental display. The jaw was heavier, slightly undershot, the ears short and located in the normal place, if a bit more pointed at the tip. Skin of a shade between Zhang's medium-gold and Rory's warmer brown. The xeno had no facial hair, but he *did* have hair on his head, roped into thick braids in which bits of metal gleamed.

Hooks, Thorsdottir thought. Those were *hooks*. Some of the braids had come loose—secured, presumably, to fit under a helmet—and hung down, loose and straight like the tail of an unconcerned cat. If cats kept hooks in their tails. Which they did not. All right, focus. This person had just gotten past a cell door that had taken two strong humans to manage and, unarmed, dispatched an armed vakar.

And now he stood between them and the door, holding the guard's weapon.

Thorsdottir tried to shove Jaed behind her, clearly a reflex and not a considered action, since in so doing she would be presenting her wounded (perhaps ruined) arm first. The effort failed, mostly because Jaed was attempting to do the same thing, and with greater success. And so they ended up making an absurdly defiant wedge of shoulders and hips. What they would do if it attacked, Thorsdottir didn't know. Well, that was not true. They would lose, and then very possibly die, if the tusk-bearing xeno decided to disassemble them as he had done to the vakar.

"Shit," Jaed said, very softly and distinctly.

At the sound of his voice, the xeno's attention sharpened and shifted.

"Grensk atalat mok." His voice was surprisingly melodic. Thorsdottir had been expecting something more gravelly.

"Yeah. Don't understand you. How about you just let us past?" Jaed sounded much more calm than Thorsdottir thought was likely, in this situation.

The xeno snorted. Definitely a snort. His lips spread, baring more of his teeth. That was a grin, Thorsdottir was certain, and not a kind one.

"You need help," he said, in clear, though accented (and possibly impeded by tusks), GalSpek. "Please tell me you understood *that*."

Thorsdottir wished she could close her eyes and perhaps settle the spin in her head. She settled for taking a gulp of blood-flavored air and stating the obvious. "You killed the guard."

The xeno's gaze snapped to her. "What, the veek? So? She was your enemy and mine."

"Doesn't mean *we're* friends, though, does it?" Jaed sounded as if he was speaking through gritted teeth. "I don't even know what species you are."

"What I—void and dust, where *are* you from?" The xeno shook his head. The braids rattled as the hooks bounced across his hard-suit. "Tenju, from the—oh, never mind what clan. Won't matter to you. Our species are friends, all right? Which tribe are you? Larish? Johnson-Thrymbe? Qing-Kovacs? Nahbib?"

Those names, Thorsdottir recognized. Merchants League corporate families, mostly concerned with making money and moving it around, all spacers, though Qing-Kovacs originated from the same homeworld as the Thornes. Rory had nearly married a Larish boy. If she had, Thorsdottir might've known what a tenju was before meeting one in a Protectorate brig. Then again, she wouldn't *be* in a Protectorate brig.

"No," Thorsdottir wanted to sound decisive. She was afraid she sounded one breath from collapse, if Jaed's alarmed glance was any indicator.

"We're Confederation of Liberated Worlds." He had inserted himself fully between Thorsdottir and the tenju now. She recalled long hours spent with him and Zhang in the SAM-1's recreational facilities, honing his skills from *determined but as dangerous as a puppy* to *might survive in a bar fight* (hypothesis untested). He might think that was enough. Or, more likely, he knew that it wasn't, but he'd make the gesture anyway.

The tenju had eyebrows. They shot up. "Where *are* we?"

"This is Samtalet. Edge of the Verge."

"The Verge, I recognize." The tenju's mouth contracted into a grimace. "Never heard of Samtalet, though."

"That's fine," said Jaed. "Don't think it's heard of you, either. Are those your friends attacking the ship?"

The tenju's features flattened, hardened, chilled. "Not mine." His tone indicated a certain finality, and a certainty, and a sort of bleak fury. "Veeks got my ship."

"Sorry to hear that. Will you please move aside?"

"Why? You got somewhere to go?"

"Not your business."

"Veek ship under attack," said the tenju, "means we wait, and hope whoever's killing them wins. That door'll hold."

"Unless whoever's attacking is worse."

The tenju gave Jaed a strange look. "No such thing as worse than the veeks."

Thorsdottir cleared her throat. "Listen."

Jaed ignored her, as did the tenju, occupied as they were with staring at each other, measuring, assessing relative strength.

"Move," said Jaed.

"No," said the tenju.

Oh, honestly. "Listen! We have a ship. Help us get there, we'll give you a ride." *Now* she had everyone's attention. "I'm Thorsdottir. This is Jaed. You are?"

The tenju regarded them through narrowed eyes. "Call me Crow," he said, after a moment. "Where's this ship of yours?"

"Docked to this one. Help us get back to it, we'll take you with us."

"Can't be a big ship, then."

"Bigger than yours."

"Ha. You're not wrong." Crow side-eyed Jaed, then thrust the vakari weapon at him. "Take this, in case we run into anyone in the corridors. What? You don't know how to use one?"

Jaed was so startled that he let the implied insult to his competence pass right by. "You're just giving me a weapon?"

"Why? You going to hit me with it?"

"I—No."

"Good. Listen, since you're Confederation and you don't know better: your people and mine don't fight. We trade. So let me trade you *this* whitefire wand for *that* damaged person." Crow jabbed his chin at Thorsdottir. "She needs help."

"She can hear you," said Thorsdottir. "She's fine. Jaed, you need to get Rory."

"Rory?" Crow snatched the wand back. "What's Rory?"

Jaed shot Thorsdottir a grim, guilty glance. "Who, not what. Our friend. The vakari took her."

Crow grunted. "Then she's dead. Or she'll be somewhere we *can't* get to. I'll help you get to your ship, but I'm not running around looking for a dead person."

"Our ship won't leave without Rory," said Thorsdottir. "You two find her. Just get me into the corridor, and I'll make it back to *Vagabond* on my own."

If she had a nice bulkhead to lean against, the journey would not be too difficult, or at least, not impossible. The medical facilities on *Vagabond* were rudimentary, no med-mecha, but Zhang would be able to patch her up. Somehow. With something. Medicine, like arithmancy, tended toward the magical in Thorsdottir's mind.

"No, you won't. Crow, all right, let's trade." Jaed took the weapon as if it might whip round to bite him. "I really don't have any idea how to use this."

"Triggered by impact. Jab someone, it'll fire." Crow shoved a brusque, ungentle, practical shoulder into Thorsdottir's ribs with a force she felt through the hardsuit. Then he heaved, and shifted her weight mostly off her own feet, and onto himself.

"I got you. You won't fall," he said, with what she supposed was an attempt at reassurance. It sounded more like a dare.

Jaed, meanwhile, tested the weapon by smacking it against the central console. A whitish-blue ball of current formed on the end, sending out curious fingers that licked over the console. Thorsdottir smelled burning polysteel.

Jaed stared with something like awe at the wand. "That's not electricity."

"No, it's whitefire. Already said that." Crow began hauling Thorsdottir toward the door. "Burns just about anything."

"You're still alive. Tenju immune to it?"

"I've got a battle-rig with good hexes. It'll turn a couple hits."

Battle-rig was a good name. Better than armor. And appropriate. Thorsdottir had a good vantage to examine the smears of soot and scorch marks, hanging as she was off Crow's shoulder. The tenju had definitely seen some battle, and more than what had happened here.

"It's like plasma, but not," Jaed was saying, with that distracted fascination he and Rory could get sometimes, when they encountered something new. It was an endearing, maddening trait, fine for meeting a new species of butterfly on a walk through the fields; it was less appropriate when escaping a hostile ship under attack from unknown persons.

But then Jaed said, "How's whitefire react with phlogiston?" and Thorsdottir forgave him.

"Explosive, if there's enough of it," said Crow. "Why? You an alchemist?"

Jaed hesitated half a beat. "Arithmancer."

Messer Rupert had said many times in Thorsdottir's hearing that mathematics underlay all the scientific arts, including alchemy. The difference between *this* material and *that* was a chemical formula, which could be rendered into an equation. In *theory*, therefore, an arithmancer could practice transmutation, if they had the correct equations and a sufficient grasp of the underlying chemistry. There would be no phlogiston particles in a ship's aether if the scrubber-hexes were working to transmute the flammable phlogiston to unburning, breathable air. Thorsdottir knew from experience what an arithmancer could do against a fixed hex, given sufficient time and skill. If Jaed tried transmuting on the fly, air to phlogiston—breaking a hex *and* performing alchemy—he probably wouldn't succeed. Math that complex did not happen in moments, particularly with the sorts of distractions that tended to come with battles. Or rather—math did not happen that fast without errors, which could be fatal if there was phlogiston involved.

Thorsdottir could not see Crow's face from this vantage. His voice, however, came out taut, gathered, coiled. "All right, arithmancer. You take point."

Jaed set himself in front of the door. He dropped the wand down, so that it hung beside his thigh. "Ready. On three. Two."

They opened the door.

CHAPTER THIRTEEN

Humanity had, in the years before first contact, spent a great deal of time imagining what other life forms might exist in the multiverse, and whether or not they would be friendly. Much fiction and art and scholarship had been devoted to speculation. As is often the case, anticipation is more dramatic than reality. Despite its apparent size and fecundity, there appeared to be a lack of sentient species in the multiverse. Prior to these accounts, humanity knew of only three: itself, the mirri, and the k'bal, and for most people (of all species), that knowledge was confined to the most cursory facts about the others. Everyone knew what their fellow xenos looked like (more or less, since no one had actually *seen* a mirri unsuited), and more importantly, that they posed no threat.

Rory's personal contact with xenos had been limited to her Naming Day, to which k'bal and mirri ambassadors had been invited, and her father's state funeral. In neither case had she personally interacted with them. Messer Rupert *had*, being the Vizier, as had her mother, but their interactions had been limited to pleasantries mediated by a translation hex. Rory knew that the Merchants League had both a more frequent and more knowledgeable contact than the Consortium, conducting commerce with the k'bal and mirri. The mirri maintained a single political entity to which all mirri belonged. The k'bal maintained several factions, loosely associated and occasionally in conflict, but the k'bal were also pacifists, and so their settling of conflicts involved the relative volume of cranial venting and elaborate dance competitions to which non-k'bal were rarely invited. No one *shot* at anyone.

Which is to say: the humanity Rory knew did not have much experience with violence other than their own, which had, until this point in their history, been more than sufficient. To discover a xeno species that was at least as violent, and more efficient and effective, was unsettling.

As Rory Thorne followed Sub-Commander Koto-rek ia'vakat'ia Tarsik, conscious that each step increased her separation and isolation in a strange vessel, among a strange people who showed great skill with violence and arithmancy, she was, indeed, unsettled. But she was also exhilarated, and because of that, unable to keep from staring around like a small child.

She had not been sure what to expect from the *Sissten's* architecture. Mirri and k'bal were not bipeds, so, predictably, their ships were not designed for two arms, two legs, and a relatively vertical posture. Vakari physiology, at least on the surface, seemed human enough, and the ship's interior dimensions did not seen unusual.

Some of the other features, however, did. The deckplates were rougher than human decks, either ship or station, and did not seem to be entirely metal. There were irregular ridges that reminded Rory of the texturing on the palace steps of Thorne, meant to prevent slipping in rain or icy conditions. Deckplate that rough must be difficult to keep clean. And what *about* the bacteria that might be living here, on a xeno ship. Or the bacteria she was bringing to *them*. There could be appalling cross-contamination.

The floor's grooves were not of sufficient depth to impede or hinder her own thick-soled steps. The sub-commander's boots looked much like Rory's own, if a bit longer in the heel, all contours of the foot smoothed out, bulked up, and concealed. The actual vakari foot, though, must look like the hand, assuming symmetry. That would mean total toes numbering four, with the extra joint, and perhaps with talons, which the fingers seemed to have since the gloves came to a curving point. A hardsuit acting as battle-armor would need to cover all the delicate bits that might be broken off in a fight. Toes qualified. Perhaps that was why the boots on Koto-rek's feet now seemed as ill-suited as Rory's to this roughed-up deckplate. Perhaps crewpersons *not* wearing hardsuits wore different footwear, as they did on human ships; Rory had a pair of slippers on *Vagabond*, and Jaed had those ridiculous socks with the individual toes, of which Thorsdottir made constant mockery.

Rory's chest hurt suddenly, as if someone had punched out all her breath. Thorsdottir and Jaed were behind her now, around a bend in the corridor (the angle of which was not human standard, and so felt abrupt, like a sharp corner). The pleasant distraction of observing vakari ship design faded.

Koto-rek ia'vakat'ia Tarsik's head turned sharply, as if Rory had made some sound aloud. The vakar's chromatophores flared briefly orange, then settled into a throbbing, dim violet.

"There is no need to worry. You will not be harmed."

It was as if the sub-commander had sensed Rory's distress. Rory supposed her aura was all manner of red and orange, but Koto-rek should not have known that. Perhaps vakari did not have to be looking at someone to read their aura. Maybe they could . . . hear it. Feel it. Sense it without looking. Smell, perhaps, or some sort of sonar that dipped into the frequencies of aether attuned to auras, like Kreshti ferns.

Rory considered about the evidence of vakari arithmancy she'd already seen, and its level of advancement, and that the sub-commander did not carry a weapon, and decided to assume that Koto-rek ia'vakat'ia Tarsik *had* sensed her aura in an arithmantic manner. She wanted to ask about it, if it was a vakari ability, or one specific to vakari arithmancers, and then remembered her resolution to be a mantis-lion, and said instead, "You speak our language well."

The sub-commander made a clicking sound in the back of their throat, somewhere behind the jaw-plates and the vibrant, etched teeth. "You speak like an ambassador, not a salvager, and certainly not a soldier, which the other two are."

"Not soldiers," Rory said instantly and fiercely. "Neither of them are soldiers."

The vakar's cheeks took on a cobaltish sheen. "They met us armed. You did not."

"*You're* not armed, either." Rory felt stupid, remarking on the obvious, when she wanted to simply ask how long it had been, how much contact, between this Protectorate and humanity. And *which* humanity, because that would make a difference, too, though what sort of difference, she was not certain.

"I am not," the sub-commander agreed. "But I am not without my weapons. Nor, I think, are you."

Leaf. *Leaf.* Rory breathed and imagined cerulean serenity spreading through her aura. Nothing to see here, move along, this is not the confession for which you are looking, Sub-Commander.

"What weapons do you believe I have?"

Koto-rek ia'vakat'ia Tarsik clamped long nostrils together so that exasperation, or amusement, hissed through the gap. The vakar said a word in their own language and speared a sly look at Rory.

Of course Rory knew the same translation hexes as Rupert, entirely because he had taught them to her, probably imagining situations in which Rory might need to scramble her own speech for concealment or privacy, or when she might need to overhear something said in an unfamiliar dialect, and *not* that she would require those hexes to communicate with a vakar.

Or rather, to respond to what was clearly a vakar's challenge. A dare. Reveal herself as an arithmancer.

Rory tilted her head and pasted a vacant smile across her lips. "I'm sorry. I didn't quite understand what you said."

Koto-rek ia'vakat'ia Tarsik's jaw-plates flared. Their facial pigments intensified into vivid violets, tinged with red. But the vakar did not press further, or say anything else in any language, and Rory was free to resume gazing at the bulkheads as she passed through the corridor on what a part of her wanted to consider an *enemy ship*, though so far, the sub-commander had not acted enemy-like. They had been courteous, had not pointed any weapons at Rory, but had merely walked a half step ahead, expecting to be followed. That was a habit of command, an assumption of authority. Rory wondered how many layers there were between sub-commander and *actual* commander, and suspected not very many.

The bulkheads, like the decking, were textured, but unlike the decking, there were discernible patterns: long, intricate branching structures rising up from the lower third of the bulkhead, becoming most complex in the middle third, and dispersing in the top third. Colors moved through them, subtle and faint and dependent on perspective, like watching the colors change on an oil slick. Decoration, perhaps, or an organizational signal, the pattern of which Rory could not discern.

The sub-commander held up a restraining arm and stopped in front of a doorway. There was a small plaque on the bulkhead, beside a keypad, white with black strokes. Very much like a sign, and entirely unreadable. Rory stared hard at the symbols, trying to commit them to memory, as the door opened.

The room was narrow, dark, consisting mostly of a porthole looking into a second, interior room. It was from that room that all illumination came, dim and faintly blueish in cast, from teslas embedded in the overhead's shallow arch in that other room, which was rounder, undecorated, possessed of a single door on one side, with no panel or controls of any kind.

But that second room was not empty. A man squatted against one side, arms dangling over his knees. His head hung between his shoulders, obscuring most of his face. He had medium brown hair, cut very short, and medium brown skin with some darker, bruised mottling. He wore a close-fitting skinsuit, standard wear under hardsuits; his had a Tadeshi flag on the shoulder and long rents in the sleeves. Rory could not see if there was damage to the skin underneath, or blood on the fabric's lips, but she thought there might be.

Rory crossed the room and put her hands on the porthole. It did not feel like glass, exactly, to her gloved hands. It seemed heavier. More dense. Some kind of transparent polysteel, maybe.

"Who is he?"

"He

Sergeant Vladimir Nash serial number 314PI1592

refuses to tell us."

Rory managed to keep the surprise off her face; Messer Rupert had drilled that habit into her, and it had proved useful with nannies and cooks and malevolent Regents. She held her breath and decided to risk deploying the tiniest, most innocuous of hexes, to distort her aura, which would have otherwise turned from a vivid, furious crimson into a terrified yellow. She watched the sub-commander as she did so, looking for a reaction. The vakar's chromatophores remained neutral, all apparent attention focused on Sergeant Nash.

Rory was not reassured.

"Why am I here, Sub-Commander?"

The vakar reached for a panel beside the porthole and pressed a sequence into the keypad with the tips of their talons. Rory made note: vakari keypads would defy all but the smallest of fingertips, and would probably need a stylus. If she should ever find herself trying to access one.

Sound leaked into the dark observation room: a man's harsh breathing, half sobs, as if he had been running.

"Speak to him," said Koto-rek ia'vakat'ia Tarsik.

The man's head came up at the sound of the vakar's voice. There were bruises on his face, and one eye was swollen and crusted with blood. He pushed himself to standing against the bulkhead at his back and, still pressed against it, thrust his face toward the porthole. He could not see through it, though obviously he knew they were there.

Rory stared at the man's damaged features. "Did you do that to him?"

The sub-commander did not answer, or rather, had no chance to do so. At the sound of Rory's voice, the man lunged at the port-hole. His fists made almost no sound as they struck the not-really-glass. Rory winced as his skin split with the force of it.

"I hear you," he shouted. "Nnedi? Is that you?"

"Ss." Koto-rek ia'vakat'ia Tarsik's jaw-plates expanded. "What is a Nnedi? He repeats the word."

Rory moved down the porthole until she could match her hands against his. "It's a who, not a what.—I'm not Nnedi. I'm sorry. I am human, though. Can you tell me your name?"

The hope on Nash's face withered, then hardened. "Who are you? Are you working with *them*? With the veeks?"

However long the association between Tadeshi and Protectorate, it had been of sufficient duration to allow the development of prejudicial racial slurs. Rory sighed. "Sub-Commander, can you let him see us?"

Koto-rek ia'vakat'ia Tarsik did something that involved long talons clicking on the panel.

There was no visible change from Rory's vantage, except in the sergeant's demeanor. His undamaged eye rounded until the whole of its dark iris was surrounded by white. His gaze flicked from her to the sub-commander and back again, landing on Rory with such force that she took a step back.

"Rory Thorne. Rory *fucking* Thorne." He backed away from the glass. His hatred was palpable, unreasonable, impersonal, and increasing with every step he retreated. His hand patted, blind and instinctual, over his chest and hips, looking for a weapon.

Koto-rek ia'vakat'ia Tarsik's stare prickled the side of Rory's face. "He appears to recognize you."

The Tadeshi's gaze flicked to the vakar. Fear twisted his features, though what came out of his mouth was rage and words which, though Rory had heard before, she was not accustomed to hearing directed at her. It was clear that Sergeant Nash held her personally responsible for the rebellion (which was not entirely unfair), and that he assumed her presence here meant the

Confederation had "allied with the veeks and against true humanity." He also had physiologically impossible impressions of her parentage.

Rory watched, trying not to flinch. The sub-commander watched as well, while their chromatophores brightened from charcoal to a rusty maroon. Then the vakar hissed and said something in their own language. The door in the other room opened, and a pair of suited, visored Protectorate soldiers entered and subdued Nash with a brutal and unarmed efficiency.

Rory watched because she thought someone ought to. Despite his misplaced malice, the Tadeshi soldier was human, though that would not have mattered to him, had *she* been within reach. But still, she did not like the odds in that cell. Nash might have shot at Protectorate troops, might have killed them, but that was war, and he did not deserve to be beaten unconscious.

But perhaps he did, by some Protectorate metric, some notion of justice to which she was not privy. She knew nothing about her captors except that their skill in arithmancy exceeded anything human, and that they appreciated art on their ship bulkheads, and what they called themselves, and that they would beat unarmed prisoners.

Which she was. And Thorsdottir. And Jaed.

Rory watched as they dragged the Tadeshi out of the cell. Nash left long, wet smears on the ridged deckplate.

"Where are you taking him?"

Koto-rek ia'vakat'ia Tarsik's long nostrils flared and clamped and flared again. "That should not be your concern, Rory Thorne."

It was not exactly an untruth; but the fairy gift was uneasy with it, and prickled Rory's scalp.

"Is the Protectorate at war with the Free Worlds of Tadesh? Is that why you destroyed *G. Stein*?"

The vakar peered at Rory through half-lidded eyes, and of course, did not answer.

Rory lifted her chin. Her heart was attempting to escape her chest, either by beating its way out, or by crawling up her throat. It was only the two of them back here in this room, no weapons except arithmancy and what physiology provided. Fight back now, and perhaps she would end up like Nash, or dead.

Or worse, because there was a worse: she could get Thorsdottir and Jaed hurt. She could leave the sub-commander with the impression that all humanity was like the Tadeshi, to be classified as *enemy*. She had to do better.

"Will you do that to my companions, Sub-Commander?"

"They are not soldiers, you said."

Truth. Oh, truth. But not much of an answer.

"Will you do that to *me*?"

Koto-rek ia'vakat'ia Tarsik tilted their head, gathering Rory into the scope of their stare like a hunting bird eyeing a sparrow and debating the worth of a strike. So much work for such small gain. "That is within your control. Answer my questions. You appear to be an enemy of the Tadeshi. Does that make you our enemy, as well?"

"I hope not."

The sub-commander made that clicking sound in their throat, the one Rory understood to be laughter. "What does *that sheep-fucking bitch on Lanscot* mean?"

"He means Dame Maggie. She's the leader of the Confederation of Liberated Worlds, which seeks independence from the Tadeshi, and which is currently engaged in armed conflict to secure that independence. Lanscot is the capital planet."

Koto-rek ia'vakat'ia Tarsik's voice remained even, quiet. "Go on."

"The Free Worlds of Tadesh was a collection of worlds, many

colonies, united under a central government. It is one of several such entities in our—in human—space. Anyway, the Lanscottar believed the Tadeshi rule was unjust. When normal political channels of appeal and reform failed, they resorted to armed rebellion."

Unblinking black eyes. Flattened jaw plates. "And your role in this rebellion?"

"Accidental. I didn't know it was happening until it did. But other circumstances made it appear as if I was in collusion, or perhaps even responsible. Clearly that is what the prisoner believed."

"What circumstances?"

"That answer is complicated," Rory began, and stopped, unsure how to go on. The account of Vernor Moss's attempted coup seemed very small and distant, petty, even though it had begun with assassinations, even though it had thrown the Thorne Consortium into war with the Free Worlds, even though it had involved marriages of alliance for herself and her mother. Even though it had led to her being here, hiding (after all, let us call it what it is) on the edge of the Verge.

Koto-rek ia'vakat'ia Tarsik's pigments rinsed from merely red to blood and fire. "Then be brief, but thorough."

So Rory hung her stare on the red smears in Nash's holding cell and told the sub-commander what they wanted to know.

". . . and then I came here, to Samtalet." Rory swallowed a mouthful of sand. The vakari atmosphere was more arid, and more acrid, than she was accustomed to. And she had been talking for some time. The smears on Nash's cell had darkened almost dry.

The sub-commander said nothing for a minute (Rory counted) while their facial pigmentation faded back to neutral grey. "Thank you for explaining," they said finally. "It is a useful perspective, when one has only heard the Tadeshi version thus far."

Rory inclined her head. She did not trust her voice quite yet.

"Princess." Koto-rek ia'vakat'ia Tarsik tried the word out. The architecture of vakari tongue and teeth made the terminal *s* especially sibilant. "You are a person of consequence. You—are a *commander*. A leader. One who makes decisions for others. One who starts wars with those decisions." They regarded Rory with new, sharpened interest.

"As I said: I renounced the title."

"Truly?" The vakar grinned at Rory, that baring of etched, dyed teeth that seemed to carry more import than a reflex of the lips.

"I don't understand what you're doing. What that means."

Koto-rek ia'vakat'ia Tarsik put the smile away as one clips a 'slinger to one's suit when it is not in use.

"Those marks say to another vakar who I am. My name. My tribe. My rank. My mothers. If I wished to renounce them, I would have to polish my teeth plain or tear them out of my head. My mothers might do it themselves, for the insult."

So they did have a notion of male and female, and a plurality of mothers. Rory made note, one of a growing mental list, to discuss with Messer Rupert on her next quantum-hex call (if she lived that long; don't think too much about that). It really should be *him* here, meeting a new species. Being the first—well, not the *first*, the Tadeshi had already made an impression—being a competing sample of what humanity might offer as an example of itself.

"That shocks you," said the sub-commander, misinterpreting Rory's silence.

"It seems extreme." Samur had not been pleased with Rory's decision, and Rory had not exactly put herself within arm's reach, either, since announcing it. She'd left communication with the Thorne Consortium to Messer Rupert. But even so, Rory could not imagine her mother's disappointment transmuting into violence. "Are you a mother, Sub-Commander? Could you do that to your own children—tear out their teeth?"

"I am, and I could. How else does one make such a renunciation permanent? Because if one does not intend permanency, there is no point in the gesture at all."

Rory had no answer for that. The silence returned, in the absence of dialogue.

The sub-commander gazed into the empty cell, unblinking. She—because claiming motherhood suggested that pronoun to Rory (correctly: vakari link gender pronouns to specific roles, and when speaking GalSpek, employ the feminine for mothers)—might have been looking through the aether. Or she might have been considering what she might say next, or do next. Who she might put in that cell next, and what she might do to them.

It was better, sometimes, to derail and distract such chains of thought, even if doing so meant drawing that unfortunate attention onto oneself. Rory cleared her throat. "Why are you here, Sub-Commander? Why did the Protectorate attack *G. Stein*?"

"Is that how interrogation works for humans? A trade of information? Sss. No. I will answer you. Though," and her plates flared wide, amused, "it is complicated. Perhaps you would like to confirm my words with a hex? Arithmancer. You are that, too, I

know

think."

Rory lifted her chin. So her little concealment hex had been noticed. The sand in her mouth had spread all the way to her lungs. "So are you. I think. Though your skills are superior."

"I am a vakar." Koto-rek ia'vakat'ia Tarsik flipped her fingers. If that gesture meant the same thing to vakari, Rory thought she'd been dismissed. No: that her *species* had been, *and* all their arithmancy. Which, when she considered the maneuvers she had seen from *Sissten*, was probably fair. The k'bal were similarly convinced of their own superiority, with more apparent courtesy to their arithmantic inferiors. Also, they had no fingers to flip.

"I think we share a mutual problem, Rory Thorne. The Tadeshi have acquired a weapon which—ss. Which should not have been made at all. *Setatir wichu*."

"What was it? Can I ask?"

"You just did, and I cannot tell you because we did not find it. We are unsure of its disposition, only that it is not *obviously* what it is. The wichu are crafty, and they would have attempted to conceal its nature from us. We emptied the Tadeshi ship's medical bay and the armory and found nothing. None of the surviving crew admits knowledge. It is unfortunate that the bridge crew was killed in our initial contact; I suspect the weapon's location was classified, and knowledge of it limited to the command staff. A salvager, however, might have found something we did not." The vakar grinned, this time without baring her teeth: a spreading of jaw-plates, and narrowing of star-spangled eyes. "Did *you* find a weapon on board *G. Stein*, Princess Rory Thorne?"

The correct form of address is Highness or Royal Highness, and I am just Rory. But perhaps she wasn't. Perhaps she *couldn't* be. The sub-commander thought her a person of consequence. That might be more useful than *just Rory*.

Sweat prickled on her scalp, on her skin, chilling in the ship atmosphere and collecting damply wherever the suit covered her. The truth—that Thorsdottir, not Rory, had found Rose—would suffice to fool an ordinary (human) hex. Whether or not it would stop Koto-rek ia'vakat'ia Tarsik remained to be tested.

Rory was still thinking of a way to answer when the ship lurched underfoot. Her boots, accustomed to decks both smooth and metal, skidded, despite the automatic mag-lock on her soles. The sub-commander spoke sharply to empty air. Empty air answered in a burst of xeno syllables, in which the collection *Koto-rek* figured several recognizable times, without the subsequent syllables (and Rory, again correctly, made a leap of understanding, that Koto-rek ia'vakat'ia Tarsik could be shortened to Koto-rek). The ship was shaking, and the vakari were speaking: a mixture of sibilants and sharp clicks and edges. The volume was higher, the cadence more rapid. Koto-rek's cheeks spiked red, orange, yellow, like a sunset on Thorne.

It had been years since Rory had seen an orange sun, much less a sunset through atmosphere. She wondered what the vakari homeworld's sunsets looked like. If Koto-rek missed them.

Those were more interesting topics for first contact than *did you find a super-weapon.* Or at least more informative, in ways that would be conducive to an amiable, long-term association between peoples.

With a final bark-hiss, Koto-rek flowed toward the door like ink spilled from a bottle. So sudden was her movement, so liquid and startling, that Rory lost all breath and leaped in the opposite direction. She overbalanced and pitched into the porthole and scraped one arm and a shoulder, making a terrible noise, leaving no marks. Then her wits caught up with her instincts and she stopped and turned.

Koto-rek was not looking at her. She had a hand splayed across the door controls, and as the door retracted, she placed her body across the opening. The light refracted off her suit, breaking pink, green, blue over the sharpest edges. Now she looked back at Rory, across the narrow width of deckplate.

"Stay here," she said, and added, almost kindly, "It will be safer than the corridors. I will come back."

Truth.

And then she was through the door and gone, even before the door had closed again. Rory had a moment to realize she could rush the opening, perhaps wedge it (with what, demanded the rational part of her, an arm? Do you think a hardsuit will suffice against a door determined to close? But there would be safeties, surely, as there were on human vessels—)

Rory got a glimpse of the corridor, of the ambient teslas tilted toward a dimmer red than they would've been on a human ship, but still flashing. She heard a brief bite of siren, cut off when the door resealed.

Soundproofing. Convenient, in that she need not hear the ship's panic. And not, in that she'd never know what was happening out there. That this was an attack was obvious; who it was another matter. She tried the door panel. It ignored her. Of course, Kotorek had locked it. Rory thought she might get past it—she was good at hacking locks. But now wasn't the time. Not with the ship rattling like a can full of bones. Running around in the corridor would not *help*, and it might make things worse if someone mistook her for an enemy and shot her.

Rory wedged herself into the corner and squatted down. There were no benches, no emergency grabholds or fasteners or any way to secure herself. If the ship lost its grav-hex, or its inertial hexes, she had only the maglock in her boots to keep her from bouncing around. It might be best to imitate a ball, which bounced without damage, instead of a spindly shape with fragile, easily snapped-off limbs.

The ship shook. Rory, now ball-shaped, pressed herself gently into the bulkhead. She sealed her visor as an afterthought. She'd been confined before. It was just a matter of patience. She distracted herself by watching the HUD catalog the atmospheric composition, temperature, humidity. Hunkered down like this, she could not see into Nash's cell, could not see the smears of blood. So that was a good thing—

The ship lurched. An alarming vibration came up through the deckplate, as if for a moment all the ship's molecules tried to storm off in separate directions. A hex, Rory thought; but before she could dip into the aether—before she'd even decided that was a good idea—all the teslas went out, and dropped her into darkness.

CHAPTER FOURTEEN ≡≡≡

Zhang remained as ordered in the rear cabin, prepared for a search and both relieved and mildly appalled that one was not forthcoming. It seemed careless, on the part of the vakari, to neglect to secure *Vagabond*. But once they had departed, and Zhang was certain that they meant to *remain* gone, she was also forced to reassess their wisdom. There was power to the ship coming from *Sissten*, which meant the hatch opened readily enough between vessels. But *Vagabond's* turings were down, both primary navigation and the smaller arms-targeting, and with them, the engines. The entire cockpit was a monument to dark teslas and dead screens. Engines weren't dependent on turings . . . but pilots usually were.

Zhang had learned piloting as part of royal service. Her qualification exam had been taken, and passed, on Royal Shuttle Two, which was meant to take people of importance from one terrestrial location to another, and occasionally to travel up to the orbiting station if a visitor was too important for the beanstalk. An atmocraft's ability to get on and off the ground relied more on engines than on turings, and an atmo-pilot's skills relied on being able to steer a metal box (cylinder, ball, or whatever geometric shape applied to the superstructure) on top of a plasma core engine without running into anything. In void, where there was less to run into, but where speeds were much greater, ships used turings to do the math required for navigation, scanning, and, if it was that sort of vessel, weapons.

Zhang knew where the primary power junctions were. She went back into the rear cabin, pried up the floor panel, and rummaged around in *Vagabond's* guts until she found and flipped every switch that she knew governed ship systems, and a couple whose purpose she did not know. The engines, which had been sulking on standby mode since the turings' demise, muttered and grumbled and began rousing themselves. Zhang allowed herself a small, explosive exhale and a tiny victory gesture.

Then, almost as an afterthought, she took the last 'slinger from its slot in the armory and clipped it to the chestplate of her hardsuit.

When she returned to the cockpit, the primary turing remained unresponsive. The arms-turing, however, had recovered. It was rebooting itself in a series of eldritch-looking lines of code scrolling down its screen.

Well. If she needed to aim *Vagabond's* limited arsenal at anything, she'd be able to do so. But—oh, *but*, the arms-turing had scanners, too. That would mean she was not flying entirely blind. Zhang sat at her station and breathed deeply and slowly and reminded herself that *Vagabond* was a very small ship, incapable of *really* dangerous high speeds, and that it, and she, did not *need* a primary turing to fly; Rory had in fact removed its original turing when they'd stolen the ship from Urse, and Zhang had flown it then, so there was the proof. She was reasonably sure she could get *Vagabond* away from the vakari ship, too, and, barring attack, limp it to SAM-1.

Whether she would attempt to do so without anyone *else* on

board, however, she had not yet decided. Zhang did not want to leave Rory, Thorsdottir, and Jaed behind, assuming they remained alive, which she could not at the moment confirm. She also knew she could not go mount a daring rescue, single-handed, armed only with the remaining 'slinger in the ship's arsenal. That was the stuff of stupidity, and Zhang, like Thorsdottir, was practical, and not prone to flights of romantic overestimation of her own abilities.

She could prep the ship and hope the others returned and that the vakari did not. And if, when, it became clear that they would not come back (Zhang was not sure how she'd know; face that fight when she came to it), she could—perhaps, with luck—detach *Vagabond* and make some kind of escape. If the tesser-hex beacons remained intact, and if *Sissten* did not blow her to dust, she might even get out of the Samtalet system. Might get back to Lanscot and—well. There, her plan hazed into *tell Grytt*, which only meant Grytt and Messer Rupert would share her distress. They had no warship of their own. They had nothing except what Dame Maggie of the Confederation of Liberated Worlds granted to them in gratitude for the parts they had played in the rebellion, and in trade for Messer Rupert's advice on political and diplomatic matters. Practically that meant political asylum and a small grant of land. Zhang was certain that Messer Rupert's value, and Dame Maggie's gratitude, would not equal a rescue mission to the Verge to retrieve Rory Thorne, Thorsdottir, and Jaed Moss from hostile xeno custody.

But, oh *but*, there was Rose: a secret and terrible weapon out there, commissioned by and stolen from the Tadeshi royalists, and now in vakari custody. That might suffice for persuasion.

Except without Thorsdottir, who had Rose stowed in her hardsuit, Zhang had no physical proof of the weapon, only the documents describing it, which someone could claim had been faked. Without proof, it was unlikely—

Oh, stop there, she told herself. Everything was unlikely from this point: Rory and Jaed and Thorsdottir returning to *Vagabond*, any kind of escape, any, let us be grim, hope of surviving. Long-term plans were impractical. Short-term: prep the ship for departure, which without the primary turing meant manual checks of the sort that kept a mind occupied.

The arms-turing squeaked an alert. Zhang went to its console and checked. The arms-turing was certain that high-velocity projectiles were inbound, and it recommended evasive maneuvers and returning fire, not necessarily in that order. Zhang perched on Thorsdottir's chair and picked through the readouts. Thorsdottir had never said the arms-turing was prone to flights of fancy and exaggeration. But if there were projectiles inbound, then that meant—

Vagabond shuddered. There was a momentary flickering of teslas as *Sissten's* power-feeds to *Vagabond* went down. Then *Vagabond's* engines took over. The interior teslas steadied, brightened.

—that the vakari ship was under attack, and that those projectiles had just made contact.

Zhang slid back to her own seat and conducted a little bit of improvised redirection so that the arms-turing sent its reports straight to the main screen. It reported that *Sissten* was returning fire (another shudder). Zhang wished that she dared patch the arms-turing into *Sissten's* transmissions, or at least into its network; but that would almost certainly alert the vakari to someone on board *Vagabond*, and while she would like to imagine that an attacking ship would demand all their attention, she could not risk nervous soldiers coming back through the aetherlock.

However, she could and did seal the hatch from the inside.

If someone *did* want to board, they would either need the correct codes or superior firepower, and she would have plenty of warning.

The arms-turing chirped and spat out another slew of reports. There were more projectiles inbound, here and here and *here*, none of which would come close to *Vagabond*, but all of which *would* strike *Sissten* unless the vakari countermeasures intervened successfully. The arms-turing estimated the probability high of some penetration, with an accompanying series of damage estimates (accuracy percentages low, since *Vagabond* had no real idea of what a vakari ship could tolerate, or how it was laid out, or, really, anything). The arms-turing repeated its recommendation, and this time it was firm on the order: take evasive, then return fire, y/n?

Before Zhang could acknowledge the recommendation with an emphatic *n*, the arms-turing transformed the main display into a cascade of orange that Thorsdottir would have recognized, a semi-sentient outburst of outrage (it *was* an arms-turing) and dread (it possessed a small arsenal and was aware of its limits). *Vagabond* had been Tadeshi once, and despite the shuffling and reprogramming of its turings, it recalled its origins in much the same way a child remembers an unpleasant classroom experience with a wretched teacher.

Zhang was not given to talking to herself, or to outbursts in general; but when she saw the arms-turing's identification of the attacking vessel, she both swore aloud and demanded of the multiverse and the arms-turing if they were, indeed, joking. That was one of the remaining Tadeshi dreadnoughts, of the sort more generally employed in trying to obliterate the fleet of the Confederation of Liberated Worlds. There was no reason for it to be in Samtalet, and yet, here it was.

Zhang made several leaps of understanding, then. A dreadnought did not run escort or courier work. It must know about *G. Stein's* errand. It had come to collect Rose. And it was prepared for resistance, which meant the Tadeshi must already know about the vakari, too. The Confederation's relative successes this past year, the ease with which they had retaken occupied systems, was not due to Maggie's leadership or her generals' skill. It was because the Tadeshi were engaging in battle (or perhaps war) elsewhere in the galaxy.

A part of Zhang (the same part which kept her quiet in most social interactions) insisted that Dame Maggie and the nebulous *they* who ran even more nebulous *things* must already know about the Protectorate. Authority always knew more than regular people. That was the whole point of it. There was no need for one former guard of a disgraced Consortium princess to insert herself as a harbinger of woe. They already *knew*. They didn't *need* her warning.

But if they did *not* know about the vakari, this nebulous authoritative *they*, then they desperately needed to; and even if they did, they did not know about Rose, and she was uniquely positioned to deliver that information.

But to do so, she would need to get *Vagabond* loose, and leave her friends on board a vessel under attack by (let us assume the worst) superior firepower, if not superior arithmancy.

Zhang squeezed her eyes closed and counted to five. Thorsdottir would say—oh, gentle ancestors, she had no idea what. Thorsdottir would look first to Rory, because that was everyone's habit, and *Rory* would put the needs of others over her own safety, but she had always had people like Zhang and Thorsdottir and Messer Rupert and Grytt to limit the consequences of her choices to her actual person.

Zhang settled into her seat, fastened the harness, and lowered her suit's visor. She was not at all sure how *Sissten* was holding on to *Vagabond*. Clamps, presumably, which would also presumably *un*clamp if the object they held proved a danger to the ship.

"All right," Zhang told the arms-turing. "You win. Target *Sissten*. I know it's point-blank and that if you actually fire, you'll blow us up, too. But let's hope the vakari ship's safety protocols *don't* know we aren't suicidal."

The arms-turing said nothing, of course, having no voice/speech capability, and though Zhang had to input the commands manually, she felt better for having said them aloud. She could imagine that Rory would hear and approve. That Thorsdottir would, too. And that they would forgive her for leaving them behind.

The arms-turing beeped, rather petulantly. Someone was trying the aetherlock, which had set off its safety protocols and interrupted its targeting sequence.

Zhang whipped around to face the aetherlock and unclipped the 'slinger in one motion. Thorsdottir would have been impressed, if she had witnessed the speed and grace of that action; Jaed would have been both impressed and envious; Grytt would have merely grunted approvingly and without surprise, since she had chosen Zhang (and Thorsdottir) for their excellence.

Zhang herself experienced a giddy moment of detachment, staring down the barrel of a 'slinger with adrenaline flooding her system. She was also expecting that hostile boarders would need to force the lock, but no, *Vagabond's* aetherlock was calmly counting the seconds to green-and-unlocked, as if whoever was on the other side either had the entry codes or (and here, Zhang's stomach dropped into her boots) had the arithmancy to hex past the locks.

A 'slinger might do very little good against an arithmancer. Still, she leveled the weapon and angled herself out of the direct line of sight. There was not *much* cover in the cockpit, but there were chairs, and she was smaller than Thorsdottir. She would have one, maybe two shots, if she fired immediately.

The hatch irised open. A siren wailed in the corridor. Emergency teslas flooded into *Vagabond's* relative quiet, splashing bloody light on the deck and the bulkhead.

Zhang did not, in fact, fire at once. She hesitated. She would think about that, in subsequent days, with a sort of queasy guilt and relief.

But so: the hatch irised open and Jaed Moss came through in a rush. It was only when he spotted her, as she rose from her pitiful concealment in the cockpit, that he realized he was on the wrong end of a drawn and aimed 'slinger, and froze, mid-step. He had a stick of some kind in one hand, black and shiny and very weapon-like.

There came a shuffling noise behind him, boots scuffing on decking, and someone who did not sound like Thorsdottir swore in what did not sound like GalSpek.

Jaed rocked just a little, as if bumped, but he did not take his eyes off Zhang, or the 'slinger, even as his own weapon drooped. "Zhang?"

"Gah," she said, and lowered her 'slinger. "*Dammit*, Jaed."

He stepped clear of the hatch. "Thorsdottir's hurt, this is Crow, he's on our side, someone's attacking the ship, we have to go."

"The attacker's a Tadeshi dreadnought." Zhang clipped the 'slinger to her suit and tried to peer past Jaed's shoulder into the aetherlock. "What do you mean, Thorsdottir's hurt? Who's Crow— ah. I see."

"I'm fine," said Thorsdottir, which was a clear lie. Her hardsuit was cracked just below the right elbow, blackened in streaks running toward her wrist. Her skin looked waxy, too pale even for

Thorsdottir, her eyes, bruised and glassy. She was draped across a xeno's shoulder and back, which was testament to the strength of the carrier. (Crow, Zhang told herself firmly. Not a what, not an it, a person named Crow, gender-designation male, and never mind that those were tusks sticking up from his lower jaw.)

"—took a whitefire wand strike to the forearm," Crow was saying. "Where's your med-kit?"

"Rear cabin," Jaed said, before Zhang could answer or ask what a whitefire wand was. "Give her to me. Take this." He thrust the weapon at Crow. "Zhang—you said a *Tadeshi* dreadnought?"

"Yes." She looked in vain for Rory, as Jaed took custody of Thorsdottir and Crow moved toward the cockpit. There appeared to be no one else in the corridor. "Where's Rory?"

But Jaed was saying something to Thorsdottir as he got her into the cabin, which left Zhang facing Crow, who grinned at her. It was not a friendly or welcoming expression. "You the pilot?"

"Yes."

Crow made as if to move into the cockpit, as if he expected Zhang to step aside. Zhang didn't. She was aware of her dimensional inadequacies, and that anyone who could carry Thorsdottir could shove her aside easily enough, but Jaed and Thorsdottir had left her alone with this person, so command of *Vagabond* must fall to her.

"Rory," said Zhang. "Is she dead?"

Crow looked at her with what Zhang could only interpret as pity and a grim discomfort. His eyes were gold with green flecks. Ordinary hazel eyes in an extraordinary face. "The veeks took her off somewhere, so good as. We have to go. Listen. Your friend back there's in bad shape. She needs help, and we need to get *off* this ship before the veeks figure out we're gone, or before the slagging Tadeshi marines board."

That was all more or less what Zhang had already determined. It was both comfort, and not, that this Crow had come to the same conclusions she had. But it was not just the pair of them, was it?

She kept her arm where it was and called past Crow's shoulder. "Thorsdottir!"

Thorsdottir did not answer, but Jaed appeared on the threshold between cockpit and cabin. He exuded dishevelment, wide eyes and sweat-matted hair and, like Thorsdottir, far too pale. "It's all right," which it clearly was not. "Crow's with us. Rory's—I don't know where she is, they took her." Then he turned and disappeared back into the cabin.

He had said nothing about Thorsdottir. And she had not answered. That—that had to be bad.

"Pilot. Zhang." Crow grabbed her arm. There was no way Zhang could have actually *felt* the grip through her suit, but she imagined she did. "This ship have weapons? I can run an armsturing."

"Yes. Right." Zhang shook herself out of guilt and immobility and threw herself back into her seat. But she was not sure anything would be *right* again.

Thorsdottir was getting worse.

There was no *reason* for the deterioration that Jaed could detect. They hadn't encountered any trouble, no fighting, no pitched battles in the journey from jail cell to *Vagabond*. (One small fireball, a joint test of transmutational cooperative hexwork by him and the fragments of Rose, which had caused a section seal to drop and blocked any pursuit from at least one direction.) Not that he was an alchemist, or a chirurgeon, or, well, *anything* remotely useful in this situation. He knew what shock looked like, from the mandatory first-aid training, but he was not sure what else was wrong under her hardsuit. He suspected burns, about which he knew very little, except that they hurt.

The contents of *Vagabond's* meager medical kit stared back at him. He knew, in theory, what all of it did. The packages were all clearly labeled. He selected an analgesic patch from the kit, peeled it open, and showed it to Thorsdottir. She turned her head obediently and let him stick it to her neck. Her eyes crawled over his face.

"We can't leave Rory."

"Shut up and let me do this."

She did, which was only proof how unwell she was. Thorsdottir should be slapping his hands off and arguing with him. She should be shouting at Zhang. She should be in charge, if Rory wasn't. They hadn't worked out a chain of command, but Jaed had always assumed Thorsdottir came second.

He could hear Zhang and Crow talking, though too softly to make out the words. They were probably planning the last few minutes of everyone's lives. Somehow get away from the vakari ship, and then run straight into Tadeshi dreadnought fire—or Tadeshi demands for surrender.

Or, *or*. Without Rory on board, Zhang and Thorsdottir weren't *anyone*. Rory Thorne's body-maids. He would be willing to bet (his life, theirs) that no one knew their names. So asking for asylum, aid, from the dreadnought might actually work.

Jaed Moss was, of course, *someone*. Traitor at the least. A useful bargaining chip, if it came to that.

"Jaed?"

He set aside the rising panic, attached as it was to an unproductive line of thinking. Most likely they would explode trying to decouple from *Sissten*. Operate under that theory. But to

Thorsdottir, as he resumed rummaging ineffectually in the medical kit, he said, "Mm."

"You're supposed to tell me I'm going to be fine."

"There's a Tadeshi dreadnought out there firing on the ship to which we are currently clamped."

"That isn't fine, Jaed."

"No, it's not."

"So you're saying, I'm probably going to die when the ship blows up, don't worry about the arm?"

"Something like that."

She chuckled, a dry sound like sand in a bucket, and put her head back. At least she wasn't watching him have no idea what to do for her anymore.

He stripped his gloves off and clipped them to his suit. You didn't leave things loose on a ship, in case the hexes went out. Unsecured debris could turn lethal. So could unsecured people. He would have to hurry and get himself and Thorsdottir strapped in before Zhang took off, which meant he'd have to deal with the wound on her arm, which meant touching it.

He felt a bit like she looked: pale, clammy, cold. He flexed his fingers and then, carefully, peeled back the edge of the hardsuit. The metal snapped like a material far thinner and more brittle than hexed polysteel. Jaed stared at the broken piece in his hand. Then, before Thorsdottir noticed, he shoved it under the medical kit. Several other pieces followed. The whitefire had somehow altered the hardsuit's composition.

It was also a bit fortuitous; he had exposed the wound in a handful of steel-snapping moments, and apparently without hurting Thorsdottir. She made a noise in the back of her throat. "How bad is it?"

"Um." He leaned forward. The cabin teslas were bright, but not obnoxiously so, and there were dark shadows under the edges of the broken suit. He leaned closer and activated his helmet's head-lamp. An unforgiving beam of white stabbed onto Thorsdottir's arm. The blackness did not resolve into anything recognizable. Was there some kind of hex, concealing the damage? He squinted and dipped his awareness one layer into the aether. As sometimes happened, when one's visual senses were otherwise occupied, the others asserted themselves. In this case, his sense of smell sharp-ened, and he caught a whiff of cooked meat.

He sat up fast. Acid boiled at the back of his throat.

Thorsdottir watched him with wise, grim eyes. "Bad."

Jaed did not trust himself to speak. He swallowed instead, which burned, and busied himself rummaging through the medi-cal kit. What did one apply to blackened flesh? The labels blurred until he had to stop, close his eyes, gasp for breath.

He was supposed to tell her she would be okay. He had already ruined any chance of her believing that. He made eyelock instead. "The skin's pretty burned."

"Thought it might be." Thorsdottir nodded. "That's fine." Her smile flickered. "There's a Tadeshi dreadnought out there. We're all going to look like my arm in a few minutes."

Jaed sputtered, caught between unexpected, sour laughter and a reflexive need to argue with her. "The Tadeshi could fix this. We get off a comm to them, ask for help. Tell them you've got *me* to trade, they won't shoot. They'll help you, if just to get custody of me."

Thorsdottir's humor dried up and blew away. "No."

He was a little bit touched, and a lot relieved, which made what he said next seem the height of poor decision-making.

"You know it makes sense. They won't know who you are, or they won't care, and they won't execute me right away. There'd be a trial. There'd be a chance for, I don't know, some kind of negotiation with the Confederation."

Thorsdottir shook her head with more vigor than Jaed thought should be possible. That pain-patch must be especially potent. "It's not about you. If they get hold of this ship, they get Rose, and we *can't*."

Jaed stared at her. He had forgotten about Rose. The Tadeshi would use it against the Confederation first, but weapons like that had a way of getting loose and finding their way into everyone's arsenals. The dismissal stung—he had been sincere in his offer of self-sacrifice—but Thorsdottir was right.

"Then we have to make a run for it." His voice felt like it came from somewhere outside of him. It sounded like his father, cold and reasonable. Running meant Thorsdottir was likely to die, too. He had, what, a handful of antibiotic patches and a few analgesics? Nothing that could treat burns like she had. If they got to SAM-1 (if the Tadeshi dreadnought did not shoot them, or the Protectorate ship, if SAM-1 was even still intact), there were med-mecha and medical staff who might be able to save her life.

That was a great many *ifs*, none of which Jaed spoke aloud. Thorsdottir already knew.

She closed her eyes. The lids looked especially fragile, wrinkled and blue-veined and swollen red on the edges. "Except that means we have to leave Rory."

She sounded like he felt. Jaed reached across her and took her uninjured hand. She would not be able to feel much through the glove except pressure, so he squeezed especially hard.

There was a Tadeshi dreadnought out there. If it took the Protectorate ship, and found Rory alive. . . .

Jaed plucked a foil of antibiotic foam out of the medical kit and tore it open, proud of his steady fingers. He squeezed it carefully into the hole in Thorsdottir's suit, where it smothered the cooked-meat smell with chemical nothing.

Jaed's visor sealed, suddenly and unbidden. The part of his brain that was void-station born and trained supplied reasons: sudden loss of atmosphere, some emergency that the hexes detected and he did not. Thorsdottir's eyes went wide as she came to the same conclusion, but her visor did not drop.

rose help

Jaed stared at the text on his HUD. Rose. Of course.

"She's pretty messed up," Jaed said. "Not sure what help you're going to be."

A targeting square appeared over Thorsdottir, on the other side of HUD and visor. He didn't like the effect.

rose help

"By what? Shooting her? What can you do?"

The HUD seemed to hesitate.

repair

Rose did not, Jaed was sure, mean the hardsuit. He was also certain that the most logical question to ask in this instance—how?—would not produce a satisfactory response. Rose was rather limited in their capacity for verbal communication. He cast back to the documentation they'd found on *G. Stein*. Granted, he had not read it closely—a lot of very small words, and very technical terms—but he did not recall any bits about repair of organic material. Destroy a biosphere, *yes*, which necessitated an ability to transmute things on a molecular level, but again, that pesky *how* rose up and demanded a response.

All right, he knew that answer, too. The *mechanism* by which Rose would make the alterations would be arithmantic, of the sort that was supposed to be confined to theory, but which someone, somewhere had managed to put into practice. Rose worked by changing the fundamental alchemy of things on the level of aether where everything was just *math*. Formulae, equations, calculations. Bodies. The actual alterations—whatever variables Rose changed—he couldn't predict. That—prediction, forecasting, probability, whatever you called it—was another sub-branch of arithmancy, and one that he had done little more than acknowledge in passing as he concentrated on the more practical hacking and reading of auras. Another arithmancer—Rory, Messer Rupert, some k'bal—would be able to say what sort of changes Rose could make—

Wait. *Rose* was an arithmancer. Rose could say, if Rose could find sufficient vocabulary. Or if he could meet Rose halfway.

So, with a breath that felt insufficient, he slid into the aether until he could see the glittering fragments of very tiny mecha who, together, called themselves Rose, and asked, "How?"

Only when he made that query here, it was not a syllable, or an utterance. It was hex-query, of the sort he might use to begin negotiations with a turing if he were attempting to talk his way past security measures.

And Rose answered.

This account will forego an exact recounting of their exchange, as the rendering and translation of arithmancy into print is an under-appreciated and laborious task best left to scholars (see in particular M. Tearle's *By Any Other Name* for what is believed to be the most exact version of this exchange), and proves to be of little interest to readers in any case.

Jaed asked, and Rose answered, and after some time Jaed exited the aether with a headache, a nosebleed, and a thorough, if uncomfortable, understanding of Rose's intentions. They meant to transmute Thorsdottir on an alchemical level. Not make her something *else*, exactly—not transmute her to, say, a different species, or a cyborg like Grytt. They meant to *integrate* themselves into her organic matter, and then transform what they found; in essence, what they had been designed to do, only this time, with benevolent effect.

"And you are certain?" Jaed asked. "You are *certain* that you won't kill her by doing this? Because that's what you're for. Killing. You know that."

Rose, we may hope, was immune to offense, or their response was simply too limited to express emotional dissatisfaction or impatience.

yes. no harm.

Until or unless someone activated Rose's command codes. Jaed remembered *those* clearly enough—seeing their mention in the documentation, if not their actual alphanumeric composition. He wished he'd been looking more closely then. He wished he dared access those documents now. But to do so might alert Zhang and Crow to his negotiations, and inject two more opinions, and at the moment, there was only one that mattered.

"Ask Thorsdottir," he told Rose. "If she says yes, you can help her."

not ask

He strangled the reflexive *why not*. Because Thorsdottir's hardsuit was a fragged mess, obviously. Because magic nanomecha had limits. He glared at his HUD and slowly, deliberately, commanded the visor to rise.

Thorsdottir was watching, waiting. "What?"

Jaed let out a breath he had not known he was holding. "Rose says they can help you. They will . . . don't ask me to tell you *how* this works, but they'll sort of . . . bond with you, on an alchemical level, and change you. Repair you. It's permanent. Rose will be part of you. But that's all I—we—know. Rose can't ask you directly because your suit's wrecked. What should I say?"

Vagabond's engines fired, then, thrumming up through the deck.

Thorsdottir rolled one bloodshot eye at Jaed. "Tell Rose, yes."

Jaed hesitated at the aetherlock. That was the story of his life, hesitation; he reflected on that, with his hand hovering over the control panel, while his guts tied themselves into cold knots of indecision. Going out and leaving *Vagabond* would be, if not lethal, then at least stupid. His chances of finding Rory in the vakari ship, with no idea of where she had been taken, were not good; and if one added the factors of *ship under attack* and the sheer brutal competence of vakari troopers *and* the likelihood that he would be seen as a hostile attacker if he was detected running loose in their corridors, then those chances slipped from improbable to infinitesimal to suicide. And then, somehow, he would have to free her and get her back *here*.

Assuming Rory was even still alive. He thought she was, because the vakari had not killed Crow, who seemed much more dangerous. They had not even bothered taking Crow's hardsuit (possibly because of the danger, or possibly because a naked tenju in the cell violated some protocol or another). The *point* was, they hadn't killed Crow, or even him and Thorsdottir, when they could have. So Rory must be alive.

That certainty made standing here, hesitating, that much worse. Someone had to leave this system and report what they'd seen, and report Rose, but those someones could be Zhang and Thorsdottir. They did not *need* him to add his voice to the report.

But what made him hesitate—if he was honest with himself, and not merely critical—was not cowardice, but the suspicion that

Rory did not need him, either. It was not that she did not regard him fondly, or find his company, if not useful, at least pleasant (though she *had* needed his expertise on *G. Stein*). He did not fret for her affection, although he had long since abandoned any hope that there would be more to her regard than just that; she had made that clear early on, before they ever left Lanscot.

I need a friend, Jaed. Not a husband. Not a lover. Can you do that?

He could. He had. They were friends. She liked him just fine. This was not about *like*.

This was, if he was still being honest, which was neither comfortable nor comforting, not about Rory at all. She was remarkably able to navigate difficult and dangerous situations. Accidents could happen; of course they could. A Protectorate soldier with a plasma—no, *whitefire*—weapon could end her life. His presence would not alleviate that risk in the slightest, and it was knowing *that* which distressed him, even more than imagining what was happening, or might happen, to Rory. He did not like feeling useless.

In the rear cabin, Thorsdottir was strapped into a seat with a cracked hardsuit and severe burns and an alchemical, arithmantic weapon attempting to rewrite its own protocols and repair her. Jaed wished he'd read the documentation more closely, but Rory had been doing that, and he had been more concerned about the vakari. He was as extraneous on *Vagabond* as he would be on the Protectorate ship. He could not help Rose. That was why he had come out here, to the aetherlock. To *do* something. He could not just *sit there* while Thorsdottir might be dying.

"Jaed."

Zhang's quiet voice came from the vicinity of his left shoulder.

He should have heard her get up, should have heard her exit the cockpit and approach him, and had not. He suspected she knew what he was thinking. Zhang was good at things like that. He also suspected she was here to argue him out of it.

He turned his head just far enough to see her face. "Aren't you supposed to be flying this thing?"

She regarded him with steady, sympathetic, bleak eyes. "How is Thorsdottir?"

It struck him then: she thought he had left Thorsdottir because she had died. Shame flamed and flooded his cheeks. "She's fine—not fine. Alive." He temporarily forgot Rory, or at least set her aside. "Rose thinks they can repair her."

Zhang's mouth opened. Then she closed it again, without speaking. A muscle knotted in her jaw. Questions piled up behind her eyes.

"Thorsdottir agreed to it," Jaed said, because that seemed most important thing to relay. "Rose volunteered, but she agreed."

Zhang leaned forward as if her boots were fused to the deck and she could only incline so far, which was not sufficient angle to *see* into the rear cabin. She took a short, sharp breath. "Do I want to know how?"

"Maybe. I do. But I think Rory's the only one with enough arithmantic theory to get it." Jaed cast a guilty look at his hand, at the aetherlock pad.

Zhang sighed audibly. "Do you think we could find Rory out there?"

Jaed entertained a thrill of hope. Zhang had said *we*. They might go together. That would give them a chance, or at least a better one than he'd have alone. But that would leave Thorsdottir on *Vagabond* with Crow, which was as good as leaving her alone, and Zhang wouldn't do that.

It was the worst choice. Leave Thorsdottir, badly wounded and in possession of Rose and Crow, or leave Rory behind, condition unknown.

Zhang let him think through it.

"I don't know," he admitted. "I want to say yes. But I don't really believe it."

"I would like to argue that Rory would tell us to leave," said Zhang. "I don't really believe that, either. What I *do* know is that you are the only arithmancer we have right now, and if anyone can explain what Rose is and what Rose does to the people who need to understand, it's you."

"You don't need an arithmancer for that. You've got the documents. And you've got Crow up there on the arms-turing. You don't *need* me."

Zhang pressed her lips together. Whatever she would have said—and Jaed supposed it would be a well-deserved admonition against self-pity—was interrupted by Crow's bark from the cockpit, "That dreadnought's launching breaching pods. We need to go *now.*"

And that settled it. Jaed jerked his hand back as if the aetherlock controls had spat whitefire at him.

"Come up to the cockpit," Zhang said. "We do need someone on comms."

It was not true, but it was a kind offer, and Jaed loved Zhang for making it.

CHAPTER FIFTEEN

Thorsdottir was still alive, a condition which, upon reflection, she found surprising. She recalled the smell of cooked self, the smell of hot metal, hazy impressions of Jaed Moss leaning over her. She recalled pain, which was entirely inadequate to describe the sensation's intensity or duration; but also fear, equally inadequate descriptor of the emotion. She remembered agreeing to something having to do with Rose, though the details of that agreement escaped her. She could only recall Jaed's face, and the palpable, smothering despair smearing his features that she knew she was the cause of, and wanting to say whatever she could to alleviate his distress.

Then there had been the small matter of *Vagabond* attempting an escape from *Sissten*, and she had not been on the arms-turing to oversee everything. There had been a xeno in her place, a, a tenju, whose name eeled past Thorsdottir's grasp.

So yes. That she was alive proved revelatory, bordering on the miraculous. *Vagabond*—because this was *Vagabond*, there was that tatty 2D poster of Jane Link from the seventh installment in the series (the one where Jane had gone undercover in a k'bal arms dealer's entourage) affixed to the side of the weapons locker—was still flying. They had not been reduced to ashes or particles. She

appeared to be unsuited, which caused a momentarily flash of embarrassment, because Jaed must have been the one to oversee that
operation. She was still wearing her skinsuit, however, and its sour
clinginess testified to its originality. Her entire right arm felt cold,
which, she realized, was because the skinsuit sleeve was missing
from the shoulder. The arm itself was not, a realization which only
compounded her pleasant surprise. Her forearm was swathed in
inexpertly applied dressings from the emergency kit, and she was
pleased to see fingers poking out of the appropriate end, and even
more pleased that those fingers wiggled when she willed them to
do so, *and* that the wiggling did not hurt. There was a pulling sensation, as if on a scab. She eyed the bandages. No need to unwrap
those just yet. The rest of the arm, the unburned skin above the
elbow, pebbled in the chill of the ship's atmosphere.

She glanced at the hatch that separated the cabin from the
aetherlock and, beyond that, the cockpit. Of course it was sealed;
that made sense, in a potential combat situation. But she was a
little perturbed nonetheless to find herself isolated. At least Jaed
had left her more or less upright, strapped into the seat, and not
attempted to maneuver her onto a bunk. (Thorsdottir did not know
that Jaed had tried, and then given up under the twin pressures of
time and a fear of doing her more damage in the attempt.) She was
only grateful for his failure, and a little jealous that *he* was in the
cockpit and aware of current events, sitting at Rory's station and—

Oh. Oh sainted ancestors, *Rory*. The knowledge that they had
left Rory on *Sissten* flooded back, washing away any lingering sur-
vivalist satisfaction. Thorsdottir slapped the harness release and
lurched to her feet before fully considering whether being alive
equaled being able to walk. It did not. She propelled herself into
the bulkhead beside the hatch, and, commandeering her almost
entirely swaddled fingers to action, coaxed the hatch into opening.

It required an authorization, since the ship was moving at high v, which in turn required time to input, time in which Thorsdottir could realize that her balance was not ideal, and that, in fact, she might end up sitting on the deck before the hatch completed its cycle.

Then, before she had quite tapped out the last of the lengthy alphanumeric string required, the hatch opened like a startled mouth. Like Thorsdottir's mouth, in fact, as she reflexively re-coiled, overtaxed her already tenuous grasp on balance, and sat down hard on the deck.

Jaed stood in the hatch, staring down at her with a matching, o-mouthed expression.

"What are you doing?" he blurted, even as Thorsdottir rolled onto a hip and, using her sleeved arm for leverage, lurched back to her feet.

Jaed arrested her forward momentum—more of a controlled stagger than the fiercely determined march Thorsdottir had intended—by spreading himself across the hatch opening. "What are you doing?" he asked again, more softly this time.

She could see past his shoulder: the cockpit hatch was open, and through that aperture Zhang and that tenju (Crow? Crow, yes, that was it) crammed shoulder to shoulder in front of the main screen.

"How is she?" Zhang called back. She did not turn her head.

Jaed did, which afforded Thorsdottir the opportunity to try to displace him. She could not shoulder him aside, exactly, given the hatch's size and placement, but she thought to propel him backwards at least, until the extra room around the aetherlock would permit her to brush by.

Except Jaed did not move when she pushed on him, and Thorsdottir realized belatedly that no, he still wore his hardsuit (there were suspicious stains on the gauntlets, reddish, which did not bear close examination) and thus was much heavier, and well beyond her capacity to dislodge even *if* she were entirely hale. Which she was not.

Jaed grimaced. "She's fine." His tone sounded more judgmental than overjoyed. "She's trying to get up."

Now Zhang *did* look, or at least she turned her head partway; she was too conscientious a pilot to take both eyes off the screens during operations. "Thorsdottir!"

That exclamation was equal parts relief (you're all right!) and admonition (why are you standing up?) and more surprised than Thorsdottir found comforting.

"She shouldn't be up." Crow lifted his voice and flung it over his shoulder "You shouldn't be up! Go sit down." Then he let out a stream of syllables whose force and invective suggested profanity.

Vagabond shifted vectors abruptly. The inertials surged, then stabilized. Thorsdottir pitched into Jaed, catching herself (one-armed) on his chestplate. It was a poor landing and a tenuous grip, and when *Vagabond* lurched again, she listed sideways. Jaed prevented any further collapse or collision and caught her in the curve of one arm and pulled her against him, where her weight and his were more centrally balanced over the maglocked advantage of his boots.

From here, at least, Thorsdottir could see all the way into the cockpit, and more importantly, see the main screen's display. *Vagabond* was moving too fast for the human eye to actually resolve much except blurriness, and the distances involved were well beyond organic capacity. Without the primary turing, there was insufficient power to render an image on the screen, which was damned inconvenient for a non-pilot observer (which was also why e-vids always pretended that pilots navigated in void-battle by sight and unaided human reflex). Thorsdottir ordinarily maintained a deep scorn for such romanticism, but right now, she wished it were true. Still, what she could see past Jaed's shoulder showed her a crosshatched display of brightly colored trajectories that meant the big ships were exchanging fire from relatively close range. There were stationary blips on the screen, too: the Protectorate ship and the royalist's dreadnought and, to Thorsdottir's surprise, two more ship-blips, hovering outside the battle's perimeter.

Thorsdottir tried to dislodge herself from Jaed's grasp and, failing the first attempt, gave up further endeavors as a waste of effort. She cranked her face around instead to stare into his. The range was uncomfortably close, particularly in an olfactory sense. There had been a surfeit of sweat lately, and a shortage of baths. Jaed's hair stuck to his forehead in sweat-matted sheaves; she supposed hers was doing the same.

No matter. "What's going on?"

"Slagging alwar," snapped Crow, whose hearing was evidently quite keen, and whose sense of conversational manners was not. "That's an Empire ship out there, *and* one of ours. What they're doing *here* right now, who the slag knows."

Thorsdottir glared at Jaed in a mute demand for clarification. His features creased in the facial equivalent of a shrug. "We're barely flying at this point. Primary turing's still down. Zhang's making do with a zombie system." No semi-sentient turing to help her, which meant calculations manually entered and a plain human brain for judgment on where to point the ship.

Zhang put the ship into a roll which did not incite disaster only because one, Jaed's boots were maglocked to the deck and two, he had a firm grip on Thorsdottir and three, the grav-hexes did their job.

Thorsdottir closed her eyes. Her bandaged arm was starting to ache a little, probably from the jostling. Her heart bounced between her ribs and the hard shell of Jaed's suit.

"Are they shooting at us?"

"Not on purpose. I think they're convinced we're debris. We've had to dodge fire from both sides, though. Listen, I really need to get back up there."

"What about Rory?"

"I don't know." Jaed looked miserable. "You really need to get back to the cabin."

Thorsdottir knew that's what they made *him* do, when it was her and Zhang and Rory up front. Jaed rode alone in the cabin, uncomplaining. She told herself she, too, could manage that task, particularly now, particularly when she was of no use in the cockpit.

The words crammed in her throat. She shook her head at Jaed, protest and plea together.

"There's no room in the cockpit," he said. "You know that. But listen: I'll leave the hatches open, all right? So you can hear?"

It was kinder than she would've been, had their positions been reversed. Thorsdottir nodded. She could not quite manage a thank you. She could, after a couple of hard swallows, manage, "I can get back by myself."

It was on the force of that promise that Jaed released her, though she noted he did not yield up his place in the hatch opening. She tried a step backward, then two. Her balance held. Zhang made no abrupt maneuvers. She chose the jumpseat closest to the hatch, not the one from which she'd come, and was glad to collapse into it.

Jaed did not offer assistance. He watched, his expression a twist of pity and guilt that inexplicably made Thorsdottir want to shout at him. She held up her swaddled arm instead, as she maneuvered herself into the jumpseat and one-armed the harness into place.

"What happened? There was something with Rose . . . ?"

"Rose offered to help you," Jaed said. "I guess they did. You survived." His gaze dropped and bounced around on the deck.

Thorsdottir swallowed the rocks in her throat. "I didn't think Rose could talk, you know. The clipping. I thought there wasn't enough left to talk to."

"Nanomecha are really tiny. There might be millions of them in something the size of that clipping. Maybe billions. And they were propagating the whole time we had them." His face collapsed. "Doesn't matter. You're okay."

Then why do you look so unhappy? Thorsdottir almost asked, but as she started to shape the syllables, Zhang's voice came floating back from the cockpit.

"Jaed! We need you."

"Got to go." Jaed wrung out a smile and hung it on his lips, where it dangled unsteadily, vulnerable to each blink as he retreated into the cockpit. He held her gaze like something precious and fragile until he had to turn around and go in and take his (Rory's) station.

He kept his promise, too. The hatches stayed open.

"Look at that." Hworgesh pointed at the central hologram.

Grytt strangled a retort that she had been looking, because there was nothing *else* to do on this bridge, except divide attention between the main display and the door behind which Rupert had disappeared. Oh, yes, and also to check the chrono, which, despite looking nothing *like* a clock, being columnar instead of circular (and what was wrong with plain digits? Bah.) still marked off the passage of time at a regular intervals. Thirteen of those little marks had gone dim while she'd been sitting out here.

But Hworgesh did have a point. There were tiny orangeish flecks streaming out of the dreadnought, which did not look like missiles or torpedoes or fast-moving rocks. "Are those breaching pods?"

"Yep. Must be something on that ship the Tadeshi want real bad, if they want to risk a pitched battle." Hworgesh slid Grytt a knowing, conspiratorial smile. "You don't want to fight the veeks on their own decks. They're all slagging arithmancers."

Grytt sat up a little straighter. That seemed . . . bad. She, like any other Kreshti marine, had encountered battle-hexes. They were awful. The only ameliorating factor was how rare arithmancers were, on a battlefield, and that they died as easily (more easily, sometimes) than a regular trooper. "*All* of them? Really?"

Hworgesh seemed amused. "Seems like. Even the regular soldiers usually know a trick or two. Or it's their arithmancers who know how to shoot. More than *we've* got, anyway. We," he added, anticipating her question, "meaning the rest of us. Human, tenju, alwar, k'bal."

Grytt had not heard a collective *we* that encompassed more than a particular political affiliation. Impressive. "You *all* fight the vakari? What, together?"

"Together?" Hworgesh looked as if Grytt had suggested he might turn into a cabbage. "No. I mean, the veeks fight with everyone except the mirri, and that's just because the mirri planets are all poison to oxy-breathers. They're mostly going after the k'bal right now. They haven't gone after the Empire in about two hundred years, but they pick off a seedworld here and there along the border." He shook his head. "Where *is* this Confederation of yours, that you don't know this yet?"

"I've been raising sheep planetside," said Grytt. "And not paying attention. What about tenju, ah, seedworlds?"

Hworgesh scowled. "We never had many. The ones we did have, the Empire annexed and colonized a long time ago. The veeks did us a favor, first time they hit the Harek ships. Got the alwar fixed on something besides us. 'Course the veeks hit *us* not long after that."

"The Expansion?"

"I guess. Or one of their gods woke up grumpy. They've got nine. Anyway, listen. Some of them raid the borders. Pick off caravans. Those are the ones *we* deal with. And yeah, I've fought 'em. On deck and on dirt. It's good practice. We all know they're coming, once they're done with the k'bal."

"But you don't have a formal alliance with anyone?"

Hworgesh's gaze slid away. His shoulders sagged a little. "No. Between you and me, we need one. Chances we'll *get* one—eh. But not easily." He thrust a chin at the alwar, clustered around their instruments. The XO had taken the captain's place; she was taller, hatchet-faced rather than lovely, and staring at Grytt and Hworgesh with evident disapproval, which Hworgesh reciprocated. His lip curled away from his tusks.

"Slagging alwar. Convinced they don't need anyone else."

Fascinating. Alarming. Grytt glanced at the still-sealed door behind which Rupert, the captain, and the adept were conducting their no doubt important, definitely private conversation, and wondered how far across the bridge she'd get, if she decided to interrupt, before security tried to stop her. Not worth an incident, was it. Rupert would come out soon enough, and she could tell him what Hworgesh had said. Or Hworgesh could repeat it.

"Hey. Look." Hworgesh pointed, this time at a small, red-ringed blip that had detached itself from the vakari vessel. It wasn't a Tadeshi breaching pod. Those pods were merely glowing blips of Tadeshi malice, too tiny on the hologram to rate rings and read-outs. *This* little blip had a ring which, as Grytt dialed in her focus, began filling itself with numbers. It hung for a moment, as if it were orienting itself, before it began wobbling away from the vakari vessel. It might have been a bit of debris, drifting on the currents of an explosion, except for its presence on the scans.

"That's a Tadeshi shuttle," Grytt said. She and Rupert had escaped from Urse on a very similar ship.

So had Rory.

"Something's wrong with its turing," said Hworgesh. "Or its pilot. It's not broadcasting any ID."

Grytt stood up and aimed herself at the room where the adept, the captain, and Rupert had gone.

Behind her, Hworgesh sputtered. "The hell are you doing?"

Starting a diplomatic incident, Grytt thought. But out loud, she said, "Need to talk to the Vizier," as much to answer Hworgesh as to inform the alwar security, which were responding to her unexpected movement with admirable efficiency. At least they had not yet drawn any weapons. But they *were* between her and her goal, and Grytt guessed that if she tried to get past them, the potential unfortunate diplomatic event would become an actual one. She diverted instead toward what looked like the communication console, and a smallish alw huddled over it.

"That ship," Grytt said, with no regard for diplomacy or titles or even an *excuse me.* "That little ship. The shuttle. We need to hail it. Urgently. Um. Please."

The communications tech did an admirable job of pretending the cyborg leaning over her was not, in fact, leaning over her. She said something quiet and urgent into the comms. Calling the captain, probably. The XO was already en route, coming around the console with surprising speed.

"Domina." Her voice was a brittle combination of courtesy and outrage. "Please return to your seat *at once.*"

Grytt cast an eye where Rupert had gone, and yes, there, the door behind which he'd vanished had opened, and a parade of Captain-Adept-Vizier emerged, in that order. All eyes on her, yes, exactly where she hated to be.

Grytt looked at Rupert. The rest of them didn't matter.

"Rory's ship just launched off that vakari vessel." She didn't point out which one, on the display. Rupert was smart. It'd take a look—there, his eyes moved, and *there*, yes, he'd seen it.

Rupert didn't ask if she was certain, or how she knew. He turned to the captain. "Captain Kahess. We need to hail that ship."

Kahess did not seem surprised. "Your princess?"

Evidently, thought Grytt, a great deal more information had been exchanged in that conference room besides first names.

"It seems probable," said Rupert, with a serenity that did not fool Grytt in the least.

The captain shook her head as if it were filled with bees. Then she snapped an order that resulted in the communications tech pivoting away from her station and looking up Grytt and Rupert with a mixture of curiosity and a wide vein of annoyance.

"I am prepared to open a channel," said that alw. "What's your message?"

Grytt traded a look with Rupert. Then she leaned over the console and glared at the machinery as if she could see through it and force contact by will alone. "Say, *Rory, it's us. Messer Rupert and Grytt*. Start with that."

Jaed was not prepared for the comm board to flare up and announce an incoming hail, nor for the beep in his earpiece. He recoiled, stifling an urge to slap his hand over the flashing tesla. His heartbeat, barely resettled after the Thorsdottir incident, came scrabbling up the back of his throat again.

"We're being hailed," he said, because that seemed like the appropriate announcement. There was more information forthcoming, a stream of identifiers on his small, crabbed scope that he did not recognize. *Rory would have*, he thought bitterly, and almost as quickly, *no, she wouldn't*, when the voice on the other end actually spoke.

"Vagabond, *this is the Harek Imperial vessel* Favored Daughter. *Please acknowledge. Uh.*" The voice sounded somewhat embarrassed. *"It's us. Messer Rupert and Grytt."*

The language was GalSpek; the accent and the voice was unfamiliar. It was definitely *not* Messer Rupert or Grytt.

"*Vagabond* acknowledges, *Favored Daughter*," he said in his best formal voice. "This is Jaed Moss. Who, ah, who am I talking to? Because you're *not* who you say."

Silence, from the other end of the comms. Behind Jaed, in the cockpit, Crow said, "*Favored Daughter* is an Empire ship. They're as close to good alwar as you can get."

"What do they want?" Zhang demanded, and then, after a beat, aggrieved, "What are alwar?"

Jaed turned away from both of them, as if to refuse to look at talking people would somehow also render them inaudible. He side-eyed Thorsdottir, whose stare hung on him like hope. The earpiece continued its quiet. He wondered if he'd lost contact, and what he should do to re-establish it, or even if he should try.

Then the channel reopened, and a familiar voice said in his ear, "Jaed? Is that you? Is everyone all right?"

Jaed felt his jaw fall open, and the color drain out of his skin before it came flooding back in a hot rush, and the prickle of tears in his eyes. That *was* Messer Rupert.

Thorsdottir, who had all her attention pinned on his face, sat up straight.

"Shut *up!*" she bellowed—or attempted to bellow. (It was more like a ferocious wheeze, but *Vagabond* was small and sound carried easily.) Nevertheless, people listened: Zhang, perhaps from habit, and Crow, from sheer astonishment.

For a handful of rapid heartbeats, the silence stretched over the subliminal hum of the engines like a translucent skin. Three pairs of expectant eyes turned toward Jaed like flowers to the sun. Jaed swallowed. "It's the *Vizier*. Our Vizier. Messer Rupert."

"And Grytt is with me," said Messer Rupert, in Jaed's ear. "Jaed. What happened? Is everyone all right?"

He meant *where's Rory*. Jaed knew he did. "Grytt's with him," he repeated dutifully. "He's asking what happened."

Jaed felt the look Zhang flung at him, like a splash of cold dismay on the side of his face. Thorsdottir pressed her lips into a line.

"You'd better tell him, then," she said.

So Jaed did.

CHAPTER SIXTEEN ===

Rory had heard, as have innumerable children, that she need not fear the dark. And, perhaps because she trusted both Grytt and Messer Rupert (who had been the most frequent and vocal proponents of bravery in the face of shadows), she bent her considerable will to overcoming that instinct when the vakari ship went *truly* dark, and did not immediately panic.

One attentive to details—or intent on eroding Rory's apparent bravery—might point out she was not entirely bound in pitch black. Her hardsuit possessed the usual power-indicator and safety teslas, and her HUD was functioning. When the ship's overhead illumination failed, she found herself staring at the tiny cool blue stars that marked the joints of her wrists, and, because of the angle at which she crouched on the deck, those on the backs of her heels, as well. That same attentive critic might also observe that the illumination put forth by those tiny blue teslas was insufficient for more than psychological comfort. She was still effectively blind, and appropriately startled, for the fraction of a second that it took her to register the darkness; then her headlamp, responding to the ambient automatically, engaged, and suddenly there was a sturdy beam carving a circle into the bulkhead across from her.

She stared at that circle of light while she gasped her heartbeat back to normal. She was, in fact, afraid of *this* darkness. Power failure on a voidship would, if it went on very long, prove fatal to everyone, and neither her HUD nor all the twinkling teslas on her suit would be of any benefit. She leaned forward and put a hand flat on the deck. It was impossible to tell, through the layers of polysteel in her glove, whether the deck still vibrated with a living engine. Or at least, it was impossible for human flesh to ascertain that vibration. But the hardsuit could and, as she stared sternly at her HUD, confirmed her fear. The engines were offline. That meant the life support was, too.

The rational portion of her brain told her that this outage was the likely result of a powerful battle-hex. That same part of her brain insisted that any people so advanced in their arithmancy as the vakari would not skimp on system back-ups and redundancies. Power *would* return to the ship, probably sooner than later. And besides, it took life support a long time to fail. There would be oxygen yet for hours.

But for the moment, it was dark, except for her hardsuit. The console, with whatever passed for vakari turings, was dark, as was the lock-pad for the door.

Rory sprang up and launched herself across the narrow room. She used the bulkhead for braking, slamming into it with force enough to rattle the teeth in her head and inspire mild alarm in her hardsuit. She ignored both, and, with her headlamp drilling a path through the dark, found the edges of the control panel. The gap was too narrow to accommodate her fingertips, so she abandoned any idea of prying it off and performing a Jaed by ripping out a fortuitous fistful of wires. Besides, she reminded herself, with no power, the door would not magically spring open with its lock released.

But the door would also not magically hold itself shut, either, without power. She directed her headlamp along the seam where door and bulkhead met. Doors, at least on human ships, had emergency overrides. Surely the vakari would include such a thing as well. When she did not find anything that was obviously an emergency release, she reverted to a maneuver she might've named the Thorsdottir and slammed her entire body into the door, as if to shift it in its track, and, spreading her hands for maximum purchase of polysteel to polysteel, tried to slide it open. It remained shut.

The chrono on her HUD ticked off the seconds since commencement of the outage. *Surely* (and Rory was well aware how often she was thinking that word, and thought that it did not seem to mean what she thought it meant) the power would return presently, and if it did before she had gotten the door open, then she was still trapped.

We may blame desperation and the lingering effects of adrenaline that it took her so long to remember that she was an arithmancer, albeit only a skilled amateur and not a professional in any of the disciplines. Arithmancy was, at its most basic, about seeing what was there, since all the multiverse could be described in mathematic equations. With auras, it was a matter of shifting one's perceptions to perceive electromagnetic emanations. With turings, the same; but there, one might alter the machine reality, rewriting lines of code.

To open a door, she needed a Thorsdottir, or a crowbar, or more strength than she had. *Or* a way to manipulate the equations she saw, when she looked, describing the mass, the momentum, the force required to move the door. She knew the most basic inertial equation, and a few more sophisticated variants besides. Surely (let that word mean what it should, this time) she could find some way to change what *was* into what *could be*.

Rory recalled Messer Rupert's somewhat battered copy of

Ben'a'di's *Ruminations*, which theorized that probability could be actively influenced, not merely observed. In essence, the theory went: *if you rewrite the equation, reality will conform.* (This theory was also practiced, and is still practiced, by the vakari, but Rory would have known that even less.) Of course Ben'a'di was k'bal; their partitioned brains could perform calculations much more quickly than the human organ. Even the best of the human battle-arithmancers required time to create their hexes. Rory, nevertheless, attempted the impossible, driven by a combination of desperation and hope.

Sometimes that combination proves sufficient for success. In this case, it did not. But, by a fortuitous alignment of probability that we like to call luck, as Rory was attempting to adjust the door's inertial equation's variables, the ship's power returned. And in that moment, when the flux of electricity returned, bringing its own entourage of equations, her alteration of those variables worked. The door moved, and because the locks had not yet received their allocation of power, and had not woken up and reminded themselves that they were supposed to prevent the opening of doors—this door opened.

Only a few centimeters, but enough that Rory could get her hands into that gap and perform a Thorsdottir—pull, push, and drag—to force the door open enough to permit a human-sized hardsuit to squeeze through.

There were no guards or sentries on the other side. The corridor was empty, both directions, as far as her headlamp could ascertain. Power might have returned, but the teslas were even slower than the locks to make use of it.

Koto-rek had promised to return, and had been telling the truth when she'd said it. That did not incline Rory to wait for her.

She made it four meters up the corridor and was in the process of turning a corner before the emergency teslas returned, dim and red and throbbing sullenly. She froze, dropping into a crouch, as if that would somehow prevent observation in an otherwise empty, open area in which any person in a hardsuit would be as obvious as an explosion. And indeed, had there been any vakari in the same corridor at that moment, they would have noticed her. The nearest vakar, however, was scuttling across the cross-corridor intersection a mere two meters ahead, and did not look sideways. Rory remained undetected.

Truthfully, her decreased vertical silhouette proved helpful. The first vakar had been alone, unsuited, unarmed. The next two who passed by were clearly soldiers, weapons held loosely. They weren't running. That suggested a lack of urgency. That could be both good and bad. Soldiers ready to repel boarders would be more likely to shoot an unfamiliar hardsuit silhouette first, and ascertain who was inside it later. But boarders, once they arrived, would add another group of people prone to shooting at everything that moved. Perhaps the lack of urgency meant boarders were not imminent. Or that the vakari were confident in their ability to repel them.

Assuming the attacking vessel attempted to board at all. Rory supposed they might not, might simply try to destroy *Sissten* outright. That was also a problem. There was, in fact, nothing about her situation that was *not* a problem right now.

Her HUD advised of increasing heart rate and respiration. Rory remained in her crouch and tried to breathe more slowly. Panic served no one.

She was loose in *Sissten*. Now she needed a destination. *Vagabond* was the obvious choice. *Vagabond* was also a labyrinth away, the corridors clogged with vakari troops, and someone shooting at the ship from the outside, which could result in a breach, either of ordnance or an actual boarding team, either of which could prove fatal.

It should be noted here that most individuals—Thorsdottir, Zhang, even Jaed—would have wished for a weapon at this moment. Rory did not, though it is not a marker of moral superiority that the wish did not cross her mind. She was simply unaccustomed to bearing arms and to violent confrontation; her first reflex was not to point and shoot, but rather to converse and negotiate. If words failed—and she had every reason to think they would, in current circumstances—then her preference was stealth and avoidance of confrontation.

She could only hope that confrontation avoided her.

Rory sank her awareness partway into the first layer of aether. She could see the numerical descriptions of the material plane—of the solidity of the bulkheads and deckplate, of the composition of the atmosphere, of the temperature and movements of aether—overlaid on the actual, physical artifacts (or, in the case of gaseous substances, sort of shimmering and floating, which made the numbers much harder to read). The probability of, say, the bulkhead dissolving into liquid was infinitesimal, though she could see which variable conditions would need to change to make it happen. The probability of *this* corridor remaining empty at *this* moment was a much more complex calculation, lines and *lines* of alphanumerics and operations.

Rory attempted to replace variables to squeeze down the probability of *will there be a vakar coming this way* to *almost certainly not*. Then she commenced creeping through (as much as one can creep in a hardsuit) *Sissten's* labyrinthine corridors.

Whether because of luck or applied mathematics, the corridors remained empty. Rory was just about to congratulate herself, having just reached the final turn into what she was certain was the corridor where *Vagabond* was docked, when a new siren howled, of a particular stridency and urgency, and accompanied by a new white and flashing light from teslas not part of the usual parade of dull red.

Breach alerts.

If *she* were part of a hostile boarding party (which she had been, though only a few times, behind Thorsdottir and Zhang) she would choose a section of the target vessel already prepared for access: it was easier to storm an aetherlock than cut a new hole in an enemy ship. She could see *Vagabond's* berth, and the glow from the aetherlock that said *occupied*. She cast a panicked look both directions. There were as yet no vakari troops. But *Vagabond* was also in the middle of that corridor. If someone caught her in the open—

Then she would be either shot or apprehended. If she remained here, she would not get to *Vagabond* at all. Rory gathered her breath, drew her awareness back out of the aether, and launched herself down the passage.

And here again we see evidence of either luck or fortuitous probabilities. It is quite possible that Rory's hesitation, for which she at the time castigated herself, saved her life.

She was perhaps five meters from *Vagabond's* aetherlock when the equations drifting across her awareness became alarmingly certain that there would be an imminent hull breach. Time works differently in the layers of aether: the greater the distance from the material plane, the more slowly observed time seems to pass. So it was that Rory had what felt like thirty very long seconds to examine a tangled pair of calculations accompanied by a frantic squirt of code through *Sissten's* local automatic safety systems. A voidship possessed reflexes, and the Protectorate vessel was experiencing the equivalent of *drop the hot tuber before it raises blisters*. The calculations that prompted this reflex seemed to be a vessel currently docked in *Vagabond's* berth, which had aimed, locked, and charged its plasma cannons.

Vagabond was going to fire on *Sissten*. Rory wanted to shout *No* and *Don't* and *What are you doing* into comms already jammed mute and did, in fact, think those thoughts in rapid-fire succession, while her own reflexes arrested her body's forward momentum and sent her scrambling back the way she had come. But even before she could finish those thoughts, she saw that the calculations had changed again. *Sissten* was releasing its clamps on *Vagabond*, and with some force, essentially ejecting from its hull a potentially injurious passenger. Zhang was *abandoning* her. And even as she *knew* that there must be a reason, that she was not betrayed—and even as she felt a fierce relief that at least one of her friends had escaped—a separate despair threatened to overwhelm her. Where would she go now, where would she hide, *what* would happen? Time seemed to suspend itself (and this was purely a subjective experience), that single horrified moment stretching into forever, even as her body propelled her back the direction she had come.

And several events appeared to happen simultaneously:

In the aether, the *Vagabond*-is-about-to-fire calculations ran back to nothing, as that ship sprang away from *Sissten* and ceased to be a threat. On the deck, the sound of tearing metal jerked Rory from her introspection. Reflex made her head turn and look back. As a result, she stumbled and careened into the bulkhead, shoulder first, which caused her to rebound across the corridor and sprawl on the deck.

So it was that Rory was both prone and lying crossways, and thus able to see both directions in the corridor, when the first Tadeshi breach team came through the hull on a blank stretch of bulkhead just past where *Vagabond* had been berthed. Smoke curled off the metal, accompanied by the blinding flicker of a plasma cutter licking through the alloy, perhaps two meters off the deck, and two thirds of the way to the overhead.

The location and the amount of smoke suggested a small cutter, which in turn told her that the breach team was coming in a pod, not a small ship. Rory had grown up reading reports of the war between the Thorne Consortium and the Free Worlds of Tadesh before her mother and Vernor Moss negotiated their ceasefire, and she was familiar with tactics and equipment and the massive Tadeshi troop-carrying dreadnoughts. Unless she was very much mistaken (which no one thinks unless, paradoxically, they are almost completely certain of their own correctness), then the invaders must be Tadeshi royalists.

At the same moment, motion on her other side summoned her attention. By now she was as flat on the deck as her hardsuit would permit. From that vantage, the Protectorate troops rounding the curve into what had been a vakari-free zone seemed particularly tall and imposing. Their rifles seemed especially nasty. And the probability of them bounding gracefully over, while ignoring utterly, a lone, prostrate human in a corridor about to be invaded did not need arithmancy to calculate.

Rory's flattened vantage afforded her another discovery, as her frantic gaze skittered along the blank inner bulkhead. There was a door, in the direction of the breach pod, which presumably opened into either another corridor or a cargo bay of some kind, and which she couldn't hope to reach without being shot. But there *was* a grated panel down where the bulkhead met the deck, directly across from her. It was smallish, narrow, likely too small for an armored vakar, but perhaps just the right size for a human in a hardsuit. It clearly led *somewhere*, into the guts of the ship or into a compartment of some sort. And the panel lay scant centimeters from her helmet and within easy reach, should she stretch out her hands and push.

So she did.

A flare on her periphery told her that the breaching pod had completed its forcible entry. A section of *Sissten's* bulkhead detached from itself and, still smoking and white-hot on the edges, clanged onto the deck. She felt, rather than saw, the Tadeshi troops dropping down, and spared all her attention for the panel, which, as evidenced by the fine mesh overlaying it, covered some sort of ventilation shaft. The panel had so far resisted her push. There must be another way to detach it from the bulkhead. She just had to find it, and quickly.

'Slinger bolts and whitefire from the Protectorate rifles began stitching the space above Rory's head. She ignored them as best she could and continued to pry at the edges of the panel. The gap had been made for vakari talon-tips, not the blunter, broader human hardsuit, and refused accommodation. She blinked sweat from her eyes and willed herself flatter and therefore invisible, which was impossible, but, like the k'bal probability theory, a comfort to imagine as reality. The bolts and beams would not strike her because no one would shoot down at the deck. They had not even noticed her. She would find access to this *damned* panel in just a moment—

She did, suddenly: a depression in one corner, which, when pressed, initiated the panel's withdrawal and retraction into the bulkhead. Rory squirmed headfirst into the gap as it opened, scraping her hardsuit and earning alarmed reproaches from her HUD. Her hopes of finding a maintenance shaft, as she and Jaed had managed on *G. Stein*, were immediately dashed. Her headlamp illuminated a narrow space, no wider than the bulkhead itself, which, though it appeared hollow from deck to overhead, was both crowded with cables and filaments and insufficiently tall for her to stand up. She was effectively trapped, with (as Grytt might say) her assets hanging out in a crossfire.

But, *but*, there was another panel directly across from this one, which from the backside proved responsive to a hard push. Rory entertained a moment's hesitation. There is a saying, *better the devil you know*, which is trotted out whenever the speaker wishes to counsel conservative action. Rory considered that the devils she knew, in this instance, were shooting bolt 'slingers and whitefire rifles at each other, and that she was unarmed and unarmored, and—

Hello, new devil. Pleased to make your acquaintance.

—she shoved herself through the bulkhead and out the far side.

CHAPTER SEVENTEEN ═══════

The new devil appeared to be unoccupied. Rory tried to reseal the panel, but no, of *course* she'd broken it. She tried for what felt like a hundred times (five, her brain corrected) before she gave up and propped the panel against the bulkhead as close to in place as she could manage. It would not survive close examination from either side, but a cursory glance might not reveal it. Flashes of plasma and 'slinger-fire flickered in the corridor behind her, accompanied by the whine of weapon discharge and the *bang* of the occasional ricocheting bolt. With luck, the Tadeshi and Protectorate would be too busy killing each other to wonder where she'd gone. Rory prodded the darkness with her headlamp. Empty deck gleamed under the beam to its limits, even when she panned up. Her experience of cargo holds and storage spaces consisted of high stacks and narrow aisles and a sense of compression. This much openness seemed inefficient. She stood cautiously, one hand on the bulkhead for comfort rather than balance, and took an arms-length step into the dark, granting her headlamp another half-meter or so of range. She found several somethings, dark and bulky-looking, squatting in the dark, separated from each other by a reasonable aisle. Rory recognized within another three steps what she was looking at. She was fa-

miliar with cryostasis units and their many variations, particularly those designed for carrying persons. These appeared to be
the vakari versions: a little longer than a vakar, a little wider, and
almost perfectly, seamlessly cylindrical. Oddly enough, they were
elevated above the deck by perhaps a meter, and lined up in aisles.
And there was another oddness: that might be a seam there, at the
top, beside the radium-blue not-quite-glow that she assumed must
be a control panel.

She took another step and revised her hypothesis on two
counts. She could see script on the panel, rather than buttons or
switches or keys. Maybe a label? Then her headlamp found and
pierced a transparent portion, which appeared to be most of (perhaps all of) the top surface of the unit. Inside was a vakar still
wearing an armored hardsuit, complete with a visored helmet,
with one of those plasma rifles lying alongside. Neither face nor
visor was intact. There was a neat hole through both that appeared
to have been made by a 'slinger bolt, and on the jagged edges of the
visor, a dull gleam of what must be dried vakari blood.

Rory was not inclined to screaming when she was startled, but
she recoiled, and in so doing retreated rapidly and without direction until she backed into the neighboring unit, at which point she
whipped around and found herself staring at another deceased
vakar, this one possessed of neither a helmet nor, in fact, any head
whatsoever about the jawline, and another massive hole in the
mid-torso. She withdrew to a position precisely between the two
cryostasis units, and while cold sweat prickled the back of her
neck, swept her headlamp around the room. More identical units
appeared under the beam's sweep, rows and columns of them.

Coffins. She was surrounded by coffins. A part of her mind
registered satisfaction (*this* was where the dead from *G. Stein* had
gone). The remainder of it behaved exactly as one might suppose,

upon realizing the place in which one has taken refuge is, in fact, the ship's morgue. The twelfth fairy had conferred upon Rory courage, but that gift had in no way shielded her from shock or its close cousin, dread.

She vanquished those herself after a few moments of deep breaths. Dead vakari posed no threat. It was the living—of any species, at this point—that presented the greater peril. Nevertheless, as she navigated through the neatly arranged corpses, she did not touch any more of the units, nor gaze at all at their contents. The transparent panel seemed obscene, somehow, since it left the dead so exposed, still wearing the armor in which they had died. Perhaps, to the vakari, it was a mark of respect, or, or—Rory cast her gaze along the bulkhead, looking for some clue, and also for some distraction: because however firmly she intended *not* to look into the coffins, she found her gaze drawn there, and her HUD was quite alarmed now at the speed and force of her heart rate when she did so.

She found instead panels hanging face down from the overhead, suspended by meter-long lengths of cord, as if the dead in their coffins were the intended viewers. Rory could make little sense of what she was seeing. Columns and rows of characters which Rory took to be words, clearly hand-created by the application of pigment to a coarse, porous surface. Perhaps a sacred text. The monarchs of Thorne had long since embraced the certainty of alchemy and arithmancy over belief in the possibility of a greater authority than themselves, and so Rory had not been raised in religious custom. But Rory's mother, Samur, *had* been raised in one of the several Kreshti sects, so she was at least familiar with the concept. She set the helmet's video recorder to work. When she got out of there, *when* she returned to safety, she could examine the texts. She could try to understand. She could—

You could what? demanded the voice. It sounded a bit like a chorus of Grytt, Zhang, and Thorsdottir (which is to say, the people Rory thought of as most practical). *Understand vakari death-rituals? Stop this conflict? Befriend the vakari? Perhaps we should begin with getting off this ship alive, hmm?*

Rory sighed and looked at the main doors, which were directly across the morgue from the bulkhead where she had come through. That meant the battle was behind her, quite literally, and that she had another convolution of corridors as a buffer. She might be able to get *out* those doors and—

And do *what*, exactly?

The fact was, there was a firefight between hostile human boarders and hostile vakari crew ongoing and her own means of escape was no longer at its aetherlock (let that mean Zhang had escaped, and not that *Vagabond* had been vaporized). She was effectively trapped and surrounded by enemies with weapons or better arithmancy or both.

Rory was not given to despair or to profanity, but she had had a very trying last several hours already. She crouched down right where she was, in an aisle between coffins, and cradled her helmet in her hands, and indulged herself in both. And so it was, when the doors to the morgue slid apart, and the red emergency lights bled inside a moment before a large, armored shape began carving shadows into it, Rory was not immediately visible.

She let out one more yip of profanity under her breath, banished her despair, and shut off her headlamp. A quick check of arithmantic probability told her that if she remained unmoving, she had a small but not infinitesimal chance of remaining undetected.

That, obviously, was preferable. But also not probable, and so— Rory reordered her thoughts with grim practicality. She would not surrender. She just needed some manner of resistance, some plan, for when she was discovered.

Rory examined the morgue from her new vantage. The coffins rested on semi-solid platforms, metal arms and bracing cross-pieces and slim, metal legs which, from this vantage, were obviously meant to fold up into the bottom. At the moment, those legs were fastened to the floor, socketed into shafts so that they would not move during any failures of inertial hexes. Rory spent a frantic heartbeat or seven pondering *how* one would detach the coffin and maneuver it, if there were suspensors or some in-built propulsion system, some source of power she could cannibalize and re-purpose into a weapon or a distraction.

No, said the chorus of practical voices in her head. *This is not an e-vid. And also, you don't have time.* The invaders had paused on the threshold such that the doors could not close, and the light from the corridor continued to poke its red, slender fingers into the dark, interrupted or redirected when one of the armored folk moved. Their headlamps dragged fat blue-white fingers over all the surfaces, lingering in the same places Rory had.

From that she surmised they must be Tadeshi. Surely no Protectorate trooper would pause in the doorway of their own morgue. Her fear wrestled briefly with her need to confirm their numbers, until they moved and solved her conundrum. Now she could clearly see that yes, those were two human-shaped hardsuits, and that their wearers carried heavy 'slingers out and ready for use. It was at that moment that Rory saw the mecha, one aisle over, tucked down below the horizon of coffins. It was a multi-limbed, low-bodied model, vaguely arachnid (did the vakari have more than one world, and did any of those have spiders? File that away for later investigation), with several ominous-looking appendages, long and multi-jointed, at the apex of its domed back.

It was also waking up. She heard the hum of machinery first, the click of its limbs on the deck. She managed to remain motionless, somehow, with her heart trying to climb out of her throat. The mecha had not reacted when *she'd* come in. Perhaps it had not noticed. Perhaps it only noticed if people came through the conventional door. Its eight limbs unfolded and extended and, as it stood level with the coffins, it uttered a high-pitched sequence of sounds that Rory recognized as machine-distorted vakari speech. Probably a query of some kind, or a greeting. *Can I help you* or *who is dead now* or whatever a morgue-mecha would say.

The foremost Tadeshi trooper promptly shot it.

The wounded mecha staggered into a coffin platform with a terrible metallic shriek and collapsed in a knot of half-extended legs. Smoke curled from its back where at least three of the five bolts had struck.

Rory knew the typical load of a 'slinger, and realized that the soldier had emptied half a clip, *if* he'd begun with a full complement of bolts. His response must be surprise, verging on panic, rather than deliberate hostility. Had Rory been able to hack into the Tadeshi comm channels, she might have heard an epic rebuke involving the second trooper's assessment of the first trooper's parentage and capacity for intellect.

Instead, she noticed that one of those dorsal appendages on the mecha *was* a plasma cutter, and that it appeared to be intact *and*, because the mecha had listed laterally during its collapse, she could probably reach it without revealing herself.

The chorus of practical voices repeated their earlier admonitions: she was not some fictional hero who would win her way out of a desperate situation simply because genre convention demanded it.

Rory reached for the mecha anyway, carefully, steadily, making certain to keep her movements beneath the coffin's level and thus out of the Tadeshi hardsuit's likely horizon of motion detection. She hooked her fingers around the nearest mecha limb and pulled. The entire mecha itself was too heavy to move, but the arm unfolded obligingly. Rory wished she dared employ her headlamp; it was too dark to see whether or not there was a way to detach that plasma cutter, and if she did manage, whether it carried its own power supply.

She tugged on the cutter, then twisted it. It seemed disinclined to detach. Heat prickled her cheeks, embarrassment and anger and a rising frustration. This wasn't going to work. She pulled harder, causing the mecha to shift slightly. Not much of a noise, even less of a movement, but enough.

A Tadeshi headlamp—they used a type of particularly piercing blue-white tesla—lanced over the mecha's bulk. Rory jerked her hand back just as the beam crawled over the mecha, lingering on the outstretched appendage, then intensifying as the soldier came closer.

Rory thought several Grytt-worthy phrases and withdrew further under the coffin platform, reeling in fingers and elbows and a recalcitrant knee just ahead of the beam's nosy probing.

The beam swept up onto the coffin. Rory held her breath, rather unnecessarily, and watched the second soldier's booted feet, which had remained comfortingly near the morgue's threshold, move to follow the first. A second headlamp lit the bulkheads on the other side of the room and stabbed at the corners. And then, finally, that which she had dreaded came to pass: both soldiers began moving in tandem, separated by a row of coffins.

Rory's own experience of military maneuvers was limited to secondhand reports, video representations, and the simulations she'd played in *Duty Calls*, but it did not take expertise to predict that they were looking to clear the room of enemies, and that they were expecting vakari troopers, and that, inevitably, they would find her instead.

Her heart commenced crawling up the back of her throat, where it lodged, fluttering, competing with her breath. Surrender would buy her—*high probability*, the arithmancy was conclusive on that matter—an arrest and an escort to whatever vessel had launched the attack, which would put her in royalist hands. (There, the probabilities broke into branches of possibilities she chose not to follow; none of them ended well.) Or she could attempt a futile act of aggression or resistance right now, and get shot, and—*high probability*—die right here, in a vakari morgue.

There was a symmetry to that. An irony that Messer Rupert might appreciate, if he ever found out, which he wouldn't because she'd be too dead to tell him. Rory squeezed her eyes closed on an entirely different sort of hot prickling.

The boots came closer. The Tadeshi were not perfectly abreast, in their separate aisles. The one coming on her left, mecha-side, was perhaps a meter ahead of the other. She scooted sideways as far as she dared. When he drew even with her coffin, she would lunge sidelong and try to strike his knees and upend him. Then, if that worked, she would try to take his 'slinger, disable both soldiers, and make her escape.

The closer soldier stepped into the same row as her coffin. Two more steps, perhaps, to bring him within striking range. She kept a metaphorical one eye on the aether, while the probabilities lined up and she got her very *best* chance.

Three. Two. One.

Rory lunged, but she miscalculated the height of the platform, scraping against it and scrubbing away her momentum. She staggered gracelessly into the aisle, well short of her target. The soldier promptly backed up a step and prepared to fire. Rory threw herself at his midline, intending to strike his 'slinger aside, and perhaps grab it.

She missed a second time.

The soldier, startled, jerked back, raised his weapon, and fired as soon as he attained sufficient range. He had not, however, waited for a target-lock from his suit and so he, too, missed. Rory surged forward again, and this time she hit what she aimed for. Both hands closed around the 'slinger's barrel, and for a sickening moment she found herself staring into the muzzle's unblinking black eye. Then she ducked a shoulder and, at the same time, pushed up with both hands and twisted just as the soldier fired. His bolt howled past her, and she found herself visor-to-visor with her opponent, close enough she could see his face and his wide, startled stare as he recognized her—if not as Rory Thorne, at least as another human being in a ship full of vakari.

It was, ironically, that moment of species-recognition that saved Rory, because it was at that moment, just before the soldier would have wrested his 'slinger out of her grasp and shot her with it, that blue-white lightning crackled over his hardsuit, jabbing forked fingers over the horizons of his shoulders and up the sides of his helmet. It *looked* like plasma, but it acted like lightning, filling the crevices of the suit, blasting the battle-hexes inscribed on the surfaces into sharp visibility before reducing them to a greyish slag. A glowing, red-edged hole appeared at the center of his chest, exactly as if something very hot had bored a hole through him from the back, which of course it had.

The soldier's fingers spasmed and he released his weapon before Rory had quite processed what was happening, which left her in possession of her original goal—a 'slinger—as he toppled sideways. There came a second flash, this one aiming to Rory's right, and she knew without looking that it had struck the other Tadeshi and, presumably, rendered him as dead as her adversary. She glanced sidelong, and discovered that he had fallen so that she could see his face behind the visor. Smoke curled from his eyes, and—no. He was very much dead.

Rory blinked hard, and looked up, and found herself staring at the business end of a vakari weapon, the tip of which throbbed redly from residual heat. She dropped her newly acquired 'slinger—which she was holding by the wrong end anyway—and raised her empty hands.

The vakar's visor retracted. Sub-Commander Koto-rek lowered her weapon. Her nostrils pinched to slits and her cheeks washed a muddy violet.

"Rory Thorne," she said, like a curse. Then she stepped around Rory as if she were an errant mecha, pausing to examine the coffins that had been jostled in the firefight. Then, gently—so gently that Rory had to blink to be sure she was seeing truly—Koto-rek touched the coffins, and whispered something. Vakari syllables, slithering and clicking over each other in a reverent murmur. Rory's familiarity with prayer was secondhand, but she was certain that was what she was witnessing here.

Rory considered taking advantage of Koto-rek's distraction to make a dash for the corridor, but the sheer physical improbability of her success aside, she was not sure Koto-rek counted as *enemy*. There were Tadeshi out there, after all, and they had already tried to shoot her. Koto-rek had not. That seemed like an important distinction. She glanced past Koto-rek. There should be more vakari, shouldn't there? A sub-commander should not be running around alone on a ship in the middle of battle. But the corridor did not disgorge any escort, and in fact appeared empty.

Then there came an ominous hum from the rear of the morgue,

like a weapon powering up. Koto-rek's weapon. She must have re-considered the whole shooting business.

Rory, still riding the tattered coattails of her last adrenaline rush, could not summon the necessary panic to spin around. It would make little difference—front or back, her hardsuit would not withstand a shot. She did not need to stare down the business end of *another* hostile weapon before she died. She stared instead at the Tadeshi soldier dead on the deck in front of her, and at the deck which was visible through the rather macabre porthole Koto-rek had burned through his back, and supposed she would have a matching wound soon enough.

But because she was Rory Thorne, and disinclined by combi-nation of nature and fairy gifts to surrender in silence, she asked, as calmly as possible, "Why shoot me now?"

"There are *protocols* to be observed. *Rules* about aliens being in this place. Your presence is a desecration. The Writ is unambig-uous on that."

The Writ. That must refer to the script on the artifacts hanging over each coffin. Religious texts. Rory was wise enough to know that one did not offer an outsider's judgment on the validity of such a text's contents to an adherent of that faith.

Rory gestured carefully, a small motion of fingers and wrist, at the door, which remained ajar on an empty corridor. "I can leave."

"It is not—" Koto-rek exhaled like a plasma core venting steam. "You are already here. It is too late. It is a matter of contamination. Of, of orthodoxy."

Contamination was a word Rory associated with alchemical accidents and leaking sewage, not the behavior of people. She noted too that Koto-rek had said *alien*, rather than *xeno*, which would be considered rude among the persons of Rory's acquain-tance. An *alien* was an outsider. A *xeno* was merely someone of alternative biology. It might be a matter of translation, and Rory would have dismissed it as such, but coupled with *contamination* and the ominous *orthodoxy*, Rory suspected she was up against something she couldn't reason with.

Still, Koto-rek had not shot her yet, which suggested *she* could be reasoned with.

Rory turned slowly, carefully. Koto-rek's visor was still raised, her face still bare. Her chromatophores had sunk back to a sullen, charcoal neutrality. Her weapon was once again pointing at Rory's chest.

Rory summoned up sufficient saliva to swallow. Her voice must be clear. It must be steady. A princess—and for the moment she quite forgot she'd renounced that role—did not *squeak*.

"Then why haven't you shot me yet?"

The vakar's weapon did not waver. Her gaze, however, did, dropping and skating off to one side, to linger on a coffin as if the answer to Rory's question were etched in that brushed metal surface.

"It doesn't seem fair. You don't know the rules, and even if you did, you clearly didn't come here on purpose." She jerked her head at the displaced shaft-cover in the bulkhead. "You came through there, probably from the corridor where your ship was, which is what I'm *guessing* was your initial destination. And I see no evidence that you've defiled anyone." Koto-rek's chromatophores rippled as if something large and toothy swam just under the surface.

Rory remained quiet and unmoving. In the distance—and it was impossible to guess specifics, in the acoustics of ship architecture—Protectorate and Tadeshi troops engaged in a noisy firefight. They might be coming this way. If they arrived while she and Koto-rek were engaged in Koto-rek's crisis of conscience, well—

Dead is dead, Rory told herself, and relied on her patience. It had carried her through Vernor Moss's imprisonment, which had lasted much longer, though with decidedly fewer 'slinger bolts. The dread of that ordeal had been worse, on balance. If Koto-rek decided to kill her, it would go quickly.

For the second time in a handful of minutes, Koto-rek lowered her rifle. "I was never especially devout."

It sounded like an apology, though to whom, Rory could not guess. "Thank you."

At that moment, an especially loud spate of 'slinger-fire rattled through the corridors.

"Sss." Koto-rek's pigmentation rippled orange, then umber. "Come on, Rory Thorne. The *setatir* Tadeshi put a missile through *Sissten's* bridge. Our captain is dead, with most of the command staff. I am on my way to the auxiliary bridge to rendezvous with the surviving command. You will come with me."

It seemed wise to cooperate. The firefight seemed to be drawing closer. Nearer Rory's feet than she liked, the dead Tadeshi's helmet crackled with comm-signal. Rory did not look at the hole in his visor, through which the sound (and bits of the soldier's cranium) leaked. A call-sign, followed by a personal name, followed by a demand for a response, a sit-rep, and back-up.

The helmet's interior, slimily visible, blinked and flashed with a half-dozen teslas. One of those, Rory knew, belonged to a transmitter. Military hardsuits were networked together to facilitate rescue and retrieval. Assuming the other Tadeshi survived the fight, they would come here, looking for their personnel.

She swallowed, held her breath, and, with a glance of *please do not shoot* me at Koto-rek, went to the dead man's side. She crouched down, eyes averted (it helped that she could put most of her attention into the aether), and, with few moments of trial and error and hexing, disabled what remained of the suit's on-board systems. The teslas went grey.

From this familiar vantage, she could see the other dead soldier, the one Koto-rek had shot through the torso. She could hear no comm-leak, which made a queasy sort of *sense*, given the perforation was not in his helmet; an aetheric check showed the suit was transmitting nothing. As dead as its contents, Rory thought. Bile burned the back of her throat.

She told Koto-rek what she'd done, and why.

The vakar regarded Rory through narrow, thoughtful eyes. "Can you do that again?"

"Hex? Yes. But not offensively, if that's what you mean."

"Sss. That is what I mean, yes." Koto-rek stabbed her rifle at the 'slinger Rory had dropped. "Then can you use one of those?"

"I—yes."

"I won't ask if you're any good. That doesn't matter. Just pick it up, and point it at any *setatir* Tadeshi you see, and squeeze the trigger."

Rory pressed her lips together and retrieved the 'slinger. She managed to prime the weapon without looking at her hands. Fortunate, that a hardsuit negated any penalties to dexterity from sweaty palms and trembling fingers. She hoped she did not look as awkward as she felt, and suspected from the long look Koto-rek leveled at her that she did.

Heat crawled up her cheeks. One did not arm oneself unless one was willing to fire the weapon: Rory had heard that from Grytt, from Thorsdottir, from Zhang, more times than she cared to recall. But she had not appreciated what that meant, exactly, until she stood among the effects of that policy, two human dead and a dozen vakari.

Koto-rek regarded her without pity. Her visor slid down, sealing her flattened jaw-plates and narrow eyes behind oilslick opacity. Her voice came from the sides of the helmet, compressed and crackling.

"Can you hear me, Rory Thorne?"

"Yes." Rory sealed her own visor and, with a nudge of her chin, activated the ex-comms.

"You will walk beside me, on my left and a step behind. If we encounter Protectorate troops, you will let me speak. And if we encounter Tadeshi, be sure of your aim."

Koto-rek poked her head into the corridor. Then she flowed around the corner like oil and not like something composed of sharp angles and talons and extra joints.

Just pretend you are following Thorsdottir, thought Rory, and went after her.

CHAPTER EIGHTEEN

I t took a very long time for *Vagabond* to reach *Favored Daughter*. Jaed, therefore, had a great deal of time to report to Messer Rupert all that had transpired. The part about Rory—how they had been separated, where the vakari had taken her—Jaed had to recount several times: first to Messer Rupert, then to Messer Rupert and Grytt (at which point he discovered how to broadcast their replies to a speaker on the console, instead of only to his earpiece), and then when *Vagabond* had drawn close enough to *Favored Daughter* to manage visual communications, to Messer Rupert, Grytt, another tenju named Hworgesh, and a small collection of alwar (Captain Kahess, Adept Uo-Zanys Kesk, the communications technician known only as *lieutenant*, and a pair of security personnel, anonymous in their uniforms and matched scowls). Jaed thought all collections of alwar must be small, if this was a representative sample of the people. It was a joke he thought best to keep to himself, in the circumstances, though he thought Crow might appreciate it; the tenju had maintained a steady, subvocal stream of disapproval until he spotted Hworgesh, at which point Jaed and Rupert had been forced to table their conversation temporarily while Crow and Hworgesh shouted at each other in a language that sounded like a severe bronchial infection carried in a bucket of rocks.

That raucous interlude provided Jaed a moment to collect himself and to arrange to the story in his head. He wouldn't reveal Rose, not to anyone except Rupert and Grytt. The part of the story from Thorsdottir's perspective he could leave legitimately skeletal. But then the tenju finished their burst of conversation, and Messer Rupert was saying in his quiet voice, "Jaed, if you'd please."

At some point during his description of climbing through *G. Stein's* guts, a banging and scuffling commenced in the crew cabin, and the unmistakable sound of one woman swearing under her breath. Thorsdottir was coming forward. Jaed kept his attention resolutely focused on the adept. Her title sounded arcane and mysterious, and Jaed was painfully curious what it meant. The woman to whom that title was attached also looked arcane and mysterious, and also sufficiently formidable—despite her diminutive proportions—that Jaed did not dare take his eyes off her to glare at Thorsdottir. He saw, in his periphery, that Zhang was aware of Thorsdottir's movement, and had in fact turned around in her seat—which seemed a little unwise, given that she was flying *Vagabond* manually—to shake her head and make exaggerated movements with her mouth that Jaed supposed were versions of *what the hell are you doing* and *get back and sit down*.

"We didn't find anything of importance, and then the Protectorate ship showed up and we ran back to *Vagabond* and got off *G. Stein*," Jaed said, in a rush, just as Thorsdottir hurled herself against the back of his chair, dragging it down and requiring him to shift forward to counterbalance. He tried to fill the lens-feed with his visage, and so prevent any stray sightings of the person whom he'd just testified three separate times was otherwise engaged and unable to come forward.

He failed, of course. Thorsdottir dropped her head down almost onto his shoulder to squint into the screen. Her fingers gripped the cushions beside his head, knuckles straining and white, as she struggled for balance.

The adept's gaze flickered. The resolution of the image—which was only two-dimensional, not holographic—prevented Jaed from seeing the finer nuances of her expression, but his stomach clenched in precognitive dread.

"And who is this?" asked the adept, at the same moment Messer Rupert said, "Ah, Thorsdottir."

"Rory," said Thorsdottir, who was finding it harder to breathe than she had anticipated. "She's alive. We left her on the Protectorate ship. We need to get her back."

Messer Rupert exchanged a stricken look with Grytt. Jaed had spent enough of his life (reluctantly) around politicians to recognize the reason for their silence. They were passengers on a xeno vessel of unknown—at least to Jaed—political affiliation and interest in this endeavor. Rupert couldn't promise military aid. Rupert probably couldn't promise them tea if and when *Vagabond* docked with *Favored Daughter*. Jaed was more concerned with the adept, whose gaze on Thorsdottir reminded Jaed of his father's stare when Vernor Moss had identified something he wanted and had worked out a way to acquire it. She said nothing, which Jaed also marked as ominous, and which convinced him that she must be an arithmancer or alchemist or perhaps something of both. Fortunately arithmancy did not work across comms (did it? Surely not). He was just being paranoid and protective. There was nothing to sense. Thorsdottir was—fine. Or not fine, but not arithmantically interesting, either.

Not that he'd *looked* since Rose's repair efforts. Jaed let his eyes slide out of focus. The first layer of aether appeared, what Rory called the aura layer, which was mostly colors and soft edges and occasional obvious hexwork (like swarming hex-shards, if there were any present, which there were not). Thorsdottir's aura seemed especially vivid, the lava and sunset swirled with a nacreous chartreuse. The entire effect seemed to sparkle a little, as if there were shards of glass in the aura.

Rose. That was *Rose*. He ducked his chin and flicked a look at Zhang to confirm. Her aura, much the same palette as Thorsdottir's, was not sparkling. Neither was Crow's, and Jaed was momentarily struck (and distracted) by the difference not just in color, but also in quality: the tenju's aural discharge appeared more *texturey* than Zhang's, as if Zhang's were painted on a flexible, clear polysteel and Crow's on a dense, woven fiber. Then he reminded himself that tenju auras were not the issue here. Thorsdottir's was, and if he was seeing Zhang clearly, then he should also be seeing *hers* clearly, which meant that what he was seeing—those chips of glass, the shards, Rose—was accurate.

Now Jaed did let slip an exclamation, which earned him a sharp look from Grytt, behind Messer Rupert's shoulder, and Messer Rupert's raised eyebrow, and a startled side-eye from Thorsdottir. He offered no explanation. Instead, he pasted a sickly smile onto his lips that he hoped might pass for apologetic.

"While we are sympathetic to your concerns, Domina," the adept said smoothly, with a chin tip to Thorsdottir, "I am hoping to hear more of what transpired on the *G. Stein*, and how those events might have precipitated a Tadeshi dreadnought and a Protectorate vessel in pitched battle. Perhaps if we understand what transpired, we can better determine how to proceed from here."

"She doesn't want a fight," Crow interjected. "That's what she means. Not unless there's something in it for her."

The adept ignored Crow, but Jaed noted the flattening of her expression, and the half a dozen other signals that, at least on a human face, would mean Crow'd gotten it right.

"All right." Thorsdottir's left hand crept onto Jaed's shoulder, as did a fair portion of her weight. The seat, relieved of its burden, sighed back to fully upright. Her right arm and hand, still swathed in bandages, remained at her side, out of the camera feed's range. "Maybe I can offer you something of interest, then."

Jaed controlled a tight, teeth-baring smile. "No," he whispered, through clenched teeth and lips and with every fiber of his being.

"Trust me," Thorsdottir said under her breath. It might have been a question, or a command. Her fingers tightened on Jaed's shoulder until flesh creaked on the polysteel of his hardsuit. "Jaed couldn't tell you this part. He wasn't there. I didn't tell him what I found in *G. Stein's* hold."

The adept hoisted an eyebrow. "And what did you find?"

"A weapon. *Plans* for a weapon. Alchemical. Meant to take out a whole biosphere. Poison a planet."

Jaed fancied he could hear the hum of the alwar ship's engines, so silent did everything become.

"You found this weapon on the Tadeshi corsair, you said?" asked the adept, in the tones of someone who wants to be very, very sure of what she's heard. Behind the adept, the other tenju resumed their rumbling mutter. The captain looked like obsidian and adamant. She did not look surprised, though. Jaed squirmed inside the shell of his hardsuit.

"Yes," said Thorsdottir, answering the adept's question. "On the *G. Stein*. In the cargo hold. It was hidden among legitimate cargo. The Protectorate destroyed that ship, but they didn't find it. We did. And we still have it. Does that sound interesting to you?"

The adept turned away from the screen and consulted with someone in rapid, xeno syllables. One of the alwar on *Favored Daughter* darted off-screen. Rupert looked as official as Jaed had ever seen him. Grytt looked like Grytt, with perhaps a bit more disapproval.

Thorsdottir, when Jaed looked at her, seemed grim-lipped and triumphant at the same time.

"You know," he said, taking advantage of the momentary respite, "we have no idea what the politics are here."

She glanced at him. Her eyes were clearer than they had been, the whites mostly void of red. "I know."

"And you might've just stepped in the middle of something really complicated."

"She has," said Crow. He sounded pleased. "Right in the middle. Both feet."

Thorsdottir ignored him. "We need to get Rory back, Jaed. I'll do whatever's necessary to make that happen."

Jaed envisioned *Favored Daughter* turning its weapons on *Vagabond*. From the look on Zhang's face, she was thinking the same thing. He and Zhang had that in common: caution. Zhang's came from a dislike of surprises; Jaed knew his reticence came from a fear of making mistakes through bold action. He envied Thorsdottir. Admired her. And at the same time, he wanted to vomit.

The adept returned to the screen. Her hair and robes were still neat, flawless in their arrangement, and yet she gave the impression of great dishevelment.

"Yes," she said. "We are very *much* interested in whatever information you might have."

"Right," said Thorsdottir. "Then here's the deal. You help us get Rory back, and we'll tell you whatever you want to know."

————

Thorsdottir knew, the moment the words slipped out of her mouth, that there would be repercussions. She read that truth in the way Messer Rupert's face smoothed over into his Vizier mask, and the way the adept with the long name's eyes (were they really a burgundy-red sort of color?) sort of . . . lit up. Not quite smiling—no teeth, anyway—but a tiny lift in the corner of her mouth that, if it meant the same thing for alwar, indicated satisfaction.

But more telling than the visual evidence was the audible: Zhang's groan, which barely qualified as a sound at all, but which Thorsdottir heard as if Zhang were sitting beside her. An effect of Rose's repairs, maybe. Or just that she knew Zhang that well.

Jaed, she could not see, except in ghostly reflection in the screen. She watched the shell of his ear go the faintest bit red, but that was the extent of his physically perceptible reaction. He didn't sigh, or groan, or even hold his breath. But she thought that, if a man could grow spikes and spines and hard edges, he had just done so.

"We will meet you when you arrive," said Messer Rupert smoothly. "Grytt and I, at the aetherlock."

"Acknowledged," said Jaed, and cut the connection.

Here it comes, thought Thorsdottir.

Jaed turned so that she could see his profile. The red that dusted the tops of his ears had found his cheeks, as well. He looked feverish. Or murderous.

He licked his lip, once and twice, with the air of a man trying to choose his words wisely.

"You can't," he said finally. "Bargain, I mean. With Rose."

On a different day, Thorsdottir might have greeted Jaed's declaration with laughter, or at least a smile: she did not take orders from *him*, of all people. Or anyone, anymore. But today, right now, she was too busy holding herself upright on his shoulder and trying to decide if she'd need his help and goodwill to return to her seat in the rear cabin.

She *would* need his help. Almost certainly. Unless Zhang volunteered, and Zhang was very deliberately focused on piloting. His goodwill might depend on the answer she gave him, for which he was apparently still waiting.

Thorsdottir cast back to what he'd said. It didn't *need* an answer, but fine. "Just did." And because her (admittedly) terse response only made the red spots on his cheekbones get brighter, she added, with some impatience, "For Rory, Jaed."

"Rory—" Jaed closed his eyes and visibly counted to five. Then ten.

And then Crow turned fully around, fast enough his hooks clicked and rattled across his armor. "You're gambling. The Empire's out for itself. You don't *trust* the alwar. Not with something like this."

Thorsdottir peered at him. She'd known what a tenju was only slightly longer than she'd known about alwar. "So we trust you instead? The—whatever your political organization is?"

"Tribal affiliation," Crow said mildly. "The name of which doesn't interest you, and yeah, you'd be better off, if what you want is *not* to use this weapon. We're not much for alchemy and arithmancy. But *they* are. And you hand them your weapon, they'll use it. Maybe not on *you*—probably not—but they *will* use it on someone, somewhere."

Thorsdottir could not find a response to that. To demand *how do you know* seemed childish and also an invitation to a biased historical treatise on interspecies relations. It was clear the tenju bore no great love for the alwar, although there seemed to be some treaty between them. Crow's account would be prejudiced, and anyway, it was clear he believed it.

She wasn't sure she didn't, but it didn't *matter*. She—they, *all* of them—needed to get Rory back.

And she needed to sit down. Now. Or very, very soon.

Jaed must have sensed it. He bit his breath off and spat it out. "You need my help getting into the back?"

"I—yes. Please."

Jaed's arm around her was steady, neither gentle nor rough. No, it was *polite*. A, a *duty*. Thorsdottir examined the sudden spike in her chest that had nothing to do with whitefire batons and burns and a nanomecha invasion.

She should apologize, but she wasn't sorry. She was just sorry he was so upset. And she was as sorry for herself to be on the wrong end of his regard as she was that she'd upset him. So she said nothing at all—that seemed simpler—and let him guide her back to her seat. She thought he would leave, but he stayed looming over her, his body across the open hatch. Then, with a sudden grimace, he whipped around and sealed the hatch behind him.

Thorsdottir felt oddly relieved. Better an angry Jaed coming at her than cold, distant, dutiful Jaed.

And yes, he was angry. "You can't," he said. "Listen. You *cannot* bargain with Rose. They are dangerous. They are a genocidal collection of arithmantic nanomecha. They are meant to kill planets, do you not get that?"

All right. Perhaps she preferred cold and dutiful after all. "I get that. I read the documents, same as you. But Rose doesn't *want* to be a weapon. Why do you think Rose turned off all those cryotubes? So the vakari wouldn't find them when they boarded again. They would've died if we hadn't taken the clipping, and they knew that."

Jaed stared at her. "How do *you* know that?"

"A hunch. My gut. They were *so scared* of the vakari, Jaed, you don't even know. Besides. This is *Rory* we're talking about. There's no price—"

"Oh stop. Rose also attempted to kill Rory. You weren't there. I was."

"If Rose'd *meant* to kill her—"

"What, then we wouldn't be having this argument? Rory'd already be dead? Do you not see how that logic doesn't work?"

"I'm saying, it should count that Rose *didn't* kill her." Thorsdottir shook her head a little too sharply for current physical conditions. "We can trust them."

"We can—" Jaed looked up, as if seeking wisdom from the cabin overhead, and tossed his hands in the air. The drama of the gesture was rather lost in the small area, where he had to mind the swing of his forearm so he did not hit Thorsdottir. "Rose is *nanomecha*. Operative word: *mecha*. Whether or not they've got true sentience, they're still *programmed*. Rose has *command codes* that trigger their programming remotely, and which for all we know the Tadeshi already have, or will be getting in a more successful delivery."

"Or *we'll* intercept them."

"That doesn't matter! Command codes. Mecha do what their program directs. Rose may not want to, but what I'm saying is, Rose won't have a choice."

"Then maybe Messer Rupert can hack them, or that adept, or someone like her."

"Sure. Then someone *else* gets control of the arithmantic bioweapon. Great plan."

"Well, what *else* was I supposed to do? Just leave Rory behind?"

"How about, wait until we'd gotten on board so we could talk to Messer Rupert? How about, wait until we had more of an idea *what* we're stepping in, here?"

"That doesn't matter. Rory—"

"Rory wouldn't want this!" Jaed's face was fully red now.

"How do you know that? I've known her—"

"No, you've been *in her service*. That's not knowing her. That's doing what you're told."

Thorsdottir recoiled. "And *you* know her better? She holds us all at a distance. You follow her around, same as we do." (Zhang, who could hear through the hatch every word, muttered "Leave me out of this," to which Crow offered a sympathetic noise.) Thorsdottir's own face was red now, her skin too tight and hot. Then she weighted her words with razors and flung them into his face. "No, take that back: not the same. We've got a *reason* to be here. You're here because you've got nowhere else."

Jaed's mouth tied itself in a bitter knot, but he neither broke eyelock nor retreated. A part of Thorsdottir was proud of him for that. "No. I'm here because I'm scared of sheep. And politics. And being responsible for anyone else. That's what *you* do: you and Zhang, you're all about taking care of Rory. For you, there's nothing bigger that protecting her. For *Rory*—there is. She doesn't think about people, she thinks about ideas. She's Messer Rupert's that way. You're Grytt's."

"And you're whose, Vernor Moss's?" It was petty, small, and Thorsdottir regretted it the moment the words left her mouth.

Jaed pressed his lips into a white, furious line. "Rose is a weapon," he said, in the tones of a teacher faced with extreme recalcitrance. "With command codes. And now Rose is part of *you*. So what do you think happens when someone activates those codes, with those nanomecha inside you?"

She had not thought about it. She was not going to *start* thinking about it right then. "I'm hardly going to turn into a *weapon*."

"No," Jaed said, light and breathless and as furious as Thorsdottir had ever seen him. "You will die. And I do not want that to happen."

The moment of revelation has been described by writers as a flash, a bolt, a violent, shocking discharge of electromagnetic energy. To Thorsdottir, it felt more like a kick to the gut. Jaed was not concerned about some larger implication of Rose's deployment, not worried about hypothetical biospheres and hypothetical people. He was worried about *her*. Not Rory. Not—all right, be fair, probably *also* the genocidal capabilities of sentient arithmancer-nanomecha, because Jaed also thought more widely than his immediate acquaintances and situation, and also Rory, but mostly about *her*, Thorsdottir.

She retained sufficient wit to keep that realization to herself. She wasn't sure if Jaed was even fully aware of it. She hoped—she did not know what to hope. That he was aware? That he wasn't? And if he was right about Rose's—not contamination, not infiltration—permeation, maybe? Decide what to call it later—if Jaed was right, then she had become as much of a threat as Rose to, well, everyone. Anyone. Until Rose was activated, Thorsdottir was the same thing as a bank of cryounits.

And if Jaed was right, Rory *wouldn't* want Rose in the wrong hands. But she'd already promised. So what to *do* about it now?

(In the cockpit, in the sudden absences of raised voices, Zhang and Crow exchanged glances. "They've killed each other," Crow said. "No," said Zhang, who was not unobservant, even if the subjects of her observations might be. But she would not hazard any further guess at the silence.)

Jaed and Thorsdottir were in fact staring at each other, as the red receded in both their faces, along with the anger, leaving a wrung-out, faintly nauseous (and in Thorsdottir's case, more than faint) ache behind.

Thorsdottir dropped her gaze first. And so she was not watching when Jaed sealed his visor. She heard the click and looked up at once, but by then he had turned away, so that she could see the precipice of his cheekbone and the curve of his lips as they moved. His gaze drilled into the HUD, and Thorsdottir could see the reflection of text across his pupils and the icy-pale blue of his eyes.

"What?" said Jaed, for although Thorsdottir believed it was his impulse that had led to the sealing of the visor, it was in fact Rose's prompting, in the form of red flashing teslas on the rim of his helmet, that had arrested his attention.

And, let us be truthful: Jaed was relieved for an excuse to temporarily suspend his conversation with Thorsdottir. On a planet, or a station, or even a bigger ship, he would have walked away, seeking physical distance and, with that, emotional perspective. But instead, he withdrew into the sealed environment of his suit, made sure of deactivated ex-comms (one only makes that particular mistake once), and snapped, at a volume too great for such an enclosed space, "What, Rose?"

need flesh

Jaed was no more comforted by the sentiment than Thorsdottir had been. He was more familiar with Rose's technical specifications, and so made a leap of intuition where the nanomecha's vocabulary failed. "You need flesh to exist. And by flesh, you mean organic matter. We kinda figured that out."

no. need flesh to . . . Rose trailed off. Jaed waited. . . . *bloom.*

That was no more comforting. Jaed supposed—correctly—that Rose meant they needed bodies as fuel to execute their unpleasant primary objective. Rosebushes were all very well and good, but nanomecha needed energy, and organic bodies were basically alchemical batteries. Flesh (ugh) made a good fuel. Break it down, remake it, and stop thinking about the details *right now.*

Jaed knew Thorsdottir was watching him. He knew she would demand a reason and recounting of this conversation, including, perhaps, some reason for its timing.

I'd like to know that, too, thought Jaed, and so he asked. "Why tell me this now?"

have flesh now

"You mean Thorsdottir."

yes

"You could've had Thorsdottir on *G. Stein*. You had her hardsuit."

no

He recalled Thorsdottir's defense of Rose. "Because you did not want to hurt anyone. But you *did* want to hurt me and Rory, and you did actual damage, so why not, um, invade us, or whatever?"

Rose hesitated. Letters flickered, half-realized, as if the nanomecha were scrolling through the alphabet, trying to find the correct symbols.

code, Rose said finally. *hex.*

Right. He and Rory were arithmancers. Not very good arithmancers, maybe not much of a threat to a vakar or an adept or whatever sort of people had created Rose, but Rose wasn't much of an arithmancer, either.

fix Rose

It took Jaed a moment to process, both because he was thinking, and thus distracted, and because when he did read the words, he did not immediately understand. Fix meant repair, except Rose had used *repair* already to refer to healing Thorsdottir's wounds. *Fix* must mean something else. You fixed what was broken—oh.

Jaed found his mouth suddenly dry. "Fix *you*. How would I do that?"

> *code*
> *fix code*
> *fix*

Jaed closed his eyes. Rose's request followed him, hanging on the back of his eyelids.

"Fix you so that you won't . . . be able to bloom?" Maybe it would be that simple. "I'm not a very good arithmancer. You want Rory. Maybe Messer Rupert."

Of course Rose couldn't answer, with his eyes closed. He opened them again.

fix flashed on his HUD. *fix no more rose*

Oh. Oh no. Jaed could feel Thorsdottir's eyes on him. He considered opening the visor and telling her what Rose had said. She would object. She would tell him, *don't you dare*, which would let him, well, not dare.

Someone would take the responsibility of the hard decision. He had just reproached Thorsdottir for offering Rose for Rory. Said that Rory herself wouldn't make that deal. He believed that. Rory was . . . not cold, never cold, but she was a princess. She made decisions for other people, whether or not she wanted to. Decide not to marry Ivar, start a civil war. Decide to run to Samtalet, find an alchemical super-weapon.

Thorsdottir had accused him of being his father's, but . . . that wasn't true. His father wanted the same power Rory rejected. Jaed had never wanted that. Never wanted anything except to be left alone, out of everyone's machinations. Free from expectation and manipulation and (painful truth) from responsibility.

Vernor Moss had made *terrible* decisions, but he'd made them. Rory Thorne had made some bad ones, too, but they were hers. Now Thorsdottir had thrown Rose out to these alwar Empire people as a bargaining chip, *very bad* decision, but her responsibility, and one that they'd all have to see through.

And now Rose was asking him to *fix* them, the effects of which might take Rose's threat out of the equation, but also Rose themself. Rose was, in essence, asking him to kill them. So yes, he could open the visor, tell Thorsdottir, let her decide. Or he could make his own decision, the weight of which already ached. There was just one further thing he needed to know.

"Will fixing you hurt Thorsdottir?"

no

"All right," he said, as if it were easy. As if this moment would not haunt him the rest of his life. "Then tell me what I need to do."

Rose showed him a few lines of code, and a brace of variables. It was an appalling vulnerability—so very *little* defense. No wonder Rose hadn't wanted to deal with him or with Rory or the vakari and their scary arithmancy. Rose was vulnerable unless Rose was completely concealed.

It was not difficult to rewrite that code—a dip into the appropriate layers of aether, that was all, a switch of variables—and it was the hardest thing Jaed had ever done.

Thorsdottir had watched the expressions crawling over Jaed's face, and come to a few conclusions about the nature of his conversation with Rose. That his face had settled onto queasy conviction did nothing to settle her own nerves.

Then his visor opened, and his eyes settled on hers, and held steady. "It's fine. Rose is—Rose isn't dangerous anymore."

Thorsdottir ruminated on the nature of *fine*, and its various meanings, and decided that Jaed's version meant *totally beyond salvage*. "What happened?"

"Like I said, Rose is no longer a danger. I mean—they're still nanomecha, but they don't, they can't, weaponize."

"The command codes won't work anymore? That's what Rose says?"

Jaed nodded: barely a movement of the head, accompanied by a jaw ratcheted so tight that Thorsdottir feared for his molars. "Jaed, *what* is the matter?"

"Rose has, ah. Deactivated the part of themself in my suit. Everything that's left is now in you."

"And that's why the codes won't work?"

"No. That's because of arithmancy. I can explain what I did to Messer Rupert. It won't make any sense to you."

There was an untruth lurking in his words, but Thorsdottir was too tired, and too worried, to dig it out. She wanted peace restored with Jaed, and she wanted Rory back, and she was not totally sure of the order of those desires. "But it's fixed? I can talk about Rose without giving this alwar empire a weapon?"

She didn't know why Jaed flinched at the word *fixed*, or why his affirmation—"Yes, it's fixed"—sounded so brittle. "But I still don't want you volunteering yourself to any xeno labs, all right? Tell Messer Rupert everything. Let *him* do the negotiating."

It was, if not exactly a reversal, at least a significant redirection of his position. Thorsdottir considered asking again what had transpired in Jaed's conversation, and once again, declined to do so. He was unhappy, that was obvious, and she guessed (correctly, though not in the way that she thought) it was because the parts of Rose in his hardsuit had decommissioned themself. Why that bothered him, she did not understand; there was more Rose, and besides, Rose had already decommed the vast majority of themself on *G. Stein* and survived.

Jaed did not enlighten her, and Thorsdottir decided that it did not matter. Jaed was upset, she was upset, *everyone* was upset. It would be better when they got to *Favored Daughter* and reunited with Messer Rupert and Grytt.

In that, Thorsdottir was wrong.

CHAPTER NINETEEN ≡≡≡≡

M uch ink, both literal and, post-turing, pixelated, has been dedicated to describing battle. There are entire genres of fiction dedicated to its depictions in lovingly lurid detail, to convey a sense of verisimilitude to a reader who will experience battle only vicariously, but who may, after reading a particularly exciting account, regret that they cannot smell the hot metal themselves, or feel the tingle of adrenaline in their fingertips. Some of those readers then seek the experience through gameplay. Rory herself had played *Duty Calls* extensively in her teen years for that very reason. And while she had told herself that a set of three-dimensional game-goggles did not convey reality, she was disappointed in hindsight by how very inaccurate the game had been. Games, after all, are meant to be fun. War, by its nature, is not.

Neither *Duty Calls* nor fiction express a nostalgia for how slippery blood can render deckplate, or the way one's nose can itch inside a visor, or how the flashing reports of a HUD can bewilder and frustrate a person trying to see past them and focus on the people who are trying to shoot her, while neglecting to place a red indicator of *enemy* over individuals for whom that designation is appropriate. At least in Rory's current context, anyone coming at her who was *not* a distinctive vakari silhouette qualified as an enemy, and thus removed ambiguity.

Rory resolved, if she survived this adventure, to write an accurate, unromantic account of battle. She had not attempted another dip into the aether to check probabilities of that survival, having her attention fully occupied with handling the 'slinger, which was larger and more unwieldy than she had imagined, and with maintaining her balance on the aforementioned blood-slick deck. The ex-comms, both regrettably and fortunately, were sensitive enough that she could detect the squelch of Koto-rek's boots through human remains.

They had worked their way through the corridors successfully so far, mostly because Tadeshi troops were not quiet, and Koto-rek knew her ship: where to hide, where to lay ambushes. Rory had watched the vakar scribe what she supposed were battle-hex traps: a flurry of equations flickering between the first layer of aether, easily visible even when one was reloading a 'slinger clip and thus paying only partial attention, and the next, slightly deeper layers, as if the vakar's hexwork stitched through several at once. Subsequent encounters with the Tadeshi, after such preparation, involved misfired 'slingers and what appeared to be malfunctioning battle-suits. Rory suspected an attack on the suits' arms-turings, which would render the soldiers inside dependent on manual aim and perhaps even disable their HUDs. As her hardsuit possessed neither armor nor arms-turing, she concentrated on staying somewhat behind Koto-rek and, when afforded an opportunity, aiming at the seams in Tadeshi armor and pretending (without much success) that she was playing an upgrade of *Duty Calls.*

As a strategy, it worked well, until it did not.

The final skirmish went badly precisely because it came upon them suddenly. A hatch unspiraled with the abruptness of mal-function or coercion. Behind it, the vakari crewpeople who had been on the other side spilled into the corridor. Only one of them armed, neither armored (nor with the limited protection of hard-suits), both injured. There was a moment of hurried communica-tion during which Koto-rek inserted herself both verbally and physically between Rory and the business end of the armed vakar's weapon, and then pursuing Tadeshi came boiling around the bend of the corridor like an infestation of hostile insects, and instead of finding two unprepared vakari, found Koto-rek instead.

From the ensuing firefight Rory learned that one could empty an entire clip of 'slinger bolts, and manage a competent reload, and *still* feel extraneous to the battle's outcome. Simple probability (barely a glance to check) assured her that at least some of her bolts had hit their targets. Rory assumed the same for the unar-mored vakar who crouched over their fallen companion, making a shield of their own body, while firing at the Tadeshi. But it was Koto-rek who turned the battle, and not with skill at arms.

Rory's experience of battle-arithmancy, until now, had been raw fantasy, the stuff of genre fiction and media, in which arithmanc-ers could, in real-time, manipulate the language of the multiverse: bend light, or turn projectiles aside, strip the phlogiston from a room or fill and ignite it. Messer Rupert had been at pains, when Rory was a child and convinced of the possibility of all things, to tell her that arithmancy wasn't *like* that. It couldn't *do* that. A dili-gent practitioner (he said, hoping to instill that diligence) might be able to, oh, read an aura, or hack her way past a turing, or, if she was not the princess of Thorne, perhaps specialize in battle-hexes, which were inscribed on the surfaces of warships and weapons. But in no way, he was clear, would she be able to *fight* with arith-mancy the way people fought with 'slingers or ships fired missiles.

Koto-rek, however, could use her arithmancy that way. And she did. Rory could not spare the attention to watch closely, much less to peer into the aether and ascertain on which layer Koto-rek operated, or what her equations looked like, but she could see the effects clearly enough. The Tadeshi's bolts slewed aside, ricocheting off the bulkhead and overhead and sometimes, *most* improbably, striking the person who'd shot it. Light from the corridor teslas transformed into tightly focused beams that did not *quite* become lasers, but which did disorient, perhaps even blind, the sensors on a battle-suit's helmet. (That was a guess only; Rory had no way to test the theory, but she could see flailing from the troopers when a beam struck them). And there was a suspicious explosion, complete with visible flames, in the corridor behind the Tadeshi, which imbalanced several of them, and which sent a wave of heat rolling over Rory's hardsuit, alarming its sensors, and which triggered *Sissten's* fire-safety protocols and pinched the hatch closed, dividing the Tadeshi forces in general and one unfortunate soldier in particular.

When it was over, Rory beheld the scorched, bloody deck, and, having raised her visor, smelled hot metal (and less happily, the burned flesh of two species), and learned that Koto-rek's competence did not guarantee her invulnerability. The vakar had taken fire despite her bolt-turning prowess. New scoring and scorches appeared on her armor, and when Koto-rek raised her visor, she revealed a scowl of especially prickly proportions.

"Are you all right?" Rory asked.

"Yesss." Koto-rek peeled off a fraction of her scowl, and donated it to Rory. "I do not see any hexes on that hardsuit to account for your good fortune."

Rory offered a tepid smile. "I stayed down," she said. "And behind you."

"A princess who follows orders. The nine dark lords smile upon us all."

Rory declined to comment on the temporal appropriateness of Koto-rek's sarcasm, and filed *nine dark lords* away for later research.

"What about them?" She indicated the other two vakari, one of whom lay prone on the deck, and unmoving, in a pool of blood which was ominously wide. The other vakar crouched over the wounded one. Now, hearing Rory's voice, they turned toward her, hissing and clicking out a series of angry-sounding syllables, which Rory took as rejection with emphatic embellishments. She wished she had time to deploy a translation hex, but the outburst was over before she could even begin the equations.

Koto-rek turned her void-cold stare at the angry vakar.

"Show respect," she said in GalSpek. "This is a *princess*." Then she spat out a stream of hisses and clicks.

Whatever she said, it did not ameliorate the other vakar's concerns. A small battle ensued, waged in locked eyes and bared teeth. The other vakar's were etched in shades of green, so that it looked like they had a mouthful of vines. Whatever the conflict, Koto-rek triumphed. The subordinate vakar flattened their jaw-plates and ducked their head as if expecting a swat on the skull. Then they thrust their wounded arm at Rory and looked resolutely elsewhere.

This vakar was a little lighter skinned than Koto-rek, a little smoother, smoky greyish brown instead of pebbled charcoal and a yellow-green wash through her chromatophores. They wore a variant of the Protectorate military uniform, though without any armor. The large, triangular panel on the elbow of one sleeve had been torn away. A set of spikes gleamed underneath, sweeping back from the vakar's elbow in a graduated ridge. Blood leaked from a gash just below the joint.

A *very* sharp people, these vakari.

"Well," said Koto-rek. "Help her, Rory Thorne."

"Ah. How do I do that?"

"Apply pressure," Koto-rek suggested. "And then cover the wound with something to soak up the blood. Is it not the same with your species?"

"It is." And so Rory did so, using a bit of uniform from the fallen (oh, just say *dead*) vakar. That earned her a flared-jaw, red-cheeked reaction from her unwilling patient. More interestingly, contact with the vakar's blood on her gloves made her HUD flare up and advise her of the presence of a mild, irritating toxin, and to keep her suit firmly sealed. Rory wished for time and opportunity for a closer examination.

The wounded vakar neither spoke nor struck and, when Rory had finished binding the wound, ground out a passable "thank you," in a more heavily accented GalSpek.

"You're welcome," said Rory. Then, because it seemed only polite, "I'm Rory. What's your name?"

The other vakar stared at her. Then she bared her mouthful of vines.

"This is Assistant Engineer Vigat," Koto-rek said, when it was clear that green-toothed grin was to be Rory's only answer. "She was on her way to the engine core, attempting to take her post when—well. You saw. This complicates matters for us. The auxiliary bridge is only accessible through engineering."

"Surely there's another way in."

"There is. But the engine *core* is in the engine room, and it is apparently the invaders' goal. If the Tadeshi compromise that, we are all dead, Rory Thorne. Seal your visor. Vigat," and then Koto-rek produced more of the bitten-off clicks, and Vigat withdrew to the rear of their trio. Koto-rek touched a gloved talon to the hatch controls, tracing the perimeter of the sensor pad in what Rory supposed was some kind of hexwork override.

The hatch opened onto a corridor scorched black by a combustion which should have been impossible, because voidship safety protocols scrubbed phlogiston from the atmosphere. It looked as if, instead of scrubbing, the filtering hexes had reversed themselves and transmuted benignly breathable aether into phlogiston. Which, Rory supposed, is exactly what they had done, at Koto-rek's arithmantic request.

Rory walked past the scorched hulks of Tadeshi armor without looking: chin up, eyes forward, exactly as if she were back on Thorne and trapped in some formal event where performance was everything. If she looked, she might gag, and there was no place for vomit in a hardsuit. This was war, wasn't it? Not what she had played at in *Duty Calls*. Not even what she had watched on *G. Stein's* recording. This was real, and ugly, and awful, and as much as she disliked the Tadeshi ideology and *everything* Vernor Moss had stood for, she just wanted it over, right then, whatever it took, so that no one else had to die in a puddle of blood and fire. Of course she knew that the royalist government would have other opinions on ending the war. The Confederation of Liberated Worlds might, too; Dame Maggie would never surrender, nor return to the old status quo. And the royalists would stop at nothing less. And where the vakari Protectorate fit into that—

Rory looked at Koto-rek, striding up the corridor, and back at Assistant Engineer Vigat trying to keep pace, with the bandage dangling damply from her arm like a sodden flag. The Protectorate was involved now, at least with the royalists, in a combative capacity. Perhaps peace lay in alliance: the Tadeshi and the Confederation might declare a truce in the face of a common enemy. Or the Protectorate might ally with the Confederation against the Tadeshi.

In no scenario that she could imagine did Rory see *everyone* sitting down and working out a treaty. Peace was simple in concept, but difficult to achieve. History said as much. *Human* history, limited to the Merchants League and the Consortium and the Free Worlds (and the unaffiliated worlds, too numerous to list here), was a chronicle of conflicts. She had no idea what Protectorate history was like, but she suspected peace was no simpler for them. Perhaps it was not even desirable. The vakari were losing this particular battle, but it was clear that they possessed superior arithmancy and weaponry, and that a long-term conflict—assuming they had the resources—would tilt in their favor.

The royalists had to know that already. If they were inclined to peace with the Confederation, they should have already made overtures. (Perhaps they had. Perhaps Maggie had declined to negotiate.) Vernor Moss had been arrogance incarnate, but Rory didn't think him so proud he'd prefer extinction to compromise.

Genocide, however: the Tadeshi royalists, which Moss still commanded (last Rory had checked), had commissioned Rose from somewhere, so it was clear he didn't mind obliterating whole planets.

Her steps faltered. She turned to look back at the dead human soldiers in the corridor. The Tadeshi command knew about vakari and the Protectorate. So what if Moss and his commanders had commissioned Rose *not* for the Confederation's annihilation, but for the Protectorate's? Then achieving peace might be as simple as handing that weapon over to the vakari—dead, sterilized, because no *live* nanomechanical bioweapons could change hands—to end all this. That meant getting back to *Vagabond*, then, and reacquiring Rose . . . and convincing Thorsdottir to hand them over. (But Rory thought that would not be impossible. Thorsdottir was reasonable, and Rory had never met any *real* resistance to her wishes except from her younger brother).

She did not realize she'd stopped walking entirely until Koto-rek said her name.

Rory trotted to catch up, past Vigat's withering stare and an aura so bright with contempt that she did not need to blink into the aether to see it (though she did, because Vigat was not hexed against observation; and here Rory found that Vigat's aura matched her chromatophores, which settled another uncertainty and, Rory thought, must make concealing one's feelings a bit frustrating for a vakar). If Vigat was typical of her people—intensely emotional, hostile to humans—peace with the Protectorate would be well-nigh impossible.

Koto-rek, if she shared Vigat's sentiments, kept them shuttered behind hexes as blank and impersonal as her visor. She waited, unspeaking, as Rory drew even with her. "You should not fall behind. There are likely stray soldiers from our side *and* theirs. You would not be safe."

"I'm sorry," Rory said. "I was—" She cast about for something to say to excuse her lapse. Then she settled on truth, which was not the best choice for diplomacy, or for protecting her pride, but which was at the moment just easier. "I was just looking at all the dead. How did this start? Between the Protectorate and the Tadeshi?"

Koto-rek's faceplate gleamed as she looked back at the carnage. Her hand flexed in a gesture that might have been a dismissal, or a vakari shrug, or just a stretching of long-jointed fingers. "How these things always start, I suppose."

"You don't know?"

"I know what I was told. What have you heard?"

"Nothing. Uh. I've been avoiding politics."

Koto-rek ground out a laugh, powdered and lethal as glass crushed between two stones. "That never works."

It had, Rory thought, until very recently, though she was no longer certain if that success could be counted a good thing. Her ignorance, which she had mistaken for comfort, had offered no defense against an encroaching reality, particularly one both armed and aggressive.

They passed through another corridor intersection without speech or incident. Rory divided her attention between surreptitious glances back at the trailing Vigat (bleeding mostly stopped, clearly in pain) and at the bulkheads, trying to identify signage or labels or some indication of what glyph meant *engineering, this way*. There were no more soldiers, nor any ambushes, nor any vakari, wounded or otherwise.

The next intersection, however, was blocked. The hatch showed no signs of damage on *this* side, but Koto-rek spent some few minutes running her fingers over the metal. In that time, Vigat caught up. She leaned against the bulkhead and let her eyes slit halfway shut.

Rory refrained from offering sympathy out loud, or any observation about Vigat's degenerating physical condition. Instead, she sneaked a look into the aether, where Vigat's aura throbbed with despair.

"Is this engineering?" Rory asked.

Koto-rek hissed, or sighed, or swore; it was impossible to ascertain which, behind the bullet-shaped faceplate. "It is. You say you are a human arithmancer. Are you skilled?"

Rory chose to ignore the faint emphasis on human, and the faint ring of contempt that went with it. "I am proficient in passive scans. I can get past most security measures, with some time. I don't know much about battle-hexes. Why?"

Koto-rek said nothing. Then, after a quick jabbing check toward Vigat, she turned and flashed her right side, against which she had been bracing her weapon.

There was a crack in Koto-rek's armor, following the edge of a pair of conjoining plates. There was nothing visibly liquid leaking out of it, and the corridor's illumination made it difficult to ascertain if the darker patches around the breach were blood or scorched metal. Koto-rek waited for a beat, then replaced her elbow and its concealing fin. The weapon she cradled in that arm did not tremble.

"My resources are somewhat stretched," she said, very softly. "And so I find myself in the unpleasant situation of needing your help, Rory Thorne. Our destination is through this hatch. There *is* atmosphere on the other side, so that is good. There is also a hex of human origin on the mechanism to prevent access, which suggests there are also invaders inside who have placed it. I can break the hex, but that will be occupying my immediate attention when the hatch opens, to our mutual detriment if there is a skilled arithmancer waiting on the other side."

Or a few soldiers with 'slingers, whose bolts Koto-rek could not divert if her attention was wrapped up in de-hexing a doorpad. "So you want me to break the hex on the door."

"If it is within your power."

Such a subtle weight on the *if.* Rory set her jaw. "I thought you said if the Tadeshi had engineering, we would be dead."

"We may yet be, if you fail."

"I see. Then I won't fail."

Rory's HUD advised of rising heart rate, of rapid breathing. At least the sweat on her palms did not matter in hardsuit gloves. She closed her eyes and took a deep breath and slid into the aether.

The hex on the pad was the standard sort a military arithmancer in the field might use, pre-scribed code meant to overwhelm, and overwrite, an existing system. Hexes like this worked by isolation, excising the target mechanism from its larger network, and then convincing both network and mechanism that nothing had changed. It was a variant of hexes that Rory had deployed on Urse during the many months of her confinement. *Then*, she had had her harp to facilitate the mathematics, and the stakes had been fooling the surveillance 'bots. *Here* . . . here she had two bleeding vakari looking over her shoulder and royalists on the other side of the hatch, which, if she succeeded, would open and permit an exchange of fire and place her in the crossfire.

Well. It would not be the first time today *that* had happened. And if she wanted to make peace with the Protectorate, her chance to prove both worth and trustworthiness started now.

Rory wormed into the hex, cracked it wide, and, as the hatch spiraled open, ducked sideways and down, as small a silhouette as the hardsuit would permit.

There was a moment of silence, pregnant and swollen with surprise and probabilities and the roiling cloud of dread from Vigat. Then Koto-rek deployed a skein of battle-hexes, visible to Rory only on her periphery. She fancied she could feel them pass over her, snaking through her hardsuit's material and sliding over her skin like she was a rock in a fast-moving stream of arithmantic malice.

Then, having hexed, Koto-rek stepped over the threshold and let loose a stream from that not-quite-plasma rifle. Bolts came from inside the hatch in the same instance, and Rory poked her 'slinger around the lip of the hatch and squeezed out a bolt. From her angle, Rory could see clearly the split in Koto-rek's armor. That was vakar flesh underneath, blasted visible in her headlamp.

A childhood pithiness about how everyone is the same inside flickered through Rory's mind, and she strangled an inappropriate, stress-driven laugh. The sentiment was meant to engender compassion by teaching empathy. Perhaps a biological approach would have been more successful: everyone's guts are red, so let's keep them inside our bodies.

(Except everyone's guts *weren't* red. Mirri didn't have discrete internal organs at all, and k'bal blood was a strange greenish-blue. Vakari, at least, shared some physiological similarities with humanity. They certainly shared the proclivity to violence.)

The firefight did not take long. Koto-rek proved more than sufficient to dispatch the invaders. Rory followed her through the hatch and found herself in a large chamber. She had been expecting engineering to be larger, more open. It was certainly the former: at least two levels higher, and one below, all threaded together with narrow metal ladders and, farther into the room, a lattice of metal platforms, around what had to be the engine core. The deck was lined with banks of what looked like turings and the strange, broken hulks of mecha designed by xeno minds to xeno aesthetics and destroyed by human ingenuity: some of the mecha had been disassembled deliberately, all their parts laid out on the deck in neat rows. The original vakari defenders, all unarmored, were stacked to the side with considerably less care than had been taken with the disabled mecha. Rory could not count from her vantage the number of Tadeshi soldiers, but she could tell that none of them remained upright.

One of the surviving (prone) soldiers gurgled, and Koto-rek's plasma rifle coughed another, final shot. A second soldier began pleading for mercy.

Rory should protest the execution. She should, oh, *help* somehow. Of course the Tadeshi would kill her, if they caught her, but they were both human, and Koto-rek was a pitiless, spikey, extra-jointed—

Not monster. Not animal. Rory stopped herself short of thinking it, in part because her gaze fell on Vigat, who had limped into the room now. She was leaning hard on a railing, jaw-plates fluttering like wings, and staring at the dead vakari. Grief and fury had replaced the despair in her aura.

Rory's guilt twisted into a new coil. It was *their* ship. The Tadeshi didn't belong here: they had breached the hull and they'd killed vakari crew—

Koto-rek shot a second time, and the pleading ceased.

—and that soldier had sounded very young, there at the end. Rory drifted toward one of the dismantled mecha. Guilt, or perhaps nausea, wormed through her stomach. She had enabled this. *She* was responsible for the dead. It was not a logical conclusion: the Tadeshi had boarded *Sissten* in the first place, had certainly accounted for the vakari dead in engineering. The fight for possession of this chamber had been brutal. There was a great deal of blood. One might perhaps argue the Tadeshi *deserved* what they got. But then Rory recalled the slaughter on *G. Stein*. Untangling who deserved what at this point was a matter for politicians and philosophers. (Or princesses, came the thought, unbidden and unwelcome. She quashed it.)

"Rory Thorne. Come here, please." The courtesy, the *please*, reminded Rory suddenly of Messer Rupert, in his former role as Vizier and Thorne Consortium ambassador to the Free Worlds of Tadesh. From Koto-rek, the courtesy was somewhat unexpected, and so was that association.

Rory obeyed the summons, and ventured out onto one of the

steel-mesh catwalks, approaching the central column that must be the core—

Oh.

Rory forgot about guilt and essential humanity and stared. She was no engineer. Her knowledge of engine cores was limited to "they use plasma," with the finer details falling into the same category as arithmancy and alchemy did for Thorsdottir. But Rory had *seen* engines before—*Vagabond's* small plasma coil, at least from the maintenance bay of SAM-1, and a diagram or two from a textbook. There would be two poles, and between them, a stream of blue-white plasma, all contained and shielded by alchemical hexes, all controlled by turing, wrapped up in an opaque cylinder, sometimes with transparent (alchemically altered) panels for viewing. An engine of the sort with which she was familiar was a horizontal affair, most of the length of a room, and massive.

This was something else. This was alchemy, arithmancy, advanced physics and engineering and, well, magic was as good a word as any. It hung vertically, suspended, perhaps stretched, between what looked like the poles on a standard engine core, with machines and wires meant to transfer the power, convert it (work magic on it) for other systems. The area between the poles was purple and flickering black on the edges. It looked like someone had pulled apart the fabric of the multiverse and *this* was what lay inside.

Koto-rek watched Rory. The vakar had raised her visor. It wasn't exactly a glow, coming out of the rift, so much as an ooze of residual light, like a cut weeping fluid after the proper bleeding has stopped. That residual weep dusted Koto-rek's features vaguely violet, while at the same time draining all variation out of her skin until she looked like a two-dimensional representation of herself.

Rory glanced down at her own hands. They, too, seemed oddly

flat in the weep from the engine rift. Engine gash. Whatever that purple thing was.

"Did they—do something to it? Are we dead, after all?" Surely that violet hole must be something gone terribly wrong with vakari physics. Some . . . inversion of plasma, or a corruption. (Inversion? Plasma didn't invert. Or corrupt.)

"They've done nothing I can detect." Koto-rek's gaze diverted, a quick reconnaissance past Rory's shoulder. "Vigat will know better."

Rory heard, now, the wounded vakar's tread on the metal grate, and felt the vibration through her soles. Vigat hissed out a string of imprecatory syllables which ended only when she ran out of breath.

Koto-rek's plates flared and flattened. "She objects to your presence here. You're not authorized to see this."

"Assure her I don't know *what* I'm seeing."

But Rory did. Or she was beginning to. She peered at the gash. It was not, as she had thought, uniformly violet inside. There seemed to be fluctuation—wait. Were those *things* moving around in there? Physical, solid shapes? Alive? Surely not solid, certainly not alive. Nothing could live in void. Except this wasn't void of the same sort that hung about outside of ships and stations, home to stars and planets. This was the void between layers of aether, or perhaps a very deep, lateral layer of the aether. Rory wished for Messer Rupert with an intensity that surprised her, not in the least because it had nothing to do with comfort and rescue and everything to do with *he'd want to see this*. As an afterthought, she added Jaed to that list. He wouldn't know any more than she did, but he'd at least gape at it like a landed fish along with her.

Vigat left off hissing and (Rory supposed) recommending Rory's execution and busied herself with a nearby terminal. Inside the engine chamber, a tiny arachnoid mecha detached itself from its rack on the bulkhead and crawled along the perimeter of the engine-rift, examining the various connections and mechanisms.

"The drive is intact," Koto-rek said finally, after Rory had come to that same conclusion, based on the shifting shades of Vigat's aura. "We are *not* dead, for the moment."

"What is it, exactly? The drive. I ask, because it *looks* like an open rift into a layer of the aether. It's *like* void, but void should be empty."

Koto-rek had been leaning heavily on a flimsy-looking rail beside Vigat's terminal, over which one could look if one wished to more closely examine the engine. Now she pushed herself off. The rifle hung in her hand, looking impossibly heavy. The edges of the hole in her armor looked freshly wet, to Rory's quick glance.

Koto-rek noticed the look. She clamped her elbow back in place and said, as sharp as her talons, "Do not ask. Come with me." She limped along the gantry, following the engine's perimeter.

Rory glanced again at the wriggling things inside the rift. In her childhood, she had loved feeding the koi in the courtyard pond; they had looked like that when she dropped bits of food into the water. A riot of scales and moving bodies, impossible to tell apart except by color and the occasional mouth. She wondered if she looked long enough at the engine if she would see mouths or—oh. She blinked. Limbs?

Don't ask. Right. Rory turned her shoulder to the engine and went after Koto-rek, who had neither turned nor paused, assuming (correctly) that Rory would follow, or perhaps hoping for enough of a head start that her limpingly slow pace might go unremarked.

Rory did not, indeed, remark on it. She adjusted her own steps to match the vakar's, and (feeling a bit foolish) maneuvered to keep Koto-rek between her and the engine and its writhing, limb-y, impossible residents.

"You didn't bring me here to admire vakari engineering. Or," she added, "to kill me for having seen it."

"This is not mere *engineering*. But no: I said we were going to the auxiliary bridge, and that is what we have done. Now let us see if anyone is still alive."

CHAPTER TWENTY

Grytt and Rupert met *Vagabond* at the aetherlock with only a pair of lightly armed escorts, and *they* made it clear they had come to escort Crow, who, with Zhang, was the first off the ship. The alwar did not quite draw their weapons, but there were some hovering hands and threatening eyebrows.

Crow scoffed, but did not otherwise argue.

"You're not taking him prisoner, are you?" Zhang demanded. When the alwar escort blinked at her, she turned sharply to Messer Rupert. "They're not taking him prisoner." This time it sounded like a declaration, possibly to be backed up with force.

"No," said the foremost alw, who was slightly taller than her fellows, and therefore came just past Zhang's shoulder. "But Battlechief Crow—"

"No," said Crow, interrupting. He scowled at the alwar, his mouth working as if he'd bitten something unpleasant and could find no appropriate way to spit it out. "Not a prisoner. This is a precaution. If I were the captain, I wouldn't let me walk around by myself. On my ship, *she'd* be surrounded."

"At least you will be able to see over our heads," said the alw with a tight smile. "Please, Battlechief. We'll take you to quarters with your people."

"Battlechief?" Zhang stared.

Crow shrugged. He might have been smiling; with tenju, it can be difficult to tell. "Fly with you anytime. Any of you." Then he turned and did not so much go with the alwar escort as he did sweep them along in his wake.

"Battlechief?" said Grytt, looking thoughtful.

Messer Rupert embraced Zhang gently, formally, his hands on her shoulders. Grytt folded her arms and scowled, which Jaed knew meant the same thing.

Then Messer Rupert looked at him. "Jaed?"

It was both invitation—*please come out here*—and query—*are you all right.* Jaed, who had been lingering in *Vagabond's* aetherlock, emerged at Messer Rupert's invitation. Thorsdottir came with him, leaning on him while pretending she wasn't. Jaed was glad of the hardsuit's support, and the proximity and sturdiness of the hatch, and not at all sure how the whole walking business would proceed once they left the narrow space.

Zhang looked at Grytt. "Where's *our* escort?"

"We don't have one." Grytt lifted her organic shoulder in a gesture that was both shrug and dismissal. "Rupert asked for a little privacy, and as the Vizier of the Confederation of Liberated Worlds, he was granted that courtesy."

Privacy. Jaed bounced a conspicuous and suspicious stare off the creases of bulkhead and overhead.

Rupert, who had noticed Jaed's suspicion, offered a faint smile. "I thought we might take this conversation back onto *Vagabond.*"

Jaed felt Thorsdottir's dread as a hitch in the deliberate, measured breaths by which she'd gotten off the ship. But all she said aloud was, "Of course," as if Rupert had asked for a cup of tea.

Jaed thought of Thorsdottir walking back inside, and then having to come out again, because of course they would be expected to debark eventually. He thought of their carefully negotiated agreement—that information about Rose was fine, even the documentation; but actually *producing* any physical evidence was not, and how that would be much harder to conceal if Rupert and Grytt laid eyes on Thorsdottir's burned suit.

Rupert, who had one foot on the ramp, paused when Jaed did not make a move to retreat. "Jaed? Is there a difficulty?"

"We just got out here, is all. *Vagabond's* really small."

"It's fine," said Thorsdottir. She turned and, pushing off Jaed, retreated into the ship.

Grytt's human eye narrowed. Both of Rupert's did, as well.

Zhang made her face carefully blank and followed Rupert onto the ramp. "Thorsdottir sustained an injury in her escape from *Sissten*," she said quietly. "She's in some discomfort."

"Which you failed to mention earlier." Grytt's quiet was far more menacing.

"There did not seem to be a good time to mention it," Zhang said. "It was not something a whole ship of strangers needed to know."

Jaed came partway down the ramp so that he could inject himself into the conversation without shouting, and because Zhang was looking rather outnumbered. "Thorsdottir's fine, and besides, we didn't want anyone hauling her off to some xeno sickbay."

Rupert's disapproval radiated. "These *xenos* have been extremely accommodating so far, and skilled."

"Because they want a new weapon, right? Or something else. They're not here for charity."

"Move this inside, please." Grytt stomped up the ramp.

At least, Jaed thought, he'd secured enough time with his

arguing for Thorsdottir to find her way to a chair, and to arrange herself so that her right arm was safely concealed between body and bulkhead. He was fairly sure Grytt wasn't fooled. He was also sure she was immune to his meaningful, pleading stare, but he tried it anyway.

Grytt was, indeed, immune. She crossed the cabin, reached over and, without so much as a *pardon me* or *may I*, hooked her mecha hand around Thorsdottir's chair and wrenched it around.

"The hell happened to you?"

"I took a hit from one of the vakari weapons. It's fine."

Jaed sighed inwardly. Thorsdottir was the absolute *worst* at lying. Which made sense, because Thorsdottir was so used to Rory, and Rory always seemed to know when people weren't telling the truth, but even so, she could *try*.

"Thorsdottir's fine," Jaed said. "I'm more interested in how *you* got here."

The look Grytt turned on him, and the subsequent heat that crawled up Jaed's cheeks, reminded him *he* wasn't good at lying, either.

"On orders from the Confederation," said Grytt, whose expression said she had only tabled her questions for Thorsdottir, and meant to come back to them. She side-eyed her companion. "Rupert here hacked a console in Dame Maggie's office. Arithmanced himself the authorization. Our new xeno friends volunteered to take us. We *thought* it was a favor to Merchants League allies, but now Rupert thinks they had an ulterior motive anyway, and we were a good excuse."

Jaed regarded Rupert with new respect. "You hacked a console *in* the office? With witnesses?"

Rupert's mouth curved up at one corner. "I told them I needed to send a message to my companion, and please, could I borrow the terminal."

"Making me an accomplice. Thanks for that." Grytt did not seem at all perturbed. She scraped her gaze over Jaed and Thorsdottir. "Tell us what happened again. Start at the beginning. Be concise, but leave nothing out this time."

So Jaed did. Zhang acted the part of assistant, producing both Rose's cutting, still confined to the empty 'slinger bolt canister, and the shipping documents, when Jaed reached that part of the story. She delivered both of them to Rupert, who held them in his lap with a look of mingled fascination and horror. He walked his fingers over the canister's seal gingerly, as if the rose clipping might tear its way loose, and his gaze slid out of focus.

Arithmancy. Jaed swallowed. He knew what Rupert would find. Or rather, what he would *not* find, which was confirmed when Rupert said, "Whatever nanomecha may have been in here, they're gone now."

Jaed let his breath out, intercepted a look from Grytt, and coughed himself into restarting the narrative. But when he got to the part about Thorsdottir's injury, he hesitated again, and looked at Thorsdottir, who looked a little frightened.

Jaed's chest clenched. "She's fine," he said. "It wasn't that bad."

Grytt raised her single brow at him. "I had a long chat with a tenju on the ride out here. He told me a little bit about Protectorate armaments. They use something called whitefire. It's like liquid plasma. So I don't think you're *fine*, are you, Thorsdottir?"

"She is," Jaed insisted.

Grytt ignored him. "Show me your arm."

Thorsdottir unwrapped her bandage, face like bleached bone. Jaed held his breath. When he had dressed the wound,

Thorsdottir had been unconscious. She had last seen her own arm when it had been black and charred. Jaed had last seen it just after Rose's migration, when it had been repaired into raw redness. And now—huh. Now it was an angry pink, and tangibly warm, but the skin was intact. Rose's repair effects were ongoing, clearly.

Thorsdottir made a tiny noise. Her stare clawed at Jaed.

He smiled with what he hoped was convincing serenity. "See? She's fine."

Grytt's eye narrowed. "That wound looks like it's a week old."

Jaed shrugged, remembered he was wearing a hardsuit, and waved his hand dismissively instead. "It wasn't a, a whitefire rifle, it was just a baton of some kind. Not as much, ah, whitefire."

Grytt stared at him. Jaed retreated to his favorite tactic, defiant silence, which had worked to limited effect on his father and brother. But he was surrounded by people accustomed to cooperation, and who did not distrust authority. Zhang said nothing, but she went to a storage locker and popped the lid and pulled out the remnants of Thorsdottir's hardsuit.

Grytt whistled. Then she swore, softly and inventively. And then, having refastened her glare onto Jaed, she said, "The whitefire burned through the hardsuit. I refuse to believe *that*"—Grytt jerked her chin at Thorsdottir's arm—"is all the damage you got from *this*." She shook the sleeve.

Jaed clung to his silent defense.

"You thought it would be worse, didn't you? You're surprised. *She's* surprised." Grytt glared at Zhang. "Are *you*?"

"She never saw the wound," Jaed said. "She was flying the ship with Crow and making sure we didn't die."

"You're not telling me everything. Start telling me everything."

Jaed paused, despite the certitude that Grytt's patience was about to snap, and flashed a guilty look at Thorsdottir. "I thought she'd lose the arm. It was . . . black. I thought we'd lose *her*."

Thorsdottir offered a small, conciliatory smile. "That's because I was dying."

"I'm no chirurgeon," said Grytt, "but I don't think you're dying now."

Jaed let out his breath. Sweat was collecting where the seal between suit body and helmet touched the bare skin at the nape of his neck. It both itched and chilled him. "She's not, because Rose repaired her."

"Rose?" Grytt looked at Thorsdottir, startled.

"Rose," Thorsdottir said firmly. "The weapon we found on *G. Stein*. That's what they call themself."

"They call *themself*." Rupert did not expound on the impossibility of sentience. He merely held out his hand, palm up, as if he were inviting Thorsdottir to dance.

"May I?"

Thorsdottir put her hand in Rupert's, whose eyelids creased with concentration.

"What," Grytt breathed, impatient. "Never mind. Arithmancy. Numbers."

"Arithmancy, numbers, and confirmation that, although there is no longer anything at all in that canister except a dead stick of rosebush, the nanomecha appear to have migrated." Rupert tapped his fingers gently against Thorsdottir's wrist. "Into you."

Grytt stared. "So the weapon we promised the alwar in exchange for aid in retrieving Rory . . ."

Thorsdottir closed her eyes for a moment, and opened them again clear, hard, and focused on Grytt. "It's okay. Hand me over to the alwar alchemists, if that's what it takes."

"No," said Zhang. She was looking at Grytt, clearly expecting some help.

Grytt, however, was looking at Rupert. Jaed wanted very much to believe Rupert was thinking of something brilliant, something no one else had yet, but Jaed *also* knew Rupert loved Rory best (which made sense; everyone loved Rory best) and very much feared Thorsdottir's life and bodily integrity might matter a great deal less to Rupert than they did to Zhang and . . . to him.

So his *no*, when Jaed blurted it out, was more forceful than he intended, thrust forth as it was by surprise at the depth of his own feeling, and followed by a fierce, "You can't give Thorsdottir up," and a perhaps improbable, unenforceable, "I won't let you."

Grytt and Rupert both looked at him, surprised. *Thorsdottir* stared at him.

He glared at her. "We left Rory on that vakari ship *because* we couldn't let them have this weapon. We're not going to hand it off now. Not even for Rory."

Thorsdottir continued to stare at him. They *all* did, with varying degrees of disbelief and hostility and, in Rupert's case, a grim sympathy.

"Jaed's right, though," said Zhang. She shot Thorsdottir an apologetic look. "The whole reason we left Rory behind was Rose, and making sure the wrong people didn't get them. That hasn't changed."

Thorsdottir looked unhappy. "Messer Rupert, Grytt: How much do we trust these people? These, these alwar?"

Rupert pursed his lips. "They have acted honorably and in good faith thus far."

"My impression," said Grytt, "is that they're cooperating with us because they're afraid of the Protectorate. I talked to Hworgesh on the voyage out here."

"Crow said something like that, too," Zhang interjected. "The alwar and tenju don't like each other, or at least, Crow's tribe doesn't like the Empire, and vice versa, but they're allied now *because* of the Protectorate and the Expansion."

"So the vakari are the problem."

"There are *three* problems." Rupert ticked them off on his fingers. "The Protectorate, who is putting pressure on the k'bal and evidently Expanding, capital E, their borders in a violent fashion; the Tadeshi royalists, who wish to re-annex the Confederation and who are doing business with whomever they can to accomplish that; and whoever *made* the weapon in the first place and sold it to the Tadeshi, because they are capable of making genocide in very small packages."

"Are we sure that number three isn't the alwar? Hworgesh seemed to think making nanomecha is within their alchemical capabilities."

"We're sure it isn't *these* alwar. They have a distinct political organization which is aware of Rose's existence, and which would like to acquire it, presumably so it isn't used on them first."

Thorsdottir yanked her hand out of Rupert's and flexed defiant fingers at Jaed. "We left Rory because the vakari can't have Rose as a weapon, and neither can the Tadeshi. But Rose *isn't* a weapon anymore." She held her pinkly healed hand up as evidence. "Rose can repair organic material. They're . . . like a med-mecha. So there's no reason we can't use them to bargain for help getting Rory back anyway. Medical tech is just as valuable as weaponry."

Her eyes flicked across Jaed's face, trying for eyelock and sliding off because he wouldn't quite look at her. She was neither an arithmancer nor possessed of Rory's perception, but she could still see through him, and under her gaze, he might crack. As it was, he drilled his stare into the space just past Rupert's shoulder.

"So this Rose is *not* a weapon now?" Grytt asked, in the tones of someone trying to head off a long, technical explanation in favor of a simple yes or no.

"No," said Jaed, but Grytt didn't relax until Rupert also said the word. But the *way* he said it—a little drawn out, his no, for two little letters—signaled to Jaed, at least, that there was a *but* coming. Or an *and*.

Grytt heard the same thing. She gave Rupert a warning look. "Then what is it? They. Whatever."

Rupert smiled faintly. "Rose is dispersed through Thorsdottir's body."

"That's *where*, Rupert, not *what*."

"Patience." Rupert availed himself of the nearest terminal and accessed the documents Zhang had delivered. His eyes flickered rapidly across a screenful of text. "Ah. All right. The original specifications indicate Rose was meant to alter the alchemy of biological organisms on a cellular level: essentially, rapid mutation leading to eventual death, passed from entity to entity. Rose appears to have altered that mandate somewhat when they infiltrated Thorsdottir. For her, they are repairing and maintaining the original tissue, rather than inducing catastrophic mutative failure. Rose is part of Thorsdottir now. I would hazard inextricably so."

Grytt sat back with a gust of breath and profanity. "Still telling me where, not what. Is Rose still a weapon? And yes, I heard you." She pointed at Thorsdottir with her mecha hand. "But healing can just as easily become damage. Just because this Rose decided to be nice to you doesn't mean it, they, whatever, can't tear someone else apart."

"True," Rupert said. He peeled his gaze off the terminal screen and transferred its squinting seriousness to Grytt. "Except I no longer believe that Rose can revert to that earlier programming, or in fact, decide anything. The entity with whom you communicated on the Tadeshi ship appears to be gone, or at least, it is not answering *me*. When I looked over Thorsdottir just now, I could find no evidence of any code on the aetheric planes that would suggest a capability to send *or* receive communication. Rose's programming appears to be fixed in a permanent maintenance and repair mode, and the nanomecha appear to be functioning, but they cannot be told to change programming again. Sentience, however limited, is required to accept the command codes which initiate the program, and without it, Rose is essentially, yes, nanoscopic med-mecha."

"Wait. Rose is . . . gone? You mean, like dead?" Thorsdottir looked queasy.

Rupert's voice was gentle. "It appears so, yes. I'm sorry."

Jaed was watching Thorsdottir from the corner of his eye; he knew when she turned to him and braced himself. He had never experienced a storm planetside, but if he had, he would have recognized the force of Thorsdottir's fury. Her anger buffeted him like a wind-driven deluge, with hailstones and sleet and a lightning bolt for good measure.

"Did you do that? Did you kill Rose?" She leaned toward him, coming halfway to her feet on the force of her anger, and for a moment Jaed thought she intended to grab his hardsuit, haul him to his feet, and shake him. He resolved to let her.

But then Thorsdottir's body reminded her that it was not, despite Rose's efforts, well enough to assault her companions, and deposited her back in her seat.

Across the cabin, visible only as movement on Jaed's periphery, Zhang arrested her own motion to intercept, though she did not retreat to her former position against the bulkhead. Evidently she did not trust her partner's temper or incapacity.

Thorsdottir was still speaking—and note that we do not say shouting, for although the force and intent were present, the volume was not. "You did something with Rose. You said you'd *fixed* them, but you *killed them.*"

Jaed had rehearsed this moment in his head under the theory that practice would render the experience easier. So far, he was not finding that to be true. The look on Thorsdottir's face *hurt.* Jaed met it anyway, chin up, eyes flat, an expression his father would have known well.

"Rose asked me to alter some of their base code. I did so, to their specifications."

"But did you know what would happen?"

It would have been easy to say no, and to fall back on claims of incompetence. Something in Thorsdottir's face and voice said that was what she wanted him to say: that he'd made a mistake, *dammit Jaed*, not the first, not the last, but forgivable. But he hadn't, this time.

"Yes. Rose told me."

Thorsdottir sputtered, face reddening around what Jaed thought would be recrimination, condemnation, a litany of his every failure, though in reality, Thorsdottir was too shocked to marshal insults. Rupert shifted position, perhaps preparing to say something, and Grytt leaned sideways, clearly intending to keep Thorsdottir from launching herself at Jaed.

Which left Zhang, standing more in the center of things than was typical, to ask, in her quiet voice, the important question: "Why?"

Thorsdottir found voice sufficient to answer her partner. "To protect me." She made it sound like a criminal act.

"I'm asking Jaed," Zhang said with unusual sharpness.

So Jaed had the space to say: "Rose asked me to. Rose said they wanted to be fixed. You were right, Thorsdottir. They didn't want to be a weapon. They needed an arithmancer to alter the base code. There were failsafes. Counter-hexes." He looked at Messer Rupert. "Rose talked me through it. I couldn't make sense of most of it."

"Then you should've waited for someone who *could*," Thorsdottir said bitterly. "Messer Rupert could've done it without killing them."

"No," said Rupert, and in that moment, Jaed understood why Rory loved him so much. "I really could not have. I don't understand the code that I see *now*. I can only imagine the level of complexity that existed when Rose was—that existed before."

"Rose didn't want me to wait," Jaed said. "Don't you remember how scared they were of me and Rory at first? Rose knew what they could do. What they were *supposed* to do. What their command codes could *make* them do. What *arithmancers* could make them do."

"As I said," murmured Rupert. "Intent was required to execute the program. Whoever made the weapon wrote a requirement for sentience into the base code. I suspect they did not intend to write in a conscience."

Because people—and Rose had been a person—did things no one expected. Because people were *better*, sometimes, than you expected them to be. Jaed had thought, once, that he'd been in that *made better* camp. Now he was not a bit sure. But what he did know was, "Rose did not want to kill anyone, and Rose knew what they were asking."

Zhang nodded, as if she understood the import of that statement. She probably did. "That must have been very hard, for both of you."

Thorsdottir recoiled. "So what, it's just okay, what you did?"

Bile burned the back of Jaed's throat. "Of course it isn't *okay*."

"But it's done." Grytt thrust her metal hand out as both symbolic barrier and a command to desist. "Rose isn't a weapon anymore, and therefore, not a danger."

"Oh," Rupert said, "I'm not sure about *that*. I would need to study a sample more closely, but I believe the nanomecha still retain the ability to replicate themselves, and to adapt to different organic hosts."

"And repair them?"

"Repair. Maintain." Rupert poked his chin at Thorsdottir's hand. "Perhaps enhance, if their presence imparts resistance to damage, or rapid healing."

Thorsdottir stared at her hand and then, slowly, rolled it into a fist. "All right. So we don't have a weapon, but we *do* have something of value to bargain with. If the Empire alwar want information, or blood samples, or whatever, then we should make sure the tenju and the Confederation get it, too. Maybe even the Merchants League, the Confederation, whoever. Jaed, *what?*"

"The Tadeshi are out there right now, boarding a Protectorate ship, presumably to get Rose, an attack that the Empire alwar have to approve of, if they hate the vakari as much as we think. But we don't know what the Empire opinions are on the various organizations of human beings. *Last* thing we want is an alwar-Tadeshi alliance in the future over a common enemy, like, oh, *us*. I don't think the xenos are going to care if the Confederation of Liberated Worlds becomes the Free Worlds of Tadesh again. Do they even know the difference? Maybe human is human, to them, especially if we're looking at vakari on the other side. So we need to get them on *our* side, specifically."

They stared at him, all of them, until he felt his skin flush. He didn't think that he'd said something stupid, but he had been wrong about that before. Zhang especially (he wasn't looking at Thorsdottir, couldn't compel himself to do so) was staring at him in something like disbelief.

Then Rupert nodded. "Those are good points. It behooves us to be certain that the Empire's alliance is with us, the Confederation, specifically. You're right. They may *not* be cognizant of the difference between the human factions, or at least not enough to play favorites."

"So we get charming." Grytt bared her teeth. It was not a charming expression.

Rupert regarded her with mingled affection and dismay. "Indeed."

Thorsdottir sucked in a breath. "Or we give them what we promised: Rose. Which is now me."

"We don't tell them *that*." Jaed waved a finger, no-no-no, and earned another startled blink from Rupert. "We promised them information on the weapon, so we give them that. The documents, the dead clipping. We don't tell them about what's happened with Thorsdottir and Rose because *why should we*."

Thorsdottir frowned. "Because the documentation and a dead plant might not be enough to win them over, or to cement an alliance that, you're right, we really need."

Rupert gazed down at the canister in his hand. He turned it over slowly, thoughtfully. "And yet, one ought not tip one's hand too early, and give too much away. If what we offer is not sufficient, then we will revise our strategy. Until then, I believe Jaed's plan is sound. Are there any objections?"

There was a round of silence. Then Zhang said, "No. None," in a faint voice.

Thorsdottir glared *damn that you're right* at Jaed and shook her head.

Grytt simply glared: first at Zhang (who flinched), then at Thorsdottir (who did not), then at Rupert. "And what are we asking for, exactly? For *Favored Daughter* to open fire on a dreadnought? For the loan of a shuttle so we can go over and board that Protectorate ship and look for Rory?"

"For what we can get," said Rupert shortly. "Beginning with an alliance that lasts longer than this crisis. Thorsdottir, I know that you are not obligated to do so, but I'm asking: please follow my lead in negotiations. Let me do the talking."

Thorsdottir held up her hands in a gesture of surrender and acquiescence. "Right. Sure."

"Jaed."

"I'm not saying anything."

"Good," Thorsdottir said, savage and *sotto*. "You've already said enough."

"Rory," said Grytt, a little loudly, "will either be fine, or she won't, and likely not because of anything *we* say in this ship right now. Fighting each other doesn't help. Let's get to work."

Jaed stayed in his seat as Grytt stood, and then Rupert. He ducked his chin as they filed past. He took a breath and held it as Thorsdottir rose and filed after them. She stopped beside him for an agonizing heartbeat. Then, without speaking, she followed.

Then it was just Jaed and Zhang left in the cabin. She moved around, tidying, replacing Thorsdottir's shattered armor in its locker, out of sight.

She paused beside him. He felt her stare on the top of his head and pretended deep fascination with the seam on the side of his hardsuit. She would move on soon. Zhang didn't make conversation, either encouraging or otherwise. She kept herself to herself, mostly, which was fine because she was a little scary.

Jaed continued to stare at his suit. Zhang continued to stare at the top of his head. Then, to their mutual surprise, she said, "All right. What's the problem?"

"No problem. Someone needs to stay and watch the ship. I volunteer."

"No." She spun the word out. "Well. Maybe. But I don't think it's politic to do so. We're supposed to be making an alliance. Besides, it's *your* strategy. Come see how it plays out."

"Rupert doesn't need me to negotiate."

"Rupert doesn't need any of us to negotiate. That isn't the point." Her brow creased. "Is it Thorsdottir? She's only mad because she knows you're right, and because she'd make the same decision in your place, and she's frustrated with both of those things. She gets mad at me, too, sometimes, for the same reasons."

"But *am* I right? Because if I'm not . . ."

"Then someone might die. And someone might die if you *are* right. That's why command is a terrible thing and I'm happy just being the pilot."

"Now I understand why Rory wanted to stop being princess."

"Tell her that, when she's back." Zhang offered Jaed a small, sympathetic smile. "Now get up and let's go, before Grytt comes back here to fetch us."

CHAPTER TWENTY-ONE ≡≡≡

Rory followed Koto-rek around to the engine's far side. The vakar stopped in front of a blank bulkhead and took a deep breath. The pigment on her cheeks purpled.

Of course she offered no explanation for either sigh or purpling. Rory, tired of enforced ignorance, and still unwilling to attempt an aura-reading on a scarily superior arithmancer, opened her mouth to make inquires.

But then, suddenly, there was a hatch in the bulkhead. Or rather, Rory could *see* one: a spiral hatch with the standard vakari panel, high enough that a human of standard height would have to reach up to it, and set with buttons just a little too small for human fingertips to comfortably manage.

Rory touched the hatch. It was cold, metal, real. "Hologram?" she guessed.

"Hex," said Koto-rek. "Although the principle is the same. It is a matter of bending light. Surely you are familiar with the hexes for that."

"Of course, yes, but how do you make the effect permanent? Because the only way I can see would be rewriting reality, and that's—" Rory stopped short of saying *not possible*, because clearly, it was. The evidence was in front of her, and in the smug angle of

Koto-rek's jaw-plates. That, Rory decided, was definitely a vakari smirk.

"That is true arithmancy," said Koto-rek, confirming her smugness with her tone. "Not just *playing* at it."

That is the end of us, Rory thought, and wondered where that thought had come from, and why she was so certain of its truth.

Koto-rek stabbed a sequence into the keypad with a talon-tip. The hatch irised open onto a cramped, circular room, stuffed with chairs and standing station-terminals. It had no central turing column, but there was a cylinder rising out of the deck to what would be waist-high for a standing vakar. The cylinder's end had been hollowed into a bowl, and in that hollow floated a hologram representation of the system, centering on *Sissten* and including the dreadnought. Two more vessels hovered on the fringe of the display, unengaged by either Tadeshi or Protectorate, and themselves not engaging. Almost every station in the room was already occupied and their occupants remained busy with their current tasks. Only one vakar reacted to their arrival. They wore an armored hardsuit with the same pattern on chest and shoulder as Koto-rek's. Another sub-commander, then. They approached Koto-rek, casting narrow-eyed looks at Rory, and the two vakari exchanged words in their own language. There were gestures, head-jabs mostly, at the holo-projection, combined with frequent repetition of the words *alw* and *alwar*.

Rory, alternating between relief and puzzlement that she was not the subject of more hostile stares, stepped fully onto the auxiliary bridge, and tried not to flinch as the hatch hissed shut behind her. She edged a bit past Koto-rek to acquire a clearer view of the projection. Her movement afforded a better vantage on several of the bridge stations, as well. The technology was unfamiliar, as was—obviously—the language of the operators; but there seemed to be more stations than should be strictly necessary for a ship's operations. That station there, with its flashing alerts, appeared to be some sort of damage assessment, and there were two operators, both intent on their tasks, which involved headsets and narrow, flat screens the surface of which Rory could not see. One of operators, wearing a pair of goggles, also held a pair of levers, one for each hand, each with multiple buttons. It *looked* like they were playing a game with a virtual interface; but when the vakar leaned hard right, muttering, and then vented their breath through flared jaw-plates, Rory realized they were watching something *else* move in their goggles, and guiding it. A mecha, perhaps, or some kind of drone.

She edged a bit closer to the central console. That station there looked like comms, maybe; *that* one might be weapons, or some inoperative system, with a screen red and crowded with grievances. As for the display on the central console itself . . . Rory leaned forward and squinted at the peripheral ships. She did not recognize the shapes of their rendering, which was both unsurprising and irritating. Jaed might have known, or Zhang. Thinking of them made her chest hurt. She did not see any evidence of *Vagabond*. Perhaps it was too small to render. Perhaps Zhang had escaped to SAM-1. Perhaps, Rory thought, she should *learn* the potential speeds of her own ship. Surely off the range of this scope. Surely. Or else they were part of that glittering dust that must be debris and that did not bear thinking.

A shadow passed across the nacreous glow of the various screens on Rory's left and stopped beside her shoulder.

"Rory Thorne," said Koto-rek. "This is Acting-Captain Zaraer i'vakat'i Brakez. Acting-Captain, the Princess Rory Thorne of the Confederation of Liberated Worlds."

Rory turned. Acting-Captain Zaraer was the same relative size as Koto-rek, but the head-spikes jutting off the back of their skull were thicker, and longer, and sharper on the tips, and their jaw-plates had an extra notch on the rear edge. Sexual dimorphism, she guessed. (Not entirely correctly; for although Zaraer *was* a male, she had not yet observed a vakari f-prime, and was still assuming a dual-sex species.) Something about him made Rory's skin prickle and her heart trip in her chest. He looked at her as though he would as soon push her into that impossible engine in the next room, or out an aetherlock. Or—her mind swerved toward what she had seen on *G. Stein's* feeds—simply rip her apart.

Rory inclined her head. It was the gesture between, if not equals, at least one individual unafraid of the other. As an afterthought, she wove together a little rudimentary hex to camouflage her aura. That, too, was reflex, unconsidered for wisdom or strategy.

Zaraer's eyes, like Koto-rek's, were a fathomless black, edge to edge. His voice, when he spoke, was deep and smooth and oddly accented, the sharp edges of syllables sliding against each other like tectonic plates. "Why are the

abominations

alwar asking for you?"

"What?" It was not the most articulate of utterances, but it had the virtue of honesty. The immediate follow-up questions should be, *what is an alwar*, but Zaraer did not look like the sort of person inclined to answer questions, only ask them, and to expect prompt answers. The only one Rory had for him was, "I don't know."

Zaraer's jaw-plates flared in what Rory had learned to recognize as vakari displeasure. "You don't know why there is a Harek Imperial destroyer, accompanied by a *setatir* tenju knarr, asking after your health and well-being? I find that difficult to believe, Princess Rory Thorne of the Confederation of Liberated Worlds."

The particular arrangement of consonants in Rory's title lent themselves to hissing, which Zaraer did to great and menacing effect. Rory noted, with the part of her brain that had not yet begun panicking, that he had not bared his teeth at her yet. Perhaps that was significant. It was probably an insult of some kind.

Her heart beat so hard that sparks glittered on the edge of her vision. She willed her voice steady and firm. "You may believe what you like, Acting-Captain, but I am telling the truth." She paused, both to breathe, and to congratulate herself on the achieving a firm, fearless tone. "I don't know who these Imperial alwar are, nor the tenju. I've never heard of either people before today."

"Sss." The acting-captain thrust his face close to hers. The unpanicked portion of Rory's brain marked that his chromatophores gave nothing away, despite his obvious agitation. A hex, perhaps, or superior physical control. Zhang and Messer Rupert could keep their expressions bland; Jaed and Thorsdottir were forever blushing or blanching. If Zaraer was more of a Rupert, that was no comfort at all.

"And yet they know who *you* are. They are offering to aid us against the Tadeshi in exchange for your safe passage off this ship. Why would that be?"

"As I have said, Acting-Captain, I don't know."

It was then Rory felt something prod at her hex, like a hand patting blindly under a piece of furniture in pursuit of some lost trinket. She jerked as if the touch had been physical, fingers made of ice thrust down the back of her neck. Did turings feel this way when they were hexed? If they did, she repented every hack she'd ever conducted.

Still, her little deflective hex held. If it were a physical artifact, it would be creaking, spidered with cracks, but it did not break.

Koto-rek, who had thus far maintained both silence and a

distance, drawn to the edge of this confrontation, made a move to intervene, both verbally and, with one hand lifted, physically.

Zaraer stopped her with a look. *This* time Rory saw teeth. His etching was red; the effect, in the dimness of the auxiliary bridge, was of a mouthful of blood.

To Rory's dismay, Koto-rek recoiled, her own teeth concealed.

"Lower your hex, Princess," said Zaraer. "Or I will *take* it down."

Truth.

It might seem that, when confronted by an angry vakar on the bridge of his own besieged vessel, wisdom should dictate capitulation: that Rory should drop the hex and permit the observation of her aura. And indeed, there is a pithy maxim, touted as wisdom, floating about which states that if one has nothing to hide, one should not mind an examination by authority, the logic being that there is never wisdom in defiance, only in submission.

The twelfth fairy had, one might recall, given Rory the courage to take necessary action (or refrain from it). And so, even as one of her gifts advised de-escalating what had become an acute situation, another advised resistance, however futile. Rory agreed with the latter. Yielding now, Rory was certain, would communicate more than her own personal weakness. She was representing humanity *other* than Tadeshi, and so—

She closed her eyes and slid into the aether and reinforced her hexes. It was ugly, her patchworking: variables stuffed into equations, supplemental proofs, convolutions of logic. Messer Rupert would cringe. Rory fully expected that Zaraer would punch through her defenses in the next offensive.

Then she opened her eyes and said, "I am not a liar, Acting-Captain. I decline your request."

The reader may hope here that Rory triumphed: that her

defiance proved successful, that sheer human obstinacy triumphed over vakari hostility.

Alas, reality did not cooperate. Rory's hex collapsed under Zaraer's next assault like a bridge made of damp matchsticks. It hurt, which surprised her. She gasped and recoiled and raised her hand to her face before she remembered she wore a hardsuit and her hand was buried under layers of polyalloy. She sniffed, instead, as blood ran out both nostrils in a fine, tickling thread. At least she could not feel Zaraer reading her aura. But because she knew that was precisely what he was doing, she looked up, and thrust her chin at him, and said loudly, "I don't know anything about the alwar, or the tenju, or why they would ask for me by name."

Zaraer spat something in his own language, sibilant and sharp-edged as his jaw-plates. Rory could not understand the words, but she grasped the essence. Zaraer was afraid, and he was angry because of that, and bitter as oversteeped tea that she was, indeed, telling the truth. He turned and crossed to the comm station in two slicing strides and said something to the comms officer, which earned a nod and what Rory supposed was a *yes sir*. Then he spat something at Koto-rek, who took Rory's elbow and guided her away from the center of the bridge and into an unoccupied patch of deck near one of the nonfunctional stations.

"What did he say?" Rory asked.

"He's telling them we're still looking for you, but that he hopes to acquire you soon."

"Which means he hasn't decided whether or not to kill me yet?"

"He wants to know what the alwar want with you, first."

"I—"

"Don't know. Yes. *He* knows that, too. Nevertheless, you are valuable to them, Empire and Confederation, and he needs to know why." Koto-rek peered into Rory's face. "Is that serious, the bleeding from your . . . nose?"

Rory sniffed, and grimaced at the taste on her tongue. "Nose, yes, and no, it's not serious."

"Sss. Why did you not simply lower your hex?"

"He would not have respected me if I had."

Koto-rek's gaze broke and skipped sideways. "He does not respect you now."

"But he knows that I told the truth, even when I might've believed myself safe to lie. Perhaps he knows I'm honest. That's why he's letting me talk to you, isn't it? You're supposed to interrogate me, and I'm supposed to confide in you because you aren't *him*."

"Something like that, yes." Koto-rek straightened in her chair with a near-breathless hiss, and Rory recalled her injury.

"You need medical attention, Sub-Commander."

"We are remarkably short of medics on this bridge, Princess Rory Thorne." Koto-rek cocked her head, that birdlike gesture again, only this time less *shall I eat you* and more *aren't you fascinating*. "The wound

hurts like knives

is unpleasant. It is not life-threatening."

While Rory did not wish Koto-rek's imminent demise, she had been hoping for more of a revelation about the injury, some reason she might have to demand Koto-rek's treatment, some reason to delay this interrogation. She supposed she should be grateful they were confined to an auxiliary bridge, and Koto-rek had no access to jail cells and the guards that would beat someone unconscious.

"If I don't cooperate," Rory said, very softly, "will you do to me what you did to that Tadeshi soldier you showed me?"

"No." Koto-rek's chromatophores darkened, violet bleeding

into deepest crimson. "There was little information he could give us. He is, after all, just a soldier. You, however, are a princess, and someone of some importance. Our methods would be more thorough."

In the ensuing gap in the conversation, Rory imagined those methods, as Koto-rek no doubt intended, and she weighed the merits of resistance. It was an option. She would not entirely reject it. But there was no need to employ it quite yet. There were other ways to control the speed of this interrogation, and Koto-rek was *not* at her best, probably less well than she had permitted the acting-captain to know. It was a weakness Rory would have traded in favor of goodwill and compassion—thus her attempt to secure medical aid—but since that option was unavailable, she would have to manage some other way.

Begin by pretending to yield. She did not entirely have to feign the tremor in her voice, or the speed with which she blurted out, "Then let me assure you that I don't even know what an alwar *is*. The acting-captain said they had been asking for me. For how long? Because you didn't look surprised *at all* by anything he said. Your face," she added, when the vakar shot her a hard look. "It changes color to reflect emotional states. Like an aura. We have ferns on Kreshti that do that, too. *His* doesn't. Is that a hex?"

"No. He's just got a better complexion for negotiation." Koto-rek's pigments, reminded of themselves, flared a yellowy-orange before banking back to charcoal. "You're observant."

"I am. And I think that *you* knew that Imperial ship was out there before we ever got to this auxiliary bridge. I think that when it asked for me, you went to find me, and when you found out I wasn't where you left me, *and* that my friends had escaped, you went looking for all of us, imagining we'd somehow escaped together."

"Yes. And it is equally clear to me that you did not, *and* that you had no idea the alwar were here. Both of which are fortunate for you."

"How would I *possibly* know what ships are floating around the void?"

"If they had sent you. If you were, in fact, allied with them."

"You mean, if I had been lying somehow, despite all your arithmancy."

Koto-rek inclined her head. "It seems possible. You managed to conceal a pilot from me on your ship, as Acting-Captain Zaraer has been at great pains to observe. Repeatedly." Her plates vented, ever so slightly. "But you really do not know who the Empire is, and that baffles me. Is that the goal of renouncing your title? Appalling political ignorance?"

"It is a result, anyway. The conflict with the Tadeshi, for instance. I know why the Confederation is at war with them, but why are *you*?"

Koto-rek's eyes remained focused on the central display, their absolute black reflecting the light, until it looked as if she had whole constellations trapped in each orb. "It is a matter of

sanctity

territory."

"Their trespass onto your territory?" Rory pressed. "Not you into theirs?"

"Yes." Koto-rek shifted her weight, the first fidget Rory had seen from her. Her pigments gleamed like an oilslick in the dim glow of the bridge, lit as it was by bleed-off from screens and the central console. "Why the interest, Princess Rory Thorne?"

"I think, when this is over, I will have to rediscover an interest in politics, and I am woefully short of information."

"You assume you will survive."

"No. I hope that I will. That we *all* will. And to that end, will you tell me about the Empire? I can't guess what they want from the Confederation if I don't know anything."

Koto-rek's long nostrils pinched nearly shut. Then she conducted a quick lesson in intergalactic xeno policies. The alwar, she said—no, the *Empire*—was a collection of planets and stations. There were alwar not part of the Empire, independent colonies on various seedworlds, but the Empire was the primary collection of the species, and was both a great economic and military power. The Empire alwar were also—and here Rory struggled a little with comprehension, because she did not dare probe for more detail in what was so clearly a sensitive matter—particularly inclined to alchemy, rather than arithmancy, and careless of contamination (Koto-rek's word, the sense of which Rory interpreted as somehow moral and not physical).

Also informative was Koto-rek's revelation of *where* the Empire sat, in relation to all the borders with which Rory was familiar. The vakar commandeered one of the stations and produced a three-dimensional map. *Here*, the k'bal, *here*, the mirri, *here*, the Harek Empire. The Merchants League made it onto Koto-rek's map (she called it the Fleet), as did the Consortium; the Confederation did not, nor Kreshti. The tenju, about whom Koto-rek could not speak without flared plates and pinched nostrils, occupied a series of seedworlds on the hinterlands, and had barely found their way into the void except as pirate fleets, and were as a species barely capable of speech or operating machinery—

"Do they also pursue alchemy?" Rory asked, having ascertained the tenju were not popular with the vakari.

"They are pirates and merchants," spat Koto-rek, as if the terms were equivalent. "They create nothing of value."

"But they are allied with the Empire—-?"

Koto-rek clamped all her facial orifices tight, and said nothing, and so Rory's gift could not help her.

"And between the Protectorate and the Empire? Is there formal war between your people?"

"No—"

not yet

"—but they have no reason to help us," said Koto-rek. "If they are willing to do so, it must be for something greater than *you*, Rory Thorne. They must be getting something from this Confederation of yours."

The Confederation had only just gained official recognition from the Merchants League and the Thorne Consortium, as well as from Kreshti and a handful of unaffiliated systems, and only *then* because the royalists were steadily losing planets, stations, and territory to the hemorrhage of rebellion. It was likely that at least some of those parties also knew the Tadeshi had run afoul of the Protectorate as well, and thus could not hope to sustain a war on two fronts. The Confederation's acknowledgement was less a matter of merit than a wager that it, and not the Tadeshi, would be around to honor trade agreements in a year.

But, *but*: the royalists had commissioned Rose's creation from someone, and taken steps to acquire it in stealth, and on the very border of the Verge. Rory had assumed they meant to deploy Rose on Confederation worlds; perhaps they had also meant to use it on the Protectorate. The vakari certainly had believed so, from their actions; and the Tadeshi attack now, on *Sissten*, suggested Rose's (re)acquisition was of paramount importance.

A weapon like Rose might just inspire an unaffiliated xeno power's involvement, although *how* the Confederation would know about Rose—Rory's breath caught in the back of her throat. At least Zhang had survived, then. She was a little embarrassed by how long it'd taken her to work that out.

Rory looked at Koto-rek, who was gazing back at her more inscrutably than usual, patient as a cat. "My ship survived its escape."

"Yes. We believe it did."

"Were my friends were on board? Thorsdottir and Jaed."

"We have been unable to locate either them or the tenju with whom they were sharing the cellblock, so yes."

"You might have said."

"I might have, except that they ran straight to an imperial alwar vessel, which suggests collusion."

"Which you know is not the case."

"Which we know," and here Koto-rek aimed a significant, two-beat stare at the acting-captain, "that *you* do not believe is the case. But truth can be divided into subjective and objective categories, Rory Thorne. And objectively, the Empire requires a motive for both being in this system now, at this time, and for its altruism."

Rory understood that the principal of successful diplomacies rested on compromise. Not honesty, exactly, but a willingness to give something up.

"I think," she said carefully, the verbal equivalent of stepping onto a frozen lake and hoping the ice would bear her weight, "that the alwar must be here for the same reason that *you* are, and the same reason the royalists attacked this vessel: possession of the weapon on *G. Stein.*"

"That is no revelation. But how did they know? You never *did* answer my question, Rory Thorne. Did you find that weapon?"

"I did not."

Perhaps it was the absence of her hex. Perhaps Koto-rek had

grown sufficiently accustomed to the use of specific pronouns, or of human expressions.

"Did someone *else* on your vessel find it?"

Rory lifted her chin. "Yes." Truth. And then *half* truth: "We acquired information, anyway. The weapon—and we didn't know what it was, at first—couldn't fit on our little ship."

Koto-rek's eyes widened. "You *lied* to me, just now."

"No," said Rory. "I told you the truth. I was just very selective in the objective facts I related. But here is a full truth: we did not board *G. Stein* expecting to find that weapon. We work for the local station, and sometimes we board smugglers' ships and confiscate their contraband. That is what we expected to find on *G. Stein*. Banned substances. Foodstuffs trying to dodge customs charges."

Koto-rek leaned close and wrapped Rory's forearm in her gloved, taloned fingers. Her breath on Rory's un-visored face was warm and somewhat acrid, a match for her tone.

"Tell me *now* what you, and your crew, know about that weapon."

They were attracting attention: sidelong glances from crew, and a stiff, deliberately turned back from Zaraer that told Rory he was absolutely aware of their conversation. "It is an abomination," she said, having gleaned that the term bore some significance to her audience. "It's genocidal arithmancy. Where did it come from? The Tadeshi did not make it, or they would not be trying to get it now. Did *you* make it? Did the Tadeshi somehow steal it from you?"

Rory had been hoping to hear about rogue factions among the Protectorate, some frailty which the Confederation and anyone else *not* Protectorate might use to resist Expansion. (Rory was not, as we said, gifted with prescience, and so could not foresee the Schism, when the Five Tribes broke away from the Protectorate, though it should be clear to a reader familiar with history that, by asking the question of Koto-rek ia'vakat'ia Tarsik in these circumstances, she planted that rebellion's seed.)

Koto-rek's jaw-plates flattened. "The makers are wichu. They are Protectorate clients."

"Clients." Rory sifted through the possible meanings. "Another political state, or another *species*?"

"Yes to both, though all wichu political entities are part of the Protectorate now." Koto-rek was watching Rory with that disconcerting, predatory head-tilt. "That upsets you."

"The Confederation is fighting a war against the Tadeshi right now because they no longer wish to be Tadeshi clients. Did the wichu also resist?"

Koto-rek performed the vakari equivalent of a shrug: a flick of her fingers, a ripple of unconcerned blue-ish teal across her cheeks. "Yes. Not for long. They are not especially gifted soldiers. They are gifted alchemists and arithmancers, though they had to be dissuaded from some of their less savory pursuits. Nonetheless: they are the architects of that weapon, which is by law Protectorate property."

Rory thought she would like to meet a wichu someday, perhaps the very ones responsible for Rose, and ask if they'd intended Rose's sentience, or if that had been an accident. If they'd known, or cared, where Rose would have been deployed. If they hated the Protectorate so much they just didn't care. But, lacking an available representative of the species, Rory circled back to something Koto-rek had said. "What do you mean, less savory pursuits?"

"You have so *many* questions, Rory Thorne."

"We are a curious species."

"So are the wichu. If they had possessed your species' capacity for violence, perhaps our Expansion would have proceeded differently."

A curious observation. And ominous. And *interesting*. The wichu, or at least some of them, must be in rebellion. *Potential allies*, Rory thought, and then, remembering Grytt's favorite saying, added *or new enemies.* Anyone capable and willing to make something like Rose might not be the best choice of friends.

"Let me talk to the Empire ship directly," Rory said. "I have no way of knowing what the state of my crew or the weapon is unless I ask. *If* the alwar have gotten the weapon from my crew, then I will see that it is returned to you."

"Why should I now believe you? Not that you are lying to me—I can see that you are not—but that you can deliver this promise?"

Because I can give part of Rose to the Empire before I hand the rest back to you, Rory thought. It was clear to her that either *everyone* must have Rose, or no one could. But out loud, to Koto-rek, she said,

"Because I am the Princess Rory Thorne of the Confederation of Liberated Worlds, and because you don't have a choice."

CHAPTER TWENTY-TWO

Rupert thought the negotiations had been going rather well, if slowly, with the vakari, until the Confederation corsair appeared.

By *well*, of course, he meant *no one is shooting yet*. Adept Kesk seemed underwhelmed by the encounter with *Sissten's* bridge: her back very stiff, her chin level, her voice as cold as an aetherlock. Rupert did not require an aura to recognize dislike, distrust, a general loathing of the Protectorate. He supposed the vakar negotiator felt the same. So far, although he assumed both sides were capable of it, and close enough that the subsequent time-lag would not be distracting, there was no visible projection.

At least the conversation was being conducted in GalSpek, so he could understand it.

"But you *had* the princess in custody?" Adept Kesk repeated. It was not the first time she had asked, nor the second. This, fortuitous third, was sharp and impatient and made Rupert wonder if the adept was overmuch experienced with diplomacy. Perhaps that was the expected attitude with vakari.

The voice coming through the speaker matched Kesk's tone. "As I have said *repeatedly*, Adept. She is at large on this vessel, which as you can see, is a contested space." There was a pause, and a clatter of vakari syllables.

Battlechief Crow, who had somehow gotten himself onto the bridge—the title revealing rank superior to Special Attaché Hworgesh, who was *not* present—leaned over to Rupert. "Something about a prison break and the murder of a guard." He was smiling, a long flat gash full of tusks and malice. "It's not true. There was no princess in that jail. Thorsdottir and Jaed came in alone."

"I had guessed as much." Rupert could not quite bring himself to thank Battlechief Crow for the commentary. He did not share Grytt's affinity for the tenju as a people, or Zhang's rather more personal regard for *this* tenju. There was a roughness to them, both of manner and attitude, that somewhat repelled him (at least, he amended, the tenju he had encountered, thus far, a sample of two; there might be very *nice*, gentle, refined tenju elsewhere who did not braid metal hooks into their hair).

Still one made do with the allies one had and his only ally on this bridge at the moment was Crow. The alwar had invited (by which we mean directed, commanded, or otherwise given no alternative) Grytt, Zhang, Thorsdottir, and Jaed to observe from more comfortable accommodations, the conference room in which they had completed the first stage of these negotiations. Hworgesh was wherever *Favored Daughter* stored extraneous tenju.

Rupert guessed (correctly) that, given the opportunity, Crow would expound at length about vakari tendency to mendacity, and (also correctly) that Crow was waiting for an opportunity to do so. Rupert was about to make such an inquiry—for purely diplomatic reasons, to better forge a rapport—when two of the bridge crew turned from their stations simultaneously and called for Kahess.

"Another ship just showed up," said Crow, who appeared to understand alwar speech. (Ask what the language is called, Rupert reminded himself, as he revised his opinion of Crow as an ally. There were so *many* new things to learn.) Crow thrust out a finger and pointed. "Ah. There. See it?"

A blip, having arrived on the very edge of the hologram through what looked like Samtalet's actual gate. "Can you tell who it is?"

"Not yet. Takes time, as far out as they are, to get telemetry. Guessing they're one of *yours*, though." Crow slid Rupert a look. "No one else uses gates."

Rupert resolved that, if he was permitted to keep his appointment as Vizier, he would make acquiring voidship technology that was unreliant on gates a priority. He squinted at the blue blip, considering relative spatial distances and velocities and how long an electromagnetic signal from the gate might require to reach *Favored Daughter*, and how long a ship leaving Lanscot might have taken to arrive here, bound by the conventional and less alacritous limits of gates. If, in fact, it might not be chasing them. Him. Oh dear.

Rupert folded his hands together, elbows bent, and attempted to look unconcerned. The other ships present—*Bane, Sissten*, the Tadeshi dreadnought (which Rupert had privately dubbed The Monster, and so shall we name it here, reader, for its real name is lost to history)—would be realizing the corsair's presence by now as well. He need merely wait, and in the next few moments, the ship's identification broadcast would arrive from the gate, and then he would know better how to react.

Captain Kahess had answered her summons, and had been hovering over the shoulders of her navigation and communications officers. Now she straightened and aimed herself at Rupert with a look he would have interpreted as standard Kahess-grim, except for the speed of her approach, which seemed much more urgent. The suspicion was confirmed when Adept Kesk hurried to intercept in a flutter of robes and more naked alarm.

Crow, too, had noticed the captain's approach. He turned subtly to face her and seemed to settle in place. It was the sort of thing Grytt would do when facing a potential threat. At least Imperial security remained at their posts on the bridge's perimeter.

"That's a Confederation ship," Kahess flung at him, when she was still a meter away from polite conversation distance. Her accent seemed thicker, more pronounced. "*Never Take Our Freedom*. Do you know it?"

Rupert inclined his head. His fingers, which had been folded, tightened down to a clench. "It is a corsair in the Confederation navy. I'm afraid I am not privy to more detail than that." He did know, however, that *Never Take Our Freedom* had been docked at Lanscot station, and that for it to have arrived here now, it must have departed almost immediately after *Favored Daughter* and *Bane*.

Kahess fetched up in front of Rupert. He found himself on the business end of her scowl for the second time in as many hours. "What do they want?"

"I have no way to know for certain." What Rupert *was* certain of was that, even if *Never Take Our Freedom* had come here to arrest him, they would soon discover The Monster; and that a corsair was no match at all for a dreadnought, *and* that without help, *Never Take Our Freedom* might join *G. Stein* in floating dead in space. (We must note that Rupert did not entertain for an instant a hope for *Never Take Our Freedom's* destruction, even though such destruction might, at least in the short term, prove personally beneficial.)

On the hologram, The Monster was already reacting to the gate's automatic, unsubtle announcement of a new arrival to the system. The dreadnought had not made much of a shift in orientation yet—it had *Sissten* to think about—but there had been a shift in readings: several of the numbers beside the ship's blip rose precipitously, which indicated systems powering up.

"The better question to ask," said Crow, "is what the *veeks* think of this Confederation ship."

"What do you suppose they think?" snapped Kahess. "They're hostile and suspicious. They think we're all already allies."

At that moment, Adept Kesk arrived, and smoothly inserted herself between Kahess and Rupert, at right angles to each, as if she were merely joining a casual conversation.

"Captain," she said, in tones designed to be reasonable and which would, in fact, only irritate, "there is nothing to worry about. The Confederation ship is some distance from us, and even when it arrives, it is hardly a threat."

Kahess stared at her. "I am not worried about an attack," she snapped. Rupert could hear that she held onto her GalSpek with the most tenuous of grips. "Not from that little thing. I am worried about the dreadnought's reaction. And what *Sissten* is going to do. We are *very* close to both of them, Adept, should they decide to resume shooting at each other."

"The Tadeshi have no reason to fire on us," Kesk said, a little less assuredly. "And you said the vakari were incapacitated."

"I said the vakari *claimed* incapacitation."

"Captain's right, Adept," said Crow, apparently immune to the blistering stare Kahess leveled at him. "The Protectorate might be lying about what they can do. But that dreadnought's a bigger problem, if they think we're friends with the Confederation. They might shoot at us. Or, if they take on the corsair, *Sissten* may fire at *them*."

Rupert was hoping in fact that the Tadeshi *did* assume an Empire-Confederation alliance, partly because he hoped to make that possibility a reality in further negotiation, and partly because he thought that an imagined alliance among Confederation, Harek Empire, and some segment of tenju might give the dreadnought commander reason to leave the system altogether.

Captain Kahess had backed off of *blistering* and was now looking at Crow with a mixture of dislike and approval. "Right," she said. "As the Battlechief says."

Crow grinned without any kindness at all. "Tadeshi're also midway through a boarding raid on *Sissten*. Let it play out."

"Play out," muttered Kahess. "Until they find what they want? Or rather, discover they *can't* find it? And what does the *Confederation* want?" But she was looking at Kesk, now, as she asked it. "I mean, why come here, now?"

"Indeed," murmured Kesk. She side-eyed Rupert. "A fair question. Captain, what will you tell the vakari?"

"Nothing, for the moment. They cut communications when they spotted the corsair."

"And the Tadeshi?"

"Still refusing our hails."

No one mentioned hailing the Confederation ship. There was not yet a point to trying. *Never Take Our Freedom* was still some distance, and thus some time, from real-time conversation capabilities. *Never Take Our Freedom's* captain would be noticing how crowded the system was about now, or very soon, and—Rupert hoped—applying the brakes more strenuously, rather than speeding into the attack.

Crow folded his arms. He no longer wore his battle-armor; like Hworgesh before him, he wore simple, practical, close-fitting clothing. That his collar (short, banded, not the sort that would bind or itch, which the Vizier envied) bore a few more shiny bits than Hworgesh's had was the only indication of rank. An informal people, Rupert decided. That made him nervous. Informal people were prone to breaches in protocol, and sometimes appalling honesty (also very much like Grytt, which was why she was not out here playing diplomat).

Crow cleared his throat in what sounded like a precursor to just such an utterance. Kahess glared. Kesk tilted her head politely. Rupert held tight to his professional detachment.

"I say—with respect, Captain, it's your ship—we hail the Confederation vessel. The Tadeshi'll know we did that, if they're monitoring our transmissions. Might make them think."

"Or prompt them to fire at us," Kahess muttered, but Rupert did not need to read an aura to know she didn't believe it. "We could do that too, though. Tell them we're neutral here."

"Except you are not," said Rupert, and found every eye suddenly on him. His attention tunneled to three xeno faces, while the ambient noise of a working ship tunneled into the background. It felt very quiet, suddenly, in this patch of bridge.

"The Tadeshi are the Confederation's enemy. One imagines," said Rupert, feeling his way into xeno politics with a little thrill and a great deal of caution, "that if you wanted an alliance with the Free Worlds of Tadesh, you might have sought one already. Your presence at Lanscot suggests a different inclination."

Crow grunted approvingly, and Rupert made a wish to the multiverse that Crow be present at all high-level negotiations, because that man hid nothing at all.

Adept Kesk considered a moment. "Captain. I believe you

should continue attempting to negotiate with the vakari for the princess's return. To that end, we need to re-establish contact. Perhaps the comm station requires a bit more supervision."

It was a dismissal, and one Kahess did not like. But she bowed stiffly to Kesk, skewered Rupert and Crow with the same suspicion, and stalked back to the primary console.

"Are you proposing a formal alliance, Vizier?" Kesk asked, when Kahess had gone out of earshot. "Because you should know"—and there was weight on her *should*—"that your government has already made that request."

Which had not gone especially well, Rupert supposed. Or had been in its early stages. Or a thousand other *ors* to which he was not privy, but someone carrying the title Vizier should certainly be.

The adept knows I am not who I claim to be, he thought, on a small surge of panic. And then, *but does that matter?*

Because even if there was reticence on the Harek Empire's behalf to ally itself with the Confederation—fair, since the Confederation was small, and at war—there was now *Rose*.

A counterfeit (no, think *acting*, and trust Maggie would legitimate the title) Vizier retained sufficient rank to negotiate broader alliances, and to decide what sorts of incentives he might offer. He had yielded up the dead clipping and the documentation with only the barest twinge already. Now he shot a glance at the conference room door behind which his remaining incentive sat with Zhang and Jaed and Grytt.

"And yet," said Rupert, "there have been developments in our relationship, Adept, since our departure from Lanscot, which can surely justify an acceleration in our negotiations."

Crow snorted. "Got something they want, do you?"

Rupert wished he knew what the Confederation's negotiations with the tenju looked like. While he supposed the Empire might want Rose to itself, he supposed equally that the tenju—*whatever* affiliation—would object to that exclusivity, possibly violently and to the detriment of the Confederation's somewhat stretched, and stressed, navy. And besides, Crow—assuming a battlechief could negotiate treaties, so *many* assumptions—had a relationship already with Rupert's remaining incentive and, more vitally, that incentive's companions. He had fought alongside Thorsdottir and Jaed. Piloted with Zhang. They had escaped *Sissten* together. Rupert hoped that sort of experience forged the same emotional bonds among tenju (tribal affiliations, not empires, not confederations: that bespoke small, tight allegiances, personal rather than idealistic) as it did among humans. If it did, then Crow might be the first of the Confederation's new allies, with the Empire to follow, so as not to be left out.

"Adept Kesk, Battlechief Crow: let us repair elsewhere, I think, to continue these discussions. It concerns," he added, as Kesk seemed on the verge of protest, "the matter we discussed earlier, Adept, and the root of the Confederation's interests here. I have further information that may be of interest."

Koto-rek did not make it a full step before *Sissten's* communications console let out a strident shriek, closely followed by an urgent speech from the officer peopling that post.

The sub-commander stopped and cocked her head in a listening posture. "Another ship has entered the system."

"Who?" Rory did not notice the look Koto-rek gave her, for what Thorsdottir and Zhang would have called the "princess tone." She was already moving toward the display, the better to see for herself.

Koto-rek thrust out an arm, reminding Rory that she was, at best, a guest and, more likely, a prisoner. The sub-commander's attention was divided between the holographic display and the rattling hiss of vakari speech as the comm officer made their report to Zaraer.

"Human," she said. "It came in through the gate. It's—" She shook her head slightly, and pitched her voice to cut through and across the ambient excitement. Rory heard the word *Confederation* tangled among the vakari syllables.

She wished, yet again, that she had been able to deploy a translation hex. She would have liked to know *why* Zaraer rounded so quickly, but only *after* Koto-rek finished speaking, and why he was looking at *her*.

Well. She would probably find out. He was coming this way. (The reader here may notice a parallel between Rory's experience of *Never Take Our Freedom's* arrival and the Vizier's, which is to say, angry captains demanding explanations of their foreign civilian passengers. Thus do we observe cross-species similarity in the tendency to react with anger and suspicion to the unknown, *at* the unknown.)

Rory tested the aether for probability and found it unsatisfyingly noncommittal. Well, that was all right. She could hazard a guess. A Confederation ship. Her mind raced through possibilities—why it was here now (herself? Surely not. To acquire Rose? But how would the Confederation know about that?), what it wanted (the same set of possibilities as the first question), if it knew what it was flying into (almost certainly not).

"Princess," Zaraer flicked her title at her like a whip. Rory was gratified to see that although several crew members flinched at his tone, she did not.

"Acting-Captain?"

"A Confederation ship has just entered Samtalet space. Why is it here? Are they here for *you*?"

"I can't say."

Zaraer gave her a look that promised, if he had time and opportunity, he would *make* her say. Rory's skin prickled cold, even under layers of skinsuit and hardsuit.

"Then what use are you?" He rocked back on his heels. The effect made him taller, so that Rory was forced to look up, and still she saw mostly the mottled underside of his throat, the blunter edges of his jaw plates, flared slightly. The acrid scent of vakar was stronger now—sweat? some other glandular effluvia born of anger?—and made her eyes burn. Acid, a part of her brain hypothesized, and marked that thought for later. Then Zaraer raised his left hand in what seemed to be readiness for a strike. She had seen how vakari pummeled their prisoners. She had rather hoped he'd ask an actual question, first.

"Sss." Koto-rek raised her own arm in more of a forestalling gesture. "Listen! She is useful. She is willing to negotiate for the weapon's return to us, if the alwar have it, on the Confederation's behalf."

Zaraer bared his teeth and snarled something in his own language. Koto-rek reciprocated, blue teeth and a hiss that made Rory's scalp go tight and cold. For the first time, she saw color in Zaraer's chromatophores. Red, to match his teeth.

At that very moment, *Sissten* shuddered. A vibration commenced under the deck. One of the officers turned and said something sharp (there was no other way a vakar could speak, evidently) to Zaraer.

Who, blessedly, turned away to shout a query at the crew, his arm dropping back to his side, the rage (or at least its visible man-ifestation) draining out of his cheeks.

"We have a return of engine function," Koto-rek murmured. "We will be maneuverable soon. Wait." She cocked her head. There was some sort of excitement among the bridge crew. "We will have limited maneuverability, though we are incapable of void-travel at the moment. And we may have whitefire batteries restored as well."

Rory took advantage of the distraction to take a step back—as much as she could, in this confined space—and lean against the bulkhead. It, like the deck, was vibrating sufficiently to register through her hardsuit. That seemed excessive for engineering that was working correctly. Perhaps the ship was in the early stages of shaking itself apart. Or that hole into the void had slopped over its containment hexes and was oozing all over the engine room.

Koto-rek seemed unworried about unsynchronized vibration, and avidly interested in the bridge-crew conversation. Rory re-frained from asking for updates. Koto-rek would, or would not, enlighten her; in the meantime, she took advantage of the absence of vakari regard, and did some regarding of her own. The gash in Koto-rek's armor did not appear to be leaking any longer. Her only ally on the vessel would not expire from blood loss, at least.

Then Zaraer turned around. The acting-captain seemed calmer now, for which Rory was grateful. "The Tadeshi are withdrawing their troops from our deck," he said to Koto-rek, although he clearly meant for Rory to understand, since he used GalSpek. "The dread-nought is starting to move. To, to turn." Perhaps not *so* calm: his GalSpek slipped on the edges. Rory wondered how it was command had fallen to him, and not Koto-rek, who seemed significantly more in control of her temper, if not her emotional complexion.

Then Koto-rek scuttled Rory's notions of calm. Her voice was nearly as sharp, her facial pigments running a red-shifted spectrum. "Withdrawing *without* the weapon?"

"Evidently. They clearly intend to engage the Confederation vessel." But now Zaraer did not seem so certain.

Koto-rek hissed objection. "But why retreat? That ship is *small.* It is of no consequence. It came through the gate. That means it is hours away. The dreadnought could launch a high-velocity rock along that ship's approach vector and force it to adjust and delay its arrival still longer, or if they were fortunate, destroy it. To leave us unattended—do they believe us already beaten, that they can return at their leisure? Princess?"

"The Tadeshi are acting as if they are disadvantaged," Rory said. "That suggests they believe the Confederation ship is, if not formally allied with the Empire and the tenju vessels, at least friendly with them."

"*Is* there an alliance?"

"Sss. That does not *matter* now, Zaraer."

Rory made note of the dropped title, and the way Koto-rek's gaze did *not* drop from Zaraer's face, and surmised that there had been some shift in attitude she did not quite understand.

That did not mean she could not use that shift to her advantage. "As I have confessed to the sub-commander, I have been intentionally uninformed about current politics. What I do understand, however, is Tadeshi tactics. If they boarded your ship intending to retrieve their weapon, and are now willing to leave without it, then they will be certain that you do not benefit from their failure. I strongly suggest reinforcing your defensive hexwork *now*, Acting-Captain."

Zaraer stared at her. Then he spun and shouted something at his crew, who began a mad flurry of pointed elbows and stabbing fingers.

Rory swallowed. Zaraer's acridity left her mouth dry and foul-tasting. She tried to gather some spit and stifled an urge to cough.

"At this range," Koto-rek said, "even if our hexes are fully powered, a projectile from a vessel that size will cause significant damage. Damaged as we are . . ."

Rory required neither probability nor fairy gift to finish that sentence. "Then you need to ally *now* with the alwar. The Tadeshi won't fire until their hoppers are clear of this ship."

"What do you think the alwar will do? Interpose their ship to defend us?"

"I don't know. Let's ask them."

Zaraer shouted, brief and furious. Koto-rek tilted her head the other direction. "We do not have sufficient power from the engines to breach their defensive hexes, nor to evade an attack, no matter how he demands it. The crew is telling him so."

"Then tell the alwar you found me. Tell them you'll give me back, in exchange for their help now. Maybe they can fire on the dreadnought, draw their attention. That will buy you time to get out of range, or, or—whatever you intend. Get your weapons online. Get Tadeshi defenses down."

Koto-rek's gaze was as blank and black as a place between stars. "*Is* there an alliance between the Confederation and the Empire?"

"Not to my knowledge." Truth, and also not necessarily reflective of political reality. Koto-rek would know that. "I didn't lie, Sub-Commander. I can negotiate. Let me talk to the alwar as a representative of the Confederation. If there *is* an alliance, I'll draw on that. If there isn't, there still must be a reason they want me, and I'll use that. I promise that I will retrieve what we took from *G. Stein* and return it."

"I thought you had renounced your title, Princess."

So had I. Rory lifted her chin. "As you observed, Sub-Commander, one cannot renounce one's lineage. I *am* a princess, and princesses can negotiate with authority." Strictly true, if not in this particular instance, as the Confederation recognized no royalty.

Koto-rek stared, and Rory braced for an invasion of arithmancy. None was forthcoming (or Koto-rek was skilled enough that, unlike Zaraer, she did not rip holes in her target). "Wait," said Koto-rek, as if Rory had a choice. Then she called Zaraer's name, and went to make Rory's case to him.

CHAPTER TWENTY-THREE

G rytt did not like the small conference room into which she and the rest of *Vagabond's* crew had been banished. No room on the bridge, *bah*. There'd been room before. Well. All right. Maybe not for Thorsdottir and Jaed and Zhang, but that Battlechief Crow fellow was out there with Rupert.

It was a matter of propriety, Adept Kesk had assured her. The vakari were touchy about—and here Kesk had fluttered her fingers at Grytt's face and arm and tied her lips up into an apologetic moue.

"So they don't like cyborgs," Grytt said. "They don't have to like me."

"It's fine," Rupert had said, and given her one of those looks which meant *please*. And because he was the only one likely to use the word, even in gesture, and because he was Rupert, she'd been dumped back here, with the—not kids, could not call them that now, nor her subordinates, nor—eh. Call them Rory's crew. That's what they were.

Still. It was a luxurious banishment. A fancy holo-projector mounted on an oblong table (made of real wood, a show of the Harek Empire's conspicuous wealth) surrounded by chairs (just a little too small), in which Zhang and Thorsdottir had deposited themselves already, Zhang with more success. Jaed was stitching a path along the rear bulkhead, farthest from the door. Grytt both sympathized and wished he'd sit down. There wasn't room for *her* to pace, with him doing it, too.

She leaned against the bulkhead instead, careful not to scuff any of the art (was it art? it was just painted on the metal, like a mural) with any of her metal bits. A hardsuit necessarily covered everything; Grytt's personal garments left her mecha arm bare, so that folds of cloth did not interfere with its mechanisms (and also, truthfully, she liked how it looked). The alwar as a whole seemed to find the prosthetic fascinating. Hworgesh hadn't batted an eye. Crow had eyed the limb with speculative appreciation, which he had transferred to her skull, her eye, and eventually the rest of her.

Interesting fellow, that Crow. *He* got to stand out with Rupert. Battlechief must outrank Hworgesh's Special Attaché. She suspected her own relegation had less to do with the size of the bridge and more to do with her mecha implants, and *not* because of what the vakari might think of them. Adept Kesk probably reckoned that Grytt could hear whatever anyone said on that bridge—which was true—and that she might just record and pass that along to Rupert—also true, because Grytt was sure *he* wasn't negotiating with the vakari.

So Grytt employed her mecha optic, instead. The holographic display hanging over the central table showed the system in real-time in an identical, but much smaller, copy of the bridge display. Grytt amused herself by focusing on the very tiny readouts beside each ship, noting the dips and surges in *Sissten's* outputs (surging now, out of the decidedly red and into more orangey-yellow). She also noticed the Confederation ship blip into the system, though on the minimized hologram it appeared first as a few lines of text that, of course, she could not read. She *could* see that this ship bore a different chromatic designation from the others, and that it was coming at high velocity from the vicinity of the gate. Not Empire. Not tenju. Another Tadeshi, maybe?

Grytt tightened the focus of her eye. The reaction among the ships already present was immediate (as much as anything is immediate, in the void). The readouts for both *Bane* and *Favored Daughter* changed, surging in all categories, as if the ships were preparing to move and shoot or be shot and then move. Only *Sissten*, which had only just recovered some level of basic function, made no changes. But the most marked reaction came from the dreadnought, which actually changed orientation, presenting its broadside battery toward the incoming vessel: a detail lost on everyone *not* in possession of a mecha optic (or in close proximity to the readouts, which at this point included only the relevant alwar bridge officers).

Thus it was that Grytt leapt (or rather, stepped carefully, but with confidence) to a conclusion about the identity of the newcomer. After a moment's mulling she shared that conclusion with the room at large; they already knew Rupert had forged his credentials, and the likelihood of official consequences. Grytt was a *little* surprised Dame Maggie had actually sent a ship to retrieve Rupert, a sentiment which Thorsdottir echoed.

Zhang said nothing, which was typical; the look she traded with Jaed, and his silence, however, were not. Grytt made a note of that new rapport, and decided that sometime in the last couple of years, Jaed had matured into someone who did not speak just to hear his own voice.

So that was something positive.

Then Grytt noticed a slew of tiny orange blips rising off *Sissten's* larger, purple shape and she quite forgot everything else.

"Those are hoppers," she said. "The dreadnought's calling the boarding parties back."

The conference room got suddenly quiet, as if all the breathable atmosphere had been sucked away.

Thorsdottir recovered first. "Do you think they have Rory?"

"I think it's because of that newcomer Confederation ship," said Jaed.

Thorsdottir shot a look at Jaed that promised a follow-up comment.

"There's no way to be sure," said Zhang, in the tones of someone trying to head off an argument. (That, too, was new: Thorsdottir had seemed to like Jaed, when Grytt had last seen them. Now there was a great deal more friction, though without any apparent rancor. Fascinating.)

And not as fascinating as the dreadnought's behavior. "You think they're going to fire on the vakari." Grytt looked at Jaed as she said it. "They don't want to hit their own people, and that's why they're recalling the boarding parties."

"Probably." He took a breath. "I think that argues they *don't* have what they were looking for, and they intend to make sure that *Sissten* is either there to come back to, or that no one else gets it."

"It." Thorsdottir sounded bitter. "You mean *me.*"

Jaed did not look at her. "Are you a genocidal rosebush of xenoalchemical origins? Then no, I don't mean you."

"We can't let them destroy that ship." Thorsdottir's gaze bored into Grytt. "Rory's still on it."

Grytt, as well as Jaed (from more practical experience), knew that Tadeshi dreadnoughts typically used mass-driven projectiles in an initial assault, with battle-hexes scribed on the stones (or metal pellets, or whatever). A defending ship's counter-measures did not typically fare well against small, very fast-moving rocks. Even though those rocks then burned up on contact with a shield, their hexes did not, and those hexes tended to hack and neutralize local shielding so that the *next* round, electromagnetic bombs, could penetrate and disable the turings. That was probably how the Tadeshi had punched through the vakari shields in the first place, and it was likely what they intended for the incoming Confederation ship.

But for the vakari vessel, which was medium-large, to destroy a ship of the dreadnought's size, well. Grytt shook her head. It was easy to punch holes in a hull and kill everyone, but the ability to render a ship unsalvageable except for scrap *and* destroy everything on board required serious ordnance. Plasma. Perhaps even atomic weapons, targeted on the parts most inclined to explode.

Or saboteurs left on board.

She said as much to Thorsdottir, and added: "It's not like we can do anything from in here. Or that *this* ship can handle a dreadnought, even with *Bane's* help."

"We don't know that." Thorsdottir pushed her chair back and splayed her hands on the table. "We don't know what they can do. The Empire or the tenju. They might have some defenses we don't. Or some weapons."

But *would* they fire, and risk Tadeshi hostility at such close range? That hung unasked over the conference room, joining the hologram in dominating everyone's attention.

"Give them a reason," Jaed said, very softly. "If we give them a *reason* to fire on the dreadnought, they might."

Thorsdottir understood him immediately. "I'm willing."

Beside her, Zhang bit her lip and offered no objection.

Grytt felt a little betrayed. She had relied on Zhang for sense. "We talked about this. Rupert asked you to let him do his job. You said you would."

"That was when we thought we just had to negotiate with vakari." Jaed looked miserable. "If that dreadnought fires on the vakari, she's *dead*, Grytt. We have to act before that happens."

Grytt looked from face to face, Thorsdottir to Zhang to Jaed. Rory's crew. Of course they'd say that. It was her job to deflect their enthusiasm, contain it. That was *really* why Rupert had wanted her back here: so that these three didn't do anything ill-advised.

So Grytt gave them her best advice: "You stay here. I'll talk to him."

Rupert, Kesk, and Battlechief Crow never made it to the conference room door to continue their negotiations.

Captain Kahess's voice cracked across the bridge. "Adept. Vizier. The vakari are hailing us. They've found the princess and they want to talk."

"Let me see her." Rupert realized the impropriety of demand the moment he made it. Kesk hoisted one of her eyebrows. Battlechief Crow hoisted both of his.

"Vizier," Kesk said, feeling her way through the words. "Of course we will ask for verification of the princess's health and well-being, but I am reluctant to include you in the negotiations." She paused again, permitting Rupert a chance to concur, demur, or otherwise retreat from his demand.

She was correct, Rupert knew, to refuse his request. The Protectorate was no doubt aware of *Never Take Our Freedom's* approach. To see the Confederation Vizier on *Favored Daughter's* bridge might undo what little rapport they—Kesk, that is—had built up so far with her vakar counterpart. He must trust the alwar, or he must explain his personal interest in Rory's well-being and undermine everything *he* had done so far. Or he must admit to Thorsdottir's nanomecha passengers *here*, in front of an entire bridge crew.

Improbably, he was saved from making a decision by Grytt, who burst out of the conference room and fired herself at Rupert like a 'slinger bolt.

"They're evacuating their hoppers," she said, with regard for neither decorum nor volume nor pronoun antecedents.

Kahess and Crow (not Kesk; *she* kept her eyes on Rupert, and he misliked the speculative gleam in her eye) turned to Grytt, who was pointing at the holographic display. The tenju recovered first, whipping around to look where she aimed.

His expression rotted. "She's right. The dreadnought's withdrawing."

Grytt ignored this unlooked for, unnecessary endorsement of her accuracy. "The Tadeshi are going to destroy that vakari ship. Fire on it, blow it up, something to make sure no one gets it."

The adept folded her face into a strict disapproval. "That is impossible to predict."

"No, it's not," said Crow. "It's what *I'd* do, if I were them."

Grytt and Kesk together fired a look of mild irritation at him.

Rupert aimed at the chrome side of Grytt's skull, with the apparently unbroken surface in which he knew very well there were sensors inbuilt. "They could have Rory," he said, partway under his breath. "The Tadeshi could have her already. Firing on them would kill her."

Grytt heard. She faltered, just barely, a hitch in her gate that someone unfamiliar with her might blame on the mecha leg. Her voice lurked at the edge of audible. "And if they don't, we can't let them fire, because she's still on *Sissten*."

"You think the veeks are lying that they've got her?" Crow also pitched his voice low. Rupert shot him a startled look. The tenju sense of hearing was very good. Better than the alwar, or Kesk was more skilled at supervising her reactions to overheard speech.

"Couldn't they be?" Rupert sought Crow's gaze.

"They want our help, maybe they would." Crow turned back to Kahess, and bowed from the waist. It was an oddly stiff, formal, respectful gesture. It also *clearly* excluded the adept from his appeal. "Captain," he said, in a voice meant to carry. "My recommendation is that you let the Vizier have the comm to talk to the vakari. Make sure this Princess is really in custody."

Rupert gathered breath to make his argument—he would know best if Rory was well, if she was real, if she was under duress—but Kahess seemed disinclined to argument. She nodded at Battle-chief Crow, and then to Rupert. "All right. Vizier, please. With me."

Rory waited through a heated and somewhat protracted argument between Zaraer and Koto-rek, involving (she gleaned, with the help of the fairy gift) the reliability of her prediction about the dreadnought and whether allowing her to speak to the alwar was wise.

Rory pretended to ignore their argument (which of course she did not) and side-eyed the bridge crew instead, who were, like her, pretending to be oblivious. She particularly watched the comms officers, one of whom seemed especially busy maintaining a constant stream of keystrokes punctuated by bursts of speech. That one must be overseeing the on-board comms, coordinating resistance or directing personnel to shelters. The other, silent, divided her attention between murmuring into her headset and more surreptitious side-eyes at Zaraer's blustering versus Koto-rek's quiet force.

There were, during this latest exchange between the vakari commanders, more bared teeth. Koto-rek did not recoil and withdraw this time, either. She appeared to be winning the argument, though whether by application of reason, or sheer personal will, or a convolution of Protectorate protocol, Rory could not say. At last, after five minutes of eternity (or perhaps less than that: perceived time is tricky to calculate), Koto-rek returned to Rory. She radiated satisfaction, even as her chromatophores pulsed with the reds of elevated aggression.

Rory peered around Koto-rek. "He seems angry."

"He dislikes defeat, even in mere argument."

"What did you say to convince him?"

Koto-rek bared her teeth. "Now you will have to trust *me*, Rory Thorne. Only know that I succeeded, and that you must produce a result or we'll both regret it."

No pressure, then. The knots in Rory's throat, chest, and gut might become permanent. At least she had not eaten in long enough she no longer wished to throw up.

Rory crossed the deck and took up position beside the silent, unbusy comm officer, who, without acknowledging her arrival, opened a channel.

Rory had been expecting an alw, though she had no idea what that might look like. What she got instead was Messer Rupert, formally robed, features composed in the bland patience of a professional courtier. He could not see *her* yet, she was certain. It was a recording, a still image, no life in it. Then Rory was grateful for the hardsuit's rigidity, and for the fail-safes that locked the suit's knees when her own turned to water.

"You know him," said Zaraer. It was not a question. "The Vizier of the Confederation."

"Yes," said Rory, and added Rupert's promotion and return to public life to the list of things she'd missed.

"And *that*?" Zaraer jabbed a finger at the screen.

Rory's face split in a smile. "*That* is Grytt."

"Is it . . . a mecha?"

"She's human with mecha prosthetics. She was badly injured in—she was badly injured."

"Sss." Zaraer recoiled. He jabbed something at Koto-rek, the tone of which sounded less angry and more revolted. Rory thought she heard the word *wichu*, more than once.

"It does not matter," said Koto-rek, finally and in GalSpek. She shouldered Zaraer aside. Her breath moved across Rory's head, raising sweat and chill together. "Now we can *all* say why the Empire was asking for you, Princess Rory Thorne. There *is* an alliance."

Rory wished she were that certain herself. She wished she could have five minutes with Messer Rupert and no one listening so they could get their stories straight, and while she was at it, a sandwich, a shower, and a nap. Most of all she wanted to get off *Sissten* alive, and that would depend on how well she and Messer Rupert could navigate the next few minutes.

"That doesn't really matter, does it? They"—and here Rory pointed at Rupert and Grytt—"*are* enemies of the Tadeshi, just like the Protectorate, and if there is to be at least a temporary alliance to deal with the dreadnought, that must include the Empire, too."

"The weapon," Koto-rek said, very softly. "Do not forget your promise." Then she barked something at the comm officer.

Rupert's image flickered, then blanked, then reappeared in real-time. He had scarcely moved, his features composed in what Rory recognized as his *I can outwait you* expression, deployed to great effect against royal children and politicians alike.

Then he saw her, and his mask cracked—only briefly, but enough that Rory's heart clenched in sympathy.

"Princess," he began, falling back on, or choosing to return to, all the formality she despised.

Then Grytt thrust her face into the feed, head tilted to give primacy to her brown, human eye. "Rory," she announced, sounding satisfied and mildly aggrieved. "*There* you are."

As if I am only late to an appointment, thought Rory. Rupert pursed his lips and slanted a look at Grytt, which she utterly ignored, being more concerned with a narrow-eyed perusal of Rory's face.

Rory recalled with belated regret that she had blood smeared from nose to chin. "I'm fine. A small matter of arithmancy."

Rupert's pursed lips drew even tighter. Had the alwar told him what sort of arithmancy the Protectorate could perform? If not, perhaps Jaed had. If Jaed had survived. Rory only knew that *Vagabond* had arrived, which guaranteed only Zhang's survival—

"My crew," she said. "They're well?"

Rupert and Grytt exchanged a glance, and after a heartbeat's hesitation, and to Rory's surprise, Grytt answered. "All three of them, yes. They're

not entirely

fine."

Rory's hardsuit, its HUD banished along with her visor, tried to signal her with flickering amber on the helmet's rim: something amiss with her physiology, likely a heartbeat gone ragged and panicked again, to which the hardsuit should be well accustomed by now. If (when) she survived, she would recalibrate the damned thing to register only breaches and perforations as serious, and leave basic human stress as a baseline reading. She wished for a chair, so that she could sit back down and signal that she was calm, collected, and prepared to negotiate.

Instead she planted her hands on the holo-projector's console and trusted the hardsuit to keep her knees from collapse. "Acting-Captain Zaraer has asked me to assure you that I'm well, Vizier. He hopes we can come to an agreement, now, on how to proceed."

The formality of her tone was not lost on Messer Rupert. His lips flattened back into their proper line. His gaze sharpened. "Is Acting-Captain Zaraer present?"

"He is, though he is busy with the ship's operations." *And I think very unwilling to speak to a human again.* "Sub-Commander Koto-rek, however, is here as the Protectorate's representative." Rory shifted sidelong, hoping Rupert (and particularly Grytt) would catch a look at the bridge as well as the individuals mentioned.

Koto-rek moved swiftly into that gap at Rory's side. Zaraer drifted that direction too, though he remained out of the holo-projector's range. That was probably fortunate. When the projector adjusted, attempting to get both faces, it banished Rory to the very bottom, with Koto-rek at the top, and a decent swath of visible bridge in the gap between their faces. Zaraer, being even taller, would have disappeared at the chin.

Look, Rory wished Messer Rupert, though she was not sure what he would see on a vakar's visage, if he would understand how to read the facial pigments, or if he would see only a collection of alien features.

Messer Rupert did look: a flicker of eyes that gave nothing away. His features were diplomatically blank. Grytt scowled, but Grytt was always scowling.

Rupert inclined his head to Koto-rek. Then, with brittle calm, he told Koto-rek that there was a Confederation vessel inbound, and that it appeared the Tadeshi were withdrawing their boarding parties, and that it was the consensus on *Favored Daughter* that the dreadnought meant to destroy *Sissten* before engaging *Never Take Our Freedom*.

"Apologies," he added, "if my explanation is redundant. We are unsure how well your instruments are functioning at this time."

"Meaning," Rory murmured, trusting to Koto-rek's ears (wherever they were on her skull), "they want to know how much help you can give in defending this ship."

"Meaning your ship's drifting." Grytt's ears, or at least one of them, was especially sensitive. She leaned forward and spoke directly to Koto-rek with her usual disregard of protocol. "At least a couple people are speculating over *here* that the dreadnought's recalling troops because your ship's going critical."

Koto-rek twitched as Grytt spoke. Then she steeled herself, a visible stiffening, and after a few flare-and-flattenings, answered, "This ship is not going to explode. Our drift is a result of an emergency shutdown, initiated when the Tadeshi attempted to tamper with the engine core. We have regained control of the engines and restored limited power. We choose to drift to maintain the illusion of incapacitation."

"Right. And weapons? Defenses?" Grytt's mecha eye gleamed. "Your ship appears badly damaged from our vantage, Sub-Commander, particularly on the central decks."

"The Tadeshi targeted non-vital systems."

"That is unlike the Tadeshi," said Messer Rupert, professionally blank. Rory wished he were holding a Kreshti fern. She wished she could see Koto-rek's very loud and informative facial pigments. She wished she could hex across holo-projections and see Messer Rupert's aura.

And then, because wishing was useless, and because Rory had learned more from Messer Rupert's tutelage than arithmancy, Rory said, "The Sub-Commander believes that the Tadeshi were seeking some sort of—contraband on board *Sissten*, and that is the reason for their deviation from standard practices. They intended to board all along."

Koto-rek folded her hand over Rory's shoulder, a visible gesture in the projection, and one which earned Grytt's sudden, pointed stillness.

Rory licked lips which were both nervously dry and unpleasantly smeared with old blood. "Specifically, she believes they were looking for a weapon, commissioned by the royalists from Protectorate clients unauthorized to make such agreements."

Rupert hesitated, and Rory supposed, from Grytt's deepening scowl, that there were questions flying about on the alwar bridge. Rupert cleared his throat. "For use against the Protectorate in particular?"

"For use against *all* Tadeshi enemies."

Rupert understood: the tightness at the corner of eyes and lips, the glitter deep in his dark eyes. "And is the Protectorate in possession of this weapon?"

Rory matched his expression. "No. They are not. It was believed destroyed after an earlier Protectorate attack on a Tadeshi military ship masquerading as a delivery vessel, the *G. Stein*. Or at least—the Protectorate forces were unable to locate it there."

Rupert nodded. "That confirms what the pilot of *Vagabond* reported, as well. The weapon on *G. Stein* was destroyed."

And oh, that was truth, of the sort that would fool a hex. *Zhang* had not been on *G. Stein*. Had Rupert said *the crew* that would have included Jaed and Thorsdottir, who of course knew Rose hadn't died entirely on *G. Stein* during their noble suicide, which meant that Rupert knew that, too. And that he'd probably seen Rose's technical specifications. He might have already examined the clipping of Rose themself.

But had he promised Rose to the alwar? Rory ground her teeth together. Messer Rupert wouldn't be that foolish. Not even for her sake would he do that—except he might, to get her back, or if there was no further danger from Rose, or for a greater purpose to which she was not privy. What she *could* observe was the alwar vessel, taken with its tenju companion, was only two-thirds the mass of the Tadeshi dreadnought. What purpose would they have to attack a dreadnought for the sake of *Sissten*, itself an enemy ship?

Rory quite forgot, in that moment, that negotiations might occur in good faith, without coercion or threats of violence; that people might work together for common good and common goals, despite differences of culture or even physiology. Fortunately, at that instant, her gaze fell up on Grytt, standing beside Rupert. Grytt did not look especially coerced. She looked a little bit bored, as she always did when people were talking instead of doing things that needed doing.

Messer Rupert cleared his throat again, with a glance flicked sidelong. "The Tadeshi appear less than convinced you don't have this weapon, Sub-Commander. They are readying their vessel to fire on yours. Presumably they mean to destroy the vessel."

"We are aware. Our systems have some functionality. We might be able to avoid incoming fire, at least temporarily. But if we do, we will be unable to return fire, or to power the necessary defensive hexes."

Zaraer spat something unintelligible, furious. Koto-rek, to Rory's surprise, said nothing, even when Zaraer repeated with both greater volume and fury. It was only at his third and loudest reprise that she answered, in cool shards of what Rory guessed must be reason, because Zaraer sealed mouth and jaw-plates and nostrils so tightly she wondered if he might not pass out.

Rupert, in the manner of all good diplomats, pretended not to notice outrage not directed at himself. He turned and, with a faint, apologetic smile, muted the output from his end, and engaged in an exchange with someone out of the projector's scope. Grytt's attention cut that same direction, and her mouth tightened into an expression Rory recognized as satisfaction, and everyone else on the *Sissten's* auxiliary bridge might mistake for intestinal distress.

Rupert nodded, and shifted sidelong. Adept Uo-Zanys Kesk (with whom the reader is familiar, so we will spare redundant description) moved into the space he vacated. Her gaze flicked over Rory quickly, then settled on Koto-rek and sharpened. "Sub-Commander."

Rory wondered if that tone and expression indicated the same thing with alwar—remarkable how similar they were to humanity, in feature and surface physiology—as they would with, say, Messer Rupert.

"Ssss. Adept."

So hostile was Koto-rek's tone that Rory was startled, and actually glanced up and back at the vakar. There had been no introductions. Did they know each other from prior contact, or was this a mutual species dislike? An adept was not a military rank. Perhaps Koto-rek's hostility was concerned with whatever this person was an adept *of.*

Rory, on a hunch, dipped her gaze into the aether. Equations swirled around Koto-rek in a glittering cloud of spiky defense, which told Rory that yes, adept involved arithmancy and also, Koto-rek was concerned about arithmancy *through* a transmission.

Rory resolved to learn how that was theoretically possible, and to acquire the skills herself as soon as was practical. If this resolution seems overly optimistic, given her current situation, we must recall Rory was, by nature, not given to despair or defeat.

"We are prepared—" the adept began.

"Is the Empire formally allied with the Confederation?"

I thought that did not matter, Rory wailed within the confines of her skull.

"—to render aid." The adept's eyes narrowed. "I'm not sure what the state of Imperial political alliances matters to you, Sub-Commander."

Rory waited for the fairy gift to confirm one way or the other, and was disappointed. Messer Rupert must be negotiating an alliance, and Rory harbored the queasy suspicion she knew what he might be offering as incentive.

Koto-rek appeared to understand the former, as well. Air whistled through the gaps in her jaw-plates. "The princess is very valuable, then."

"She is," said Messer Rupert, and Rory's heart clenched. There was no untruth there, but it was personal. Purely, solely personal.

Rory leaned forward, conscious of Koto-rek's tightening grasp on her suit, as if the vakar feared she would leap through the comm unit and escape.

"Of greater immediate concern than my value," Rory said crisply, "is the withdrawal of Tadeshi troops from this ship. I suggest that the Tadeshi may *not* wish to engage three hostile vessels simultaneously. If you could send your own boarding ships, perhaps—transmit your intentions to the dreadnought, tell them you are rendering humanitar—ah, compassionate aid to *Sissten*, perhaps they will refrain from firing, seeing such an alliance."

The adept and Rupert looked at each other.

"If you will loan us a vessel, adept," said Rupert, "let me propose a joint venture, with some of our personnel accompanying yours to the Protectorate ship."

Grytt, too, was looking off-screen. "And some of the Battle-chief's personnel, too," she said, which Rory did not understand, but which elicited from Koto-rek another quiet hiss.

"Acceptable,"

filthy tenju

said Koto-rek.

The negotiations proceeded in like manner for some time, Koto-rek (with occasional unspeaking, hard-stares consultations with Zaraer) speaking directly with Grytt and the adept. Rupert and Rory held themselves quiet and on the perimeter and conducted their own nonverbal communications, which, on Rory's part, in-volved much holding still to better permit Rupert to look her over, while trying to project reassurance and confidence. She suspected, from the barely veiled dismay on his face, that she was failing.

Or perhaps he was dismayed that negotiations had moved out of his hands and into Grytt's; perhaps he had expected Rory to better steer her end. Perhaps he just wished she'd stayed on Lanscot and not attempted to remake herself from princess to privateer. He most definitely knew something she didn't about Rose, alwar, vakari, and the current state of multiverse politics.

What Rory knew, that Rupert didn't, was that Zaraer was ex-tremely unhappy with Koto-rek's ongoing negotiations, and his heretofore undifferentiated complexion had acquired a range of crimsons that promised the sub-commander a dressing down later, if not a court-martial.

Unless we save the ship and get Rose back. Then she'll be a hero. There might be that worry, too, in Zaraer's range of scarlets. The Empire and the Protectorate were, if not formal enemies, at least cordially hostile. Perhaps there were taboos about armed foreign troops on Protectorate decks. Perhaps Koto-rek was committing treason by inviting the alwar on board.

Rory recalled Koto-rek's hesitation in the morgue and her mention of a doctrine which had demanded a death penalty on intruders. She had thought then that Koto-rek had spared her because there had been no intent, on her part, to violate the taboos, and indeed that was what Koto-rek had implied. But now, seeing this bridge, and the ships on the holo-screen, seeing Acting-Captain Zaraer's ire, Rory thought otherwise. Koto-rek had spared her because practicalities of this situation overrode doctrinal concerns. The sub-commander was a pragmatist, not a dogmatist.

That had to mean *something*. That there was room for reason, even between cordial enemies. The Tadeshi were the agreed-upon problem: if *they* acquired a terrible weapon, disaster for all. So if she could just get them to work together, the Protectorate and the Empire and the Confederation and *whatever* the tenju collective political entity was, perhaps they could still work this out so that everyone went home happy.

Or, because Rory was not entirely a romantic idealist—at least go home alive.

CHAPTER TWENTY-FOUR

"What do you think you are doing?" Grytt asked, in tones of great patience and great exasperation.

Rupert, who had been expecting Grytt's arrival from the moment she realized what he intended (which was the moment he had excused himself from the bridge and returned to their quarters), did not pause in his task. Hardsuits were complicated matters that required his full attention. He concentrated more intensely than was strictly necessary on the seals of his left glove. It was fortunate that the alwar kept various sizes of hardsuits to accommodate the species who might be on board. Sensible safety measures. Human ships would have to start doing that as well. Or perhaps they already did. He could ask Samur, if and when they spoke again, if Consortium and Merchants League ships carried alwar and tenju sizes.

When he was satisfied with the left glove, and only then, he said, "I am coming with you to retrieve Rory."

Grytt did not sigh. Sighing, for Grytt, would imply surrender. Instead every syllable came out like diamond. "No, you are not."

"You can hardly forbid me." It was a childish retort, and he regretted it at once.

"I was *going* to attempt an appeal to your better sense, but I see that would be a waste."

Rupert began to draw on the right glove, but slowly. "Well, then what shall I do? Wait here?"

"Yes."

"Grytt! You saw them. These, these *vakari*, hovering over her with their, their—" Rupert stopped himself, appalled.

"Go on. You were going to say . . . their weird facial features, maybe? Those creepy eyes that just don't look human?"

Denial welled up hot in his throat, both reflex and dishonest. He swallowed the dishonesty back down before he could utter it. Very bitter. He stopped drawing on the glove and turned to face her.

"She looked—Grytt, you *saw* how she looked. We don't know what they've done to her."

"No, we don't." Grytt peeled herself off the bulkhead and crossed to him. She took Rupert's right hand, tugged the glove off, and dropped it to the deck.

"She's afraid!"

Grytt took his left-hand glove and, with considerable more deftness than he had, undid the seals, pulled it off, and sent it to join its partner. "Of course she is. *She's* not an idiot."

"And I am?"

"You're worried. And so am I, before you start fussing at me. But." Grytt put her hands on his shoulders with a weight and force that made his hardsuit creak and his bones with them. "*But*, Rupert: we have an agreement with the Protectorate."

"Which Adept Kesk suggests will last exactly as long as they find convenient."

Grytt rolled her human eye. "They'll find it convenient as long as that dreadnought is out there. We've been *over* this. For the love of small *fish*, you were in the room when we worked this out. You *said* you thought this plan and all the reasons behind it were sound. You gave us your official viziery blessing."

"That was when I thought I would be going along."

"You never thought that. Not really. You know better. This isn't your kind of battle."

Rupert found himself short of breath. He tried to breathe deeply and slowly and ended up coughing instead. It was a dry sound, thin, squeezed out by lungs more accustomed to a damp planet's atmosphere than rarified voidship aether. An old man's cough.

Grytt was at least as old as he was. *She* didn't cough. Grytt was also a good portion mecha, and those components were much younger than her original organic set, *and* she spent much of her time maintaining the original parts in, with no irony, fighting trim.

Not sitting behind a console. Not puttering around in gardens and kitchens. Not talking, endlessly talking. Sour regret and recriminations burned at the back of his throat. Grytt was, of course, correct. His weapons had never been 'slinger bolts, but words, and it was largely due to his version of warfare that they had come to this place at all.

He *knew* all of it, without Grytt having to say any if it, but his heart ached anyway.

She knew it. She always knew, even without the aid of arithmancy and auras. Her mouth tightened into a rueful, incomplete smile. Her brown eye softened. The blue tesla optic burned, unblinking, like a star. "We'll get her back, Rupert. I promise."

You can't promise that, he wanted to protest. *No one can foretell the future.* But instead he returned her smile, and walked with her to the door. He would get himself out of this hardsuit, and then he would go down to the bridge and wait for events to spin themselves out.

Grytt was, truthfully, relieved that she hadn't been forced to lock Rupert in his quarters. She was worried enough about taking Jaed, and was even more worried about Thorsdottir, whose insistence on accompanying the mission should have been an easy *no*: she'd sustained massive and recent injuries, even if they weren't visible anymore. *Because* they weren't visible anymore. It would look pretty suspicious if, of all the crew on *Vagabond*, capable-looking Thorsdottir stayed behind citing injuries no one could see because of an invisible infiltration of nanomecha that were supposed to be extinct.

Yet that became the precise reason she could not be left on board *Favored Daughter*. Jaed's plan for how much to reveal about the weapon's transformation had held up so far, but Grytt didn't think it would last. Adept Kesk was too smart, and asked too many probing questions, and was probably arithmancing everyone. If Rupert could suss out the nanomecha in Thorsdottir's blood, then surely someone called *adept* could, too, if she thought to look.

That had been Rupert's argument for Thorsdottir's inclusion on the retrieval team. It was probably why he'd thought he should come along, too.

Grytt glanced back at his closed door once before she trotted toward the armory. Truth: she didn't have *time* to stay and wait and be sure that his better sense had been restored. She could only trust that it had. Rupert had never been prone to heroics.

Then again, neither had the Jaed Moss she had known, and *now* look. The armory was full of people of various species and sizes equipping themselves with experienced efficiency, and somehow Jaed fit right in among them, suiting up between Zhang and Crow.

Now *that* one worried Grytt a little bit. Rupert had made a deal there, too, with the tenju. They, like the alwar, had gotten access to Rose's documentation and the dead stick of rosebush. But Crow, unlike the alwar, knew about Thorsdottir's very tiny passengers, or at least suspected, and Crow had made it clear that the tenju *would* like biological samples from Thorsdottir when this mission concluded. The intimation was that not only would the tenju like the samples, they would like even better if the alwar never got any, nor found out that the tenju had.

Grytt suspected Thorsdottir would end up parceling out her blood to everyone by the end of this business, to Empire alwar and tenju whatever-they-called-their-political-units, to the Merchants League and the Consortium and the Confederation, in the name of keeping peace, which really meant making sure everyone had access to the same level of destruction. Grytt (and Thorsdottir) considered that just fine, if doing so got Rory back *and* won Dame Maggie a few more allies so that she wouldn't toss Rupert in prison when they returned to Lanscot.

Thorsdottir, at least, had gotten a new hardsuit. Grytt admitted to herself a little envy: it was a tenju frame, welded with armor plating etched with alwar hexwork that had made Rupert's eyebrows climb when he'd seen it.

"That's alchemy," he'd said, "as much as arithmancy," and then launched into an analysis that had made as much sense to Grytt as the noises sheep made. Maybe less.

"Does it stop 'slinger bolts? And plasma?" Grytt had asked, interrupting. And when Rupert nodded, "All right, then, good enough."

"You have no sense of wonder."

"Correct."

But, Grytt thought, that wasn't entirely true. Her sense of wonder just focused on different miracles, such as how two young

Royal Guards and a feckless second son of a would-be dictator ended up preparing for battle so calmly and competently. Zhang, checking a plasma weapon's charge. Jaed helping Thorsdottir with a gauntlet.

Good teachers, ha, that's what some people would say. Grytt knew very well that was part of it, no false modesty as to her own role in that. But at some point, students and children have to take on some independence. She hadn't been worried, exactly, when Thorsdottir, Zhang, Jaed, and Rory had gone kiting off to SAM-1 to try being salvagers and privateers or whatever romantic name they'd thought up. They'd be fine, she'd told Rupert.

And they had been. They were.

Grytt cast her gaze around the armory, at two species of xenos she hadn't known before last week, on her way to render aid to a third, and decided that, once this was over, she'd go back to Lanscot and her sheep and *stay* there, and take Rupert with her. Thorsdottir and Zhang and Rory and Jaed could handle the multiverse now. It was theirs.

Thorsdottir had worn armor as a Royal Guard, but that had been ballistic weave panels as part of a uniform, subtle by design. This new hardsuit, which Grytt had so admired, was anything but. Flashy hexwork, all alwar, all aftermarket.

"We don't want you injured," Adept Kesk had said, when she'd presented it.

And Thorsdottir thought, *you don't want Rose injured*, though Adept Kesk couldn't know (could she?) that Rose's remnants floated through Thorsdottir's blood. Nor was Thorsdottir certain if Rose was still even *Rose* in there. There hadn't been any communication attempts. Messer Rupert, who had a better skillset for determining such things, had said definitively that Rose-the-entity-that-hacked-hardsuits was gone. Jaed had concurred, for what that was worth. It was clear that no one thought Rose's self-sacrifice any kind of tragedy. Rose had saved Thorsdottir's life, and *that* was fortuitous, lucky, a good thing. That a sentient weapon had perished in the process, well, that was fine, since no one had been sure what to do with them anyway.

Fine for me, thought Thorsdottir. Not for Rose. That they had agreed on that sacrifice—Rose asking, Thorsdottir consenting—did nothing to ameliorate Thorsdottir's guilt. She hadn't *known* Rose's offer meant Rose's death. If she had, she might've said no.

Maybe. *Definitely.*

"It's no different than you'd do for Rory," Jaed had said, in an attempt to comfort her. "Or for Zhang."

"Or for you," she'd snapped, which had made him turn red.

So it was just as well that Jaed had Crow to help him with his hardsuit (which had alwar hexwork too, they all did, but the standard human design underneath), and even better that they'd all been quartered on *Favored Daughter* in separate cabins. Privacy for a change. Solitude. No need for discomforting conversations—

"You all right?" Zhang handed Thorsdottir a plasma rifle with a Qing-Kovacs stamp and proportions designed for tenju hands and tenju hardsuits. There was a business relationship there, between Merchants League and the tenju spacer clans, clearly longstanding enough for design alterations to the weapons.

"Fine," Thorsdottir said absently, reflexively, and took the rifle. It was true. Her hand and arm did not hurt, and of course, that wasn't what Zhang was asking.

"Huh." Zhang's features stayed carefully neutral.

"Don't you start."

"I'm not starting anything."

"Because if you're going to say something about what I do with my life now is how I prove myself worthy of Rose's sacrifice, I might scream."

Zhang shook her head slightly. "I don't need to say that. You already believe it."

"I don't even know what I am anymore."

"Stubborn. My best friend." Zhang pursed her lips. "Also, contaminated with a weapon of unknown origin, so maybe a biohazard, too. Don't bleed on anyone."

"*Thank* you. You're such a comfort." Thorsdottir checked the weapon, which of course Zhang already had, and found it fully charged, primed, ready.

"You all right?" Zhang asked again.

"Yes," said Thorsdottir, and this time she meant it.

Somehow, probably because the multiverse didn't like him, Jaed ended up beside Grytt on the transport. He had Crow on his other side, but on *Crow's* other side and across the aisle sat tenju, all talking in—tenju. There had to be another name for their language, but he didn't know it, but that didn't matter. Conversation with them was right out.

He might've been safe from interaction if it were Thorsdottir sitting beside Grytt, but it was Zhang, with Thorsdottir next to *her*, and they had their heads together in the way old friends and partners did.

So Jaed thought to try just staying silent. Grytt wasn't much of a talker. She might let him be. But then he noticed her expression, which, bifurcated as it was between mecha and organic parts, still seemed a little bit *lost*.

That shook him. Jaed's experience with Grytt was primarily

filtered through her effects on his companions, with one exceptional, personal conversation which had involved her pinning him to a station bulkhead until she convinced her of his sincerity. So *no*, she was not a comfortable benchmate, but she had also seemed, well, unshakeable. Constant. Rory might be everyone's sun, but Grytt was some other massive gravitational source holding the system together, like dark matter and—Jaed sighed, both inward and out, and discarded the metaphor.

The sigh is what did it, he thought later. *That* was why she spoke to him.

"You nervous?" she asked, in a tone which implied she expected he was.

Jaed almost said *yes*, because then she could offer encouragement, which he could accept, and then everyone would feel better. Except he had learned not to lie, even politely, around Rory, and so he said, "No. Not really. I mean, *yes*, but not about boarding that ship."

"Huh. What then?"

Jaed flicked a look at Thorsdottir, over Grytt's shoulder. She was a worry, of course she was, but the root of it was: "What Rory's going to think? We left her behind. She might've said we should do it, but we never exactly asked. We just did it. I mean, she could've been dead, yeah, but we didn't *know*. We didn't even check." He grimaced at the bitter, sour truth of it.

"You made the right choice. Saved *her* life, leaving like you did." Grytt turned her head partway, tilted it, so that Jaed knew she meant Thorsdottir. "Rory would agree with that."

Jaed shrugged, and bumped his shoulder on the inside of his hardsuit, and made a fist instead.

"I wanted to go back for her. Zhang talked me out of it."

"Huh. Well. Zhang's got sense. No, don't make that face. You've got heart. You're loyal. Those aren't bad things. And you're here now, going back to an unfriendly deck, trusting the people who took you prisoner once won't do it again. Bravery's not a problem for you." Grytt offered a smile, hideous and genuine and almost gentle. "Guilt is, though. Leave that behind. Could have, should have—that will get you hurt. Or someone *else* hurt."

That would be—well, not the *worst*, but definitely bad, if he came to rescue Rory and ended up needing a rescue himself. He laughed a little, and when Grytt cocked her head, said as much.

"Ha," said Grytt. "Rory doesn't need rescue. We're here to pick her up, that's all." She swept her eye over the tenju and alwar. "And we're all here to render aid to the Protectorate."

"Yeah. Well. *They* can go help the Protectorate. I'm just here to get Rory back."

Grytt eyed him. "You say *Protectorate* the same way you sometimes say *Tadeshi*."

Yes. "Can't make friends with some people. What they did on *G. Stein*. Grytt, if you'd *seen*—it's not *that* they killed people, it's *how* they did it. It was easy for them."

"They're not invincible." Grytt jerked her chin in the general direction of *Sissten*. "Clearly."

"That's because the dreadnought surprised them. They're different, and I don't mean how they look. There's something about them. I know, *something*, be more specific, but I can't. But I think, just because we share a common enemy doesn't mean we're all friends."

It took Jaed a moment to realize the gargling noise boiling out of Grytt's throat and nose was laughter.

"You sound like me."

"Is that a compliment?"

"It's a warning. Means no one's ever going to listen to you, and you'll get to say *told you so* a lot. Means everyone will think you're wise as hell when you're dead, and not before."

"Messer Rupert listened to my advice already." God, *why* was he arguing with her?

It had been good advice but they both knew Thorsdottir's anonymity wasn't going to last. Jaed knew she'd promised blood samples to Crow. Grytt probably knew it, too. And from there, the adept would get some, and the Confederation certainly wouldn't just *sit* on it. At least, maybe, the Confederation having Rose, and the Tadeshi *not*, would put an end to that war.

"Listen. None of what happened after was your fault. Let me give you more advice you won't believe until it happens: the best plans don't survive implementation. Never as we expect."

"I hope you're wrong."

"Me too," said Grytt. "But I won't be."

CHAPTER TWENTY-FIVE ≡≡≡

Perhaps the reader hopes here for a HUD-level view of the battle: how a Harek imperial breach-hopper (one of several) slid out of *Favored Daughter*'s launch bay and crossed the debris field that lay between *Sissten* and the dreadnought, a labyrinth through which the hopper's alwar pilot and nanny (which is much the same as a human turing, with perhaps more sass) navigated with apparent ease and at greater speeds than *Vagabond* and Zhang had managed. It is fortunate that hoppers are not armed; the alwar ships pass Tadeshi ships returning to the dreadnought. But there are tense moments, nevertheless—

Or, no, skip the journey. Perhaps the narrative should resume when the hopper seals itself to *Sissten*, in the very berth *Vagabond* had vacated. Listen to the hiss of aetherlocks, the rattle as a suddenly silent hold full of armored people stands up. The teams prime their weapons. They know where they're going. They have orders. Their debarking is orderly, precise. Visors seal, HUDs flicker to life, comms murmur coordinates, objectives, orders.

Or perhaps we should begin *here*, when it is discovered that Grytt is a little bit prescient, in the way that experience confers, and that there are lingering Tadeshi on the ship: who could not return to their hoppers, perhaps, or who are operating under other orders. Sabotage, general mayhem. Their orders are unknown, though they are, upon contact and successful defeat, found to be carrying explosive devices.

But to acquire those explosive devices, one must first have a battle, which leads to warfare in the corridors. Bolts exchanged, plasma burning through polysteel and the flesh underneath: *all* sentient flesh, because the Tadeshi have picked up vakari whitefire weapons from the bodies of Protectorate fallen.

But we have seen this, reader, already. One battle is much like another. People will live, and people will die. Here are the universals: fear, flashing HUDs, roaring breath in the helmet's confines, sweat slick under a skinsuit that develops itches in inconvenient places which are forgotten the moment bolts fly.

Let us skip to the salient details: Jaed, Thorsdottir, Zhang, and Grytt survive unharmed; Crow sustains minor injury.

We will not include details of *what it is like*, because although it is a chronicler's job to sift through such details, it is also their job to decide which to include. The personal experience of battle is recounted in interviews and testimonies, or perhaps conversations with too much alcohol, late at night. Such details, such stories, are important. This chronicler wishes to make that very clear. But battle, war, is not the point of this story. *This* history is about how and why things come to pass, how and why people like Thorsdottir, Zhang, Jaed, and Grytt have to fight at all.

And so.

Rory followed various battles to retake the corridors of *Sissten* from the rear of the auxiliary bridge. The central holo-display divided itself into hemispheres, one dedicated to the tableau of voidships, the other to an interior map of *Sissten*, where the Tadeshi resistance was marked out in red, and the Protectorate personnel in blue, and the combined Empire and tenju forces in a green which, if it had been seen in an aura, would've meant dishonesty, distress, and potential malevolence.

She could not understand most of the words spoken, but body language, even bodies as unfamiliar as the vakari, employed a language which needed no translation. The battle was going *well*. Nor did she need arithmancy to know that the color designations for the various parties were deliberate; the same instinct that permitted her to understand vakari body language and tone also told her that this alliance wasn't going to last.

"It's time," Koto-rek said. "Come with me, Rory Thorne, and let us see if your friends are still willing to make the exchange."

That was an odd way of putting it. Odder was that Koto-rek seemed to be Rory's sole escort. Rory suspected some punishment on Zaraer's part for ordering it, to inflict some petty horror on Koto-rek by forcing her to deal with *aliens*. Again, she had no proof, no evidence, only a gut-deep certainty.

She glanced back at Zaraer, at the bridge hatch; the acting-captain was watching her.

How many of you are like him, Koto-rek? How many are like you?

But that was not something she knew how to ask, nor something that Koto-rek was likely (or able) to answer.

Rory was not sorry when the hatch irised shut, cutting her off from Zaraer's hostility. Even the creeping horror of the vakari engine—*that was not a core, don't call it a core, it was a rift, a tear, a weep*—was preferable to Zaraer's malice, suspicion, and contempt.

"What did you mean, if my friends are willing to make the exchange?" she asked, to give her brain something to do besides imagine the worst possible scenarios.

Koto-rek did not answer immediately. They walked past the engine core, and Engineer Vigat, and several vakari Rory had not seen before, similarly attired, and similarly stuffed into consoles and first-elbow deep in equipment. Vigat said something as Koto-rek passed, which the sub-commander acknowledged.

"Repairs are proceeding
we'll be able to fire
ahead of schedule," Koto-rek said, apparently casually.

Rory's stomach dropped through the deck. She did not want to ask, did not want to know, but a princess didn't run from discomfort. "Sub-Commander. I need an answer, please. What you said before, about the exchange, and the willingness of my allies to make it. What did you mean?"

Koto-rek stopped there in the middle of a deserted, blood-spattered corridor. The red emergency teslas had been banished in favor of the harsh, cold blue-white the vakari seemed to favor. Except for the ship's ambient hum, it was quiet.

"Zaraer does not want me to give you up, Princess Rory Thorne, unless I gain some new advantage from our bargain." Koto-rek's chromatophores were muted, roiling greens and yellows.

"You mean, you're going to break your word to the Vizier and to the Empire. You're changing the deal. That seems unwise, with the dreadnought out there, and your ship's need of allies."

Koto-rek made a circular, all-encompassing gesture. "*Sissten* is one ship in the Protectorate fleet. Our defeat and loss today would be painful, but ultimately insignificant. Likewise, our survival. So Zaraer believes Empire intervention—and this new apparent alliance with tenju, and with what seems to be a weaker partner, your

Confederation—must bear some greater significance than we have understood. He believes you are a great deal more important than you have thus far indicated."

"I am not that important to the Confederation."

"I know that. But the weapon we failed to acquire *is*. Zaraer believes it is the price of the Empire's cooperation, when by all political sense, the alwar should delight in our defeat today rather than offer their aid."

"I told you—"

"I know what you said, and what *they* said. The Empire's adepts are skilled at the simpler forms of arithmancy. It's a small matter to lie in negotiations, and make the lies seem true."

"And what do *you* think?"

"I think . . ." Koto-rek shook her head, another of those apparently universal gestures among species with the requisite physiology. "I think you are a more skilled politician than you seem. I think you have not told all the truth, though I am not sure how you concealed it. And I think you are honorable, which is not the same thing as honest."

"You know the acting-captain is wrong. Going back on the deal now is a bad idea. You have a Confederation-Empire alliance on your ship, *helping* you clear your decks of Tadeshi. If they realize you've gone back on your word . . ." Rory had no idea what would happen, practically and immediately. Nothing good. Violence, surely, with so many weapons in so many hostile hands. "People will die."

Koto-rek's chromatophores soured a deep greenish-gold. "And I should do what, then? Defy him? Sss. Would you encourage *your* servants to do the same, if they disagreed with your orders?"

"I don't *have* servants anymore, but when I did, *yes*, I expected them to tell me if they thought I was wrong."

"And I have done so. Zaraer declines my advice, and he is my commanding officer. I am disinclined to mutiny."

"Is it mutiny to avoid a war? Killing me—threatening me—won't get him that weapon, if the Empire already has it. Which they *don't*."

Koto-rek did not answer at first. Then her jaw-plates fluttered before sealing tight to her face. "Zaraer believes that. But he also thinks that without you, the Confederation will not yield it up at all. I would kill you with regret, Rory Thorne. So let us hope that your friends are more willing to part with information than you are, and let us hope that *someone* has more than just a shipping manifest to exchange for you."

Koto-rek resumed walking, long vakari strides that rapidly opened a distance between her and Rory, who considered staying right where she was, mag-locking her boots to the deck and refusing another step until—

Until what? She had talked Koto-rek into mutiny? That seemed unlikely. It seemed *more* probable that, if she resisted, Koto-rek would either drag her bodily or, worse, summon someone to *help* drag her bodily to the rendezvous.

Rory shook her head—regret, resignation, and anger—and hurried to catch up. She followed Koto-rek through familiar corridors, past the morgue and intersections now unsealed and vacant, until they came to the row of berths to which *Vagabond* had been tethered. This location showed particular damage: ugly circular patches in the bulkhead where a breaching pod had locked on and punched through. Two of the berths had aetherlocks unsealed and open to *Sissten's* corridors. Rory knew from her observations on the bridge that the majority of Empire personnel who'd debarked here were still dispersed in the upper decks, but that the Tadeshi threat was, in military jargon, *neutralized*, which really meant dead people on both sides.

There were troops waiting at the far end of the corridor, near the berths. Ten, perhaps, though Rory did not stop to count. She did mark the breadth and shape of the collection, the variation that told her some were xeno. All of the hardsuits bore unfamiliar plating, covered with hexwork visible even though Rory was not peering into the aether; it glittered like snowflakes in moonlight, and had Rory been a fraction less sure that her survival depended on her absolute attention to the next few minutes, she would have risked a closer look.

The corridor stretched perhaps ten meters. Koto-rek slowed, but did not break stride, when a single individual peeled away from the rest of the troops and stopped halfway up the corridor's length, a clear obstacle, holding a plasma rifle more comfortably than Rory found comforting.

Then his visor retracted, and Rory thought she'd never been so glad to see Jaed Moss in her life.

"That's far enough," he said.

Koto-rek took a final, insolent step before halting in the middle of the corridor, equidistant from the bulkheads, perhaps two and a half meters from Jaed. She held her empty hands out wide, both to show that she was unarmed, and to prevent Rory's easy passage around her.

Jaed leaned slightly to one side. His eyes sought Rory's. "You all right?"

"Yes. You?"

He nodded. "We're good." He laid emphasis on the pronoun.

The intensity of her relief bordered on pain. Rory let a breath out she didn't know she'd been holding. "Listen, Jaed. We have a small problem. The Protectorate would like to amend their agreement."

Jaed's eyes narrowed and shifted to Koto-rek. "No. Don't think so. Rory, come here."

The subtle shift in Koto-rek's stance said any attempt to do so would turn rapidly violent. Rory did not move. "Jaed, listen. They know about the weapon. The captured Tadeshi soldiers they took from *G. Stein* told them."

Jaed stared at her. She could imagine the outraged monologue in his head, the *but you confirmed it, why* succeeded by a slow drain of color and indignation into something more like horror. *What did they do to you?*

Jaed said nothing, however, and so Rory's fairy gift could not aid her with revelations. All she had was her own native intuition, and Jaed's complete attention, and his miserable skill at keeping his thoughts off his face.

"I'm not authorized to negotiate for the Confederation." Jaed's voice climbed the twin peaks of desperation and frustration.

Truth, said the fairy gift. Koto-rek would read *truth,* too, if she was looking at his aura, which of course she must be.

The small cluster of hardsuits waiting at the berth's aetherlock stirred. Faceplates retracted, one-two-three. Rory closed her eyes against a sudden, stinging relief. Thorsdottir. Zhang. *Grytt.* A savage glee surged through her, pushing fear and dread to the margins. Koto-rek did not stand a chance. One lone vakar, and *these* people, the fight would not last more than a shot—

The fight in this corridor, no. That was an easy victory. The war begun between Confederation and their allies against the Protectorate, however, would last much longer, and to much less certain outcome.

That will be the end of us.

It was on her lips to say, *Then I will negotiate.* She let them hover there, caught on her held breath.

She had come out here to *avoid* politics, having renounced her title. And anyway, she had been a princess of Thorne, not the Confederation. She was—nothing to the Confederation at all. A citizen. A, a reminder that they'd needed her help once, however unwitting, to launch their war of independence. Dame Maggie wouldn't thank her for usurping political authority to which she was not entitled.

Nor did Rory want to do so. She wanted to wait for someone who did have Maggie's endorsement. Maybe on that incoming ship. Or call for Messer Rupert to do it. He could negotiate. Rory had no inkling, then, of what official powers Rupert had (or did not); these were the thoughts of a young woman who very badly did not want to do a thing that she was uniquely positioned to do. Because she knew she was in a good position: the vakari *knew* her—well, perhaps that was an exaggeration. She had some traction with Koto-rek, anyway, and that might help. Dame Maggie was nothing if not practical. She would forgive. Or understand. Or arrest and incarcerate, but damn sure she'd stick to any agreement Rory made, too, if it gained her more allies against the Tadeshi.

Then Rory thought about the engine core, that weeping rip into a deep layer of void, and the arithmancy it would take to *do* such a thing. She thought about how such arithmancy was so commonplace among the vakari that they powered ships with it. And she recalled her own certainty that a war with the Protectorate would be the end of everyone. Her own comfort seemed petty, next to that. Her own wants, selfish.

She could do something. So she would.

Rory raised her voice for Thorsdottir, Zhang, and Grytt's benefit. "I'll negotiate the new terms for the Confederation. I am, after all, a princess. Is that acceptable?"

"It is." Koto-rek sounded entirely self-possessed, as if she were not outnumbered, as if firearms accidents might not happen in this corridor so far from other vakari.

Rory did not think Zaraer expected the Empire to start something overtly, but if they did, fine, they'd kill Koto-rek, whom Zaraer did not love overmuch. Or maybe he wanted to observe how the Princess Rory Thorne acted when she was not held under compulsion, and from her actions, judge the entire Confederation. It was both unfair and exactly the sort of judgment people made all the time.

Rory took a deep breath and eyelocked Jaed.

"The Protectorate is concerned about the weapon that the Tadeshi were smuggling on *G. Stein*, which was made by their clients," she said. "They believe that the Empire has possession of it now."

"Huh." Jaed's glance tore free and speared Koto-rek with contempt. "The way I understand it, when the Protectorate says *client*, they mean *slave*."

"That allegation is false. Client-species have rights. Slaves do not." Irritation thinned the Koto-rek's voice. "Your subordinate has been speaking with the battlechief, I think."

I don't even know who this battlechief is, Rory thought. Jaed did, clearly, from his tight, unfriendly smile.

"Jaed. This is important. Is the sub-commander correct? *Has* the Empire been promised this weapon in exchange for coming here to retrieve me?"

Jaed closed his eyes for a little too long. He was trying some kind of arithmancy, a hex on his aura. Rory winced inwardly. Of course he was. *She* would have. "I don't know anything about those negotiations. We're just here for Rory."

Koto-rek did not move. She did not even blink. But Jaed flinched, startled, and a line of blood threaded from his nose.

"The sub-commander is an arithmancer," Rory said rapidly, softly, urgently. "Please, just tell me why the Empire agreed to assist the Confederation. I can't negotiate if I don't *know*."

Jaed worked the words around in his mouth for a long moment. "They wanted the documentation we found on R—on the weapon, yes. And, ah." Another trickle of blood emerged from his nostril. "Shit. Fine. They also wanted the remnants of the original biological organism."

"You told me the weapon had been physically destroyed." Koto-rek did not turn her head. Did not sound angry. And yet Rory's skin tingled as if she stood naked in a thunderstorm.

"It was. Most of it, anyway." Rory ignored the raw indignation on Jaed's face, the naked betrayal. "Except for one small salvaged remnant. Not enough to *do* anything."

Koto-rek's voice sharpened until the air itself bled. "Does the Empire now possess this remnant?"

The red on Jaed's cheekbones was spreading, and his eyes held a dangerous glint. "Yeah, they do."

Koto-rek's jaw-plates flared wide, exposing the teeth in her jaw. "The Protectorate claims ownership of the sample. It is proprietary information illegally obtained from our clients. We want everything returned to us."

Rory felt a pang for Rose. But there wasn't a choice, was there? War, or one sentient weapon. It was an easy decision. "All right. We'll get the sample back from the alwar."

Jaed's jaw squared and knotted. *That* wasn't good. "No," he said. "That won't be possible."

"Sss. Let me be clear. This is not negotiable. Our stolen property and all data, returned to us, in exchange for your princess."

"You're pretty outnumbered to be making threats." Jaed gestured broadly. "You know. *Out there.*"

"And *you* are outnumbered in here."

"I think what my associate means," Rory interrupted smoothly, "is that the Empire will insist on retaining copies of all data and documentation, as part of their prior negotiation and agreement with the Confederation. Sub-Commander, the more people that have this information, the less of a threat the weapon becomes. You know this. Of *course* we will return the physical sample, but even you must acknowledge the impossibility of what you're asking."

"No. What I *mean*," Jaed snapped, "is that *Rose* is dead. The sample's inert. You can't use it. No one can."

truth, said the fairy gift.

Rory dropped a sliver of attention into the aether, barely an eyeblink; it was thick with equations, knots of vakari hexwork, through which Jaed's aura glowed like a sun. Rage-red, agitated orange, a growing filament of green she didn't like, green as any rosebush. "*Whatever* remains, we'll return to the Protectorate," she said aloud. "Again, minus any samples already extracted, or copies already made of data. Agreed?"

"Ss. Acceptable."

"Jaed?"

Two spots of color appeared on Jaed's cheekbones, a sure sign of defiance. To Rory's surprise, and Koto-rek's frustration, he said nothing that an arithmancer's hex (or a fairy's gift) might reveal as untruth. But Rory knew, as did Koto-rek, what that silence meant.

"Don't lie," Rory wished him. "Just tell me—why won't you

agree? There's nothing left to protect, especially if Rose is dead. This is a matter of *war*, do you get that?"

"Of course I get that. But we can't give up all the physical remains. *Some*, maybe." Jaed cut a glance at Koto-rek.

"*All* physical remains, or there is no deal." Koto-rek's hand closed on Rory's shoulder.

"Jaed." Rory didn't like the pitch of her voice, rising into panic. She didn't like the way Grytt had raised her rifle, down the corridor, or the way Thorsdottir had taken a step in their direction.

Or the way Koto-rek's talons were biting into her hardsuit, physically biting.

Jaed looked like he wanted to throw up. "Listen. When we escaped, Thorsdottir got hurt. They"—he jabbed at Koto-rek with the tip of his rifle—"burned her bad. She was dying. Rose saved her, but they—they're gone."

"Saved *how*?" Rory asked, before Koto-rek could.

"I

nanomecha

don't *know*. Repaired her, somehow."

Of course. Rose's nanomecha, made to transmute and transform. Alchemy verging on magic.

"What do you mean, the weapon *repaired* this Thorsdottir?" Koto-rek tripped over the syllables. "How?"

Jaed shook his head and set his lips in a stubborn line.

And because Koto-rek could read untruth in any denial Jaed made, and because she did not want to see him bleed anymore, Rory said, "The weapon we found on *G. Stein* was a decorative flora that had been infused with nanomecha. *They* were the weapon. Upon triggering of the command codes, those nanomecha were intended to infiltrate, and then destroy, a biosphere. Evidently the nanomecha could, in the right environment, *choose* to act. And now, having done so, those nanomecha are . . . dead?"

"Right," Jaed said, in the flattest tone Rory had ever heard from him.

Koto-rek became very still and quiet, the way cats do before leaping on some unfortunate creature, or the way bombs do before they explode. "Are you saying this weapon

contaminated

chose to render aid? That it was

abomination

sentient?"

Jaed peeled the vakar a look of contempt. "They were. Now they're dead."

"But the *nanomecha* themselves. Do any remain?"

Rory's heart dropped. "I think what my associate means to say is—the sentience is gone? Right, Jaed?"

"Right."

Truth. Rory's chest ached, not for her own grief, but for Jaed's. She felt only a guilty relief. To hand Rose over to what would likely be their own execution had been an unsavory proposition. But if they were already *dead*—

"You said that the weapon *repaired* this Thorsdottir," said Koto-rek. "Unless the nanomecha are entirely gone, they may still infest her. Whether or not they are sentient any longer, whether or not they are a weapon, they remain Protectorate property. Therefore, because there is no way to completely extract nanomecha, we will require her, as well."

"The hell," Jaed said. "No."

"We could arrange for a biological sample," said Rory. Thorsdottir might object, but—

"Are you *serious*?"

—Jaed certainly was objecting.

"I am," she said, and pinned him with a stare. "Be quiet."

"Because Thorsdottir—"

"Will do what she's told," Rory snapped, in her best princess voice. She would ask, of *course* she would ask, but in the end, Thorsdottir would have to agree. This was a matter of preventing war.

Jaed stared at her, and in that moment, something broke. Rory saw it: a shattering, like a glass dropped from a great height onto stone.

Inside her chest, something similar happened, but smaller, quieter.

"No," Koto-rek repeated. "The agreement was the return of physical material, and copies of all stolen data. We offer this compromise: the Empire may keep the samples it has already extracted. But the rest, this Thorsdottir and whatever nanomecha remain in her, belongs to us."

Jaed took a step back, two, and pointed the rifle at Koto-rek. "Thorsdottir belongs to *no one*."

Koto-rek ignored him, though her pigments spangled an uneasy yellow. "Princess Rory Thorne," she said. "Control your subordinate."

I'm not sure I can. I'm not sure I want to. Negotiation. Reason. Jaed might be beyond both, but Koto-rek was not. "Sub-Commander, please. Jaed was telling the truth. The sentience is dead. Whether or not there are any remaining nanomecha is immaterial. The *weapon* is gone."

"And yet," said Koto-rek, "potential remains. The Empire adepts could find a way to recreate it. Perhaps its flexibility of purpose means it can be adapted into weaponry again, or into something worse."

A rose by any other name is still nanomecha meant to alter biological matter to new forms on a genetic level. And a rose by any other name was also Thorsdottir.

"You don't believe that the Empire is capable of harnessing that level of arithmancy." Rory let a small, Rupert-shaped smile fall onto her lips. "I *know* you don't believe that."

"Zaraer does. And Zaraer is not the only one who will. And I could be mistaken, Rory Thorne, about what the alwar adepts can manage."

Truth.

"Then if we return every bit of Rose to you, including what remains in Thorsdottir—you will what? Destroy her as an abomination?"

Perhaps that was sympathy on the vakar's face. Perhaps a trick of the teslas, refracting on the oilslick pigments. "One contaminated individual, Princess. Let the Empire keep what data it has; but surrender the rest to us, and maintain this truce."

Rory looked down the corridor, where her friends waited with their tenju and alwar allies. There was a conference, Zhang and Grytt and Thorsdottir together, conducting what Rory supposed was an argument waged too quietly to carry. But then Thorsdottir stepped clear, and started walking up the corridor. Zhang and Grytt let her go. Trusting Thorsdottir's judgment. Allowing her sacrifice. They were *good* at sacrifice, Grytt and Zhang and Thorsdottir. (Not Jaed. Not anymore. Somehow, when she wasn't looking, Jaed Moss had decided to *fight*.)

One woman's life, for peace. For the potential thousands of lives, millions. Rory did not yet know details about the Expansion, how many k'bal were dead in the Verge. She knew no details of wichu clientage, what happened when a people surrendered to the Protectorate.

She *did* know the Free Worlds of Tadesh would not last much longer, waging a war on two fronts. It might be a year, two, three, but the Protectorate would finish them, or the Confederation would accept their surrender. And either way, then the Protectorate would be down to one front to their Expansion.

She thought about what she'd seen in the morgue, and what might be contained in the Writ, and the words abomination and contamination. She thought about a very sharp people, inclined to violence.

She thought about whether, even if she could reason with Koto-rek, any agreement they made would hold once it got to Zaraer, or others *like* Zaraer.

"Rory," said Jaed. Pleading with her.

Oh, it would be easy to let Thorsdottir walk into vakari hands, and say *but she chose it*. Except sometimes a woman could not choose only for herself. Sometimes she had to choose for many people. That's what being a princess meant. Being a leader.

Rory drew a lungful of breath, and of courage, and pitched her voice to carry. "No. I'm sorry, Sub-Commander. We will transmit the information we collected, so that you and the Empire have that, and we will return what remains of the inert sample. We will *not* part with Thorsdottir."

Down the corridor, Thorsdottir stopped. Perhaps she felt relief. Perhaps pride. Perhaps grief. But she did not protest.

Koto-rek tilted her head, first one way, then the other. Her cheeks cycled through a spectrum of disbelief, distress, outrage, fear. She looked at Jaed, and past the leveled menace of Jaed's rifle at Thorsdottir. Something passed over her face, a ripple of blue, deepening into cobalt, then violet. Her talons spasmed on Rory's shoulder, and the hardsuit wailed a breach warning.

"Then I am afraid, Princess, that you will stay here."

"No," Rory said, softly, as Jaed's finger tightened on his rifle. No wars started in the corridor.

Not *another* one, because of her choices.

"I'll go with the sub-commander, Jaed. Those are the terms we agreed to."

"The hell. We are not leaving you behind."

truth, said the fairy gift.

Then Grytt's visor sealed, and Zhang's. Thorsdottir, face still bare, watched her with steady, burning eyes. Or perhaps it was Koto-rek she looked at.

Then, sudden as catastrophe, the vakar released Rory and stepped back, so quickly the hardsuit chirped an alert. Koto-rek raised her hand—ignoring Jaed's indrawn breath and the twitch that said he'd almost fired on her—to touch something on her helmet.

The comms, Rory thought. *She just cut the comms in her suit.*

"So we see the worth of the Confederation's word." Koto-rek's voice carried the corridor's length. "There will be war because of your decision."

"It's not the first war I've caused," said Rory, though the words cut her like slivers of glass to say aloud. Truth was, is, can be—a painful thing.

"Not because of you, Rory Thorne. Because of *them*."

Grytt, who had just drawn even with Thorsdottir, stopped, and Zhang with her. Grytt raised her visor. "What did *we* do, exactly?"

"You are—" Koto-rek groped for the word.

Rory came to her aid, a combination of the fairy gift and prior experience. "An abomination."

"Grytt." Jaed included Rory in his generalized outrage. "Her name is *Grytt*."

"Not just . . . Grytt." Koto-rek flicked her too-few, too-jointed fingers. "That one, *Thorsdottir*, is contaminated with nanomecha. I can *see* what has happened, in the aether. The wichu weapon is dead, Rory Thorne, that is true. But what it has *become*, what remains in that person, can spread. *Will* spread. The Protectorate will not tolerate that. Can never tolerate."

"Maybe the Protectorate needs to try." Jaed bared his teeth, white and unmarked and, to a vakar, ominous in their blankness, offering no hint of heritage, of *who this person was*.

Koto-rek's own lips lifted, baring her gleaming blue testament to a lineage and tradition so very different. So very *alien*. "Perhaps it does. Perhaps it may yet have the opportunity. But now, you need to leave. Quickly, before Zaraer sends troops to investigate my silence. Withdraw and return to the alwar ship."

"Why?" Rory asked. "Why are you letting me go? Letting *us* go?"

Koto-rek ground out a laugh. "How could I stop you, one vakar against so many?"

"I think you could stop *me*."

"I could. But I still do not think you deserve to die, and your death today will not stop anything that is coming."

Rory set her teeth against nausea and despair rising bitter in the back of her throat. "You mean, war was always inevitable with the Empire. With *us*. No matter what happened here."

Koto-rek's cheeks darkened to ashy black. "The Expansion does not recognize borders. But today, I am tired of death, Princess Rory Thorne."

Rory shook her head, not because Koto-rek was wrong, or because she disbelieved her, but because she *wished* she did. "What will Zaraer do to you?"

"Sss. Not what you imagine. We are not tenju, to kill our rivals without trial or process. I will survive today."

Rory swallowed her own throatful of razors. "Then I should thank you."

"No. You shouldn't. I have done neither of us any favors." Koto-rek began to retreat, backing down the corridor one step at a time, hands raised, empty, open and weaponless. It was a symbolic gesture—arithmancers did not need hands to hex—but symbols are sometimes enough. She flung a look at Rory like an entire clip-ful of 'slinger bolts. "This war will be the end of your Confedera-tion, of your species—and it will be a slow, unkind ending. It will cost many lives, ours and yours. Let us delay it as long as we can."

Then the vakar turned and strode briskly away, back bare to Jaed's rifle, to Grytt's, to an array of hostile xenos clustered at the aetherlock. The gesture was equal parts *you cannot harm me* and *you don't scare me at all.* An arrogant people, the vakari, to go with their sharpness.

Rory heard Jaed's indrawn breath—not unlike a vakar's hiss—and supposed he was reading that arrogance, and reacting to it. Perhaps that had been Koto-rek's intention: to provoke, and thus keep her enemies (*because that is what we are now, and maybe always were*) reacting, instead of acting. It was a Protectorate strat-egy, and it was something the xeno and human alliance would need to learn to counter.

Rory opened her mouth to tell Jaed not to shoot, however tempting a target. Then she looked and saw that he wasn't point-ing a weapon, nor looking at her—that he was, in fact, gazing after the vakar with a stubborn-jawed thoughtfulness she hadn't seen before.

The corner of his mouth twisted like a wet rag wrung out. "Great. Like the multiverse needs another war."

Rory took a bite of air. "I couldn't give them Thorsdottir." It was not an apology.

He shifted that thoughtful, furious gaze to her and his lips leveled. "I wouldn't've let you, so I'm glad you didn't try."

He gestured with the rifle as if it were an extra hand. Rory looked where he pointed: at Thorsdottir and Grytt and Zhang, back to a waiting knot of xenos with whom her friends, and therefore she, were now aligned, both circumstantially and apparently politically.

"What do we do *now*?"

"*I* figure out how to fight vakari," said Jaed. "You—I don't know. You're a princess, Rory."

"I don't know if there's any place for *princesses* in the Confederation."

Jaed cocked an eyebrow. His eyes were very blue, and much older than Rory remembered. "Then be something else. You're good at deciding things. At getting other people to decide things."

She laughed, a little hysterically. "Does the multiverse really need more politicians?"

Jaed was not laughing. He wasn't even smiling. "It needs you."

And the thirteenth fairy's gift said, *truth.*

CHAPTER TWENTY-SIX ≡≡≡

The Confederation corsair *Never Take Our Freedom* took four hours, twenty-seven minutes to travel from the Samtalet void-gate to the place where *Favored Daughter*, *Bane*, and the remains of *G. Stein* waited. When it drew close enough to hail *Favored Daughter* without obnoxious time-delays, it did so, with a greeting and subsequent demand (barely framed as a request) for the remanding of the Vizier into Confederation custody, which the captain promptly withdrew upon learning of a formal alliance between Empire and Confederation. The presence of the Princess Rory Thorne (whom the captain had only seen in person during the very early days of the Confederation, and then at formal events and in the company of Dame Maggie) added to the captain's conviction that whatever orders she might've left Lanscot with, the situation had changed radically, and until Dame Maggie confirmed that yes, she was to arrest what was clearly the negotiator of an advantageous alliance, and possibly run afoul of one of the heroes of the rebellion, she was content to accept the Vizier's word and authority. The whole business smacked of politics far above her pay-grade.

Thus did Rupert avoid immediate arrest. He did eventually acquire his title legitimately, though accompanied by a dressing-down behind closed doors that left metaphorical blisters, and a permanent cooling of relations between himself and Dame Maggie, which would have been more of a problem if Maggie herself had not been replaced as head of the Confederation shortly after the Tadeshi surrender and before the Expansion war's formal declaration.

The astute reader may be wondering what became of *Sissten* and the dreadnought. The latter, after re-acquiring its hoppers, spent an hour or so making everyone wonder if it meant to start a fight despite being outnumbered (and despite multiple attempts to communicate, all ignored) before it accelerated away and passed there out of the system and this chronicle.

Sissten departed shortly thereafter, also with no further communication, retreating toward the nearest gas giant behind which, presumably, it meant to shelter until it solved its wobbling and could depart. It must have succeeded, because the name *Sissten* does not reappear in battle reports until several standard years in the future, when the first wave of Expansion crashed into the Confederation's shores.

Although the first actual exchange of what would be called the Expansion War—whitefire lancebeams from the Protectorate vessel, mass-driven metal shards from a Confederation ship, which swiftly and decisively lost that battle—did not take place for almost a year, and happened in a system far from the k'bal Verge, this chronicler contends, and believes that you, reader, will agree, that the war had already begun.

Rory met the green fairy for the second time in her life in a lavish, if diminutively proportioned, guest cabin on the Empire warship *Favored Daughter*. She had just returned from a meeting with

Messer Rupert, Adept Kesk, Grytt, and Battlechief Crow, and upon entering, found a small, green woman seated on the settee, legs crossed, hands in her lap.

Rory knew exactly who and what she was, despite having been an infant at their first and only prior meeting. But knowing in no way ameliorated the shock, nor in any way kept her heart from lurching up into her throat. She slapped one hand on her chest to remind that rebel organ of its proper location, and hit the door controls with the other before a passing alwar crewperson chanced to look inside.

"Hello," Rory said, because that seemed polite.

"Huh," said the fairy. She did not seem concerned with etiquette. "Princess Rory Thorne."

Rory had accepted that her days of untitled anonymity had ended, but she had not made friends with that knowledge. She grimaced at the word princess. "Green fairy. May I inquire the reason for your visit?"

The fairy peered at Rory through narrow, verdigris eyes. "I came to tell you that you have well and truly
destroyed the multiverse
broken things this time."

Rory blinked. The fairy gift had seemed unusually loud. "I'm sorry?"

"You're not. That's the irony of it. Even though you keep telling yourself that you are."

It had been exactly two days since Rory's ordeal on *Sissten*, and only a little less since *Never Take Our Freedom's* arrival, and she had already spent several (too many) hours on quantum-hex conference with Lanscot and Dame Maggie, both reporting on her experiences and the alliance, and arguing for Messer Rupert's retention as the Vizier, and also, please, don't arrest him. She had succeeded, but in so doing, she had talked herself nearly hoarse. Rory wanted a cup of hot tea, a little solitude, and some sleep. The sooner the fairy finished whatever she meant to say, the sooner she might get all three.

One did not expel a fairy from one's (borrowed) quarters because of a little exhaustion, however. There were not many places to sit in the cabin—the fairy occupied the primary location already, and seemed disinclined to share—and so Rory sat instead on the edge of the small table in front of the settee, meant to hold beverages or handheld tablets or, if one was untidy, plates absconded with from the mess hall and not quite returned.

Rory pushed those plates to one side and sat down, mindful of any creaking or tipping that might indicate alwar tables might not bear the weight of a human woman.

The fairy watched this, silently. She did not seem angry, exactly (though Rory knew herself no expert on fairy expressions). Resigned, perhaps. A little aggrieved.

Rory weighed the wisdom of attempting to tease out the cause of the fairy's discomfiture, or just making some educated assumptions and going from there. She folded her hands in her lap and pasted on her best politely impenitent smile.

"If you mean, do I regret my choices on *Sissten*, I do not. If you know anything about the Protectorate, then you know I couldn't give Thorsdottir to them. Or Rose. Or what was *left* of Rose." Rory had done some research about what was actually contained in the Writ, and what vakari considered abominations, and—by examining what was known of wichu clientage outside the Protectorate—what happened to those on whom fell that designation.

The green fairy, who was also aware of those things, said, "And so you put one woman's life above the lives of millions."

Rory was becoming accustomed to a sort of permanent

queasiness. She was also accustomed to people demanding an account of her actions, and she was becoming rather tired of it. She decided to make her own demand, and see what happened.

"I did. And now you have come all this way to tell me I'm responsible for destroying the multiverse why, exactly?"

"I never said that you—ah. Right. Thirteen's curse."

"I think it's a gift."

"Think what you like." The green fairy smiled with small, sharp teeth. She looked a little bit like an alw, Rory thought, now that she'd seen a representative population. They were also a sharp people, though their spikes were concealed on the inside, and emerged only in alchemy, politics, and conversation. "But no. I'm not here to chastise you. You didn't *fail*. You survived. That was the point."

Rory blinked. "I—Wait. That seems somewhat at odds with what you suggested to Messer Rupert. He thought he was supposed to recover Rose and prevent them from falling into the wrong hands."

"He was supposed to recover *you*. You were supposed to recover the weapon. The vakari would have destroyed the nanomecha. The Tadeshi would have used them as they were. But you will use them as they *are*. And you will share them among human, alwar, and tenju." The fairy ticked them off on her fingers.

That begged an obvious *how*. Rory rolled the word around in her mouth, and elected to leave it there. "But you believe I've destroyed the multiverse anyway? Because I thought that's what all this was supposed to prevent."

"Change always comes with a measure of destruction, and without guarantee of something better coming afterward. You were *always* going to break things." The green fairy cocked her head. "I always wondered if I'd made a mistake, giving you harp-playing instead of physical prowess. Imagine what would've happened if you had learned to hit things as a first response."

They stared at each other for a long moment. Rory was reluctant to look away—to even blink—lest the fairy disappear the same way she'd arrived. She supposed it must be some kind of personal tesser-hex, some arithmancy so advanced it looked like magic, or something inherent to whatever fairies *were*. It was on her lips to ask, even knowing the fairy would not just answer (fairies, it seemed, tended toward cryptic utterances, just as they did to coming and going without regard to physics).

But then she said simply, "Thank you. For making the choice, and for giving me the gift that you did."

The fairy looked surprised, then pleased, then a little bit sad. "You're welcome."

CHAPTER TWENTY-SEVEN ≡≡≡

J aed and Thorsdottir converged on the transparent platform at the top of the arboretum, in almost exactly the
same place Rupert (now officially Vizier to the Office of
Alliances and Treaties) had encountered the green fairy. It was
neither a chance meeting, nor a prearranged tryst, but rather the
half-hearted attempt by Thorsdottir to "be alone."

Zhang had, when informed where Thorsdottir was going, rolled
her eyes. "Shall I tell Jaed where you've gone, when he comes by?"

"You can, sure, but why would he?"

Zhang produced another eyeroll, this time accompanied by a
faint, knowing smile. "You aren't answering his messages."

Thorsdottir had frowned, on the edge of protesting she'd had
no *time* to answer messages. Since they had all returned from
Samtalet, Thorsdottir's days had been a confusion of tests, medical and alchemical and probably arithmantic (those, at least, did
not employ needles), conducted by both tenju and alwar on their
respective ships, in their respective medical bays, which had involved a lot of traipsing back and forth through aetherlocks. And
then, after Dame Maggie finally made Rupert Vizier and Rory
into *whatever* her new title was (not princess, but something that
required a lot of meetings and no personal security), human

chirurgeons from the Confederation conducted their own examinations as well in the station medical bay. Thorsdottir was very tired of needles and disrobing in front of strangers, and when granted freedom from those obligations, she had been seeking refuge in the quarters she shared with Zhang. If, after a day of bloodletting, she did not want to answer a small queue of *message received: J. Moss* then surely that was forgivable.

Instead, she'd said, "What do you mean, *when he comes by*? Has he been coming over here?"

"Oh *honestly*," Zhang had said, and made little shoving motions with her hands. "Go. *Go*. Just don't leave the arboretum until he finds you."

The platform on which Thorsdottir was perched had been intended to facilitate stellar observations. It also worked well as a vantage for observing incoming visitors. She saw at once when Jaed passed through the doors. He looked up immediately—which most visitors did not—and seeing her, stuttered to a pause. There was a moment of eyelock, strained by distance, during which neither of them made any extraneous gestures, neither waves nor smiles nor other modes of acknowledgement. Then, visibly setting his shoulders, Jaed dropped his gaze, minding where his feet were, and set a brisk pace for the stairs.

He was moving a bit less briskly when he finally achieved the platform (having discovered, as Rupert had, that there were a *great* many steps). Thorsdottir, who had found herself not half as tired as she should've been at the end of her own climb (she credited Rose's remnants for that, based on things overheard from various medical professionals), watched him come, and pretended that her own heart was not thumping and flopping about in her chest in a manner that had nothing to do with exertion.

"Do you know what she's doing?" Jaed blurted, when he was

still half out of breath and two steps from the top of the platform. He meant Rory. There was no other possible referent for that tone of *she*.

Thorsdottir felt her face knitting into a frown she had not pre-approved. "Hello, Thorsdottir. How are you? Oh, *fine*, Jaed, how are you?"

He hauled himself the rest of the way onto the platform and teetered toward her, a little shaky in the knees. He stopped in that strange no-man's land of personal space that was a little too close for stationer politeness, and a little too far for the close-quarter intimacy of crew on a ship *Vagabond's* size. It was as if he was not quite sure where he belonged, which, Thorsdottir supposed, was *her* fault. She had not been very welcoming since the Rose Incident, even before the excused absences of all her medical testing.

Now, from this undecided, uncomfortable distance, he offered her a headshake-and-glare combination. "I asked how you were in the first, oh, *dozen* messages I sent. Which you ignored. I thought— never mind what I thought. I just started asking Zhang how you were. Did you even read them?"

"No," said Thorsdottir, who of course had. "I just saw them in the queue. I've been *busy*, Jaed. Everyone wants a piece, or a few drops of blood, or, or *whatever* of me."

That diverted him for a squint-eyed, searching moment. "And? What are they saying?"

She nipped back a snarky *Oh, Zhang didn't tell you that, I see* and said, perfectly civil: "The consensus is that I'm harboring nano-mecha of xenobiological origins, formerly sentient, that appear to be maintaining me at optimal health. Maybe even a little better than optimal. Nothing we didn't already know." And then, because Jaed had flinched a little, because they had been over and *over* this and Thorsdottir was bored with her own resentment, she added, "I'm fine. I'm *good.*"

Jaed's eyes gentled, and he looked on the verge of saying something Thorsdottir decided she did not yet have the courage to hear. She trampled over his indrawn breath and said in a rush, "To answer your original query: I have not heard what Rory is doing exactly, but I imagine it's her job. Another title starting with *p.*"

"President of the Allied Confederation Council. Except, typical Rory, she's put out a resolution to expand the Confederation to include the xenos, the Merchants League, basically anyone who wants to join, and drafted a proposal to make the Council into the ruling body, doing away with prime ministers. Dame Maggie's not happy, but the idea's pretty popular with the public and some of the other Confederation members."

"So?"

"So . . ." Jaed paused for another lungful of air. "*So,* as part of this newly expanded Confederation—assuming the Harek Empire goes along with it, *which they will,* because at least three tenju battlechiefs just signed on—she wants to form some kind of multi-species group? Specifically to gather intelligence about the wichu situation inside the Protectorate. I don't think it has a real name yet. All those messages were me *trying* to ask you if you'd heard about it, and if you were going to sign up."

He paused. Thorsdottir peeled her attention away from his face and threw it into the void, where it landed between the curve of Lanscot below and the scattered stars and let the expectant silence hang, unfilled.

Jaed said a very Grytt sort of word. "I had to ask *Zhang*—"

—who had not, Thorsdottir was sure, yielded up any confidences—

"—and she said that not only did you *know* that, you'd already signed up. Both of you. That *your* acceptance was just waiting for medical clearance. Which, she said, you'd just gotten."

She heard Jaed move closer, a squeak of boot on the clear poly-alloy. She was glad that the porthole's mysterious alchemical composition didn't permit reflections. Bad enough she could feel his stare on the side of her face.

"I did some checking around. Seems like Battlechief Crow is one of the commander-types Rory's asked to lead this joint task force. And there's an alw, though I don't remember her name. Did you hear she tapped Grytt, too?"

"Grytt turned her down."

"Oh, you *can* speak."

"We've *been* talking, Jaed."

"Good. That's *great*. Because I thought you'd just lied to me about knowing what Rory's up to, when clearly you *do* know, so maybe you can tell me why."

"I didn't lie. I wasn't sure what you meant. I *do* know about the task force. Obviously."

"All right. Then maybe, since we're have an attack of sudden honesty, you'll also tell me why you've been avoiding me."

"I haven't been—you're here now, aren't you? I know Zhang told you where I'd be."

"Yes. Yes, she did. She said, *Thorsdottir's run off to the arboretum and she's hoping you'll look for her there.*"

"She did *not*."

"She actually did." Jaed huffed, halfway between amusement and exasperation. "Anyway. *Point* is, I signed up, too, and I think we need to settle whatever this is between us before we all ship out."

Thorsdottir's head snapped around. Jaed was *right there*, a handspan from her shoulder, staring out the same porthole with the same unfocused determination. "You did *what*."

A faint flush dusted his cheekbones, there and gone in a breath. "Signed up. I'm coming with you and Zhang. Joining this *whatever it is* Rory's thought up, whatever she's calling it. We need to know what's going on out there. Who these wichu are that made Rose. Whether they're another enemy, or maybe an ally."

"We're probably going to get into *fights*, Jaed. With the Protectorate. With *vakari*."

"That's possible, yeah."

"And blood makes you sick."

"After what we saw on *G. Stein* and *Sissten*? I honestly don't know if I can get sick again."

"I'll take that bet."

Jaed lifted his chin and jabbed his gaze at her like a spear. "Why are you arguing with me? After *Sissten* and *every other damned thing*."

"Maybe *because* of all that."

There was a time he would have flinched, hearing that. Assumed fault, assumed guilt. Now his eyes narrowed. "Are you still mad about Rose? Because if you are, we need to talk about that."

"It's not about Rose."

"Is it *me*?" His face did not change, but there was something so raw in his voice that Thorsdottir's chest ached.

"Yes. But not the way you think, Jaed. Listen." Thorsdottir found it very hard to keep looking at him. She made herself do it anyway. "What happened, what we did—that wasn't intercepting smugglers trying to sneak contraband apples past station customs. That was *dangerous*. That was, that was *war*."

"Says the woman who showed us all what whitefire can do to a body."

"That's exactly the point." She made a fist of her right hand, which didn't hurt and which, if she looked at it, would show no scarring. "What happened to me? I don't want that to happen to you."

"Oh for." Jaed rocked back on his heels. His brows crashed together. "You're worried about *me,* but not Zhang?"

Of course I am, she nearly said, because that was what he expected to hear. Then she recalled the relative smallness of their society, and how very *good* Jaed was at reading people, with or without arithmancy. She grimaced instead. "That's different."

"You're *not* worried about her." Jaed nodded like he'd won a bet with himself. "Because you trust her more."

"It's not that. Not trust." Thorsdottir examined the sliver of glass lodged under her chest, which only hurt whenever she thought about it. Like now. "It could've been you, in that brig, getting hit by that guard. Could've *easily* been you, and if it had? I don't know, Jaed. I don't know."

"Don't know . . . what?"

"If you'd still be alive."

"Because . . . ? What, you wouldn't have sacrificed Rose for *me,* and you would have for Zhang?"

"No!"

"Then . . . what?" He raised his eyebrows, his shoulders, and his open, empty hands. "I'm not following."

"I *couldn't* have done what you did with Rose. Arithmancy. Turning off their code. I would have just had to sit there and watch you die. I couldn't take that."

"For the love of—how do you think *I* felt? Or, or *Zhang?* Because that's what we thought we were doing."

Thorsdottir did in fact know how Zhang felt, having had this conversation. Zhang was not a demonstrative woman; she had given Thorsdottir a hard hug and admonished her never to *do* that again.

And still, "That's different. No, it is, you listen to me. Zhang and I, we signed up to be Royal Guards. That means being ready to die, or get hurt, or hurt people, for someone else—for Rory, obviously, but it was King Philip when we joined. Anyway. That's what we *chose*. To make our lives this thing that we'd risk, if we had to. And maybe we didn't have to do much risking that, before now, before *Sissten*, but that's always been out there as a possibility. Jaed, listen. If Rory'd told us to fight back on Urse, when your father came to arrest her, we would have, and we'd probably have ended up dead or hurt, but that's just, you know. *What we do*."

She braced for a retort, for indignation, for Jaed to turn around and walk back down that very long series of steps, having decided he'd rather be somewhere else than with her, planetside with Grytt, maybe, and Ivar.

Instead Jaed laughed, a bitter, sharp-edged thing, cousin to Thorsdottir's sliver of glass, though for once, it was not turned inward. Then he snapped it off and leaned forward, until she could count every pale lash ringing the plasma blue of his eyes. His tone was silk stretched over barbs.

"You're not a, a battle-rig, Thorsdottir. It's never been just about protecting Rory for you. It's everyone. When are you going to get it through your head that you aren't the only one who has to take risks?"

"What? I just *said* Zhang and I signed up to die if we had to. That's a *we*."

"Sure. You said. But you'd throw yourself between her and trouble, too, and she knows that. She and I talk about *you*, too, you know."

Thorsdottir had *not* known that. She had assumed that she and Zhang were a unit, and Rory was a law unto herself, and Jaed was—well. Jaed was Jaed, extra even after two years of close living.

Before *G. Stein*, before *Sissten*, she would have defended that thought. But *now* . . . to Zhang, clearly, he was part of the *we*. To her, too, if she thought about it.

Now Jaed was not only staring at her from an uncomfortably close distance, he was also making uncomfortably accurate observations, and seemed disinclined to retreat without some sort of response.

The truth backed up in her throat. She swallowed, took a breath, and made room for it to escape. "I don't want to be the last one left alive."

"Well *that* at least makes sense."

"It does?" The admission had sounded like a subgenre of fear, to Thorsdottir, and she had never found fear to be especially practical.

"Yeah." Jaed smiled, faint and sure as an approaching dawn. "It's how I felt, sitting back there with you in *Vagabond*. I've never felt more helpless, or more awful, or more useless. Definitely not recommended."

The laugh burst from her chest like a startled rabbit. "But then why volunteer? Go planetside. Go, oh, raise sheep or something."

"Planets scare me worse than vakari. All that sky. And sheep? *Brr.* Sheep." His smile faded. "Truth? Because I would rather be *there*, whenever *there* is, if something happens." He took a deep breath. "With you."

That pronoun was slippery, as a collective, able to refer to two, or three. Or two of three, in particular contexts. But *you* didn't include Rory, and Thorsdottir realized with something like pain that it might not ever again.

And looking at Jaed, with Jaed looking back, she thought that might be all right.

EPILOGUE

History remembers Rory Thorne as a great leader, whose powers of negotiation continued what her mentor, the Vizier, had begun in creating the inter-species alliance, which eventually adopted the name of its most influential member's home association, the Confederation, and stood alone, and somewhat battered, against the Protectorate's brutal Expansion.

Popular historical accounts focus on the legend Rory Thorne, former princess, then interim president of the Confederation Alliance Council, then founding member of the Synod and first Prime of the Aegis, as a human woman whose decisions, if not *saved* the multiverse, at least enabled its survival past the first savage wave of vakari Expansion. These popular accounts ascribe to Rory a sort of prescience (which this chronicler hopes to have definitively disproven): relating the events as if her actions were always aimed at the result which she achieved. These accounts also overlook Rory's role in the breakdown of the multiverse in the first place: her responsibility in the sundering of the Free Worlds of Tadesh first, and later, her part in earning the Protectorate's ire. They prefer instead to relate events as if she had always planned on success, as if the risks were accounted acceptable. As if we should not, in hindsight, examine those choices, and judge them.

Such accounts make a better story, by some metric, because they are cleaner and neater than what we have recounted here: that Rory was a woman who made choices that mattered to her, personal choices, bound up in her loves and her fears, and that these choices were sometimes mistakes.

The lesson here is that accuracy, however uncomfortable or unsatisfying, is necessary to the chronicles of history, because when a story is particularly compelling—when its lessons are more than *this is how our ancestors did something, how quaint!*—it may transmute into legend, and its actors into heroes. Legends and heroes can be inspirational, certainly, and culturally important—but they are not *truth*.

It is the fervent hope of this chronicler that the reader comes away from this version of the story with a greater understanding of that truth: that the principals in this tale—because Rory would not have succeeded at all without Thorsdottir, Jaed Moss, and Zhang, even Rose—did not set out to be heroes or legends. They were too busy trying to survive, and the decisions they made that changed the course of history were made with the primary goal of helping each other.

That is the truth so often lost, amid debates about effects, ramifications, and motives; and, in this chronicler's opinion, the only truth that matters.